Readers are gripped

'This is a first-rate thriller with ...

Sunday Telegraph

'Sharpe is a welcome addition to British fiction's police service' *Observer*

'Top notch . . . meticulous attention to detail and complex characterisation' *Daily Record*

'John Connor's debut novel *Phoenix* starts as just about the most impressively detailed police procedural that I've ever read . . . I have high hopes that this new series will turn out to be something a bit special' *Morning Star*

'Leeds-based barrister John Connor drives his complex tale of secrecy and betrayal along at a cracking pace. Not for the faint-hearted, but highly recommended' *Irish Independent*

'It'll be the rare reader able to put *A Child's Game* down after a chapter or so . . . the police procedural novel is given the kind of spruce-up it has been in need of for some time'
Daily Express

'He's created a beguilingly complex character, perfectly suited to his taut thrillers' *Daily Mirror*

'A riveting tale, with a thrilling climax' *Yorkshire Post*

John Connor left his job as a barrister to write full time. During the fifteen years of his legal career he prosecuted numerous homicide cases in West Yorkshire and London. He advised the police in numerous proactive drugs and organised crime operations, many involving covert activity. He now lives in Brussels with his wife and two children. His novel *Falling*, a part of the Karen Sharpe series, was shortlisted for the prestigious Portico Prize for Literature.

Also by John Connor

Phoenix
The Playroom
A Child's Game
Falling
Unsafe
The Vanishing
The Ice House

Phoenix

A Karen Sharpe Thriller

JOHN CONNOR

ORION

First published in Great Britain in 2003 by Orion
This paperback edition published in 2019 by Orion Fiction,
an imprint of The Orion Publishing Group Ltd
Carmelite House, 50 Victoria Embankment
London EC4Y 0DZ

An Hachette UK Company

1 3 5 7 9 10 8 6 4 2

A CIP catalogue record for this book is
available from the British Library.

ISBN: 978 1 4091 8875 9

Printed and bound in Great Britain by
Clays Ltd, Elcograf S.p.A.

MIX
Paper from
responsible sources
FSC® C104740

www.orionbooks.co.uk

This is for Mark Hayward and Jane Cryer

With very special thanks to Detective Constable John Markham, Detective Chief Superintendent Max Mclean, Elaine Merrington.

Thanks also to Detective Inspector Jonathan Hoyle, Clare and Sophie Abboud, Jill and Grace Gowar.

SHEPHERD'S BUSH, LONDON
6 MARCH 1988

She was numb, inside and out. The stuff running out of her eyes came without emotion, without control. It didn't mean anything. She placed the child clumsily on the floor at her feet and lay back against the sofa. Inside her the weight was crushing, relentless. It was somewhere in her chest, around the heart, pressing against her lungs. Breathing was an effort. She wanted to close her eyes, roll into a ball, forget about it.

But when she closed her eyes she could feel the blood racing through her veins, see bright lights dancing across the lids like fireworks. She had not slept properly for days, weeks, maybe longer. Time had blurred. She couldn't even recall how long she had been sitting there.

The thing was wrinkled, staring at her from ugly flaps of wrinkled, loose skin, screaming. She could hear the noise in its throat, see the contorted expression. But when she reached out her fingers to touch the blue skin at its cheeks she could feel nothing. Everywhere she looked, everything she touched, every sound that entered into her brain, even the lumps of food she placed inside her mouth – everything had become dulled. It was as though something grey was pulled down across her senses, cutting her off, insulating her.

Its eyes were milky, unfocused. She didn't know whether it could see her or not. She had no idea what it wanted. She pulled her legs up to her chest and felt something slip from her hand and spill across her thigh. When she looked down she saw that it was a plastic bottle of milk, lukewarm. Far away, from beyond the door into the room, she could hear a key turning in a lock.

The television was loud, but not loud enough to drown it out. The incessant crying. The thing had been attached to her insides, sucking her blood. She had stood in front of the mirror and seen the effects. She had been too thin for it, a tall, skinny child with a pot belly and everything else drawn, jutting, skintight over the bones, black rings around her eyes.

She had not desired this baby, did not want anything to do with it. On the outside its demands were obvious, the grating, noisy needs – food, attention, warmth – *any* body would do.

It had come out slippery with her blood, wailing, underweight. She had turned her head away, reeling with the drugs. He had called it Mairead – his dead mother's name. But it had looked more like a skinned rabbit.

She could hear him pleading with her now. She opened her eyes and saw him leaning over her, face dark with concern, confusion, the baby in his arms. She couldn't make out what he was saying. *'Please, Sinead . . . please . . .'* She could hear the desperation. Behind him the house looked as though it had been bombed. There was a smell in the place she remembered from her youth, from council estates where her classmates had lived. A background odour of soiled nappies, boiled cabbage, dirt. Where had he been?

She could see the love in the way he held it, cradling it, gently placing the bottle inside its mouth. When it stopped crying he put the bottle down and reached out to close his fingers around her own, understanding.

4

His hand felt like rubber. She shook her head slowly. She felt nothing inside. Nothing.

He told her he was going to get her help, call a doctor. He had always spoken gently to her, never shouted. He was telling her that they would move away, go somewhere else. Half of the problem, he thought, was this place, where they lived, a stinking, drug-infested high-rise.

Halfway through telling her this, something on the TV distracted him. He turned his head, watching the pictures, listening. Where his hand held hers she could feel his arm trembling, as if he were shivering with cold. Somewhere deep inside her brain she realised she had been waiting for this, had known.

She heard the names being read out by the newsman. The same names she had seen seven months ago, written on the slip of paper he had in his wallet. *Farrell, McCann, Savage* – one woman, two men – the newsreader said they had been planning to set off a bomb. She listened to what had happened to them and watched the blood draining from his face. They were dead, all of them. Shot dead that afternoon in the bright sunlight, in Gibraltar.

The words on the piece of paper in his neat, ordered, unmistakable handwriting had said '*Spain/Gibraltar*' and there had been three other names listed beside the first three. She had overheard him on the phone talking about passports for them. The three other names were aliases, false names that they were to use on the documents. The details seemed so distant it was as though she was having someone else's memories.

When the news item finished, he stood up from the sofa. He was frowning, breathing heavily, a thin layer of sweat on his forehead. He looked at her, into her blank eyes and she saw, even through the veil of numbness, that he was frightened. The baby began to cry again and he gave it the bottle.

'We shall have to go away, Sinead,' he said, very quietly. 'There's no choice now.'

For a moment she wondered who he was talking to. Then remembered. *Sinead*. That was her name. *Sinead Collins*. She nodded to him, watching the child sucking on the teat like a massive leech. In the back of her mind she could hear the pieces falling into place.

What had started seven months ago was over. That was what it meant. If she could find the energy to see it clearly, to work it out, then this too could be over. She could walk away.

She looked at the child and tried to recall whether in the five weeks of its short life she had felt *anything* for it. Anything at all.

But her mind had only images of its gaping mouth and toothless gums.

APRIL 1996
WEST YORKSHIRE

ONE

They stopped her car before she got to the wind farm. They had cordons across all the roads, isolating the scene. Where they had blocked the road above the village two big crime scene investigation vans were parked on the verges, as if it were the location shoot for a TV series. One of them was the catering truck – preparing coffees, refreshments, breakfasts, though no one was taking as yet (they would bus the probationers in later) – from the other she got her suit and pass.

When the man handing them over spoke to her she couldn't make out his words. Her heart was racing, thumping in her chest like a steam hammer, her ears filled with a rushing noise. She asked him to speak louder. He began to talk irritably to her, asking her for her name and ID.

'DC Sharpe,' she said. 'Karen Sharpe.' Her voice was slurred, defensive. She held up her warrant card, hand shaking, but he barely looked at it.

'They're expecting you,' he said.

Back outside she felt nauseous. Getting the suit on was difficult. She leaned against the side of the van and forced the chill morning air into her lungs.

She had to walk about a kilometre from the road blocks to the scene on a poorly kept road, the white sterile overalls squeaking like polystyrene as she moved. She tried to keep a straight line, but her head was spinning.

Above and in the distance, in a wide, overarching, cloudless sky, she could hear X-Ray 99, the air unit, the chopping sound from the blades increasing and fading as it searched the heights between Cock Hill Moor and Lancashire.

It had started fifty-five minutes ago. She had awoken fully clothed, lying on her bed, an upturned glass sitting on her chest, the stink of spilt brandy in her nostrils. The phone ringing. As she had moved to answer it, something massive had shifted inside her skull, a weight, sliding from one side of her head to the other.

She had struggled to ignore the pain, trying to focus on the calm male voice on the other end of the line, which was asking her to come to a place called Wainstalls. The man had told her why, speaking slowly, carefully, waiting for her reaction. He was starting to tell her where it was before she spoke, cutting him off. 'I know where it is,' she had said, and hung up.

In the bathroom, the night before – Monday, 8 April 1996 – had come back in a rush, flashing past her eyes as a string of half-formed images and sensations.

It was the same every year. It began as a tiny, hissing voice, a muttering that would start without warning in the back of her head and mount steadily in intensity. There were no words to it, nothing comprehensible. Just as insistent, background pressure, threatening to throw her into a blind panic. Beneath it a feeling in her stomach like the acid of ulcers, burning. Every year she dealt with it in the same way. Sometimes she needed drugs, but usually alcohol was enough.

That was what she had done yesterday, why she had fallen asleep fully clothed and why she now felt as if someone had shot the back of her head off. She had woken up with it yesterday and had started drinking immediately. She had kept it up right through the day, wherever she was, whoever she was with. The details were sketchy.

Beyond the hangover and the dizziness, the morning after should have brought relief. Another year when the anniversary was past and gone. Another year she had survived it. But not this year. She had listened to the voice telling her to come to Wainstalls, stood up and felt it starting all over again. A whisper of madness trying to drag her back into the blackness.

She tried to remember the last thing that had happened the night before, when Phil Leech had left her. They had met Fiona Mitchell in a pub somewhere, early evening. She could recall that. Leech had been annoyed with her because by that point it had been obvious she was trashed. They were on duty, working. Leech was her DS, Mitchell his most important snout. There were rules.

He had given her a lift home in moody silence. She had started on the brandy as soon as she got in. Usually she drank very little and the brandy was all she had in the house. That was as far as the memories took her. She couldn't even remember lying down on the bed.

As she set off up the dirt track she tried desperately to focus on what she *could* remember, working back from known details to get to others. She felt as if she were being drowned in something, some clinging viscous liquid that sat in front of her vision and obscured everything. What had happened was going to be important. She had accomplished what she set out to achieve every year on 8 April – she had blanked it. Now she had to get it back.

Wainstalls itself was a straggling collection of squat, stone cottages in the hills above Halifax. There were about thirty houses along the main and adjoining streets, more spaced out over the hillsides below and above. At the edge of the village there were the remains of a mill – redbrick walls dug into the slopes, a crumbling chimney, the hillsides above stained black with old pollution. The building had been converted into factory premises more recently, with bright metallic corrugated roofing.

But when people spoke of Wainstalls usually they meant the area above the village; the moor, the valley head, the high expanse of barren heath running up to the watershed and over the top to Cock Hill. Or sometimes the wind farm at the valley head where twenty-five gigantic wind turbines had been constructed. Gleaming white, industrial structures, they were as aesthetically apposite as the factory below them, or the massive row of electricity pylons that marched up the other side of the valley and over the top to Lancashire.

Wainstalls meant somewhere lonely, deserted. Windswept enough to have attracted wind turbines, but little else.

Ahead of her the South Pennine landscape was desolate, rising and falling in a featureless pattern of green and grey. There were no trees, few bushes, hardly any paths or walls once you got out above the valleys. The sheep they turned out to graze here were tough, scrawny – dirty balls of wool dotted in amongst the stiff stretches of marsh grass and peat.

As she came over the top of the rise below the wind farm, a group of murmuring, white-suited uniforms passed her, walking in the other direction, bent against the wind whipping down from the tops. She could hear one of them saying something about 'a double tap'. He sounded like he didn't know what it was. She walked past them in silence.

She knew what it was. Her heart skipped like a frightened animal.

They had let the Scenes of Crime Officer, forensics, the pathologist, the Senior Investigating Officer, his Deputy and an Armed Response Unit drive up there. Everyone else had to walk. Scene Management Priorities; she could remember the order from her training: *Preserve Life, Preserve the Scene, Secure Evidence, Identify Victim, Identify Suspects*. In this case, the whole moor appeared to be a major crime scene. They had secured it, roped it off, restricted access. The more people they let up, the more contaminated it became.

The cars they had allowed up were parked off the track just at the top of the rise, tucked up tightly against each other beneath a solitary clump of hawthorn bushes. She walked up to them, came over the rise and looked at the scene below her. She was standing on a rim of higher land, the wind cold in her face, her eyes stinging, looking down at a wide, black sheet of water, the surface shifting in ripples as the wind fanned over it.

A reservoir. There were a group of maybe eight people by the edge of it, white shiny figures against the green and black. A little apart from them, parked up on a flattened area of land, she could see a single motor vehicle, a Rover, driver's door open, stalled and abandoned by the water's edge.

A dirt track led off from the road down towards the car. The rutted, pot-holed road she had followed up continued to the wind farm and beyond to Cock Hill, about three miles distant. The track down, which the Rover would have followed, was cordoned off. Instead, they had used a line of metre-high metal rods to stake out and tape off a new track down through the tussocks of marsh grass and sphagnum moss. It was narrow, barely enough room for one person at a time. She began to walk down.

They saw her coming and someone must have recognised her. A man broke away from the main group and came up to meet her. He was tall and muscular, easily over six foot with strong broad shoulders. He looked about forty, but well looked after, athletic. Because she was focusing on the car, trying to see if it was empty, she didn't recognise him until he was standing right in front of her, introducing himself, but also blocking her path.

'You're DC Sharpe? I told someone to meet you at the road block. You shouldn't have had to walk it by yourself. I'm sorry. Thanks for coming up. I'm John Munro. I'm the SIO here.'

She looked up at him. He was about four inches taller than her. Clean shaven, piercing blue eyes. Hair that was thinning slightly. He had spoken with a faint Scottish accent. She had met him maybe ten times in the last five years. He wouldn't remember her though. She wasn't important enough. In West Yorkshire the SIO – the Senior Investigating Officer – on any Category A homicide was always a Detective Chief Superintendent.

'Have they told you what has happened?' he asked her. He moved closer to her, lowering his voice, eyes on hers, his hand reaching out to touch her arm, giving reassurance, support. His voice sounded concerned, careful. A side-effect of the accent, no doubt. And years of practice. Beyond him she could just see that the others had fallen silent and were watching. She recognised only one of them – Graham Dawson, the pathologist.

Her mind switched back suddenly to the night before, to Leech and Mitchell. She remembered Leech touching Fiona's arm in the same way; reassuring, gentle. It had happened when they were in the pub, when he had been trying to get that extra bit of information out of her.

'Yes. I've been told,' she said. Her voice sounded steady. She met his eyes. 'Let's get on with it.'

'Okay,' he said, nodding, but uncertain. 'I'll go over with you. Remember not to touch anything.' He hadn't let go of her arm.

She allowed herself to be walked the distance from the end of the taping to where the car was. On the way over he asked her once if she was sure. She hardly heard him. She said something to him about having seen dead bodies before and thought he said, 'Good girl,' but by then they were alongside the car, moving towards the open driver's door.

She saw that there was an arm hanging out, just outside the door frame, the fingers long, slender, relaxed. Then the legs. She recognised the shoes. There was a furious, deafening banging in her ears. Small splashes of black substance across the intact windscreen. She moved round, realising that Munro still had hold of her arm, that his grip had tightened and almost hurt.

There was one person in the car, sitting in the driver's seat, upper body slumped towards the passenger side and head lolling backwards between the seats so that she couldn't see the face.

The driver's headrest was a mess, covered in a thick, blackening substance that had run down the back of the seat in long, coagulating gouts. It looked like a tin of black paint had been sloshed across the headrest and into the rear of the vehicle. Stuck within it were what looked like clumps of papier mâché, streaked in with a thicker liquid, green or grey in colour, like mucus. Past the headrest she could see the rear passenger side windows were completely obscured with it. The smell was overpowering. An abattoir smell. Stupidly, she turned to ask Munro what it was.

Munro met her eyes without saying anything. She

15

looked back to it. Her brain fitted it together. It was blood. The back of the head had been shot away, spraying the rear of the car with bone, hair, blood, tissue, brain.

She swallowed, stepped forward, almost leaning into the vehicle, feeling the stench rising around her. She looked at the face. This was what she was here for, this was what they wanted her to do.

There were two small, black holes in the front of the head, above the line of the eyes – one at the right temple, the other towards the middle of the forehead. The skin was burned around the edges, blistered. A near perfect double tap from point-blank range. Not even a trickle of blood had come out of the entry wounds. His face was completely clean, the features untouched.

The eyes were open, but dull, sightless, the facial skin already stiff like a latex mask. But she could recognise him. No doubt about it.

'That's him,' she said, voice steady.

'Who do you say it is?'

'It's Phil Leech.'

TWO

She turned away from the car, her head reeling. For a moment she felt as if she were outside herself, watching everything happen. Nothing was connected to her. She saw it from above herself – Munro beside her, leaning towards her, hand on her arm, the huddle of figures a little apart from them, waiting. For a split second she felt convinced she was watching someone else.

At some level she knew the person Munro was touching was herself, Karen Sharpe, yet the figure seemed alien to her, a woman she didn't recognise. She couldn't even feel the point where his arm had contact with her.

Was this what she looked like? Tall – almost as tall as Munro himself – and thin. Beneath the steriles she was wearing a black, thigh-length leather jacket, a pair of scruffy, faded jeans and black, flat-soled shoes. Her hair was a mess; a nondescript brown, hanging to shoulder-length in thick, untidy strands. She could see herself constantly brushing it from her eyes. The face was so white as to look unwell, the eyes green, tired, squinting.

Memories came back to her unbidden. In the pub, the night before, she had gone into the toilets to look for Fiona Mitchell and had stared at this very person in the mirrors behind the sinks. She remembered thinking then that she was ugly.

As a teenager her mother had not let her leave the house without her putting on lipstick. As if lipstick were an essential item of clothing and the naked face – like anything naked – ugly. That much was obvious. Yet how many men had said otherwise? About her face, her figure, everything that she was?

Even her eyes. Her mother had told her that her eyes were too small, too close together. *You have little piggy eyes*. Those were the words she had used. Yet, men had always commented on her eyes. Bright, intelligent eyes. Eyes that would undress you. That was what they said.

She had remembered this as she was looking at herself, face devoid of make-up. At the time, Fiona had been hunched over the sink, vomiting, mascara running in thick black stains from her tear-streaked eyes. Karen had placed an arm around her, tried to convince her that everything was fine. What had been going on?

The pub had been off force, somewhere in Lancashire. Leech had driven her there; Fiona had been waiting for them. They had got there about eight o'clock and been out by nine. Leech had been expecting Fiona to pass him some information about a heroin dealer in Manchester who was about to set up a deal with Mark Coates. Had she done that?

The detail was gone. She needed to recall why Fiona had been sick in the toilets, why she had gone in after her, why she had been crying.

Leech's relationship with Fiona was complicated. He had picked her because she was Mark Coates's girlfriend and Coates was his target, the point around which his life had been arranged. Fiona was meant to be passing back information about Coates's heroin dealing. Leech gave her no payments for this, though, and there were none of the usual snout/handler relations between them. So why was Fiona doing it?

She looked back at Leech's shattered head and felt a

dull sadness. She heard Munro say to the others that the ID was 'positive'. Scene Management Priority number four: *Identify the Victim*. He still had his hand around her arm, continuing to hold her, but at the same time was giving instructions now, setting things up. She waited for him to finish, then asked if she could go.

'Not just yet, Karen. I need to ask you some questions. Really important. We'll go up to my car, shall we? Get out of the wind.' He didn't wait for an answer. 'Tony,' shouting back to someone else, 'my car, please.'

They walked back up between the tapes. He let go of her only because there wasn't enough room there to hold on to her. They had to walk through the gap single-file.

His car was a big four-wheel-drive thing. She sat in the rear, Munro beside her, not touching, about two foot between them. 'Tony' went into the front passenger seat and twisted round to watch.

'I'm sorry to have asked you to do that, Karen,' Munro started.

'I've seen it before,' she interrupted him. 'Don't worry.'

'Yes. But am I right that you knew Philip Leech?'

'I worked with him.'

'He was your partner. That's right, isn't it?'

'More or less. He was my DS.'

'But there were only two of you in that drugs unit?'

'Yes.'

'So you will have been close?'

'Yes.'

'That's why I'm sorry to have asked. That's all.'

'Better me than anyone else.'

'Like his wife. Of course. But it's bound to be upsetting.'

'Yes.' She was conscious that she didn't sound upset.

She rubbed her fingers together. She couldn't feel anything. 'I'm numb,' she said, matter-of-factly.

'It's cold out there,' Tony said, watching her hands.

'Not numb like that,' she said.

'You'll be shocked,' Munro said. 'We're all shocked.'

'He was a police officer,' Tony said. 'That makes a difference.'

She nodded.

'You say you've seen it before, Karen,' Munro again, voice very quiet. 'Where was that?'

She frowned.

'Do you mean in the job? You mean dead bodies?' he clarified.

She looked at him, expression blank.

'Or bodies like that? Killed in that way? Shot?'

'I've seen hits before,' she said. 'Professional killings.'

He nodded. 'Yes. That's what it looks like,' he said. 'Why would anyone want to do that to Phil?'

She looked down at where her hands were resting in her lap. For some reason she found it irritating that he had called him Phil. He hadn't known Leech, after all.

'They wouldn't,' she said. 'We're not looking at anyone big enough. We're not looking at anyone with the clout to do that. Not to a policeman.'

She noticed her use of the present tense.

'Who was it you were looking at, then?'

'Mark Coates.'

Out of the corner of her eye she saw him frowning. 'Do you know him, Tony?'

Tony nodded. She looked up at him.

'Sorry, Karen,' Munro said. 'This is Tony Marshall. My Deputy SIO.'

'Drug dealer. Middle range,' Marshall said. 'Nothing big.'

'Just Coates?' Munro asked her.

'Coates and Varley. Luke Varley. He's Coates's brother.'

'Brother? The names are different.'

'Half-brother. Different fathers, same mother.'

'Right. No one else then? Just Coates and his half-brother? That it?'

'That was it. That was the Operation. Operation Anvil.'

'Who else besides yourself and Phil on that? Who was SIO for it?'

'Alan Edwards is SIO. There was just me and Phil, usually.'

'For how long?'

'Phil has been looking at Coates for nearly three years. I've been on it just over a year.' Suddenly something slotted into place. Nothing had happened at the pub. That hadn't been it. It was later it had begun to unravel, when she was in bed, asleep. There had been a call around midnight, waking her up. She tried to get it back, letting Munro and Marshall wait.

Fiona had called her after Leech had dropped her off, and had woken her up. She had been screaming about Coates threatening to kill her, saying he had found out about them. Karen ran through the call in her head, feeling her breath quicken. It wasn't the first time it had happened, but she shouldn't have forgotten it. It was important.

Fiona had wanted to meet her, had told her to drive to 'the reservoir'. The phonecall had been cut short before she could ask her where the place was. 'The reservoir' had meant nothing to her.

She looked out of the window at the surface of the water below. She had called Leech immediately afterwards

21

and told him she was too pissed to do it, too drunk to drive. He had told her he would go, that Fiona had already called him as well.

She turned to Munro. 'He was meeting someone connected to it last night,' she said. The words came out rapidly, with a trace of panic. 'They were going to meet up here, I think.' She nodded towards the reservoir. If they had killed Leech they would have killed Fiona too. 'She might be in there,' she said, aloud. It felt as though there was a block of ice in the pit of her stomach.

'Who might be, Karen?'

'Fiona Mitchell. She was an informant. Coates's girlfriend. She rang me and Phil last night. Said Coates had found out and was threatening to kill her. She wanted to meet.'

'Was Phil with you when she rang?'

'No. I called him after she rang me. It was just before midnight. She had already called him, separately.'

'Did *she* tell you that?'

'No. Phil told me, when I rang him.'

'She wanted to meet you both?'

'Yes. But I was pissed. I couldn't drive.'

'So Phil came here to meet her?'

'I think so. That's what he said he was going to do. Assuming this was the place.'

'But the threats were against Fiona Mitchell? Not Phil?'

'Yes. There have been threats in the past against Phil. Nothing I would count as serious, though. They'll all be on the intelligence database, on OIS. There was a rumour about a year and a half ago that Coates had put a contract on him. But not to kill him. Just to frighten him, I think.'

'A rumour? How do you mean?'

'Phil had informant info, I think. It was before I came in on it. I'm not even sure it was true. Phil was obsessed with Coates. The whole thing was too personal. He thought Coates had left messages on his answerphone, sent him stuff through the post.' She shook her head. 'I'm not so sure.'

'You think Phil was imagining it?'

She looked down towards the car. 'Maybe not.'

'Was any of this investigated?'

'I don't know. You should ask Alan Edwards. At one point they put security cameras in Phil's house, monitored his movements. He thought he was being followed. But this was two years ago. Nothing has happened since then.'

'Until now,' Tony said.

She shook her head. 'This isn't Coates.'

Munro leaned towards her. 'So who else do you think it could be, Karen?'

She ran a hand through her hair. Her brain felt fuzzy, unclear. 'I don't know. Not Coates.'

'But Coates knew Phil? Knew his face, knew who he was?'

'Undoubtedly.'

'Would he have known what car Phil was driving?'

She nodded. 'Phil thought he was paying someone in the job. To check his cars on the Police National Computer – the PNC. I forget the guy's name. Some PC in Wakefield. That will be on OIS as well. Phil was paranoid. He did his own audit trail, every week. He thought they were trying to get details of where he lived, what he drove, what his phone numbers were.'

'Did DI Edwards know all that?'

'Yes.'

'But there was no investigation?' Tony again.

'I don't think so.' She looked up at them. 'I don't think he believed Phil. Phil used to say that Coates had wrecked his life. That his wife left him because of it all. But he didn't give that impression. I think this *was* his life. I think he enjoyed it.'

Munro nodded, watching her. 'That's excellent, Karen. Can you move on all that, Tony? Now?' His voice hadn't changed at all. Softly spoken, calm, even-paced.

'You want them in?' Marshall asked.

'Yes. Both of them. Coates and Varley. We need to toss their houses. Fast.'

Tony let himself out of the car door. Munro waited for it to close.

'How are you feeling, Karen?'

'Fine.'

'I need you to be with me for a while. Talking to me. You understand that?' She nodded. 'I need to know everything there is to know about you, Phil Leech and Operation Anvil. We'll go back to the incident room, get a coffee, something to eat. Is there anything else you need to sort out?'

She shook her head. 'What about the reservoir?' she asked.

'Already in hand, Karen. Don't worry about things like that. If she's in there, we'll have her out in a couple of hours.'

THREE

Fiona Mitchell wasn't in the reservoir.

The Incident Room they were setting up was at Richmond Close, in Halifax, the nearest station to the scene. They had been there all of ten minutes before Munro's mobile went off. Karen sat at a table in the first-floor canteen, sipping half-heartedly at a coffee while he paced around speaking *sotto voce*.

'Another body,' he said when he had finished. 'Three, maybe four miles away. Over the other side of Cock Hill. It might be your woman – Mitchell. I'm sorry, Karen, I need you to come up there with me.'

They drove the long way around, to avoid contaminating the road over from Wainstalls. By the time they were driving up the other side of Cock Hill, from Oxenhope, it was coming round to nine o'clock. A clear, bright day, ruminations of spring in the air.

She stared out of the car window and tried to fight a feeling of blind panic she had not felt so badly in nearly eight years. If she had not drunk so much the night before she would have been sitting there, with Leech, bullets through her face.

Munro talked the whole way, oblivious to any difficulties she might have been experiencing. The subjects ranged from trivial attempts at some perceived need for consolation – 'At least it was quick, Karen. He would have known nothing about it' – to endless detailed questions about Anvil, and Leech's past.

'You understand,' he kept saying to her, 'the most important thing? To try to recall anyone, no matter how trivial, who might have a *motive*. These are the people we have to get at quickly. Before they're on their toes and the evidence is burned. You understand that, Karen?'

But there was nothing else. No major criminals Leech had recently locked up (Munro was having all his cases resulting in a custodial sentence researched separately, he said). No personal or family problems that might lead to a grudge.

'The crazy thing is,' he told her, 'it only costs about five grand to have that done. You don't have to be rich. Just big enough. Or mad. Those are my two main lines: someone big enough, *criminally*, to think they can get away with this, or someone unhinged. Right now it could be either, but it's looking strong for Coates, from what you've said.'

'He's not big, though,' she said, feebly. 'Not big enough to do this.'

'And probably not mad enough, right?'

'No. Phil has been looking at him for three years without him putting a foot wrong. There was no need for him to do this.'

'Drugs, though, Karen. It's a funny world. Big fish eating little fish, all rubbing up against each other. Maybe someone higher up than Coates needed this done.'

A *funny* world, she thought. She noticed that as he talked, he forgot to be serious, sensitive. He was at work, as normal, the weather was good, things were working out. Why should he be otherwise?

'I think we would have had a warning,' she said. 'Something would have come back. Through Fiona, through the jungle drums. It takes time to set up something like this. We would have heard.'

'Maybe Coates pulled the trigger himself. Found out about Fiona passing Phil info. Set them up and did the business himself. There are too many options at the moment. Don't close things off. Whatever you think of, *whatever* it is, you tell me. Okay?'

It was worse than a good mood, she thought. Underneath the false sympathy he was completely untouched, cheerful even.

On the way down from Wainstalls she had already gone into the basics – the history between Leech and Coates – the rumours of threats and contracts, the security measures Leech had taken, the names of the informants (if she knew them). Another detective had sat in the car with them, taking notes. As soon as they got down to Halifax he had been sent off to chase up detail.

Walking into the station with her, Munro had said, 'The death of a policeman has never gone undetected in West Yorkshire. Did you know that, Karen?'

'No. I didn't,' she replied.

She wondered how long she would be able to bear his tone.

There was an unmanned weather station on the summit of Cock Hill. A collection of two or three bunker-like buildings, a wooden tower, satellite dishes, weather vanes, aerials, antennae – all ringed with a six-foot barbed-wire fence. The place had the look of a prison compound – low concrete buildings with barred windows, a brutal functionality to the design. They left the car by the roadside about four hundred metres below it, put on fresh overalls and galoshes and walked up. As they got near to the top, the tips of the wind turbines above

Wainstalls, two straight miles to the east, came into view.

'It's not far to walk, straight over,' Munro commented.

He left her by the fence to the weather station and walked ahead, off the edge of the road by a line of telegraph poles that ran down a steepening gully, still swollen with rainwater from the afternoon before. She could see that there were a group of people putting up a scene tent on the bare hillside, a little to the left of the gully.

The view beyond was panoramic; vast stretches of flattened, wind-battered heath stretching to the lip of a high horizon. The gale was a constant roar. She could see for twenty or thirty miles in a one-hundred-and-twenty-degree arc and in the entire distance there was not a single tree. The isolated dwellings on the slopes immediately opposite, three to five miles distant, were abandoned and broken, crumbled like the lines of the walls leading away from them.

To get to this place with motorised transport there was only one road up – the one she was standing on. She looked down at it, followed its line as it snaked away towards Calderdale, to the south, or back over the ridge to Airedale, to the north. It was blocked, he had told her, over three miles further down the valley, just to be safe. She looked at the single smear of rubber intersecting the curve of the road and angled directly at the gully Munro had walked down. A skid mark. He had stepped carefully around it.

When he called up to her she followed him down, sticking to the route he had taken as best she could, using the line of the telegraph poles to guide her. The wires carried over the poles came from the weather station, down the gully, into the valley below. So far they hadn't staked and taped this scene. They had the tent up by the time she got there, a low white plastic thing – more like a tunnel than a tent – heavily pegged against the wind, guide ropes already singing. There was barely enough clearance to stand within it.

She stood with her head touching the fabric, the wind buffeting the sides so strongly that she could hear nothing of what was being discussed in front of her. She felt like an intruder. Up ahead they were busy, active, at work. She was interrupting them, contaminating things. The earth beneath her was soft and wet, like a sponge. There were no reeds here, just hillocks of soaking sphagnum. Nothing to obscure the corpse. She wondered that it had taken so long to find it.

They had sited the tent so that most of the area immediately above the body was covered and furthest from the entrance. She entered from below the site and someone – not Munro – shouted in her ear that she should not stray further than a foot inside the thing. 'Keep your back against this side,' he advised. She saw why.

Even with the rain the quantity of blood on the ground between where the gully would have been (outside the confines of the tent) and where she assumed (from the huddle of white-suited figures) the body to be, was considerable. In the car the blood had looked almost black in colour. For some reason, out here, sunk into the bright green sphagnum, matted through the tussocks, it looked crimson. At certain points the quantity was so great it had gathered in a fold of ground and coagulated where it lay, like a jelly.

She stared at a line of muddy indentations leading back through the blood towards the rear of the tent. Out here it was impossible to walk without the ground sinking under foot and a puddle of water forming around your shoes. When you moved away, the sphagnum you had stepped on remained sunk below the water, leaving a faint but unmistakeable trace. Not good enough to yield a tread pattern, she guessed, but adequate to trace the route.

Munro had hold of her arm again, pushing her towards the entrance. When they were at the threshold he placed his mouth against her ear and whispered into it, 'I'm sorry. This one is a bit messier than last time. We have some ID from her clothing – credit cards and such like – so if you can't do it we can work around it. What do you think?'

His mouth had been so close her ear was moist when he backed off. His lips had been against the skin. She looked at him, saw that he was conscious of the intimacy, embarrassed.

'Was there no ID on Phil?' she shouted. The wind was too strong. He leaned his ear towards her and she shouted into it, careful to keep her lips from touching.

'No,' he said, shaking his head. She cupped a hand around her ear, leaning towards him. 'Nothing at all. *She* has his warrant card on her. In her pocket, along with the other stuff.'

'Should we be here at all?' she asked, mouthing the words to him. She pointed down at the muddy holes they were leaving in the bog. 'Are we not messing everything up even being here?'

She saw him smile. 'Leave that to me,' he shouted. 'It's all choices. Speed is the first thing with dead bodies. Without an ID you can't get on to stage two. You can only preserve a scene so much. That's life. Will you do it or not?'

She nodded.

The body was sprawled out on its back, one leg twisted

and folded beneath the other, both arms stretched out to either side. Arched slightly, or at least it looked like that – perhaps there was a clump of sphagnum right below her. It was Fiona. She was wearing the clothes she had worn the night before, when they had met. The top had been pulled up around her neck, exposing her chest. As if it were something sexual.

It was hard to make out the details because the wound in the centre of the chest was large, the flesh and clothing around it completely saturated with dried or congealing blood. From the size she guessed it was an exit wound, which meant she had been shot in the back.

They moved away to let her closer. The scientists, the pathologist, the experts. They would know already whether it was an exit wound. She stepped carefully, skirting the sump of blood on the ground immediately around the body.

A portion of the face was missing – the top left quarter, running from under the left eye in a line to the rear of the skull – shot away. She could see the pieces sprayed out across the marsh behind. As if he had stood where she was standing now, leaned forward at a slight angle and discharged the weapon into her left eye.

She followed the line of the left arm and saw that a gun was lying in the hand. The fingers weren't gripping it, still less on the trigger. It looked as if the thing had been placed there, on top of the open palm. An automatic, a 9mm Beretta. It was stained, wet. But she could read the words on the barrel; Pietro Beretta. Underneath, clear and untouched, the serial number. The thing looked heavy in her hand, like Fiona would have had difficulty even lifting it.

Fiona. She was too small for this. The tent made her seem larger, restricting the space around her. Her angular,

31

bony body would have looked lost without it, flat out on her back on the roof of the world, arms open to the sky. A child. How old had Phil said she was? Twenty-two. Alive and talking to her twelve hours ago. And now this; all the blood emptied out of her, washed into the heath.

She stepped back, turned round and walked back to Munro, nodding. They stepped outside and walked away from the tent and the wind noise. She had the feeling he was watching her, waiting for her to break down, or cry.

'It's Fiona,' she said. 'I recognise what's left. The clothes as well, the hair.'

'You sure?'

'Certain. Where did you recover the cards from – her pocket?' She hadn't noticed a handbag of any sort.

'From the jacket.'

'No handbag?'

'Not so far.'

She nodded. Fiona had been holding a small, cheap-looking handbag when she was with her the night before. She wanted to ask – so where did she keep the gun? But he had no doubt already thought of that.

She waited until they were right back at his car before asking him where she could vomit.

'Vomit?' He looked surprised.

'I don't want to contaminate the scene.'

She sat down at the side of the road, legs like jellies. From the car he brought a plastic bag and a box of tissues. She waited until he had returned to the vehicle, then gave in.

FOUR

He kept her for the entire day, right through until nine in the evening.

Halfway through the morning he told her they had brought Coates in. She had given them lists of properties and on Section 18 authorities or warrants they had searched them all. The quantity of material coming in was massive. Throughout the day they kept feeding Munro questions, details they wanted him to put to her.

He had taken a decision to tape record everything, so, apart from breaks, they spent the day in an airless, windowless interview room just outside the custody area. There was always one other in with him, taking notes. Whether they were recording or not, everything was noted.

Frequently he sent them to follow up details or check something. Sometimes Marshall sat with him. Munro didn't smoke, but he drank so many coffees his pupils looked dilated. At three in the afternoon he broke off to do a press interview.

All the time he was with her he was also setting up the enquiry, managing it. Taking calls about personnel and premises, arguing with someone about money, discussing the evidence with the SO13 – the Scotland Yard Anti-Terrorist Unit – in London. All on the mobile. It would ring, he would switch off the tape, deal with it. In any hour with her he probably spent twenty minutes talking to her, the rest on the phone dealing with something else. At first he was apologetic. But as the day wore on it got more functional. At one point she had a delusion, that she had been arrested herself, was being accused.

At nine he received a report about Luke Varley, who was still at large. He decided enough was enough and had someone take her home.

'We'll start again tomorrow,' he said. No gratitude, no comforting words. He had grown too tired for it by then.

She stood in her house and felt the silence coming up to meet her. It was almost exactly twenty-four hours since Phil Leech had dropped her here and she had watched his Rover bouncing away up the track. She recalled asking him about Fiona. *What is going on?* she had asked, meaning between him and her.

Nothing at all, he had said.

She wondered briefly what his wife was going through.

She hunted for drink. The brandy bottle was empty, but in the freezer she found some overproof vodka. Ideal. She switched the TV on and watched a meaningless pattern of images flicker in front of her. She had downed barely two shots before she heard the sound of a car outside.

She lived in a converted barn in open country west of Skipton, just outside the National Park boundaries. The nearest neighbour was just under a mile away, an ageing farmer called Sutcliffe. The track that ran to her door went on to his place, so not every noise meant a visitor. She stood up and went to the window. The car was Munro's. For some reason she wasn't surprised.

At the door he was apologetic and at first she thought something else must have happened.

'No,' he said, still on the doorstep, 'I just wanted to

apologise. I let you go without saying thank you. I'm sorry about that. You've been really, really helpful today, Karen, considering everything. I mean that.'

She shrugged. 'You want a drink?' she asked. Expecting a refusal.

'A tea, maybe,' he said.

'Something stronger?' Another memory. She had said something similar to Leech the night before, as he was dropping her off.

'I can't. I'll be working all night.'

He followed her in. She walked through to the kitchen, switching the TV off on the way. Behind her she could feel his confusion. She turned to see him standing looking at the place, frowning.

'Have you just moved in?' he asked.

'Five years ago.'

He held his arms in the air, questioning. The room they were in was long, running straight into the 'dining area' and kitchen, with no partitions, the ceiling low and beamed, enforcing a sense of constriction, of untidiness. In the kitchen there was a huge oak table, with two chairs, but nothing else. The plates, cups, saucers, bowls and glasses she had brought with her were stacked behind the table or on it. The units running the length of the kitchen had been unfinished for nearly two years now. Some were on the walls without doors, some still on the floor waiting to go up.

The TV she had bought was still standing on top of its cardboard box. Since she hardly watched TV she had yet to work out why she had bought it in the first place. Her books – nearly all cheap paperbacks and enough of them to fill a small library – were stacked against the walls in untidy piles, some of which had reached chest height. It wasn't a routine picture of female domesticity.

'I haven't got round to buying much,' she said. 'A question of priorities.'

He sat at one of the kitchen chairs. There were no other chairs to sit on. She filled a pan with water and placed it on the stove.

'You don't have a kettle?'

'I don't really drink tea or coffee,' she said. She could see the thoughts building up behind his eyes. *Weird*, he was thinking. *I have misjudged her. She is mad.*

'I don't normally drink alcohol either,' she said, filling the shot glass again.

'There's nothing I'd like more right now,' he said. 'A nice single malt. Or six.'

'When will you finish tonight?'

'I won't. It's all critical right now. We'll get something preliminary from ballistics in a few hours, the PM for Fiona around three. Plus, I've got to finish getting the teams together and keep them moving on Varley.'

'Still nothing?'

'No. A few leads. He'll come to light though. They always do.'

'So what can I do for you? I don't expect you're here to keep me company.'

He smiled. 'You know me already,' he said. 'It's the first briefing tomorrow. Ten sharp in the Incident Room. I'd like you to be there if you can. I want you on the team. If you're not up to it now, fair enough. But when you are—'

'I'm a witness.'

'I've checked with the lawyers. It's fine. Practicalities, Karen. It's like walking over to the bodies. You have to make these choices all the time. With you it's simple. You know too much to leave out. I can try to get it all off you – out of your head and on to paper – but that's only halfway there. I want you with the Statement Readers, looking at the stuff as it comes in.'

She nodded. 'I'll be there.'

'Good.' He stood up.

'You don't want that tea?'

'Better not, on second thoughts. I'll have to get back.'

She switched the flame off, downed the vodka, followed him back to the door.

'I read your file,' he said, exactly as she was opening the door for him.

She sighed.

'There's not much to it,' he said.

'Depends which version you had.'

'I must have had the short version.'

'Ah.'

'I'm not important enough for the full thing.'

'I'm sure if you ask . . .'

'No need. I know what it means. You must have done something big down there.'

'Down where?'

'In London. I hadn't realised that today. I'm sorry.'

'I don't remember,' she said, flustered. 'I'll see you tomorrow.'

She went to close the door on him but he remained where he was, blocking it.

'You live alone here,' he said. Not a question. 'Do you not have family you can go to?'

'Why?'

'Tonight. I mean. Rather than be alone. Family? Or friends?'

'I'm fine. I can look after myself.'

'Do you want me to send someone up?'

'Like who?'

'Whoever you like.'

'Male or female?'

He saw that she was playing now.

'I'd invite you to mine,' he said. 'But I won't be there.'

At the table she sat with her head in her hands, trying to control the thoughts. First the date, then the violence. An eruption of violence. It had been like that in the past. Exactly like that. Long periods when it didn't even exist. Then sudden, total carnage. So much blood she felt filthy. Like she would never get it out of her eyes.

And now this. Munro knew. He had seen the file.

It was coming back at her.

FIVE

The full autopsies were knocked back eighteen hours to get a gunshot expert from Belfast in. That was Brian Butcher's decision. Butcher was technically head of CID, though nominally only the same rank as himself. On the other hand, he had a lot more experience of these things and was worth listening to. (He had also taken it upon himself to speak to Mitchell's mother; the Chief Constable had done Leech's wife.) He already had cause and rough time of death from Dawson, their own pathologist, who had attended the scenes. But the delay on the full post-mortem meant he would have to do the briefing with less information than he liked.

It was after four in the morning before ballistics got back to him. Sometime between two and four he fell asleep in a chair in the Incident Room, waiting for them. A poor, frequently interrupted slumber in a position that left his neck stiff.

The ballistics reports surprised him. He sat staring at the faxed sheets of paper, trying to put together scenarios that would account for everything he knew so far. It wasn't easy. He checked the position on Varley (the latest being that they were setting up an armed arrest action on a house in Odsal, which he could safely leave in the hands of the DS running the liaison with the Firearms Support Unit) then drove back to his home in Shipley feeling strained and disconnected, a part of his brain still shut down from the earlier doze.

In the house he ran a bath but dropped off again before he could get into it.

It was a rush to get back to Tony in time for the pre-brief at eight. When he had dragged the razor over his stubble he stood in front of the mirror and looked at himself. Bloodshot eyes, skin breaking out in patches of irritation, tired.

It was always like this. He had been called out at four the previous morning and it was likely to be the same pattern for the next few days. The first few days were make or break. If you didn't break the back of it in seventy-two hours, the evidence dissipated and you were looking at something that would take months. That couldn't happen here. The deceased – at least, the one that mattered – was a police officer. It had to be wrapped up quickly.

On the way out he caught himself looking back at his house. Not quite a home. Superficially, at least, it resembled the disorganised shell Karen Sharpe lived in. Except he knew from her records that she had never been married, never had children. The reason his own place looked so uninhabited and untidy was because it was only half the picture. His wife had taken the other half with her – including the kids – nine months before.

He closed the door behind him, set the alarm. It was no life for a family man. That was the truth of it. The thing with Anne Shepherd had been a distraction from that, an excuse. He made a mental note to do something about seeing a solicitor.

F Division had donated three large rooms in Richmond Close. It was a Category A enquiry and Command had promised him at least forty detectives for the first two weeks. He expected nearly all of them to make first briefing. Tony would have to mop up the stragglers later. Of the three rooms they had, none was really big enough for a forty-man briefing. In the end they settled for clearing as much space as possible in the Incident Room itself.

On a portable whiteboard he wrote up the date and time when Coates's custody clock would expire, assuming they got all the extensions they asked for, including one twelve-hour extension due up at 11.20 that morning and two maximum warrants of further detention from a magistrate. Underneath he wrote the time at which the twelve-hour extension would expire. That was all they were certain of – that they had Coates until twenty-one minutes past eleven that evening. So far, they hadn't even tried to interview him. Given the ballistics, he would seriously have to consider bailing him without charge or interview. There was no point in wasting time on the clock unless they had something they could put to him.

As the team filed in to the room, helping themselves to the coffee he had organised, he watched out for Sharpe. She wasn't difficult to spot. Every force in the country had abolished height restrictions in order to get more women applying. The result was that you could look down the line of a Public Order Serial, suited up with pads, shields and helmets, and tell immediately which were female – the short ones. But Sharpe was older than that. Her file said thirty-five. That probably meant she had joined the Met – where she had come from seven years ago – when height restrictions were still in. Her file put her height at six feet, exactly. Compared to most men on the force, that made her tall. For a woman it was unusual.

She carried it well. He had noticed the day before.

Straight back, not a hint of embarrassment, sure, confident step. At six four himself, he had to resist a subconscious urge to stoop slightly, to come down to their level. It had been the same throughout his childhood. But not Karen Sharpe. She looked as though she liked being tall. Her eyes had been more or less at the level of his nose when he was speaking to her. He remembered he had leaned towards her, placed his mouth against her ear. The smell came to him again – the scent she was wearing, or the warmth coming off her skin. He couldn't be sure.

By comparison, his wife had looked like a child standing beside him, the top of her head barely reaching the height of his shoulders.

He watched Sharpe waiting to get into the Incident Room. She didn't look any different to any of the others. Same hard face. She was dressed in jeans, a white, open-necked shirt, a suede jacket. Dark hair cut to shoulder-length, exactly like the day before – an untidy effect, as if she hadn't had time to do anything with it, or just couldn't be bothered. It was an illusion, he thought, a deliberate effect. Because it looked *just* right, *just* like that.

She seemed the same, but she wasn't. He had looked into her eyes long enough to notice the shade of green. Searching eyes, full of intelligence and irony, unmistakably unimpressed by rank, height, masculinity, authority or physical attraction. A strong personality. The sort of person he was invariably attracted to, precisely because she appeared so distant, untouchable. She hadn't looked away from him, hadn't broken eye contact when they spoke. That wasn't his normal experience. He was more than aware of the effect his own eyes could have. Her lack of reaction throughout the day might be attributable to shock, but he doubted it. That wasn't the whole story.

He had been surprised when she had been sick at the second scene. Already it had seemed out of character.

And here she was today, in line to get in, bright and early, talking to the others as if nothing had happened. He had seen her file. It was a work of fiction. The editing said more than the little they had left in.

There would be something hard at the centre of Karen Sharpe, something she kept only for herself.

He stepped up to her and pulled her aside, into an empty room off the corridor outside. 'I just want to run something by you,' he said, closing the door. 'Before we kick off.'

She nodded, waiting. Those eyes on him. Watching.

'Are you okay today?'

'I'm fine,' she said. 'You look whacked.'

'I am,' he said, slightly fazed that she wasn't bothering to address him properly. Yesterday he had let it pass, but it wasn't usual. He had a rank, a title. Most people either used that or called him 'sir'. She was doing neither.

'Didn't you get much sleep?' she asked.

'Maybe an hour or two.'

'I slept fine,' she said. 'Although I might have slept better at yours – like you said.'

He looked at her, for a moment mute. 'Yes,' he said, faltering. He was embarrassed. What was she doing? It wasn't that she might be flirting with him, it was that she was doing it *now*.

'I don't think my wife would approve,' he said, the words coming to his mouth before he could stop them.

'You've been separated for nine months,' she said. 'Everyone knows that. You live alone.'

Silence. A moment of complete silence, her eyes on his.

'Just like me,' she said, smiling at him.

He looked away. 'I was worried about you,' he said. 'That was all.'

'Right.' A slight touch of amusement in her tone.

You are some kind of monster, he thought. You worked with Leech for nearly a year, every day. You should not be capable of this. Not so soon.

He handed her the ballistics report, told her what it was. She began to leaf through it.

'Tell me what you think,' he said. 'You knew them both. I just wanted your opinion on the most obvious scenario – to which that report clearly points – before we take the whole thing in the wrong direction.'

He watched for a reaction as she was reading it. He could see where she was up to on the page. He could tell when she had got as far as the conclusions, but there was nothing, not even a raised eyebrow. Control, he thought. What she is about, the key to her, is control.

'No,' she said, when she had finished. She handed him the papers.

'No?'

'No. Not a chance. You know that. Not her. Not him.'

'I thought so,' he said. 'Just needed to check.'

'Was there no residue analysis?' she asked.

'Yes. Inconclusive. They were both near it when it was discharged. That's it.'

She nodded. 'Besides,' she said, 'it's too easy.'

He opened the door.

'Did you tell SO13 about that?' she asked.

'SO13?'

'You were talking to them yesterday.'

'Yes,' he said, trying to work out where she was coming from. 'No. I haven't told them. We already decided yesterday that it was crime, not terrorism. It doesn't have the profile for terrorism.' He frowned at her. 'Besides, a terrorist group would have claimed it. Don't you agree?'

'Not always. Not when it's a cock-up.'

'So what are you saying?'

'Nothing,' she said. 'What would I know?'

She moved to get past him.

'While you're here,' he said, halting her right in front of him, so close she was almost touching his chest, 'I've thought better of putting you with the Statement Readers. I've allocated you to the team looking at Coates and Varley instead.'

'Good,' she said, looking up at him, breath warm on his face. 'It'll be just like old times.'

SIX

At nine fifty-five Brian Butcher, Head of CID, arrived. Munro had already briefed him by mobile and had passed on Tony's latest news – that Varley was on the move again and under observation. He walked to the front of the room and turned to face his team.

They were sitting on the tables as well as behind them, leaning against the walls, in groups, alone, smoking (if they had grabbed the space near the open fire doors), drinking coffee, chewing gum – all watching him, waiting for his words. Only seven were from this Division and knew the place. The rest had been drawn from teams across the county.

Not surprisingly, there was a buzz in the air. It didn't sound serious or respectful. It sounded like a crowd gathering before a sports fixture. This was their job. Investigating the shooting of a colleague was about as interesting, involved and exciting as it was likely to get. He couldn't complain about that. The minimum he needed was that they were interested.

The conversation died out as he waited. He took time to count them, scan the faces, nodding at some, greeting others. Fresh, young faces mainly, eight or nine old school that he knew. Forty-three in all. Only four women in the whole group, one of them Sharpe. Three black or Asian faces, one of them female. The usual poor mix.

He walked to the empty table in front of the

whiteboard and sat on it, facing them. Tony sat down beside him; Butcher remained at the back. To their right, along the walls, were blow-ups of the two scenes.

'Good morning, everybody,' he said. 'Welcome to Operation Phoenix.'

He waited for their murmured responses to subside. They had assigned the codename centrally, at random, as with every other operation.

'For those of you who don't know me, I am Detective Chief Superintendent John Munro. I'm the Senior Investigating Officer on this enquiry. My Deputy, sitting here beside me, is Detective Inspector Tony Marshall. The Office Manager will be DI Dyson. You'll get our contact details and those of everyone else here before the end of today if you've all handed in your details to Julie, as requested.' He pointed to a woman sitting near the front. 'Julie White. Detective Sergeant. She will run Enquiry Admin and Criminal Justice Support. We will have our own team of File Preparers brought in once we get to that stage. Which we will. There has never been an undetected murder of a serving officer in the entire history of the West Yorkshire Police Force. This one will be no different. You will see to it.'

He paused, scanned the faces, let the intent sink in. As with every time he did this, he reflected that he probably wasn't very good at the motivational part, the words. The press interview he had done yesterday – full of indignation at the death of a serving officer – had been largely conscious, deliberate. Not things he felt. It would be the same with the one he would have to do later today. At bottom he was no different to anyone in the sea of faces in front of him. This was the job.

'A few of you will not have been on a major enquiry before. I hope you'll find me easy to work with. I like –

and want – everyone to contribute to policy formation. Your ideas are as good as mine or DI Marshall's. Equally valid. However, I do have one rule. You must attend briefings. This is a Category A enquiry with in excess of fifty personnel involved. In a little while we will divide you into teams under nine sergeants. If you don't attend briefings you will not get the bigger picture, you will not understand what we are aiming for and you will not have a clue why you are being tasked to do certain things. That will make you less effective.'

He stopped momentarily, for emphasis.

'You *must* attend briefings. Murders are solved by meetings. On a big enquiry like this, the people with responsibility – me and Tony – are the *only* people who don't actually do anything. The *only* way we get to keep on top of what *you* are doing, to maintain the enquiry running in the correct direction, is via these meetings. Is that understood?'

A few nods, a few murmurs. Not many writing anything down.

'Of all the meetings you will attend this is the most important. The first briefing. Take notes. After this there will be a briefing every day at ten and a de-brief at five. In case you missed anything. You will be there – at both – unless you give a valid prior excuse to your sergeant and he or she permits it.'

He stepped up to a massive enlargement of an aerial photo of Cock Hill Moor and Wainstalls.

'What I am going to do now,' he said, 'is tell you where we are so far. Pay attention. I will assume you know nothing, because some of you don't. This is our scene.' He pointed to the photo. 'The area known as Wainstalls, to the bottom here, and Cock Hill Moor, at the top. Within this area we have two major crime scenes – here and here. The first we will call "Wainstalls", the second "Cock Hill". Easy to remember that way.'

He moved over to a series of photos of Leech's car, the first from above and behind, the second showing the inside after Leech had been removed, the last complete with ballistic rods showing bullet trajectories.

'Wainstalls. Just after four o'clock in the morning, Tuesday, 9 April 1996, a witness,' a pause to point back to the whiteboard where Tony had written out and colour-coded the names of all significant witnesses, suspects and victims, 'Muriel Horsfall, came upon this scene here,' pointing to the car, 'while taking her dog for a walk. An ungodly hour, I know, but it *is* light up there at four-thirty – I saw that for myself this morning – and she *is* clean. Nearly seventy-five years old.'

That didn't make her clean, he thought. Everyone was capable of it. Even pensioners.

'One deceased inside the vehicle – Philip Andrew Leech. Age thirty-seven, a Detective Sergeant on this Force. Recently separated from a wife and one child, a daughter aged six. Cause of death – gunshot wounds. Two nine-millimetre casings recovered from right here, right beside the open door of the vehicle. Two shells expended and recovered from the body of the vehicle, making this trajectory reconstruction possible.'

He pointed to the two long rods inserted by ballistics, showing the downward angle of the bullets into the rear of the vehicle.

'Both bullets passed through the deceased's head. You'll get a briefing pack giving details. The photos are available now on the desk near the door.'

He stood back and pointed to his own forehead. 'Here and here. Death will have been instantaneous. We have a ballistics expert coming in from Belfast to do the post-mortem later this morning. For now we can say that this *looks* very professional. Two rapid, accurate and purposely lethal shots, both fired from extremely close range. That is important.'

He stepped forwards until he was beneath the pictures of Fiona Mitchell, caught where she had lain, before they put the tent up. The lab had blocked out the detail from the head and the chest for the blow-ups. They could *choose* to examine the photos at the back – with all the details – if they needed to, but *forcing* the images upon them was a Health and Safety issue. Detectives had sued some other force for the shock and distress it caused.

'No ID on Phil Leech,' he said. 'No wallet, no warrant card, nothing. The only reason we were able to get going is because the car was his and is registered to him. At eight-forty the same morning, X-Ray 99 found this young lady. Fiona Mitchell. Age twenty-two. About three hundred yards into a gully running away from the road near the summit of Cock Hill. In the pocket of Mitchell's jacket is Leech's wallet, warrant card and all. In her *left* hand – or rather, lying on top of her left hand – a nine-millimetre Beretta with one live round in the clip, one chambered up in the breach. The clip holds nine. Cause of death – gunshot wounds. She has one large wound in her chest and her back. Clothing pulled up over the wound, to expose it – you can't see that on this one because of the blocking out – chest exposed in a way you might normally associate with some kind of sexual motive. Puzzlingly – and I'm hoping our Belfast expert will help with this – the injury has the characteristics normally associated with an exit wound, but to *both* sides of the body, front and back. Now, obviously one is an entry and one is an exit, but at this stage we can't get any further than that. Directly beneath that wound – and, as you can see, she is face up there – buried deep within the peat bog, we recovered a bullet confirmed as coming from *that* gun, the one in her hand. Her second injury is to the top of her face and head. Another wound with the characteristics of a close-range discharge, fired while she was in *that* position, on her back. Once again, the bullet recovered from within the bog, confirmed as discharged from *that* weapon. Two shell casings recovered from within six feet of her body.'

He paused, stepped back, took a breath.

'And as if that's not interesting enough, the bullets in Phil Leech's Rover also came from *that* weapon. The one in her hand. Confirmed.'

A murmur broke out at once. He spoke over it, raising his voice. 'One gun, four bullets, four casings. Two deceased. Make no assumptions at all.'

He waited until they had stopped.

'In particular, do *not* assume that Fiona Mitchell shot Phil Leech. Do *not* assume that Fiona Mitchell then shot herself. Do not *even* assume that Fiona Mitchell died after Phil Leech. At the moment we don't know enough to say any of that. For instance, *can* someone inflict that kind of significant chest injury on themselves and *then* go on to fire a second round into their face? That is, assuming the chest injury pre-dated death, which we don't, as yet, know. No possibility of Fiona Mitchell doing anything *after* the head injury. But someone else could have. Surprisingly, the serial number on the weapon is intact, so if we're very lucky it might turn out to be traceable. The weapon itself is completely clean, not used in any other incident on the database, including Northern Ireland.'

From the front someone asked a question. He had forgotten to tell them to keep their questions to the end.

'I'll take this one question now,' he said. 'Keep the rest for when I'm done. What did you ask?'

A male detective, not one of the sergeants. 'Do we have a time of death, sir?'

'Nothing definite yet. They were both drinking the night before though, so we might get something from the alcohol levels. Later today for that. We know it was after midnight and, trivially, before they were found. That's all so far. I don't want assumptions at this stage, but there are two pieces of evidence suggesting that Mitchell may have died after Leech, and was present when he was shot.' He counted them off on his fingers. 'One; we recovered what is probably Leech's blood from Mitchell's clothing and hair. There's a match to type at the moment, the DNA ETA is Friday morning. Two; no blood from Mitchell on Leech, that is, no type other than her own has been found, though once again DNA is expected back Friday morning. Plus what we know of their movements.'

'Why after midnight, sir?' They were keen, at least.

'I'll tell you that now.' He caught Sharpe's eye. She was seated on a table near the back, not far from Butcher. No expression on her face.

He gave them everything Sharpe had given him. From Operation Anvil and the former threats against Leech, right through to the meeting the night before and Mitchell's hysterical phone call just before midnight. He finished by telling them that Coates was in the cells not twenty feet from where they were sitting and Varley was being followed across Bradford by three Armed Response Units just looking for a chance to strike.

'DC Sharpe, incidentally, is on this squad, sitting at the back.'

Another murmur as they all turned to find her. She raised her hand, frowned, coloured slightly. Not quite so untouchable.

'Now,' he said, 'scenarios. This is the way we do it. We

gather evidence, construct scenarios, make policy decisions as to which are worth following or eliminating. The aim, always, is to get it down to one story that makes *all* the evidence make sense. The best fit. If successful, we take that story to the CPS and if they like it they employ an expensive barrister to sell it to a jury. But *we* write it. And the central bit of it – which makes all the rest work – is *motive*.'

He stood up and pulled across the second whiteboard.

'At the moment I am working with two possible scenarios. For one I have a motive, of sorts, for the other I don't. Scenario one goes like this: Mark Coates discovers that his girlfriend Fiona Mitchell has been passing information to DS Leech so he puts a contract on both of them. Many variations – as you can see from what Tony has written up here – but essentially that's it. Simple. Easy to understand. Scenario two, on the other hand, has Fiona Mitchell possibly having a sexual relationship with her informant handler – DS Leech – and, *for some reason*, becoming embittered and depressed enough to arrange to meet and kill him, after which she walks off and kills herself. The latter fits what we know of the forensics and scene examination so far. But the *for some reason* bit is crucial. So far, we don't have a reason why she should do any of that. And the idea that Phil Leech and Mitchell were having anything other than a purely professional relationship really is, at this stage, speculation. Does that matter, you might ask? After all, if scenario two is true there isn't going to be a jury to tell anything to. The Defendant is dead.'

He looked at the back row, daring them to answer.

'It does matter, because scenario two might be a red herring set up by the killer to waste our time. I have spoken to DC Sharpe about it,' a nod towards her, 'and she confirms my view. The scenario does not fit with any of the information she has about the two deceased persons' behaviour or plans just hours before all this happened.'

He paused, smiled, looked over to Tony Marshall. 'Over to you, Tony.'

Tony stood up, clearing his throat. 'Thanks, sir. What we are aiming to do over the next few days – rapidly – is develop as many scenarios as we can. Including these two. There are a lot of us, as well as others not here right now, who are equally essential parts of this team – the scientists, for example – so the information is really going to flood in as we get going. To stay on top of it we will have the benefit of a team of statement readers and the Home Office Large Major Enquiry System, HOLMES. Everything will go through both systems – on to the HOLMES computer and then to the readers. The readers will report to us, the SIO team. They will be reading what you have produced from following up the parameters set in these meetings. To organise all this we're going to divide you into the following nine teams, each under a DS.'

He stepped over to the flipchart placed beside the second whiteboard and turned the first sheet back. 'Team one. DS Smythe and these four detectives. You're HOLMES, Statement Readers and Unused Material.'

Munro watched him running through the remaining teams. They had carved up the numbers earlier. Five on the HOLMES team, a minimum of six on each of six other core teams. Three under Julie White on CJS and Admin, and three on General Research and Antecedent info.

The six core teams would change names, duties, numbers and tasks as the case developed. But at the outset there were two central teams largely reflecting the personnel already involved at both scenes during the last twenty-four hours, a Wainstalls team and a Cock Hill team. They would manage all the area searches already underway using the Operational Support Unit, probationers and army, plus anything else that came from the scenes themselves.

Then a team of six to deal with wider door-to-door enquiries and CCTV seizures. The 'Surrounding Area' team, for want of anything better to call it. They would seize anything and everything that might have a remote connection to the scenes, victims and individual suspects.

Those were the scene teams. From there they moved on to people teams. They had decided to fund a (short-term, until the idea was discredited) 'suicide' team, to look at Fiona Mitchell's background in detail, focusing initially on negating the suicide idea, thereafter on what remained of her background and connections.

The team Sharpe would be a part of would unearth all the background pertinent to Coates and Varley. This was the largest task and as the scene teams finished up they would help out. To begin with, nearly half the Coates and Varley team was taken up with the business of locating and arresting Varley and processing the premise searches that would follow. There were to be two Detective Sergeants running the Coates and Varley team, with a DI in overall control.

The last team would look into Phil Leech.

Officers would be pulled off the most appropriate teams as and when interviewers were needed.

That accounted for nearly all the officers Munro had been promised, once the Exhibits Officer, Forensics Liaison, Receiver and Office Manager were included.

He listened as Tony's flat South Leeds voice gave them all this with names and details and watched them taking notes. Then he stepped up again.

'We've put five on the HOLMES team,' he said, 'because of the Unused Material aspect. We don't want any cock-ups here. I know you are all anxious to get out of here and get back to it – especially the three scene teams when we have the OSU and nearly two hundred personnel up there waiting to start fingertipping – but can I ask you, as you leave here, to keep these first crucial lines in mind, in order to stop ourselves making assumptions.

'One; if Fiona was at Wainstalls, *how* did she move from there to Cock Hill? Was transport involved? There is a nice skid mark on the road above Cock Hill. Any connection? Two; if scenario one is true, someone else was at one or both scenes. How did they get there? Both these scenes are remote and difficult to get to without transport. Three; Fiona told DC Sharpe she was going to drive up to the reservoir at Wainstalls. We recovered her car, undamaged, from a pub car park in Keighley. How did she get up there? Four; DC Sharpe has told us that earlier in the evening Fiona had a handbag with her. This has not been recovered from her premises. She has a gun when we get to her at Cock Hill. Did she tuck it down the back of her jeans? Or was it carried in a bag of some sort? If so, where is that bag?'

He stepped back. 'There are many other lines that Tony has put together in the briefing pack. Please read it. It's meant to help you play a wider role in policy formation. You don't have to worry about which actions are your responsibility as they will be assigned appropriately by DI Dyson. I know there are already piles of paper actions in the team trays. Check. They might have your name on them. More will be coming from HOLMES before long. That's it. Any questions?'

As they started he reflected that one thing was certainly different from almost every other briefing he had set up in the past. This one had been entirely free of interruptions from mobile phones.

SEVEN

It wasn't that she had held things back from them, it was just that – given the state of her head – it was difficult to recall everything at once. She remembered now, for instance, that Fiona had told her on the phone she had broken a window to get out to Haworth, to escape. And while she had remembered most of the information Fiona had provided to Leech about the supposed Manchester deal involving Coates, she had forgotten that Fiona had also given the name of the Manchester dealer. *Liam Toomey*. She had forgotten the name. Given the pressure, it wasn't surprising.

Just those two details, but they kept coming back at her. Jammed in the back of her mind, like a little, stubborn lump.

Worse still, she could now recall part of her own conversation with Fiona in the toilets. As she had tried to console her Fiona had turned to her and, inexplicably, asked her where she was from *originally*. The question had thrown her.

'Why do you want to know that?' she had asked.

'Because sometimes,' Fiona had replied, struggling to speak clearly through her tears, 'I think I can hear an accent.'

She could feel the depth of her frown even now, thinking about it.

'An Irish accent,' Fiona had said.

She hadn't passed any of that to Munro. But why should she? The conversation was bizarre. The one thing she knew for certain about her voice was that she *definitely* did not have any trace of an Irish accent. Munro would have been puzzled if she *had* passed that on.

But something in the back of her mind wanted to connect these three things. A trivial conversation – from Fiona's viewpoint, at any rate – a name, and a detail about a window. There was something about them she was missing.

Coates and Varley was the biggest team. There were fourteen detectives on it, expected to rise to twenty-six as things progressed. They had a separate room in Richmond Close, on the first floor, two levels up from the Incident Room.

In that room, she had a desk. On one corner of it was an in-tray, already full of paper actions, generated largely, she saw when she examined them, by information she had passed on to Munro. The top one, for example, was a request to recover from the Anvil paperwork the ownership details of Fiona's one bedroom flat in Ilkley. (She had told Munro that Coates provided her with the flat.) There was a three-day turnaround on that. Not urgent.

Beneath it, with a twelve-hour turnaround, a request to scan the CCTV footage taken from the security system in Coates's home to check for Fiona's presence between nine p.m. and twelve p.m. on 8 April. Wrongly allocated. That should have gone to the Mitchell/Suicide team. It was about Fiona, not Coates, Varley or Anvil.

DS Bob Harris was in charge of the sub-team she was attached to. His desk was at the front of the room, facing them as if it were some sort of classroom. On his desk was an in-tray for them to submit completed actions. He would check them, take them downstairs to the

HOLMES team, who would input them on the computer and pass them to one of two Statement Readers. They would read them, decide whether anything else needed actioning and, if so, pass a request back to the HOLMES operators who would input it and then pass it to DI Dyson, for allocation. And so the wheel went round.

Given she had now remembered previously forgotten things, what was meant to happen was simple. She should take a minute sheet out of the drawer, write down the two things she had remembered and put the minute into Bob Harris's in-tray.

But she didn't. Instead she picked the action already in her tray, which requested, 'Check authenticity of Fiona Mitchell's information concerning an imminent drugs deal with a Manchester dealer' (three-day turnaround) and told Harris she was off to visit Greater Manchester Police to follow it up.

Harris was a mild man, probably due for retirement, no doubt experienced in running murder research teams. But he had the sort of gentle features that suggested he wouldn't be good with spaced-out informants and wouldn't handle confrontation. When he looked at her she saw concern and fear in his eyes. Concern that, despite appearances, she must be cracking up and fear that she was going to do it in his office, that he was going to have to deal with it.

He didn't want her to visit GMP. She could tell from his half-hearted response. What he wanted her to do was help find PC Oliver Williams – the man Phil Leech had down as having checked his car number plates in the past.

'It will be a quick enquiry,' she told him. 'Half-day maximum.'

'It's not priority. Williams is.'

'It will be done in an hour. Then we can get on to Williams.'

'I'll come with you, then,' he said.

'You need to stay here, Bob. To organise us.' She walked off.

'Take Ian, then,' he called after her.

'I'll be okay. Don't worry,' she shouted back, flashing him a smile.

She found the normal CID office and logged on to an OIS terminal to access the force intelligence database. Anvil was still marked as restricted. She used their password and searched for any reference to Liam Toomey. Nothing. She did a general check with the same result.

In the Incident Room, in the basement, it took her nearly half an hour of sifting through photos, statements and exhibit logs – and fifteen quick minutes enquiring of the search teams – to discover that there were no broken windows at any of the properties they had searched during the last twenty-eight hours. She had given them the list of premises. She had given them anywhere either owned or frequented by Coates, Varley or Mitchell.

Fiona had lied to her. Why?

Starting the car in the back yard, she tried to work it into perspective. One lie didn't mean a conspiracy. There were readily available explanations. She ran through them as she drove out of the station and began following the road out to the motorway.

Three small details. No obvious connection between them. But they were shouting at her, putting up warning signs that had probably been there two days ago if she had been looking. She could reason her way around it, find excuses, but the feeling remained. A piece slotting into

60

place? Or more like sitting in a darkened house waiting for something to happen.

As she joined the near stationary queues of traffic on the M62 westbound she used the mobile to call MANCRO, GMP's Force Intelligence office. She identified herself, gave her mobile number, cut the connection and waited for them to call back.

They didn't take long. She listened as a civilian operator gave her the info in a deadpan, flat voice. They had a Liam Toomey. But he was blocked.

She pulled over into the lay-by and spoke as calmly as she could. 'Blocked isn't good enough. I'm on a murder enquiry. You'll have to clear it.'

'I can't do that.'

'The victim was a police officer.'

'I know that. You told me. But it comes up blocked. I'm not authorised to clear it.'

'*Can* you clear it? Do you know how?'

'No. You need higher level clearance. I don't have authority.'

'So who does? How do I get past the block?'

Silence.

'Did you hear me?'

'Yes. I'm trying to think about that. Probably put in a request through your SIO. I don't know.'

'A request to who?'

'The Director of Intelligence.'

'Who's he?'

'She. Detective Superintendent Green. Sue Green.'

'Where will I get her?'

'Here. Manchester HQ.'

'Do you have a number?'

She waited while the operator read off the number.

'Any indication why it's blocked?'

'No. I'm just reading from the screen. Sorry.'

She cut the line. Pulling back into the traffic she was set to turn back at the next junction, but the mobile went off within minutes, before she got there.

'DC Sharpe?'

'Yes.'

'Eric Sutherland. MANCRO. You called a few minutes ago.'

'Yes?'

'You were asking about a Liam Toomey. I think we gave you wrong info.'

'You gave me no info. I was told he was blocked.'

'Yes. Sorry about that. That's not right. We just don't give details over the phone.'

She thought about it. She had got telephone responses countless times in the past.

'So if I come over, will you give me what you've got?'

'Of course. How about tomorrow?'

'I need it now. How about half an hour?'

EIGHT

Sutherland wasn't with MANCRO. She could see that just by looking at him. She knew the type too well. Special Branch. From tip to toe. That or worse – something military, perhaps. Once she'd worked it out she knew exactly how to play him.

'So what's your interest in Liam Toomey?' he asked her, features relaxed. Nothing more than a casual, conversational enquiry. He spoke with a clean, public school accent, clipped Sandhurst vowels.

She smiled helplessly, shrugged her shoulders. Stupid female. 'It's an action I was given.'

He nodded, allowed himself a thin smile. 'Which enquiry?'

'Phoenix. The dead DS. You might have seen it on the news.'

'Yes. Terrible business.'

They were in an office that had someone else's name on the door. The papers littered on the desk in front of Sutherland had nothing to do with him. She doubted he had ever sat there before.

'It's good of you to see me so quickly,' she said.

'So what do you need?' he asked.

He was a thin man, tall and wiry. Very straight back, sharp little eyes. Maybe mid-fifties. He wore a tweed jacket and slacks, a thick, expensive-looking shirt, perfectly pressed. She reflected that it had taken him less than a minute to contact her. Which meant there was a flag on the screen telling the operator to notify him of each and every enquiry about Liam Toomey. Urgently. Though he looked comfortable behind the desk he could have arrived only minutes before her, unless they were based here, in Manchester HQ. Which she doubted.

'I'm checking up the background of the operation the deceased was working,' she explained. 'It was a drugs job called Anvil. Looking at a small-time dealer in Bradford called Coates. There was some information that Toomey might have been a link in his supply chain.'

Sutherland shrugged. 'So what? How will that help?'

She shrugged back at him. 'I've no idea, sir. They give me the action and I chase it up.' She called him 'sir' deliberately, though he hadn't bothered to introduce himself other than by name. In front of him she could see a thin, buff folder with a photo clipped to the corner of a CRO sheet.

He saw her looking at it, reached a hand over and picked it up. 'You've no idea how Toomey would fit in to the death?'

'No. I suppose they're working on a drug thing.'

'A drug thing?' Slight tetchiness in his tone.

'Yes, sir. Like maybe the dead officer was getting too close to Coates? So he had him killed.'

'And how would Toomey fit in to that scenario?'

She shrugged again. 'I've no idea.'

He placed the folder back on the desk, photo face down, leaned back in the seat and frowned at her. 'So how do you know what you're looking for?'

'I was just going to ask Toomey about it. Ask him whether he was doing business with Coates.'

'Just ask him?' He gave her the thin smile again, this time derisory. 'Just walk up to him and ask him?'

'Why not?'

He nodded. 'Indeed. Why not?' She saw him relax a little. First impressions confirmed. 'Do you have a copy of the action I can see?'

She dug it out and passed it over to him. 'Is that Toomey's file, sir?' she asked, while he was reading it. He ignored her.

'Check authenticity of Fiona Mitchell's information concerning an imminent drugs deal with a Manchester dealer,' he read from the slip of paper, then looked up at her. 'It doesn't mention Toomey,' he said.

'No, sir. Someone on the Mitchell team told me the deal was to be through Toomey.'

'*Through* Toomey?'

'Or with him. I'm not sure. If you give me the file, I'll happily look through it myself.'

'Look through it for what?'

'Addresses.'

'So you can go up to him and ask him?'

'That's right.'

'How long have you been a detective, Officer?'

She looked away from him, colouring slightly. Smiling at herself even as it happened. 'Three months, sir.'

She watched him swallow it. Not a hint of suspicion in his eyes. Why should she lie to him?

'I thought so,' he said. 'I want you to promise me something.'

She waited. A fatherly tone now.

'If I give you his last two addresses, will you promise me you will not simply drive over there and knock on the door? Will you promise me you will first take the information back to your supervisor?'

She feigned a look of confusion.

'I don't want responsibility for a second shooting,' he said. 'Who is your supervisor?'

'DS Harris.'

'Not him. The SIO. Who is SIO on this enquiry?'

'John Munro. Detective Chief Superintendent Munro.'

'Very well, Officer.' He opened the folder and looked down at it. 'I can tell you this much: Toomey is a bottom-range dealer who worked until recently for a Manchester mister called Skelly. An errand boy. That's all. The information we have is that they had a fairly major fall-out about four months back. We don't know why. But Toomey had to leave Manchester. The last address I have for him is in Bradford.'

She took out her notebook and wrote it down as he gave her it. *Flat 15A Manor Park Road, Manningham.*

'Do you have a phone number?' she asked.

He shook his head and passed her three thin sheets of paper. 'That's his form. You'll note the violence conviction three years ago. But there's nothing big. Nothing for firearms, for instance.'

'No?' She glanced briefly at the print-out. 'Is he Irish?' she asked, without looking at him.

'Irish? Why?'

She could feel him tensing. She glanced up, looked into his eyes. 'The name. Toomey. It's Irish, isn't it?'

He stared back at her. 'Half of Manchester has an Irish name. It doesn't mean they're all Paddies.'

'Quite,' she said. She raised an eyebrow, waiting. 'Is he, then?'

He shook his head, closed the folder. He was irritated now, unable to conceal it. 'No. He's not.'

NINE

Boyd – the Belfast gunshot expert – was younger than Munro had expected. Certainly younger than both himself and Graham Dawson, their own pathologist. He was about five eight with black hair falling across his forehead in a lank fringe that reminded Munro unfortunately of Adolf Hitler. He spoke in rapid, blunt sentences that were sometimes difficult to keep up with. The Northern Ireland accent was heavy, giving his words a weight that matched the content.

There was a reason why Brian Butcher had seen fit to bring him in and it was apparent when he spoke; whatever the type of gunshot injury, Boyd had seen it before. In his experience of this type of thing, he was twice their age. The worn expression at the back of his eyes confirmed it. Explaining the idea that it was theoretically possible for someone to shoot themselves twice, he sounded to Munro like the Reverend Ian Paisley's twin brother.

'It has happened. Certainly it has happened.'

'With so large a first injury?' Dawson asked.

'There are accounts of it. Certainly. From all wars. The First, Second, Korea, Vietnam. You name it. Even our own little local war in the Province – as you call it. Wounded soldiers with injuries as severe as this or worse, in traumatic terms – legs blown off and such like – have lain in the field of battle screaming to be put out of their misery, calling pathetically for their mothers until a comrade who could not bear it any longer put a gun in their hand and permitted them to despatch themselves with dignity. It *has* happened.'

'And it could have occurred in this case?'

'Theoretically. But I doubt it. It wouldn't be your first theory.'

As he delivered this opinion, they were standing in the Bradford city mortuary. The remains of Fiona Mitchell and Philip Leech were set out on tables before them. As usual, the atmosphere was getting to Munro, a persistent weakness he had been unable to master in five years as an SIO. It wasn't so much the odour of stale blood, the hint of putrefaction behind it – with Leech and Mitchell it was early days for real decay (and usually, with the really bad ones, it was the incidental gases bubbling out of them that knocked you back, the stuff that popped through the holes when you moved the corpse, rather than the stuff that fell off) – nor was it even the overpowering combination of formaldehyde and disinfectant. What got to him every time was a stench some people didn't even notice in the place – the background odour coming off the stomach and bowel contents, usually bagged up and placed discretely to one side. He didn't mind, conceptually, that cut-up, rotting bodies should smell like a butcher's shop, but that they should reek however faintly of faeces and vomit made the bile rise in his throat.

It didn't help that the Bradford mortuary was a particularly dingy and airless location. There were no windows in the room they used for autopsies and the theatre lighting was correspondingly harsh to make up for this. Pack six people – himself, Boyd, Dawson, Tony Marshall, Dawson's assistant and the DC Tony was using to take notes – into a room that was barely large enough for the two tables holding the corpses, and the effect was very quickly unpleasant, even without the corpses and the stench.

Mastering the urge to turn out his stomach left him with a feeling similar to a hangover. A need for air and aspirin, a dizziness when he moved quickly. In this condition he watched Dawson retracing for Boyd each step of the post-mortems already carried out on both Leech and Mitchell. Apparently there was nothing amiss in what they had done. Once he had known Boyd was coming, Dawson had been careful to preserve the gunshot areas without much destructive analysis.

Notwithstanding, the body spread out on the metal table in front of them bore no obvious resemblance to the photos Munro had seen of Fiona Mitchell alive, nor even to the body he had recovered from Cock Hill Moor. A post-mortem was nothing if not intrusive. To get access to everything he needed, Dawson had cut her torso into three distinct pieces. He had left the head and chest relatively intact for Boyd, but the rest of the process had been standard. Everything inside had come out.

Dawson was as interested in Boyd's help as the rest of them. He had relatively little experience of close-range gunshot injuries of this type. In particular he was as hopeful as Munro that Boyd would have something to say about the size of the entry wound to the front of the chest. They had determined already that it was far too small to have been caused by a different weapon – a shotgun, for example – but they needed help. In both their experiences, entry wounds were usually small and relatively clean.

Working around the bullet wounds, Dawson had carried out all the standard procedures with medical records and general examination before Boyd's arrival, most of it, in fact, the day before. There were no other underlying or non-apparent conditions that might have caused or contributed to the deaths; both were healthy, well-nourished individuals, and the blood and urine samples yielded nothing more poisonous than alcohol traces, in both. For Leech this wasn't surprising, but for Mitchell it was confirmation of the information she had repeatedly given to Leech and Sharpe – that she had been clean for nearly a year – which Sharpe, at least, had doubted.

There were no injuries to Mitchell apart from the obvious – two gunshot wounds. No defensive injuries. Similarly with Leech, though that was less surprising. The best Dawson had been able to do with time of death had been predictably useless, given what they already knew from Sharpe, though it did more or less confirm her timings. The back calculation on blood alcohol for both had been rendered speculative by the period of just over three hours between last sightings by Sharpe and the phone calls before midnight.

So far they had been unable to adequately piece together what either deceased had done in that time and whether it had included alcohol. Until they knew for certain, the back calculation wasn't going to help discover which of the two had predeceased the other. For that it looked like they were to be dependent on the DNA results, the ETA for which had come forward to midday Thursday. If – as the typing suggested – Leech's blood was all over Mitchell but there was nothing of Mitchell on Leech, then it looked likely that Leech had been the first to go.

It didn't take Boyd long to confirm cause of death on Leech. He spent a long time looking at the ballistics report and the photos from the scenes, asking various questions.

'Do you have compounds on Mitchell's hand?'

'Yes,' Munro replied. 'Lead, antimony and barium. But

the gun is in her hand. If it was placed there, the compounds could arise through contamination.'

'Gun in left hand?'

'Yes.'

'No compounds on right hand?'

'Yes. Residues on both hands. In fact, all over her clothing and face, as well as within the nasal passages and hair. But once again, if she was sitting next to Leech when the gun was fired into him, she could have taken up the residues that way. I've been told that she could even have become contaminated simply because she herself had been shot at close range.'

'True. But she is clearly right-handed?' Boyd looked to Dawson for confirmation.

Dawson nodded. He had already pointed to the evidence indicating this as a high probability, most clearly the small lump of hardened skin on the right index finger built up by writing.

'So the gun was probably placed there. If she gave herself this head injury she wouldn't be changing hands afterwards. Obviously.'

'Is it obvious?' Munro followed Boyd over to the table where Mitchell lay. 'I didn't think it was possible to shoot yourself twice like that.'

'This head injury has killed her, almost instantaneously. She will have lost consciousness immediately. Normally the heart would stop beating within seconds of this kind of trauma. The chest wounds are different.'

'Wounds?'

'Yes. I think there are two wounds to the chest, two separate points of entry.'

Munro glanced at Dawson. He shrugged, equally in the dark.

'It's easy to miss,' Boyd continued. 'You get yourself

puzzled by the injury type and you forget to wonder about the obvious – *is* it only one injury? Assumption, you see. That's what sidetracks us. In this case, I assume it was meant to.'

Munro smiled at him. The experts were never much good at plain English. 'You'll have to be clearer than that, Mr Boyd. You've lost me.'

'I won't be sure until I've taken the tissue apart a bit, but it is an obvious explanation for this particular type of "entry" pattern.'

'Meaning?'

'It's not an entry pattern at all. It's a standard exit wound. Just like the one in this woman's back.'

'Two exit wounds?'

Boyd nodded, brushing the fringe from his eyes. 'I've seen it before. Something similar can happen when paramilitaries attempt to disguise torture injuries on executed informants. But clearer than that, I dealt with a case two years ago where a chap had been arrested by a clandestine military unit, down near the border. Before the helicopter got in to get them out they claimed he had come at them trying to disarm them, so they had shot him. Right here,' he pointed to the hole in Mitchell's chest, 'front chest. About three inches right of the heart. That man had an injury profile almost exactly the same as this, except the calibre and velocity of the weapons were greater. But the same rough size to the exit and entry wounds, front and back.'

He paused, looking at Munro as if to ask, do you see it now? Munro didn't.

'We started with blood pattern analysis. From that we began to build up a different picture to that given by the soldiers. When I went into his chest I found fragments of bone from his posterior rib cage buried in the anterior intercostal muscles.'

He looked up at Dawson, who nodded, apparently understanding.

'In other words, he was shot through the back – while trying to escape, perhaps – and then, quite deliberately, shot through the exit wound in order to conceal the nature of the first injury.'

'Shot through the back first and then shot into the same wound – from the front – in order to disguise the back injury?' It was Marshall who asked the question.

'I believe so.'

Munro frowned. 'Why?'

'It's clumsy, of course. It's not going to stand detailed analysis. But it might slow you down.'

'Slow me down? How?'

'You understand that at this point I am speculating?'

'Yes. Go on.'

'Whoever killed her placed the gun in her hand. To make it look as if she had killed herself. I don't know why. But if she was lying there with an exit wound in her chest – clearly shot through the back – well, it doesn't take you long to smell a rat. No one shoots themselves through the back. So he – or she – shot this woman through the chest to disguise that. That is why her clothing was pulled up – to locate the exact position of the wound.'

Munro shook his head. 'It's too speculative. What about other explanations? A different weapon type, for instance.'

'I don't think so. But it's easy enough to prove. The ribs are broken in her back. The entry point, according to Mr Dawson's analysis, is right here – through the seventh rib, breaking it and, on a fragmentation effect, the sixth and eighth ribs as well. But the trajectory is slightly downwards – interesting in itself – causing this exit wound just below and to the right of the sternum in the front of the chest. No broken ribs in the anterior aspect. If I'm right, you will find bits of the rear ribs near the exit wound in her chest. No more than pieces, of course. Most of the fragments will have been blown clean through her body. Hence the very ragged look to the wound in her chest. But if she was only shot at this point in the chest then there should be no bone fragments there at all. As simple as that. If it turns out there are areas of broken rib to the anterior aspect, then you will still be able to chart my theory by matching fragments to specific bones in the back. It just takes a little longer that way. I suggest Mr Dawson start with that work while you take me up to the scene.'

TEN

Boyd asked Munro whether he would mind if he smoked the minute they got into his car. Concealing his reluctance (the cigarette was between Boyd's lips) Munro told him he didn't mind at all. Then, unable to stop himself, added, 'You know those things can kill you?'

Boyd didn't even bother acknowledging the comment.

He didn't want to see Wainstalls, wasn't interested. 'Nothing difficult there,' he said, between drags. With the fag between his lips he looked less self-assured.

Munro took the long way around, down through the valley and back. They would be starting to fingertip at Wainstalls. He didn't want to get in the way if it wasn't necessary. He tried to make conversation to fill the time, but Boyd wasn't much for talking unless it was about work.

'Did you speak to SO13 about it?' he asked, as they were coming into Hebden Bridge.

'Yes. You must have a lot to do with them?'

'Not really. They're London. Sometimes they come over for advice. We have our own people.'

'RUC Special Branch?'

'And others. What did SO13 think?'

'In what way?'

'About terrorist involvement.'

'That there wasn't any.'

'Too quick. They didn't know what I know.'

'No. But since Mitchell wasn't in the IRA – as far as we know – and her killer is unlikely to have been a soldier, I guess we can put that one to bed.'

'I would say so. PIRA would have claimed by now. Though you never know what the SAS will get up to. If what I'm saying happened pans out, of course, then you get the start of a profile.'

'Someone who was panicked?'

'A little more than that. Someone not completely ignorant of ballistic issues, for example, who knew an exit wound would be fairly quickly recognised but perhaps didn't know that we can equally quickly get past the first indications. Or maybe he – or she – wasn't thinking at all. Or not thinking clearly. Didn't intend to kill her perhaps. Not originally. When it happened didn't quite know how to react. Panicked, as you say. Either way, not someone for whom something specific like this is second nature. What you have is a hit – a targeted killing – but with a novice on the trigger. Not uncommon where I come from.'

'I imagine not.'

He was quick to explain, Munro thought, to match speculative facts to theories. If they were this incautious in Northern Ireland, it was a wonder they had ever caught anyone.

At Cock Hill, standing by the car looking along the line of telegraph poles that led down through the gully to the scene tent, Boyd became visibly excited.

'I didn't notice from the photos,' he said, voice raised against the wind. 'It's an incline. That's why the trajectory is downwards, through the chest.'

'But we've recovered the bullet,' Munro said. 'It was in the ground beneath her.'

'Not that bullet! You've recovered the one he put into her as she was lying there, flat on her back. I'm talking about the one he put into her from here!' He gestured wildly in the air. 'As she was running from him. Running down there!'

He paced off towards the tent, turning through the album of scene photos Munro had given him. Past the gate on to the moor he quickly covered the three hundred yards to where the first yellow flagged stake marked the beginning of the blood pattern. When Munro caught up with him he was comparing the scene photo to the spot at his feet, lining up the photo edge with the marker stake.

'Excellent marking. Really first class,' he was saying. Munro watched him. It was like taking a sighting along a compass. There was no longer any blood visible on the matted hillocks of sphagnum – it had rained the night before – but the stake had four radial prongs, which SOCO had aligned to the four compass points as they fixed it in place. The same stake was in situ in the photograph of the area, showing the fresh blood spattering. Comparing the two it was possible to work out exactly where the blood pattern had lain on the ground.

'Clearly where she was first hit,' Boyd said. He was slightly breathless. 'A typical exit pattern.' He looked back up towards the road they had come from. 'Night time . . .' He was thinking aloud. Munro watched. They had already been through a similar process. 'How would he see her to aim?'

'He?'

'He or she.'

'A torch?'

'No. I don't think so. Hard to pull that one off. Gun in one hand, torch in the other. More likely the moon. Have you checked the phasing?'

'Yes. Almost full.'

'I thought so. What about cartridge cases? Two further down, right? Near to the body?'

'Yes.'

'The distance from here to the tent is another ten yards though. How would a case get carried there if she had shot herself here?'

'I don't know,' Munro said. 'Caught up in her clothing?'

'And other coincidences. I don't think so. Did you recover anything from back up there?' He was sighting with his arm along a precise trajectory taken from the photo, pointing not back towards the road, but towards the weather station, to the right of the line they had followed to come down.

'In that exact direction?'

'Yes.'

'No. We've searched in a line from where we are now back to the skid mark on the road.'

'Why?'

'SOCO told us the line was consistent with the blood pattern analysis—'

'Rubbish. They've been sidetracked by the skid mark. The skid mark might have nothing to do with it. *This* is the line from this exit pattern. Right here.' He held his arm up again.

'That's not what SOCO said. They were—'

'I'm the expert, Mr Munro. I *am*. Believe me. I am indicating the correct line for this exit pattern, give or take ten degrees. Have you searched it?'

'No. Not that line. Half of this hillside is underwater anyway. We fingertip it tomorrow, if we're on schedule.'

'You should bring it forward. Unless he removed it, it will be there.'

'A cartridge case?'

78

'Yes. Anything between ten and fifty feet from where we are standing now. Any further and it would be a really lucky shot.'

'You're sure about this?'

'Almost.' He turned around and pointed back down the moor towards the tent. 'And in this direction – anything between fifty and two thousand metres – somewhere in that moor, you will find, if you are very, very lucky indeed, the shell itself.'

Munro looked at him, looked back in the direction he was pointing. Over the top of the tent the land fell away towards the valley. The far side was perhaps three kilometres distant. A vast open expanse of featureless hillside. Was he serious?

'Do you think we should fingertip for it?' he asked. A joke.

'Absolutely.' Boyd didn't look up from the photos. He was serious.

'The entire moor?'

'No. Find the spent cartridge first. After that I can help you. In Northern Ireland we have a computer model that does just this – computes fall trajectories. I'll send a man over to get the data. It won't be a small task. The chances will be slim. But it won't be the whole moor. It will narrow it down. And at least you'll have tried.'

Munro shook his head. 'We'll see. I'd be happy if we found the cartridge case.'

Back at the station he left Boyd with Dawson and took a call from a frustrated DS from the Coates and Varley team called Scother. Apparently the Firearms Support Unit had cocked it up, at least, that was how Scother described it. For four hours they had been tailing Luke Varley across Bradford without making any attempt to take him just because they were terrified he might actually be armed. He gave instructions to Scother and then found Chris Greenwood, the DC Bob Harris had tasked with sifting through the video material culled from Coates's house in Haworth.

They watched nearly an hour of CCTV clips seized from the security system inside Coates's house on the evening of 8 April. Greenwood had watched the tapes several times over. What he had discovered was significant. He had needed to be certain and flicked quickly through the footage to find the parts he wanted Munro to see.

At ten twenty-seven p.m. Fiona Mitchell could be seen on the external camera driving up to the building and entering it. Inside, about ten minutes later, Varley prepares and snorts two lines of a drug. Presumably cocaine. (They had recovered a small quantity in one of the bedrooms.)

Mitchell appears at the back end of this session, sitting down on a sofa opposite Coates. They are seen to argue about something – possibly where she has been. Munro thought the sound quality was useless. Greenwood was on to it though. It would be another day before they could get it enhanced.

Varley offers Mitchell what appears to be the same drug he has taken, but she refuses and leaves the room. Varley leaves shortly after her and drives off. All prior to eleven-ten p.m. Coates remains sitting in the same room, with very few interruptions, apparently watching TV. At some point he falls asleep. The tape runs on. At eleven thirty-three p.m. Mitchell leaves the house and drives away. Coates unaware. Nearly four hours of footage follows. Coates slumped in a chair. He wakes up just after four, replete with alibi.

'Definitely the night of the eighth and ninth?' Munro asked. 'No chance of doctoring or setting it up?'

'No. It's genuine. Coates was there throughout and it's all on film.'

'The perfect alibi.'

'As good as it gets.'

'We'll see. It's good work, Chris. Well done. We know now Coates wasn't on the trigger. Varley is bang on time though. That's a start.'

'Coates sets it up; Varley is on the trigger?'

'Maybe. Is there a camera in his bedroom?'

'No.'

'And we have – what? – three months' worth of these recordings?'

'According to the labelling.'

'Very strange. Why do that? Why record and *keep* recordings of stuff going on in your own home?'

Greenwood shrugged. 'Paranoia?'

'Whatever. Put up an action for someone to check how often he falls asleep on camera. Not often, is my guess.'

ELEVEN

DS David Scother watched the FSU vans moving into place with a growing sense of despair. They had thrown two cordons around Varley's cousin's home in Odsal and Varley had walked out in broad daylight, got into his car and driven away unchallenged. As usual, involving the Firearms Support Unit had meant nothing but bureaucracy, caution and delay.

His own team had tracked Varley to his cousin's by ten the night before – the Tuesday. It had taken Firearms until one the following morning to decide (a) there was a risk sufficient to warrant an armed 'solution' (Varley had previous for armed robbery and was linked to Coates and Leech), (b) the exact structure of the solution (involving a rapid entry action), and (c) that it would be 'outwith the risk assessment parameters' to execute the solution during the hours of darkness. Instead the FTT had put covert observation teams in and they had set about overbriefing the three Raid teams. The psychological profile and risk assessment alone had taken nearly two hours, all during the early hours of the morning.

Though the sun was up by five, it took them until six-thirty to finally clear the proposed operation through the Command Team at Wakefield. The delay had been because several different levels of permission – including that of the Chief Constable – had proved problematic. He didn't know why. By seven they had the strike cordons in place.

No one was going to get into the Inner Cordon until they had gone in. However, because the houses were back-to-back terraces with no gardens or yards, the Inner Cordon was cast fairly wide. That involved a slight risk of interference from within the cordon. Slight because at that time of day not many people were up and about in Odsal.

The strike was fixed for seven-fifteen. At seven-twelve the 'slight risk' miraculously materialised when the next-door neighbour left her own adjoining terrace, walked the short distance to the target front door, knocked and entered. In her arms was a small child.

The effect in the command vehicle – an unmarked van three streets back (from where Scother had been listening to all this unfolding over the radio traffic) – could not have been much more dramatic if a hand grenade had rolled through the open back doors. Within three frantic seconds the whole thing was closed down and called off. There was to be no question of setting the blower and rolling in safety-off if there were 'third parties' anywhere near the place.

'Just too dangerous,' the Inspector running the operation had told him. He had seemed relieved.

All Scother could think about was the evidence. If Varley was involved, everything even vaguely useful would be cinders by the time they got to him. Every hour they delayed reduced the chance of a forensic hit. Fibres were especially short-lived. The chances of recovering fibres diminished rapidly as time passed. Within three days the chances of a hit would be non-existent.

'Just too dangerous for who?' he asked, trying to keep his voice even.

'For the third parties. There's a child in there now. That changes everything.'

'So what's Plan B?'

'We go back to Command.'

Another two-hour delay, he thought. As it turned out, however, Varley changed the shape of it before Plan B ever saw daylight. Within twenty minutes of the neighbour entering he was out on the street and heading for his car.

'Take him now?' Scother had suggested. They hadn't even bothered responding.

So the Force Tactical Team had ended up picking it up again.

Four hours later, a long series of rolling observations on his movements had ground to a halt in a pub in central Bradford. Naturally, a firearms response was not going to happen there.

'So where do you think it's safe to do this strike?' Scother had asked.

'All manner of locations. But not a busy pub.'

Scother called John Munro to complain. Munro told him to put a man into the pub without telling them. Scother lined up two Leeds detectives (they were less likely to have run into Varley in the past) and sent the first in to scout. He was in fifteen minutes before returning to report that it looked very unlikely that Varley was armed, from his movements, demeanour and clothing. There were about fifteen people in the place and Varley was with a group of men – all mid-twenties – gathered beneath the TV in the bar, watching a satellite sports channel. Varley was drinking lager.

He was not behaving like someone who knew he was wanted for shooting a policeman, although given he was watching a television, it wouldn't be long before he saw something about it and put two and two together. For that matter, if he had a mobile with him it probably wouldn't be long before someone got the news to him that his half-brother was already inside. Time wasn't on their side.

Scother sent the second man in to keep a watching brief and lined up another five officers from his team who said they had never come across Varley before. By the time they arrived it was just past midday.

He sent them in ahead of him, waited five minutes, then walked straight past the FSU vans and into the place.

The Leeds officer he had sent in with the watching brief – Geoff Evans – was large and immediately noticeable at the bar. 'Varley is a small-time Bradford scrote,' Scother had said to him. 'I will put money on it that he is not armed, that we could have pulled him last night without any of this fuss.'

The place was dingy – an old pub the brewery hadn't yet got round to theming. Brown paint on the walls, wooden bar and floor, wallpaper a discoloured floral pattern. It was just after midday and the place still smelled of the night before. Varley was sitting on a stool at one end of the bar, back to the entrance of the gents toilets, watching a foreign soccer match on the TV. There were three other males stood around him. None of them looked at Scother as he entered.

He took some time to take in the details. He recognised Varley at once, from the photo in the briefing pack. He was a slight individual, no more than five seven in height and skinny with it. There would be a wiry, street-hard kind of strength there, no doubt. But no weight behind it. He was the sort of person who would have learned the hard way that he was too little to win fights without a weapon. But carrying a gun was something else entirely.

Scother thought there was something slightly effeminate

85

about him – the rolled-up sleeve showing the tattoo (an eagle?) at his biceps, the single earring in the left ear, the way he smoked the cigarette, cocked lazily between his fingers, pursed lips as he took the drag, even the gel or lacquer or whatever it was that ran his lank red hair back from his forehead. His skin was too smooth.

During the psychological profiling, an incident a few years back had been mentioned during which some black Leeds drug dealers had come to collect a debt from Varley. They had beaten him a bit, then put a rumour out on the street that they had buggered him as well. The story was part of the background to a firearms incident involving one of the dealers. Someone had shot him in the legs about three weeks after the rumour began to circulate. They had been unable to pin anything on Varley. But the story would be useful wind-up material when they got him into the interview room.

Scother picked out the five-man back-up, still ordering their drinks at the other end of the bar, then moved up beside Evans. Standing beside him he made eye contact and nodded that he should follow him. Then he walked past Varley (without looking at him) and into the gents toilets. Thirty seconds later Evans came in behind him.

'What do you think?' he asked him.

'Not sure, boss, but he doesn't look like he knows what's going on.'

'Right. That's my view, too. And if he doesn't know Coates is in the tank, why would he be armed?'

'He doesn't look armed. No bulges, no movements.'

'Exactly. Here's what we are going to do. We walk out of here now, go straight for him, take him to the floor. Just like that. Got it?'

Evans looked indifferent. 'Why not?'

Scother led. Once past the second door to the gents

Varley was no more than eight feet away. Scother crossed the boards quickly, moving up behind one of the men between him and Varley's stool. Slipping between him and the bar, he used his shoulder to shunt the man away and almost jumped the gap between himself and Varley. Varley was bringing his drink to his lips and Scother saw him pause in the action, as the man he had shunted careered across the floor, drink sloshing all over the other two in front of him. Then Scother was into him.

He had a clear swing to his face and was six one, seventeen stone; Varley was probably two-thirds his weight. The punch caught him exactly where he intended it to – his left cheekbone. Varley's head snapped sideways, the pint glass slipping from his hand. The stool toppled and Scother put his weight against it, following through with a short jab as Varley went down.

As he stepped across the fallen stool he could feel Evans behind him, muscling in. Across the bar the five detectives were running, bearing down on the other three, shouting out identity. He watched Varley's body hit the floor, watched the head bounce off the boards. Before he could come back up he had one knee in his back and the cuffs out.

Varley began to shout. Scother smashed his free hand into the back of his head, knocking the face into the floor. Then Evans was with him, knees on Varley's shoulders, pinning him. He moved back and found his arms, wrenched at them and got the cuffs on. Behind him Varley's legs were kicking out. He saw Evans raise both hands above his head, clasped together like a cudgel, then bring them down on to the back of the head. The blow sounded devastating. The kicking stopped.

When they got him to his feet he looked out of it. Not unconscious, but disorientated. There was blood all over his face. Scother told Evans to search him and called in back-up using his mobile.

When he went back to them he saw that Varley was looking at him through glazed, shocked eyes, blood running from the lips, nose and forehead. The cut to the forehead looked nasty and would need stitches. He told him he was under arrest for the murder of Detective Sergeant Philip Leech. He didn't bother with the full caution. What was the point? Varley didn't look like he was up to understanding anything. There was no reply.

When they told him the van was there he marched him out and handed him over. Then he got into his own car and got out quickly. As he drove off he could see the FSU Inspector shouting after him from the pavement. Varley had been unarmed.

At Halifax he waited for Evans to join him in the canteen before filling in his pocket book.

'Did you hear his response to caution?' he asked Evans.

'No reply.'

'Maybe you were too far away to hear.' He passed his book over to Evans to read.

Evans nodded and passed it back. 'Now you mention it,' he said, 'I did hear something like that.'

'Write it down, then.' He read aloud the words he had written into his pocket book, Varley's response to being told he was under arrest for murdering Leech: 'He deserved what he got. But I'm not your man. I've got form for it, I know the score. I wouldn't be that stupid.'

It was a good verbal, he thought. Apparently exculpatory – and therefore possibly genuine – it got in enough side lines to make it useful. Later, when they interviewed Varley, he would offer him his pocket book to sign. Varley wouldn't sign it, of course. Because he had said nothing of the sort. But that didn't matter. As long as it was spontaneous, as long as you wrote it down and offered it for signing. That was enough for the lawyers. The defence would object to Varley's reference to his own previous convictions. But the pure malice – *he deserved what he got* – would be more difficult to get out. And the jury would go for that.

TWELVE

Manor Park Road was a back street that cut up towards the part of Manningham predominantly populated by Pakistani Asians – Muslims, mostly from the Mirpur area of Pakistan. So far as drugs were concerned, there were no more than two or three big names in the area, and they ran the place tightly. If Toomey had stirred things up back in Manchester, they would have known about his arrival.

It would have been helpful to have been given information as to why Toomey had moved into their sphere of control – to a bedsit at the edges of a location that would bring him into immediate contact (and probably conflict) with the Manningham hierarchy the minute he attempted any kind of deal. But Sutherland hadn't told her any of that. She doubted even the story he had given her about Toomey's connections with 'Skelly' the Manchester mister, and the argument that had forced him from the city. When she had asked for a copy of the photo she could clearly see attached to the front of Toomey's file, he had simply refused to let her even look at it.

'It's not him,' he had said, staring at her.

'The photo on the front of his file is not . . .' She had left the challenge unfinished, thinking betting of it. She would find Toomey without his help. It would just take a little longer.

She wondered how long it would take Sutherland to put in a call to Munro, calling her off. That would be the test. She would know from speaking to Munro exactly how much had been said. If Sutherland left Munro in the dark, then she would be sure who and what she was dealing with.

As she drove up Manningham Road, it began to rain again, the water streaking suddenly across the windscreen, distorting the shapes of the big Victorian houses off Park Road. Mansions for mill owners and their foremen; massive, gabled structures, set in stands of sycamore and beech. White wealth. Once upon a time.

Most of them were either broken into multiple occupation now or converted into schools and care homes for the elderly. On Manor Park Road they were mainly semis, built in the same era, but for the less well-off in the mill hierarchy. Yet even these had been converted into flats. The demand for cheap housing was high.

There were parts of Manningham with a depressingly decayed, rundown air. Rows of factory terraces with boarded windows, broken roof tiles, multiple lines of washing hanging across the tiny back yards, rubbish littering the streets, stray dogs, unkempt gardens, vacant lots overgrown with nettles and thorn thickets, peeling paintwork on the shop fronts. And with the decay, it seemed, came the crime.

Not half a mile from Toller Lane police station, gangs of bored, unemployed youths could be seen hanging about, smoking dope, grouped around flash Japanese cars (the Subaru Impreza was the latest favourite) with bright metallic paint and lowered shocks, exhaust pipes the size of small cannons, trim. The driver was nearly always some bottom-range dealer (bottom feeders, Phil Leech had called them) with gold chains at his neck, music thumping out through the open windows. The message clear.

Leech hadn't liked it. The few times she had been in

Manningham with him he had tried his best to provoke confrontations, staring back at the dealers, slowing down as he passed them. One or two had been stupid enough to say something that would give him an excuse. But the arrests had usually proved fruitless. At best a couple of wraps and a possession charge. They knew better than to walk around loaded. 'Disruption', Leech had called it. 'At least that way they know we're here.'

The pattern was the same on the Thorpe Edge and other high-rise estates now earmarked for demolition. Except on the Thorpe Edge the dealers and punters were white. Leech had been more careful with the white dealers.

Karen knew herself better than to pretend she didn't share his prejudices. They were standard, a part of the job. There was no getting away from background and education. Maybe it even came with the colour. She was white. She was racist. That simple. But at least she was conscious of it. Leech wasn't.

In her book, goading dealers wasn't helpful. It wound up the tension, added to the problem. It gave an impression they should have been seeking to avoid in Manningham. Less than a year before there had been riots around Toller Lane; the alleged cause – heavy-handed policing. For two days, parts of the city had been virtual no-go areas, businesses in flames, cars burnt out, barricades and petrol bombs.

To get informants, you needed support from the community. Muscling in on dealers achieved the opposite. To be successful you had to do it quietly. Infiltrate, tease out the embittered, the jaded, the jealous, the sump of life *below* the bottom feeders. Find a way into it and take them from the inside. Ironically, Leech had been capable of it with the white trash – the Coates and Varleys – but when it came to Manningham, colour had somehow got in the way.

The landlord had a 'representative' at number 15, Manor Park Road, a small Asian woman in a screened-off office behind a counter in the main hallway, like a concierge. Sharpe held her warrant card up in front of tired, bespectacled eyes. She asked if Liam Toomey was in, smiling down at the woman, polite. The woman took her glasses off.

'You've just missed him, luv.' Strong, broken Bradford accent.

'Know when he will be back?'

'He won't be back. He got a phone call about half an hour ago. Took it out there.' She pointed back out through the open front door. 'They have to take them outside. The reception is poor inside. That's how I hear them. He was agitated. Ran back upstairs, left about ten minutes later, gave me this.' She held up a roll of notes for Sharpe to see. 'All the rent he owed me.'

'You mean he's gone, checked out?'

'It's not a hotel. You don't check out. But he's gone.'

Sharpe thought about it. 'Did you hear what he said on the phone?'

'He was asking questions mainly.'

'Like what?'

' "Who? How have they got my name? Why me? What's behind it?" That sort of thing. Swearing as well. Obviously. Very violent speech. Not a nice man. What's he done?'

'Maybe nothing. I don't know. Do you recall anything else that was said – the name of the person he was speaking to, for example?'

'No. No name. "I'm out in ten," he said. I remember

that. Because he was. Ten minutes and he was gone, bags and all.'

'Many bags?'

'Two. One over his shoulder, the other in his hand.'

'How did he go? Did he have a car?'

'Not that I saw. He just walked off.'

Sharpe nodded. 'Can I look at his room?'

'Of course you can, luv. We help the police here. Flat A. Top of the stairs.' She passed her a set of keys, then commented, 'But you won't find anything. I've already been up. There's nothing there.'

The room was small; almost completely taken up with the double bed and the makeshift wooden counter construction that signified where the 'kitchen' began and the bedroom ended. Behind the counter a small, two-ring electric hob and a half-size fridge. There was another flimsy partition leading through to a toilet and shower cubicle.

Had Eric Sutherland made the call, warned him? If so, why? What was the connection? Toomey had left quickly, but he had left it neat. Bed made, toilet clean (still smelling of the bleach he had used). She checked the cupboards in the kitchen, checked under the bed, in the bed, in the toilet cistern. She didn't really know what she was looking for.

On top of the bathroom cabinet she found a discarded container for a protein supplement, the type used by body builders. For all she knew it might have been there months. Her mobile rang as she was checking behind the curtains. It was Munro, the reception so poor she had to tell him she would call back. She finished up and went back downstairs.

'How long was he here?'

'This was his fourth month.'

'Any idea where he will have gone?'

'I know nothing about him. I just sit here and make sure they don't wreck the place. You need to speak to the landlord. He deals with references and deposits.'

'You need references to live here?' She tried not to appear surprised.

'Of course.'

She wrote down the landlord's details, tried a few more questions (did he have visitors, listen to music, meet people), all with a negative response. The woman gave a description, but it was general, useless. She wrote it down then walked back to the car.

'Where are you?' Munro asked her. She didn't hesitate. She knew what was coming.

'Manningham. Looking for Liam Toomey.'

'Liam Toomey? I don't recall the name.'

'I told you about him. He was the guy Fiona said Coates was setting up a deal with.'

'No. You definitely did not tell me that.'

Silence. She waited for a few seconds, absorbing his mood.

'Sorry, sir. I thought I had. In fact, I must have. I have an action to verify the info.'

'Verify a drugs deal with a *Manchester* dealer. That's the action. You couldn't remember the name of the dealer. That's what you told me.'

'Did I? Sorry. I thought I had told you the name. Anyway, I can't locate him.'

'No?'

'No. I think maybe the name is false.'

'Is that right? Can you come in, please? Now. I want to talk to you about this.'

'Of course. No problem.'

Munro cut the line.

On the way back out she called the landlord, a Dr Mohammed Hussain, on the number the concierge had given her. It was an answerphone. She left a message about Toomey and her mobile number. The references would probably be false, but it was worth a try.

THIRTEEN

They found the fragments Boyd predicted they would find. The results were not one hundred per cent, however, so they would have to go off to Scientific Support along with pieces of Fiona Mitchell's fractured rear ribs to get evidential matches. But given there were no broken rib bones in the front of her chest it was, on the face of it, significant that there were shards of bone buried there. They could have come only from the broken ribs in her back, meaning she had certainly been shot from behind at some point.

Munro drove back to Halifax with Boyd. They collected his belongings and were in the process of going out to the car laid on to return him to the airport when they passed Karen Sharpe on her way back in. They were in the narrow corridor leading from the Coates and Varley team Incident Room, on the first floor – just Boyd, himself and Sharpe – she coming from the opposite direction. He was about to tell Sharpe to wait for him, but Boyd spoke to her first.

'Helen Young?'

She stopped alongside him and looked at him uncomprehendingly. Then shook her head, eyes bemused. 'DC Karen Sharpe. I'm sorry. Do I know you?'

Boyd stepped back a pace, clearly puzzled.

'This is Karen Sharpe, Mr Boyd. She's on the squad.'

Munro said. 'Ian Boyd, Karen. He's a gunshot expert from Belfast. He's done some invaluable work for us.'

She nodded, looking at him.

'You look like somebody I once knew,' Boyd said.

'Like Helen Young?' Sharpe smiled.

'Yes. We were students together.'

They stood for a moment staring at each other. Sharpe laughed, slightly uncomfortable. Boyd apologised. Munro told her to wait for him, he would be back in a few minutes.

Outside he put Boyd in the car that was waiting for him, shook his hand and thanked him.

When he got back up to his office, Sharpe was leaning on the window sill, watching Boyd's car drive off. As he entered, she turned to face him. There was perspiration across her brow, a bloodless pallor to her skin. She looked unwell.

'Are you okay?'

'Fine.'

Munro sat behind his desk. 'Sit down.'

She looked away from him, not moving from the window, silent. He waited for a moment. Still she didn't respond.

'Karen?'

She had her hand over her face now, turned away from him. He couldn't be sure, but he thought she might have been crying. Her shoulders were shaking slightly.

He stood up and walked over to her, rested a hand on her shoulder, gently. 'Are you sure you're okay?'

She nodded, still not looking at him.

'Maybe you shouldn't be working, Karen. Maybe it's a bit too soon.'

'I'm fine,' she said, drawing the hand across her eyes. She turned suddenly to face him, so quickly that his hand dropped away from her shoulder and for a second he was left standing far too close to her. Her eyes were on him, bright, puzzled, but not filled with tears. She looked more confused than upset. The colour returned rapidly to her cheeks as he stepped away.

'I thought you were upset,' he said, stupidly. He felt awkward. It was as if she had tricked him.

'Were you going to console me?' The question came back quickly, cheekily.

'Tell me about Liam Toomey,' he said, voice deliberately cold. He moved back behind the desk and sat again. She remained where she was, leaning back against the window. There was a time, in the past, when she would have been spoken to about insubordination. The time when lower-ranking officers had been required to salute Detective Chief Superintendents. Long before he made the grade.

'There's nothing to tell,' she said. 'I was hoping MANCRO would have given you more than they gave me.'

He thought about this answer. 'Sit down, Karen,' he said. Third time he had asked her to do so. This time she did.

The phone call that had told him she was tracking Toomey had been from a Superintendent called Sue Green who had said she ran the Intelligence Office for GMP. It had been a friendly enough call – purportedly a harmless query – but it had left him puzzled. Green had told him that an officer called Sharpe had requested details about a Manchester nominal called Toomey, but said that Sharpe had been unable to give any explanation as to why the details were wanted, except that it was in connection with *Phoenix*. Green was ringing out of professional curiosity, allegedly.

'What did Manchester give you, then?' he asked.

99

'An address in Bradford. No sign of him there.'

'That it?'

'That's it.'

'Why did you tell them you knew nothing of why we wanted Toomey?'

'I didn't. I showed them the action.'

'That doesn't say much. Or so they tell me.'

'Who did you speak to?'

'Superintendent Green.'

'I didn't see him. He's got it wrong.'

'She. She's in charge over there. You will have seen someone lower down.'

'So what's the problem?'

He sighed. What *was* the problem? 'Did you forget to tell me about Toomey?'

'I thought I did tell you. Maybe I forgot the name at the time. But I remember it now. I checked it out. Why are you worried?'

Why *was* he worried? 'I got the impression,' he said, 'and I could be wrong about this, that they had maybe closed up on you because you had closed up on them. Do you think they had more on Toomey?'

'I don't think so. They would have given me more if they had more. Why keep it back?'

'So why say to me just now that you were hoping MANCRO had given *me* more than they had given you? And why did you think I had spoken to MANCRO at all?'

'Didn't you tell me you had spoken to them, when you called me?'

'No.'

'I think you did.'

'I didn't.'

She shrugged. 'That's how I remember it. What does it

matter? I hoped they might have called you to give you sensitive stuff, if they had any. Did they?'

'No.'

They sat looking at each other for a moment, a niggling trace of nameless suspicion somewhere in the back of his mind. But *why*?

'I'll put somebody else on Toomey,' he said, testing for a reaction. Again, not quite sure why he was doing it.

She shrugged again. 'Fine. Tell them to speak to me. I'll give them what I've got so far.'

'Which is nothing?'

'More or less.'

'I want you to talk to PC Oliver Williams about the checks on Leech's details. That's the priority. If we can get Williams to help, and connect him to Coates, it will be strong for motive.'

Again, no discernible reaction. 'Have we spoken to him yet?'

'He's gone astray. He didn't show for duty today. His wife doesn't know where he is. My guess is that he knows what's going down and has panicked. You seem to like that kind of thing – hunting people out. I suspect you're good at it. And this is more important than Toomey. This is what Bob Harris wanted you to do first. I think he told you that. *I* want you to do this now. Do you understand?'

She nodded.

'Bob is in charge of you,' he said. 'You realise that, don't you?'

'Of course.'

'When he asks you to do something, you do it. You don't do what *you* think is priority. You understand that too?'

'Perfectly.'

'Good. Let me know when you find Williams.' He stood to open the door for her.

'Why do you think he's on his toes?' she asked him.

'What else could it be?'

'He might be dead. Shot.'

He felt a prickle of sweat on the back of his neck. He hadn't even considered that. What if there *was* something bigger going on? Should he have considered it?

'You're right,' he said. 'I shouldn't assume. I'll think about that. Meanwhile, you find him for me.'

'Dead or alive?'

'Yes,' he said, looking down at her as she passed him, smiling. 'Dead or alive.' He shut the door after her.

Joking. She was joking about it. The man she had shared her working life with for the last year was dead and already she could smile about the whole thing. He sat at the desk thinking about it, wondering why that side of her didn't shock or repulse him.

FOURTEEN

In the ladies toilets on the first floor she locked herself into a cubicle and leaned back against the door, head pounding, breath too quick. She felt dizzy. She leaned forward, suffering a rush of blood to her brain, waiting until she could feel it prickling at her face before straightening up. Not enough oxygen. She took deep breaths. What was going on?

Toomey. Fiona's lie. The Irish accent. Sutherland. Special Branch. And now this. *Helen Young*. Could it be a coincidence?

She couldn't think clearly about it. She was missing something.

The bodies had been shocking. Because she had known them. But that was all. Like looking at joints of meat in the supermarket. Not the same if it was your pet pig lying there. Or cow. But that was all. She had liked Phil Leech once, but not very much. Now that he was gone, for his life, his death, she felt nothing. Absolutely nothing. She felt more for Fiona. No one was thinking about her.

She sat down on the toilet seat and ran her hands through her hair. Other people would have been ill, sedated, hospitalised, or at least off work. It was acceptable to have a certain level of depression if something like this happened. Expected, even. You weren't normal if you didn't. She had looked in Munro's eyes as she was flirting with him and seen it. He thought she was some kind of monster.

They wanted her to be depressed. They thought about depression as some kind of vaguely black feeling. They didn't have a clue. She remembered. It wasn't some kind of fuzzy, low mood. It was physical. It stopped you eating, sleeping, moving. It reduced you to something that shivered with cold and fright, incapable of feeling *anything* but fear. It was lethal. She had the marks to prove it. The mental scars. She was never going there again. No matter what.

She stood up. Took a breath. She didn't care about Leech dying. She could go through the motions. She knew how to act it out. But why bother? She had lost more than herself in the past. She knew how it felt. She wasn't on this enquiry to avenge his death, to find justice for his poor cheated widow. They hadn't even been together. People were born, lived a little, died. That was the way it was. Why mourn it? Even sleeping with Leech – eight months ago now – had been insignificant. Like putting something into her mouth and tasting it. Before taking it out again.

'I don't think you're capable of love,' he had told her. (A restaurant somewhere?) 'Not real love. Not like normal people.'

She hadn't even wasted time thinking about it. What was *real love*?

She wanted to know what had happened on Cock Hill. But not for Leech. Not even for Fiona. Not really. This was about *her*, Karen Sharpe. Of the three of them in the pub that night she was the only one left alive. She needed to work it out because a tiny lump of doubt, a connection already made, was telling her to do it. To find out, quick.

She opened the cubicle door, walked over to the sinks, washed her face. Looking at herself in the mirror she saw calmness, normality. The moment had passed. She held her hand in front of her and inspected it. Steady.

Finding Toomey *was* the priority. Not theirs – not the entire fifty-five man Phoenix squad, from Munro to Harris and back again – because they knew even less than she did. But it was *her* priority.

She rang Hussain again. Got the answerphone.

Sutherland had given her an old address for Liam Toomey in Manchester as well. Did she dare go there?

She walked up to the Incident Room. Harris wasn't around. She sifted through the growing pile of actions in her tray, replaced them. Logging on to the HOLMES machine on Harris's desk she worked her way through the progress so far, action by action, looking for anything that might have something to do with Toomey. She passed the details for PC Oliver Williams's home address as she was going, and noted them down, along with the name of his wife.

It looked as though they had asked his wife where he was, got no help. It wasn't the first time he had done this, she said. She suspected he was 'having an affair'. So instead of kicking his door in they had gone off to consult Marshall about getting a warrant. Marshall had noted it up for a Section 18 search when and if he was arrested.

Dithering. Williams was a policeman, after all. It wouldn't do to treat him with the same degree of suspicion as an ordinary punter. There were ways of proceeding when it was a colleague in the frame. (They had even put a request to the Federation for permission to go through his locker.) Questioning him about checks he had run over a year ago on Leech's car was a long way off implicating him in murder. His wife had promised she would call when she found out where he was. That was that.

Stupid. She looked at her watch. She would need to be

quick. Munro had asked her to do it, so she would do it. But there was no need to make a meal of it.

She needed Munro off her back. Already she had lied to him, hidden things. That couldn't go on for long. She needed to appear normal to him, obedient and pliant. Was that the kind of woman he would want? He had tried to be nice to her, to empathise. She had wanted to respond, touch him, say something that would open that door.

But all that ever came out was derision. Most of the time she felt like an iceberg. Not just frozen. But moving around in the midst of more trivial objects. The people around her were too visible, their lives and characters written all over the surface. There was nothing to find when you looked closer. But she was dragging it around behind her. Two-thirds beneath the surface.

She was heavy with it.

FIFTEEN

A short woman in her late forties opened the door.

'Brenda Williams?'

'Yes?'

'DC Karen Sharpe. I'm looking for Ollie.'

The door was open about eight inches, on a chain.

'I said I would get him to call when he rang.'

'I know. Can I come in?'

'Why?'

The woman had a small, pinched face. The sort that looked suspicious of everything. She was wearing a dress that looked as though it were made in 1940.

'To speak to you. Nothing dramatic.'

Karen stepped back, looking around her. The house was a three-bedroom semi on a quiet cul-de-sac in Wibsey, an inconspicuous Bradford suburb. Further down the road someone was washing a car. It was a mild spring afternoon, now that the clouds had cleared. She took the folded sheets of paper from the pocket of her jacket. As usual, the magistrates had barely bothered to check her ID before issuing the warrant.

'You going to let me in?' she asked. Brenda Williams looked back over her shoulder, openly nervous. Karen could hear movement from within. 'Is Ollie in there?'

'No. It's my sister. You can't come in. I've said all I can say—'

She started to close the door. Karen placed her foot against it, holding the piece of paper up in the gap.

'I've got a warrant,' she said. 'It would be easier if I didn't have to kick my way in.'

The woman blanched. Behind her someone, a female, was speaking.

'She says she has a warrant,' Mrs Williams said, her voice vague.

'I'm going to move my foot now. What you should do is take the chain off. Okay?'

The woman nodded. Karen took her foot away. The door closed. She counted to ten, slowly. No movement. Standing back she kicked at it with a deliberate action, striking the wood just below the lock. It splintered and gave immediately, then caught on the chain. From inside she could hear raised women's voices, panicking.

The second kick took the chain off and smashed the door off the inside wall. Something hanging on the wall behind it broke. She stepped into the hallway to find another, taller woman coming straight towards her. She was shouting something about an outrage.

'You had your chance,' Karen said. She stepped past her. In the front room there were a stack of boxes in the middle of the floor and a hearty fire in the grate. Brenda Williams was taking papers from the boxes by the handful, throwing them on to the flames. Karen told her to stop and took hold of her arm to reinforce the point.

'Step over there. Now.'

Williams was crying. Karen removed the sheaf of papers from her shaking hand and placed them on top of one of the boxes. She steered her back towards the doorway, where the other woman was still shouting at her.

'Spring-cleaning?' she said. The other woman fell silent. 'Do you want to tell me what's in these boxes?'

Neither replied. Brenda Williams was sobbing silently. Karen moved past them, back into the hallway, warning them about touching anything. The phone was on a small table, just inside the door. She picked it up and dialled 1471; it came back number withheld.

'When did you last speak to Ollie?' she asked Williams.

'Don't say anything,' the other woman snapped at her.

Karen stepped over to her. 'Let's not be stupid about this. Whatever he's been up to, he's not here. You two are in the firing line.' She looked down at Brenda, by far the less aggressive of the two. 'I'd like a coffee, Brenda,' she said, smiling at her. 'Can you go and do that for me?'

The other woman started to speak again. Karen cut her off. 'Shut up. I'll speak to you in a minute.'

She looked at Brenda again. 'Let's keep this pleasant, Brenda. I don't want to upset you.'

'I don't know what's happening,' Brenda said, voice forlorn.

'No. But don't worry. If you give me what I want, there won't be a problem.'

Brenda nodded. 'A coffee.' She went through to the kitchen.

Karen turned to the sister, leaning her hand against the door frame by her head. 'What's your name?'

'Do I have to tell you?'

'If you don't you'll spend the night in custody.'

'Elizabeth Horner. I'm Brenda's sister.'

'Well, you can stay or go, Elizabeth Horner. But if you stay, you stand right where you are now with your mouth shut. You understand that?'

She walked back into the front room and began to look through the boxes. It didn't take long to work it out. The first handful of papers she picked up were loose leaf copies of a personnel file. She found the name. A civilian

Despatch Centre Operative. She didn't recognise her. The next set was the same, but for a PC called Smythe. Once again, no one she recognised. She dug at random through the box. At the bottom she came across entire files, copied complete with jacket. Oliver Williams worked in Wakefield, in the department that handled firearms licences. Clearly he had access to force records.

The box underneath contained copies of firearms applications, carefully stacked in alphabetical order. She looked quickly for Coates's and Varley's details. They weren't there. But that would have been too obvious anyway. The way it would have been done was on false ID. Part of the application procedure involved passport photos. Williams had used a colour copier to take a copy of each photo. She estimated there were perhaps two hundred applications in the box, all complete with copy photos.

Brenda came back in with a mug of coffee.

'These are all Ollie's, I suppose?' Karen asked.

'Yes.'

'Why burn them? Aren't they just part of his work?'

Brenda didn't answer. Too bright to take the bait.

'I'm going to search the house,' Karen told her. 'I can do it with pick axes, a team of men and drugs dogs. Or you can tell me now whether there is more of this kind of thing.'

Brenda didn't think about it for long. 'Upstairs. In the spare bedroom.'

'Good. Thanks for the coffee.' She took it from her, stood up from where she had been squatting, took a sip. 'This is going to take a little time,' she said. 'You might as well sit down.'

The third box was similar. She left it and walked upstairs. In the smallest bedroom she found five office filing cabinets stuffed with copied or original paperwork.

On a desk in the corner of the room there was a computer. She switched it on. Both the women followed her upstairs and stood in the hall, in silence now, watching her.

What she was looking for was in a cabinet marked 'Operations'. In the top drawer, she found a dropdown folder labelled 'Anvil'. Pages of information printed off OIS, all relating to Anvil, all requiring a restricted password to gain access. Ollie Williams had been busy.

She turned to the second cabinet with a feeling of growing nausea. She knew what she was going to find.

Her personnel record was there in its entirety. Alphabetically filed. She pulled it out and leafed quickly through the forty or so pages. The hairs began to stiffen on her scalp. This wasn't the doctored version Munro had seen. This was the full thing. She tried to work out how Williams could have got hold of it. This version should not have even been sent up from London. Either they had forwarded it by accident, or he had access to someone there.

Halfway through she found a set of ten photographs. They appeared to have been taken with a long-range telephoto lens. Her legs felt weak. She sat down on the chair in front of the desk and paused, waiting for her breath to settle.

They were recent. Certainly since she had started on Anvil. She could tell because it was only after starting with Leech that she had cut her hair. Previously it had been halfway down her back. In these photos it was short.

They were mostly close-ups of her face, good enough to identify her. No doubt about that. It took her a while scrutinising the background details to work out where she was. Inside her own home. They had been taken through the windows.

She leaned back and looked across at the two women. 'Where are his cameras?'

They looked at each other. 'He took them with him,' Brenda said.

'When?'

'He hasn't been back since Sunday. He left to go bird watching.'

'Bird-watching? Is *that* what he does for a hobby?'

Williams shrugged.

'Does he do this often? Leave for days on end without telling you?'

She nodded.

'He's a twitcher,' the sister said. 'There's nothing sinister about it. They get news of some rare bird and they travel. Immediately. Doesn't matter where it is.'

'Is that right? So where're his bird photos?'

Silence.

She searched for nearly an hour for records relating to Leech. Apart from the stuff in the Anvil folder, there was nothing. If he had phoned his wife and told her to burn it all, it was likely he had told her to burn Leech's folder first. Or perhaps the folder was more important, or, more probably, recently used. If so, he could be keeping it elsewhere. The computer yielded nothing using standard Windows search programs. She clicked her way through his hard drive without finding a single photo of a bird (or anything else) and she couldn't get his internet connection up because it needed a password to get through. The lab would pick that apart later.

In a separate set of drawers, under the desk, she found bank statements, payslips, letters from solicitors, building societies, clubs of which he was a member and such like. There was no obvious fund of money, but he wasn't going to be collecting West Yorkshire Police personnel and operational details for fun. What she was looking at was power. Placed in the right hands it would certainly bring him money. There would be a trail back to that somewhere in this room.

She took everything she could find relating to herself, then called Harris. She told him where she was, what she had found. The only details she left out were those relating to her file and the photos.

'I think we need a team over here,' she said. 'To seize all this.'

'Yes. I agree. Now that you're in. How *did* you get in, as a matter of interest?'

'A warrant.'

She heard him sigh. She cut the connection before he could start.

She turned back to the two women. She wanted to ask them about documents she had found (and left in place) relating to membership of Berman's Gym in Leeds, but thought better of it. Besides being a gym (a very exclusive and expensive one) Berman's was known to be favoured by a sizeable quota of ex-cons who weren't short of cash. New money. The kind that came back covered with brown powder when you sent it off to the lab.

Berman's had featured more than once in the Anvil enquiry. Coates was down as a member, known to be a regular user. When Leech had dug into the PC who had checked his car number plates over a year before, he had come up with information that Coates had a friend on the Force whom he had met at Berman's. He had not known then that Williams was a member. If Berman's was a significant connection, she didn't want Brenda Williams passing that on to her husband when he rang.

'Tampering with evidence is a criminal offence,' she said, standing in front of them, voice hard. 'I have to go now. Other people will come to take all this away. I am aware of what's here. I will know if you destroy anything. You understand?'

The sister looked at her with something close to hatred. Brenda started sobbing again.

Standing by the front door she had a thought, something half formed which had been nagging her for days. Maybe longer. She turned back to them.

'A motorbike.'

They looked blankly at her.

'Does Ollie have one?'

'No.'

'You sure?'

'Yes.'

'Can he drive them?'

Brenda Williams shook her head. 'Not that I know.'

SIXTEEN

Two months back. She had the exact day written down somewhere. She had been travelling back from Bradford Central, in the car, night-time. It had been wet, cold, visibility poor. Sometime in mid-February.

As it happened she had taken three detours she would not normally take. That was how she spotted it. Two had been planned, ordinary functions of life. The third had been deliberate, a tester. Somewhere in the recesses of her brain the training had kicked in; first spotting it – not hard, because it was a motorbike, at night, a single head-light – and then checking it. She had tried to forget that she had learned these things. But the lessons had been thorough, drilled into her.

Her normal route from Bradford Central to home took her straight up the Aire Valley, through Shipley, Bingley, past Keighley and out to Skipton, then into the country just north-west of there, between Settle and Skipton. A straight enough route, slow in rush hour as you came through Manningham and Shipley, speeding up once you hit the trunk road to by-pass Keighley and Skipton.

She hadn't thought much about security before joining Leech on Anvil, hadn't thought much about it even after that. Phil had audited the PNC every week for checks against his cars. That was how he had turned over Williams's name. She didn't bother. These days she didn't check her mirrors, or watch for repeat sightings. All simple things. But why should she? Those days were gone. Or so she had thought. If she had been asked about it before this week she would have said that Leech lacked perspective.

It had started before she ever met him. About two years back. A friend of Coates – someone who knew him from schooldays – happened to live on one of the estates Coates was setting up with an outlet. Eric Roberts. He had come to Leech out of the blue, through normal channels. That meant three or four phone calls passed on through the CID room, a mention to the DI, registration and a log. It should have been safe enough. It was all within a police station.

It wasn't. Within a week Roberts had been dropped from a third-floor balcony on the Thorpe Edge. He was lucky to survive.

Leech said he had been careful with him. Between the first contact and the subsequent attack he had met him only twice. Both out of area, in safe circumstances. Only the DI had known.

The DI, Alan Edwards, was a zealot. When Edwards spoke about drugs, Karen wondered if he was all there. She found talking to him disturbing. Like arguing with someone religious, knowing that *reasons* just weren't going to do it for him. So it was unlikely to have been Edwards who had picked up the phone to Coates. But someone had told him. In hospital, fractured skull and two broken arms later, Roberts made that clear. Coates had hung him out of the window until he had given the name of the officer he had met with. Then he had 'let him go'. There was a case in it all, but not without forcing Roberts into the witness box.

About six months after that, Williams had checked the registration numbers for two different cars belonging to Leech, both within a period of days. But Williams worked in an office. He wasn't out and about fighting crime. So someone else had obviously phoned him with the numbers. That meant someone had been following Leech. Then the threats had started coming in. Messages on Leech's answerphone at home, letters pushed through his door by day. Some garbled, some vague, some very clear. *Watch your back. It's coming* had been a regular one.

And informant info from street level. Rumours of a professional contract. They were telling him that Coates had put down money to hurt him, maybe worse.

So Leech had backed off, got the security cameras into his home, thought about it, watched his friends. Williams had not been number-one suspect. He didn't work at Bradford. And despite the fact that he had only told Edwards about Roberts, for some reason Leech was still thinking that the betrayal was there, in Bradford, close to him. He hadn't thought about the data Edwards might have sent to the centre, to Intelligence, to HQ, over the ordinary 'secure' force computer systems.

Six months later he had Karen brought in from the other side of the area. (Thinking that way she would be clean.) She had listened to his fears, but it had been hard to take them seriously. At the level they were operating – mid-range heroin dealers – that sort of thing didn't happen. Anyone could put a rumour out about contracts, but nobody would see it through, not at Coates's level.

That was how it seemed. So checking her back hadn't been a priority. Even when she had virtually caught someone on it.

She had noticed the bike when she turned into Keighley to get food shopping. At that stage she hadn't realised she had seen it, but when she pulled out on to the trunk road and saw the single headlight again, hanging back about three hundred yards on her tail, no traffic in between, she realised that a part of her brain had picked it up already. As she turned off at Steeton to get petrol she lost it. Within thirty seconds of getting back on to the dual carriageway it was there again.

She had tried to get the details then. Difficult, in the dark, to see the registration plate. She had slowed down a little, sped up, nothing dramatic. She wanted it close enough to be able to get the plate, but she didn't want to panic it. It hadn't taken the bait.

On the dual carriageway it dropped back three cars. Once it was so far back she thought it had pulled over. When she turned off into the narrow country lanes she detoured immediately. She took a steeply hedged lane she wouldn't normally use, pulled over to wait for it, killed the lights and engine. It was nearly thirty seconds before it appeared (quite a distance at the speed it was going), shooting past the entrance to the lane, too fast for her to pick out anything in the mirrors. She pulled out after it, her heart picking up a little, wary, but still not sure.

It had not been in sight when she had come off the main road. Which meant – if it really was following her – that it already knew where she was going, which route she took. Yet what other reasons could there be to follow her? Only those too dramatic to seriously consider.

It passed her at speed, coming back in the other direction. About three minutes after she started after it. Even then she wasn't sure. The driver had a black visor. That was all she could see. It didn't look to be a particularly fast or flash bike. He wasn't sitting on it in any particular way. No indication that he even looked at her as he passed. And she was assuming it was a male rider. In truth she couldn't even say that with certainty.

There was no front plate and at the speed it passed, in

the rain, through the interior mirror, she didn't stand a chance with the rear plate.

She had thought at the time to check the CCTV from Keighley. She had even written down the date and time. But in the end she had gone home and felt certain of nothing. Not even that it was the same bike after each time she had lost it. So she had done nothing. Even when that feeling had persisted for weeks afterwards, of being watched and followed, she had not wanted to believe it.

She sat in the car outside PC Oliver Williams's house and looked at the date on her watch. Not so much to remind herself – how could she forget? It was two days after the eighth – but to put her mind back to then, to mid-February. What had been the exact date?

The local authority were running an experiment in Keighley with the CCTV. Recording everything on to CDs and retaining them. She knew because Coates's route from Bradford back up to his house went through Keighley town centre. They had seized material in the past, to check movements, registration numbers. The Control Centre recorded and kept images from every single camera they had. But only for three months. After that the CDs were wiped and reused.

She leafed through the thin black diary that was as near as she got to an organiser. (Leech had had an electronic thing – had they recovered and checked that? she wondered.) It didn't take long. On 21 February, there it was. 'Motorbike. 7.15 p.m.' That was all she had written. It was enough. She was in time. She found the Control Centre number and called them.

'You're too late,' a woman told her, not too fussy about checking her ID.

'You've destroyed it?'

119

'Everything has been seized already.'

'By who?'

'DC Hoyle. He's on the enquiry into the shootings. Phoenix.'

SEVENTEEN

A motorbike.

There was a pub – one in the middle of nowhere, halfway between West Yorkshire and Lancashire, in the Pennines – a place so isolated he wondered how they stayed in business (at least, without aiding and abetting the driving of motor vehicles with excess alcohol). It was about a mile and a half further up the road from where the motorbike was found.

What would they do without dogs on this enquiry? The landlord of the pub walked his dog – some big grey thing that looked like an overgrown sheep – every day, same route. The dog had passed the wall, started sniffing, the landlord had looked over. And there it was.

The road led from Hebden Bridge up a long wooded valley to a place called Widdop. From there it twisted through a small gorge before dropping down into Lancashire. Hebden Bridge was no more than four miles from the summit at Cock Hill Moor. In effect the road was two valleys over. To drive from Cock Hill, or Wainstalls, to where the bike was dumped, would take no more than twenty minutes maximum.

Munro stood watching the SOCO moving carefully around it. It was leaning upright on the other side of a five-foot, dry-stone wall. They had already determined that it had got there by being pushed through a gap in the wall about ten yards back. Then through tall grass to a spot where there were gorse bushes growing up against the wall. With what must have taken considerable effort (it was a 250cc Suzuki, not a massive model, but heavy enough to put the action down to a man, not a woman, all other things being equal), it had been wedged between the gorse bushes and the wall, out of sight from both sides, unless you were a dog.

The wall hemmed in a chapel of some sort. Squat, ancient yew trees ran from behind the gorse and long grass to the edge of the building. Even from the other side it was difficult to see it.

'I want everything off it,' he said. 'Every trace in the book. And quickly.'

The SOCO – a woman called Bernie Harris – nodded. Beside him Dave Binns, the DS running the Wider Scene Team, was discussing things with a couple of his DCs.

'Two days,' Harris said. 'For *most* of it.'

'For *everything*,' he replied. 'If this has nothing to do with it I don't want us running around for any longer than that before we know.'

He looked up at the skies. It had been a fair enough day earlier on. Clouding over now, though.

'It's going to rain,' he commented. 'You should get cracking now. You'll need help.' She wasn't moving fast enough for him. 'I want fibres, DNA, rubber compounds from the tyres, petrol impurity analysis, fingerprints, glass, soil, pollen, gunshot residues – you name it.'

He looked at his watch. Nearly four-fifty. He needed to get back for de-brief. 'Is there any blood?' he asked her. She was bent over it now, pawing at something with her pen.

'Yes,' she said. 'I think so.'

'Much of it?'

'Enough. If that's what it is.'

'Have you got help coming?'

She straightened up. 'I'll call them.'

'You need to be quick, Bernie,' he said, fretting, irritated. He walked back to where Binns was standing. 'No plates,' he commented.

'No. But that's no problem. There's a number on the engine block. We can find out about the plates from that.'

'Not quite. You can find out about the *original* plates. He will have been running around on false plates if he has sense.'

'True.'

'We need CCTV. It will have gone through somewhere, sometime on CCTV.'

'It's matching it that's the problem,' Binns said. 'Most CCTV is shite. One bike looks like another.'

'You'll have to try. Skip de-brief. You need to get cracking. Assume it's linked and that the skid mark at Cock Hill comes from this machine. Work to trace it back. Is there CCTV through Hebden Bridge?'

Binns shook his head. 'A few shops. No local authority system. I'll check though. We already have everything they kept. If it's on them, we'll find it.'

'Good. Why would it be dumped here?'

'A vehicle switch?' Binns suggested.

'Ran out of petrol?' One of the detectives with him spoke.

'Or lives near?' Munro said, looking around him. Beyond the churchyard the hills rose steeply. Between where they were now and the pub the landlord had walked from, he had seen no houses at all.

'Check this chapel as well. Full forensics and prints – footwear, the lot. Door to door every farm within walking distance.'

'How far is that?'

'I don't know. Use initiative. Be sensible about it. If he abandoned it here he might have walked, or stopped somewhere to steal another vehicle. Maybe the owners haven't noticed yet. I don't know. Ask yourself – why here? Why dump it here? Your Wider Scene just got wider. At least until we know it's definitely not connected.'

'I might need more men.'

'Just let me know. What's at the other end of this road?' He pointed back in the direction of the pub.

'Colne, Lancashire. Nine miles distant. Small town. My sister lives there. Usual petty stuff, nothing organised.'

'If it's got CCTV, get it all. Same with any other towns on the immediate route out of here. If SOCO gets cracking I would hope to get something from that skid mark reasonably quickly. Meanwhile we have to assume it's ours, that this is our getaway vehicle.'

EIGHTEEN

DC Sam Fisher didn't like it. He was chasing a fairly standard action from his tray. The SIO – Munro – had appealed for witnesses on the very first day in a media interview and they had so far received something in the region of 150 calls, mostly useless. One of them, which he had been tasked to chase up, was from a man called Mohammed Iqbal. Munro had asked for anybody who had been near Cock Hill Moor or Wainstalls. Iqbal's phone call said he had been near Cock Hill around midnight. Those were the exact words – 'near Cock Hill around midnight'.

Fisher was a thorough detective. He was new to the role and could remember his training. He had called Iqbal and taken his address and details all over again, just to be sure. Then he had checked him on PNC.

Iqbal was a smack head. That wasn't good. Addicts didn't make good witnesses. But there was worse. OIS said he had connections with the Khan brothers. The Khans ran the heroin trade in Manningham and Keighley. They were in direct competition with the likes of Varley and Coates. Iqbal was down as doing more than merely taking his supply from them. On occasions he cropped up as a collector and enforcer. He had antecedents for both violence and drugs, the latest being a supply charge from November 1995, for which he was still on bail awaiting crown court trial.

When Fisher called him, on a mobile number, Iqbal had hung up on him and then called back, taking more than ten minutes to do so. His voice was sullen, reluctant, aggressive.

'What would you like to say?' Fisher had asked, pen at the ready.

'I was there.'

'There. Where?'

'Cock Hill. That place. It's the truth.'

Fisher sighed, wrote down the words, word for word, scrupulously accurate. 'Did you see anything?'

'Yeah. A car. It came down from the top, stopped in the road, a fella got out with a bag, took two steps away from the car and lobbed it. Got back in, drove off.'

'Lobbed what?'

'A bag. I told you.'

'What kind of bag?'

'I don't know. A bag bag.'

'Like a lady's handbag?' The SIO had said the DC who met Leech and Mitchell the night before said Mitchell had a handbag with her.

'Yeah,' Iqbal replied, then spoiled it. 'Or a carrier bag.'

'Which? A handbag or a carrier bag?'

'I dunno, man. Whichever. It was light in colour.'

'Light as in?'

'As in light. White. Like white skin.'

'Like white skin.' He wrote it down. 'Where was it thrown to?'

'On to the grass.'

'And what time was this?'

'Just after one. I told you.'

He hadn't. In fact, the record of the original phoned report said just after midnight. Fisher paused, thinking quickly through the possibilities.

'You still there?' Iqbal asked.

'Yes. Would you be able to take me to where this happened?'

'Yeah.'

'Okay. You might have to do that. Did you see the car?'

'Yeah.'

'Did you get a registration number?'

'It was dark. It was an H reg. That's all I know.'

'Colour?'

'Dark.'

'Black, blue, brown?'

'Blue. An Astra.'

'An H reg dark blue Astra?'

'That's it.'

'Did you see the face of the man who threw the package?'

'Clear as day.'

Fisher bit his tongue. 'So you would recognise him again?'

'Line them up. I'll pick him out.'

'Tell me what he looked like.'

'What do you mean?'

'A description. Did you see clothing?'

'It was too far. I just know I'd know him if I saw him. Put me on a parade.'

'To pick out who?'

Silence. Fisher could hear him thinking.

'The suspect,' he said finally, unsure.

'How do you know we have a suspect?'

'I don't. Your fella said call so I'm calling. Do you want it or not?'

'You can't give me a description?'

'No. But I would know him if I saw him.'

It was, he thought, total bullshit. So obviously a set-up

he wondered whether it would be worth chasing it further. The Khans had heard about Coates's and Varley's difficulties and they were trying to help them along. Eliminate the opposition. The registration, make and colour of the car were correct for Varley's vehicle, the timing useful. The Khans – especially the older brother – were bright. They had thought about it, fed their donkey the lines. It was a cheap way to improve business.

He showed his pocket book to his DS, told him what he thought. The DS was called Scother and came from the Drugs Squad in Leeds. Scother read through the pocket book, looked behind him, then casually dropped it into a wastepaper basket.

'How long have you been a detective?' he asked.

Fisher closed his mouth, cleared the frown from his forehead. 'Nearly a month.'

'Nearly a month, sir.'

'Yes. Nearly a month, sir.'

'It shows. Lesson one: don't do the other side any favours.'

'I don't know what—'

'Those notes were – as I'm sure you already knew – the first description of a suspect. If we hold parades with this Iqbal character then we will have to serve that garbage on the other side prior to doing so. Ring bells?'

'I am aware of that.'

'Of course you are. You've just been trained.' He stood up, walked from behind the desk and put his arm around Fisher's shoulder. 'You lost that pocket book a couple of weeks back,' he said. 'You will need to fill out the forms reporting the loss.'

Fisher nodded, swallowing.

'What you have to do now,' Scother continued, voice warmer, 'is forget all the shite they fed you at training

128

school. We are here to bin villains. In this case, the villain has slotted a brother officer. The last thing we therefore need is to have to serve the defence with a first description that totally undermines the identification witness. Do you understand?'

Fisher said nothing.

'You stay here and mind the shop. I'll take the statement from Iqbal.'

Fisher waited until Scother had left before retrieving his pocket book from the bin.

NINETEEN

Berman's Gym did not advertise. You had to know. You didn't just walk in off the street and ask to join, either. It was invitation only. Berman himself was rumoured to be gay, though you would have to be a very close friend to say that to his face. Even in his sixties, he was a big man. Convicted in the early seventies on three counts of armed robbery and one Section 18 (shooting a security guard in the legs), he had learned the value of good fitness training over an eight-year spell at Her Majesty's Pleasure. He had run the gym facilities in three major prisons he had passed through, including Armley, where he had met the core clientele for his present business.

Rumours abounded as to where he got the money to set the place up. From the obvious (the proceeds of his last job) to the absurd (Special Branch had him on the books and had set him up with a grant to pull in info on the big misters, in Leeds). Karen had never seen an entry anywhere on OIS crediting information to Berman. But that didn't mean some more credible version of the story wasn't true. Certainly, during the mid-eighties, before she had been anywhere near West Yorkshire, it was well known that an incestuous closeness had developed between the CID at Leeds City and the punters who got into Berman's.

An exchange system. The big misters came to Berman's to work out, stay fit, keep connected. The detectives came because the bar in the place was, basically, an all-hours illegal drinking club. So much so that Berman had never bothered applying for a licence. The villains threw choice titbits to the 'seventies detectives', who in turn kept off their back and enjoyed Berman's booze for free. Karen had heard stories about Masonic connections as well.

The bar was gone now, the gym open to the general public provided an existing member sponsored you. Amongst a certain class of Leeds professional the place had acquired a name for itself – a notch up the exclusivity scale. Money alone wouldn't get you in – you had to know someone. Usually somebody slightly dodgy. There existed social circles within which that was a plus.

Berman left his younger nephews to run the place now. They were less sniffy about drugs connections than he was. At that level a drugs connection came out as nothing more alarming than a little problem with the laundry. Even lower-tier pushers like Coates were making so much that cleaning it became the number-one priority. Karen knew of at least six major importers who were on the books at Berman's, rubbing shoulders with the bankers, lawyers and police officers who were, by day, under obligations to report them. If a little recreational coke made its way from one side to the other, who was to complain?

Coates would *just* fit; Varley never. Oliver Williams would be in because he had some connection with Leeds City back in the 'good old days'. It was a guess – she would have to check his file to be sure – but, on his own account, Williams was too small to get into the Berman's of the mid-nineties.

The place itself looked distinctly unprepossessing from the outside (another weird inversion that increased its value to the city types freshly emigrated from the smoke).

On the Leeds Road, sandwiched between a condemned row of terraced shop fronts and a less than exclusive nightclub, the place looked like a bomb shelter, with a floor above and a floor below ground, all done out in dirty seventies concrete and complete with flat roof. Steps down to an anonymous red steel door with a single security camera were easily mistaken for the entrance to a council storage depot, a telephone exchange or a nuclear bunker. There were no windows.

She rapped on the door and held her warrant card up to the camera. Within seconds she heard the lock click back, pushed the door open and went in. She had been in the place twice before, though some years ago. Not much seemed to have changed. She stood at a counter manned by pretty young girls and thick-chested males, explained who she was and asked to see the manager.

'Mr Armitage is busy at the moment.'

'Armitage?'

'Yes. He's Duty Manager. He's doing an interview. Can I help you?'

'No. I need a manager. If you want this place to remain open, it's important he see me. Please tell him that.'

The girl nodded, frowning. As if she were unused to impoliteness. 'If you'll wait a moment . . .' She disappeared through a door behind the desk.

Karen sat down on a chair to one side of the entrance area. The place looked and smelled like any other gym. Faint odours of chlorine from the pool, staff in neat tracksuit uniforms, piles of towels on the reception counter. It was cleanly and simply decorated, carefully fitted out with tropical plants, original oil abstractions and pre-war fitness posters. Everything looked careful, uncluttered, expensive.

After a while Armitage appeared. He was tall, tanned,

toned and attractive. Wearing an impeccably pressed, lightweight suit (if she had been better at this she would have known the designer label), a soft, cotton shirt, open-necked, no tie. Maybe five years younger than her. With a serious expression, he came from behind the counter, walked over to her, held his hand out.

'Can I help you?'

She stood up and shook it, looking into his eyes. He was puzzled, concerned, but he was also interested. Attracted. She could see it in his eyes. The male chemicals doing their thing.

'I hope so. DC Karen Sharpe. I need to speak to you in private.'

'Of course. Come through.'

His office was small, but tidy. A single desk, no papers, a computer terminal. She took the chair opposite.

'Would you like a drink?' he asked. He had a public school accent.

'What kind of drink?' She smiled at him.

'Whatever you like.' He smiled back. A nice smile, she thought. Probably, at home, he was a nice person. If that idea made any sense. No rings on his fingers.

'I'll have a mineral water. Fizzy. No ice. No lemon.'

He picked up the telephone on his desk, ordered it.

'Now,' he said. 'They tell me you are to close us down.'

She laughed, trying to inflect it with nervousness, a trace of self-consciousness. 'I'm sorry. That was just so I could get to see you.'

'I see.' He was staring at her. Eyes constantly on hers, never breaking contact. She found it unsettling enough to blush slightly. A similar thing had happened with Munro.

'I'm on a murder enquiry, Mr Armitage.'

'Joe. Please. Call me Joe.'

'Joe. Okay. I'm Karen, by the way.'

'Karen. Yes. You look too young to be a detective, Karen.'

He left the sentence hanging there, like a question. She smiled stupidly at him. Same old thing, she thought.

'Go on,' he continued. 'You're on a murder enquiry.'

'Yes. I'm investigating the shooting of a policeman. You might have heard about it.'

'Of course. It was on the news. A terrible business. How can I help?'

She smiled at him. Looked at her feet, looked up again. His eyes never moved. Every time she looked they were there, waiting for her. Her mother had told her, she remembered (though not without difficulty), that not to look someone in the eye was a sign that you were lying. But then her mother had also thrown a vacuum cleaner at her when she was ten, breaking her collar bone. Could someone who could do that be trusted to give insights into human behaviour? The difference between Armitage and Munro, she realised, was that with Munro it was all genuine, unconscious, natural. That was just how he was. She had the impression with Armitage that he was deliberately doing this, deliberately staring her out – and not simply to convince her of his bona fides. He was doing it to unnerve her. It was something she would have to get past.

'Do you really think I look too young to be a detective?' she asked. 'Or was that just your way of flirting?' She said it seriously.

He frowned, but the eyes didn't move. 'How old *are* you?' he asked. There was something else in his tone now. A slight relaxation. He was sure he could control the situation.

'Older than you,' she said.

He smiled again. 'That doesn't necessarily mean you

have more experience. Depends what you've done with the extra years. How long have you been a detective?' Still confident.

'How long do you think?'

'I don't know.'

'Take a guess.'

'Why don't you just tell me.'

'Then you can get on to the speech? How important you are? How important this place is? How the ACC works out here? What things I still have to learn? Is that it?'

He frowned again. 'I don't think so.'

'No?'

'No. I'm sure you know already the answer to these things. No matter how inexperienced you are, relatively speaking.'

She held his gaze, smiling. 'I've been a detective seven years,' she said. 'Does that help?'

She saw the eyes flicker, the brain adjust. 'That's interesting,' he said. 'I don't know you. I don't recall coming across you before.' He was being more cautious now. A hint of uncertainty.

'Nor I you.'

'You're not a member here, obviously.'

'Obviously.'

She stared at him, face blank. He stared at her. She let the silence settle, grow awkward.

'So,' she said, when she'd had enough. 'Flirting or serious. Which was it?'

'Flirting? Not at all. It was a throwaway comment, Officer. A pleasantry. I'm sorry.'

'Don't be.' She smiled again. 'I've thrown it away.'

She leaned forward, resting her hand on the desk so that it was no more than an inch from where his own was resting. In terms of intimacy, she might as well have rested it *on* his hand. The proximity was deliberate. He would be aware of that.

'What kind of club is this?' she asked, voice soft, suggestive.

His eyes broke contact momentarily, looking down to check the position of her hand. 'A fitness club,' he said. He sounded slightly irritated. Worried she was off limits, out of control.

'One with a history,' she said. 'Do you know the history?'

'Of course.'

'So do I. We should be honest with each other. I'm sure we want the same things, at heart.'

The door opened and the same girl she had spoken to at reception set a drink down in front of her. Karen watched her looking at the position of their hands on the desk. It looked like they had been interrupted in something. There was a faint visible pulse at his temple now. She waited until the girl was gone, then took a sip from the drink.

'Probably this place suffers from its history,' she said.

He sat back in the chair, moving his hand away from her. Silent.

'In the past you had to be a blagger to get in. A blagger or a bent copper, as they said then. Quaint old language. I'm talking twenty years ago.'

'A long time ago.'

'Yes. It's all different now. Big shots and big money. Discretion. A little coke in the locker rooms. In the Drugs Squad – where I normally work – we regard this place as a meeting place set up to facilitate the laundering of drugs money. It's a source of embarrassment that there are officers from other departments who are naïve enough to be members. One day we will have to do something about that.'

'Other departments?' he said. 'Mr Rawson has been a member for five years.'

She took another sip from her drink. Rawson was her DCI. The idiot that fronted the Drugs Squad. The information was new to her. She tried not to let it show. She didn't doubt that it was true.

'Like I said,' she said, 'at heart, I'm sure we want the same things.'

His face betrayed nothing. Eyes on hers again. Silence. Waiting for the point to it all.

'I need your help,' she said. 'I'm looking at a PC called Oliver Williams. He's a member. But not the sort of member you would want these days. He's the bent copper variety. If he applied now, you would tell him where to go. My guess is he got in way back. The Leeds City days. He will know a few people, but mainly low-level stuff. If he is – as I suspect – implicated in shooting a policeman, then you would not want to be helping him. You would want him out of here.'

He shrugged. 'I couldn't agree more.'

'I want to get into his locker. Without him, or anyone else, knowing. That's the first thing. You might want to make a call about that.'

He nodded, features impassive. 'Do you have a warrant?'

'That would give the wrong impression,' she said. 'I want your help. I don't want to trash the place.'

'I see. And the second thing?'

'Does Mark Coates have a locker?'

He shook his head. It was impossible to tell whether the name meant anything to him. 'I don't know. Is he a member?'

'On my information.'

'I can check. If he does, you want to see that as well, I suppose?'

'That's right.'

'Is there a third thing?'

'That depends what's in Williams's locker.'

He stood up. 'Well, now we know where we are, at least.' She thought he was about to refuse. She stood up with him. 'If you wait outside, Officer. I'll make that phone call.'

She sighed a little, privately. Berman – or the nephews – would throw Williams to her without thinking about it. Coates was a different matter. There would be a reluctance about that. But she would cross that bridge when he put it in front of her.

Ten minutes later it was like she was talking to a different person. He came back all smiles, expansive in his offers of help. As she stood to meet him he rested a hand on her arm, leaned forward and spoke *sotto voce*, ostensibly so that the staff at reception couldn't hear.

'I'm sorry I was a little unhelpful earlier. A little frosty, perhaps. I didn't wish to be. In fact, from the moment I saw you, I thought we would get along just fine. It's just . . . well, you have to be careful these days. Police officers aren't always just doing their job.'

'Quite.'

'I'm authorised to help you in whichever way I can.'

'Whichever way?'

'Exactly.'

They cleared out the men's changing rooms and he showed her Coates's locker first, opening it with a small plastic key. It was empty. She smiled, understanding. When she had asked him about Coates, he had already known this. That was why he hadn't asked how Coates fitted into her enquiries.

Williams's locker was a different matter. It was stuffed to the gills with paperwork. It took less than a minute to find what she wanted. A complete copy of Phil Leech's personnel folder, a set of photographs of him and two reports on his movements covering periods over a year in the past, completed by two different firms of Private Investigators. She took some notes then closed the locker. Armitage was at her elbow, watching.

'Did you find what you wanted?'

'Yes. And there is a third thing.'

'I'll do my best.'

'My guess is he will come back for this stuff. I'm slightly surprised he hasn't already been.' She dug out a battered business card with her mobile number on it. 'Will you call me when he comes?'

He took the card from her, glanced at it. 'I have your phone number now,' he said, grinning.

It was tedious. She waited.

'I'll do better than that,' he said, growing serious. 'I'll make sure he remains here until you arrive.'

'I don't want him hurt.'

'Of course not. Trust me. I'm more intelligent than that. There are certain account difficulties I need to discuss with him, though. Anything to help root out corruption in the force.'

TWENTY

Munro was late for de-brief, his first on this operation. There were about thirty detectives in the basement Incident Room as he walked in. He took time to scan the faces, memorise them, try to work out who was and who wasn't there. Sharpe wasn't. He searched for Bob Harris's face and beckoned him over while they were all still talking amongst themselves.

'Karen Sharpe,' he said. 'Where is she?'

Harris shrugged, looking slightly embarrassed. 'I need to talk to you about her, boss.'

'Again? We're missing about fifteen men, Bob. Do we have excuses for all of them?'

'I think so. Most are out on the moor with the fingertip teams.'

'Any results there yet?'

'Nothing.'

'We'd better get cracking.'

He made a mental note to get Tony to set up a supervisors' meeting for the morning. Which reminded him that he hadn't seen Marshall anywhere. He saw Peter Dyson and asked him.

'Where's Tony, Peter?'

'He'll be late. They're about to start interviewing Coates. He's briefing the team.'

'They should be at this briefing before they do *any*

interview. Can you go up there and get them all down, please? Tony included.'

He leaned back against the table in front of the large whiteboard with the scenarios, turning to the faces in front of him, waiting for the whispers to subside.

'Right then. Can we get started? It's been a busy day. We've made a lot of progress. I'm really pleased with you all. I haven't had time to follow it all on screen so this de-brief is important for me. My plan for these de-briefs is that I will go round each DS in turn. That way we will keep it to a reasonable time frame. If you want to say things – and I sincerely hope you will – in future run them by your supervisor beforehand. When I pick on him or her, they can bring you in. Understood?'

A few nods, a few smiles. More generally, non-committal silence. Perhaps they were tired. He turned to Bob Harris.

'I'll start with your lot, Bob.'

'Some really good work from DC Firth,' Harris said. 'He's not here. He was on the original teams out at four this morning, so I've let him go. He's been on to Firearms in London to try to trace the serial number on the weapon. No joy. This afternoon he went over to our own place in Wakefield and got them to trawl through the local records. We've got a match.'

'Licensed in West Yorkshire?' It was almost too good to believe.

'Correct. Licensed to a Mr Peter Cryer. Address in Keighley. He doesn't exist. This is why.' He held up a small, clear exhibit bag, passed it round to Munro. Munro looked at it. Inside, folded so that the top sheet was visible, was a Section 1 Firearms Licence Application Form. There were two passport photos attached to the top sheet. The face looked familiar.

'Who is it?' he asked.

'Mark Coates.'

Munro almost fell off the table. 'We have Coates on the Section One licence for the weapon?' He stared at Harris in astonishment.

'I would have told you,' Harris said. 'But we only just got this back in the last few minutes.'

'Are you sure?'

'Certain. He'll deny it, of course. But look at the name of the officer who dealt with the application.' Munro tried to find it. 'It's Oliver Williams,' Harris said, while he was still looking. 'He works over in Wakefield. Part of his job is Section One licences.'

'Williams? The PC Phil Leech thought had checked his car?'

'The very same.'

'I put Karen Sharpe on to that. Has she—'

'That was one of the things I needed to talk to you about. She got a warrant for Williams's home address this afternoon.'

'A magistrate's warrant?'

'That's right.'

'I would want to be asked about that kind of move. To my knowledge, no one asked me.'

'No, sir. In fact, DI Marshall decided we didn't have grounds to get a warrant. This was before we found out about the Section One licence for Coates.'

'Communication difficulties?'

'I don't know, sir. But she found a whole lot of stuff in there. She jumped the gun, I realise that. But she got a result.'

'Like what?'

'Masses of copied records on Operation Anvil. And

others. So much stuff he must have been using. Possibly selling it. I don't think he will be coming back to work.'

Munro took a breath. 'Okay. I'll speak to you about the warrant later. But for now, are you telling me we can link PC Williams, this Section One licence application and Coates?'

'I'm sure of it. We haven't recovered the actual licence yet. Still double checking the seized material for that. But even if we haven't got it, even if he denies it's him in the photo on the application form, we will still have the connections. The postal address is being chased up now. I guess it's false. This form will go off for prints, DNA, the lot. But ultimately, when push comes to shove, we have the photo. We can let the jury decide.'

'I've not actually seen the man. Are you certain it's a good resemblance?'

'Absolutely.'

'In that case, Bob, that is fantastic work. We have the gun linked to Coates and, if Dave's lead follows through, Varley near the scene at the right time. What could be better?'

Marshall, apologising, came in with two or three others. Munro waited until he had joined him, then turned back to the group.

'I have a few less certain things to report,' he said. 'I want to tell you about a motorbike we've just recovered about twenty minutes from the Cock Hill scene. But there's a whole lot of detail from the autopsies that I'll let Tony give you first. Some of it is helpful in that it is beginning to point away from the Mitchell suicide scenario, though we won't know for sure until tomorrow. Tony?'

He let Tony get started then beckoned to Bob Harris to

143

follow him from the room. Outside, in the corridor, he asked him about Sharpe.

'What did you want to tell me?'

'She's out of control. I don't know where she is now. She hasn't told me. She went over to get that warrant without consulting anybody. Tony had already made a decision not to get it.'

'Maybe the wrong decision.'

'Maybe. And she got a result. It was good work. I accept that. But that's not the way we do it. It will work once and get us all into shit the next time.'

TWENTY-ONE

She had eaten nothing all day. Now, coming back from Leeds at nearly seven-thirty in the evening, when she finally felt something like the stirrings of appetite in her belly, it was the usual Bradford dilemma. She could think of nowhere, absolutely nowhere in the entire city, where she would be happy to sit down and pay for her food.

Restaurants weren't something Bradford did well. If you didn't mind sticky linoleum floors, greasy tabletops, a background toilet smell and food that was submerged beneath two inches of oil, you were in the right city; there was an abundance of restaurants serving entire meals for under three quid in just those conditions. Guaranteed mild food poisoning every third try. If you were less worried about the price and more about the sustenance, however, you were wasting your time.

It was one of the things she missed about London. Not eating out expensively. Just eating out at all. To feed herself now she would have to stop at a supermarket and buy a sandwich. In London? What would she have done? She tried to think back.

A memory of eating something, somewhere in London. It should have been easy. If she missed it – and she had *just* thought that, *just* had that feeling – then surely she had somewhere in mind.

Blank. No memory at all. It was like looking at a white canvas. As she came over the top of Dudley Hill and the view to Lister's Mill opened out in front of her, she slowed the car down, struggling with the thoughts.

Why couldn't she remember? The frustration began to irritate her. A car passing her to the left let out a long blast on the horn. She saw vague faces through the windows, mouthing at her. What was she doing? Straying across the lanes? She pulled over by a service station and sat there trying to think, to work her way back to it.

Take it one step at a time, she thought. Where had she been living in London, for the last few years she was there? West London. She brought the words up like little pebbles from the depths, held them out in front of her, turned them over.

West London. Was it *Hammersmith*? No, not Hammersmith. She remembered slowly, the words forming in front of her eyes. For half a minute they meant nothing to her. Then they fell into place. The last link in a long chain. She realised at once where it would end.

It was like a bitterness in her mouth, warning her. Something physical. The memory was there, she could *feel* it, a shape, heavy at the bottom of her consciousness. The taste in her mouth was what happened when she was panicking. Don't go there, it said. Don't pull it up. Leave what is buried underground.

She was a different person now. Everything she had been then was dead. The cloud of memories swarming to get up at her were dysfunctional reminders. The product of a biological accident, that what she was now and what she had been *just happened* to share the same body. She had to control it.

She realised her mobile was ringing. The sound swept over her in a wave. Relief. Work. Pulling her back. It was all she had now.

She put the phone to her ear. 'Hello?'

'Hello. Is that DC Sharpe?' A foreign voice, accented. Asian?

'Yes. Who is speaking?'

'Dr Mohammed Hussain. You left me some messages.'

'Dr Hussain. So kind of you to get back to me. I'm on a murder enquiry and I'm trying to trace one of your tenants.'

'Toomey. Has he killed someone?'

She laughed, though it wasn't funny. 'No. I think he will want to help us. Do you know where he is?'

'I have no idea. I knew only today that he had moved out. Mrs Khan told me this afternoon. I knew he would be trouble.'

'Did you? Why was that?'

'He paid everything in cash, double.'

'Double?'

'Yes. He had no references, so I refused him. He offered double and I accepted. I should have known better.'

She felt her heart sink. 'No references.'

'No. I'm sorry.'

'Did you know anything about him?'

'Nothing at all. He paid up front, double. You won't mention the house, will you? It will get a bad reputation. I could lose business.'

'Mention it to who?'

'I don't know. The press? The court?'

'No. He's not involved like that. Can you tell me what Toomey looked like?'

'Tall, normal build, normal clothes. He looked normal to me. That's why I took him on.'

'Without references?'

'Yes. I will not do it again. Regardless of the money. This is terrible.'

'Did he have anything noticeable about his appearance?

147

Scars, limps . . . I don't know. You're a doctor, aren't you? Did you not notice anything else?'

'I'm not a medical doctor.'

'No?'

'No. My field is business management.'

She sighed. 'I see. Did you notice anything else?'

'No. I only met him once.'

'Spoke with an accent?'

'Yes. Manchester, I would think. That was where he said he had come from.'

'Did he say why he couldn't give references? Why he would have to pay in cash?'

'He said, "No questions, double rent." I knew he was dodgy.'

'Did he say anything else? Anything you can recall?'

'Yes. He asked me if I knew any car dealerships in the area.'

'Car dealerships? What did you say?'

'I gave him details for the Lister Park Garage. But that's a BMW place. He wanted to trade a Merc.'

'He had a car?'

'Yes. An expensive car. A Mercedes SLK.'

'Are you sure? Your woman at the house said he didn't have a car.'

'Mrs Khan knows nothing. She is a silly old woman. Probably she lied to you. She is suspicious of the police, you see. Her son was arrested in the riots last year. Anyway, she wasn't there at the time. When I first spoke with him his car was outside. I could clearly see it. In fact, he pointed it out to me.'

'Did you see the registration plate?'

'Yes.'

'Did you write it down?'

'No. No need to. I have a good memory for numbers. Sometimes. MIL 1122. A Northern Irish plate, if I'm not mistaken.'

'MIL 1122? You sure?'

'That's it.'

She wrote it down on a scrap of paper. 'That's excellent. What colour car?'

'Silver, metallic. But he may not have it now. Like I said, he wanted to sell it.'

'Was there anyone else with him?'

'No.'

'Not in the car?'

'No.'

'Okay. That's really helpful, Dr Hussain. If you think of anything else, no matter how small it may seem, ring me. Please.'

'Of course. You will not mention the house?'

'You have my word.'

She sat back in the seat and watched the darkness forming over the city in front of her. MIL 1122. A Northern Irish plate. Not that it meant anything. There were scores of them running around the UK. Toomey clearly wasn't Irish. But at least the plate was distinctive. People might remember it.

On the way out to Halifax she called in the number, using her mobile. The response was predictable.

'A black Ford Orion. Scrapped 1995.'

'Last keeper?'

'David Dungannon. Ballymena, Northern Ireland. Do you want the full address?'

'No. Not now.'

If he had sold it, they would have re-plated it. It would be virtually untraceable by now.

*

149

It was after eight-thirty by the time she got to the basement Incident Room. The place was empty. She scanned the board for who was on. There were thirty detectives authorised for overtime. All out and about. She noticed that her own name had a question mark beside it.

She sat down in the corner office Marshall and Dyson used, pulled on a pair of sterile rubber gloves and started to look through the bags of exhibits they had seized the day before from Varley's home address in Eccleshill, checking for any references to Toomey or MIL 1122. There was nothing obvious. She did the same with Coates's exhibits. The lights went on in the main room and someone peered through the door at her, without coming in.

There was a plastic key in amongst Coates's stuff, similar to that used by Armitage to open the lockers at Berman's. She checked the exhibit number, logged on to HOLMES and searched for actions against it. As yet, there were none. She replaced it. She had already been inside Coates's locker.

There were two diary notebooks in the bags from Varley's place. She took some time looking through each page. In one book there were lists of numbers, set beside letters. '70/EM' occurred a few times. Also '50/JDM' and '80/PB'. Dealer lists, without a doubt. The initials would probably be false, coded. At a later date she might have to think more carefully about them. For now, there was nothing obviously linking them to Toomey. The other book contained rising tallies of amounts, presumably takings or savings. The figures ran on to December, by which point the amount had got as high as 5K. Small fry. Probably his little business on the side.

Sandwiched between various pages there were scraps of paper with scrawled letters on, unintelligible. One from the page for 18 February looked strangely familiar to her. Possibly some dealer's handwriting she had come across before. She replaced it, stood up and made to leave. She had got as far as the light switch when a ripple of shivers ran down her spine. She stopped. Someone walking on her grave, her mother would have said.

She brought her hand up and rubbed the back of her neck, looked at the clock. Nearly ten-thirty. Time had passed without her realising. There were perhaps twenty detectives in the larger room now, most of them talking amongst themselves. She opened the door, switched the light off and stepped out. The hairs on her neck were standing on end, prickling. She paused.

After a while she realised some of them were looking at her. She was standing by the door to the little internal office looking at her feet. What was she trying to work out? What had she just missed?

'Are you all right there, Karen?' one of them asked. She didn't recognise him.

'Yes,' she said, unsure. 'Just tired, I think.'

'We're just done with interviewing Coates,' another said.

'Yeah? What did he say? No comment?'

'No comment.'

They looked disappointed.

Why should he comment? she thought. This probably had nothing to do with him.

TWENTY-TWO

She wasn't in. Nearly eleven-thirty and she wasn't back. Munro sat in his car outside her house and wondered what he was doing there, second night running. He had an excuse both nights, of course. Last night to invite her on to the squad, tonight to give her a final warning about team work. But that wasn't why he was there, not at this time of night.

Her house was small, old, dark. As far as he could see there were no other properties within half a mile. Isolated, surrounded on three sides by some kind of very tall tree. Massive black shapes in the darkness. Maybe sycamores or chestnuts. He wasn't good at identifying nature. His wife would have wanted them cut down. The sort of tree that in a storm would fall right on to the house and crush you in your bed.

No street lighting here. Parked up on the dirt track outside her front door the sky was clouded and moonless, the night black.

Feeling slightly foolish he started the engine to leave. She could return with a man. A woman even? (Was she like that? Was that possible?) How would he explain himself? He had her mobile number, he could have called her. He was the SIO on this enquiry, he ought to have known better.

He had reversed between two trees and was pulling round to turn back down the lane when headlights appeared at the end of it. He paused, slipping it into neutral. The car came past him, pulled up in front of the house. Her Volvo. She got out and walked towards him. He could see her frowning through the darkness, peering, trying to get a better view of who it was. He started to lower the window, but by the time it was halfway down she was standing there, right by the driver's door.

'It's only me,' he said.

'I know,' she said. 'I was expecting you.'

She was smiling at him. Ironically. Not with warmth.

'Expecting me?'

'Yes.' She held up a carrier bag for him to see. 'I bought this for you.'

He frowned. 'What is it?'

'Whiskey. Your drink of preference, sir.'

He felt himself colouring in the dark.

'Do you want to come in?'

He sighed. She hadn't even asked for the excuse.

The house was the same. A curious combination of clutter and emptiness. Cold. It didn't much seem like a home. He sat down on one of the two chairs, keeping his coat on. She hadn't taken her jacket off.

'Are you cold?' she asked, getting glasses out of a cupboard.

'Yes. Don't you have central heating?'

She shook her head. 'Not yet. I'll build the fire for you, if you want. Meanwhile there's a gas heater behind you. Do you want a drink of this or not?'

'Yes. I'll have one.'

'Then you'll be going, right? You've got to drive.'

He tried to ignore her mocking tone. 'It was kind of you to buy it. What is it?'

'No idea. The most expensive one they had. I don't drink the stuff.'

He watched her as she poured it and felt uncomfortable. She was attractive, but not in the standard way that usually got to him. It was something more than that.

'You don't seem like a police officer,' he said, as she brought the drink over. That was part of it. She was not what she seemed.

'Maybe I'm not,' she said.

He frowned, took the glass from her. Did she know how to converse? How to just chat, person to person? 'Meaning?'

'Meaning all that they are, their attitudes, desires, ways of reacting to the world, maybe that's not me.'

'Speaking philosophically, you mean?' he said. He tried to be light-hearted, stating the obvious. 'But in reality, you *are* a police officer. Just like the rest of us. That *is* your job.'

'Yes. But only my job. Not my life. Just how I earn a living.'

'Not your life?' He looked around him at the mess. Apart, perhaps, from the copious quantities of paperback books, there was no sign in her home that she had any life at all outside the job.

She saw him looking. 'Don't judge what you don't know, *sir*.' The title came as a sarcastic afterthought. 'Just because you can't see anything like *you*, doesn't mean there's nothing there.'

'Not like me? You make it sound distasteful.'

She shrugged. 'Do I? You told me I wasn't like a police officer. What kind of reply did you expect?'

He felt himself tightening up within. Why had he come here?

She sat down on the other chair, very close to him. She had poured herself something that looked like vodka. He took a sip from the whiskey. Jameson. Unmistakable smooth flavour. Not his favourite, too understated.

'It's nice,' he said, trying to get back to politeness, at least.

'But not your favourite?'

He stopped in the action of bringing the glass to his lips. 'No.'

She was looking at him so intently he thought it might not be beyond her to read his thoughts. 'It will warm you up though,' she said.

She was unnerving, he decided. Too intense.

She stood up and walked over to the portable gas heater behind him, lit it. She had switched on one light in the place, a small table lamp on one of the counters in the kitchen area. They were virtually sitting in darkness. Fully wrapped. She sat down again.

'Are you *sure* you live here?' he asked her, meaning it as a kind of joke. He regretted it at once.

'I'm certain. This is my house. That is why I'm here. Why are *you* here?'

He put the glass down, moved his chair a little away from hers. He couldn't read her at all. 'I came to ask you where you were this afternoon.'

'You came at quarter to midnight to ask me that?' She sat back in her seat, eyes on him, faint smile playing at the corners of her mouth. Not the slightest pretence of respect.

'Why not?' he replied. 'I won't sleep for hours yet.'

'No? Aren't you tired? I thought you hadn't slept in days.'

'Yes. I'm tired. That isn't enough to make you sleep though. Not always.'

'I sleep well,' she said. 'The sleep of the innocent.'

There was a bitter tone to her voice. She raised her glass to him. 'Cheers.'

He touched the rim of his own glass against hers, took a sip.

'Why *are* you here? It's hardly professional,' she said.

Distance, antagonism, defensiveness. He grew tired of it. She was always one step away from it all. Whatever was happening, she wouldn't relax. He finished the drink and stood up, decision made.

'I don't know,' he said. 'It was a mistake. I'll leave. Please see me first thing in the morning. Before you do *anything*.'

He looked down at her. There was a look of unexpected panic on her face. He turned to go. She stood up quickly, placing a hand on his arm, stopping him.

'Please. I'm sorry,' she said. 'I don't want to be like this with you. I'm sorry.'

He paused. She was standing about a foot away from him, one hand on his arm, looking at her feet. He felt confused. She had thawed, suddenly. The hand on his arm, the look in her eyes. He frowned. Was she being serious? In his office she had done something like this to him, pretended to be upset. Was she playing with him again?

'Please stay,' she said, quietly. 'Have another drink. I'll try to be civil.'

'Civil?'

'Human. Whatever.'

'Human?'

She looked up at him. Her eyes looked black in the half light, wide open. 'I want you to stay,' she said. 'I mean it. I'm not messing around. I'm sorry. I don't know why I act like that.' Where her hand was on his arm her fingers squeezed slightly, willing him. 'You have been nothing but pleasant to me,' she said. She sounded miserable.

He let his shoulders sink. 'I'll stay if you light the fire,' he said.

He reached out a hand and touched her hair with the tips of his fingers. At her left temple, momentarily. A matter of a split second's contact. But done. Too late to take it back. She smiled at him. Still no warmth in it, but no mockery either now. She looked sad, he thought. He couldn't understand why. He could feel his heart beginning to thump. He wanted to put an arm around her, hug her, but he couldn't. He shouldn't even have touched her like that.

'It's a deal,' she said.

TWENTY-THREE

He poured himself another whiskey (hand shaking slightly) and watched her making the fire. She did it quickly, with practised movements. Within ten minutes she had it roaring in the grate, flickering the walls with red light. He moved over and stood behind her while she was stoking it, feeling the heat on his face.

'It will warm up quickly,' she said. 'I'm sorry. I'm not in the habit of lighting it. Not just for me. It's hardly worth the effort.'

'Have you always lived alone?' he asked.

She finished what she was doing then turned round, still squatting on the floor. 'No. Not always.' The defensive tone was back.

'Here, I mean,' he said.

'Yes. I moved here by myself.'

'A long time ago?'

'You already asked me that,' she said. 'Five, six years ago. I told you.'

'So why *is* the place so . . . so makeshift? Like you can't be bothered with it.'

He tried to make his voice sound mild, gentle. Maybe there was some terrible reason, something he shouldn't disturb.

'You asked me that too.'

'And you told me it was a "question of priorities". I don't know what you meant.'

She was thoughtful for a moment, looking up at him. He felt uneasy, standing above her. But there was nowhere to sit. 'You look uncomfortable,' she said. 'Why don't you sit down?'

Same thing again. It was unsettling. 'Where?' he asked.

'On one of those?' she suggested, pointing behind him to three large cushions, propped up against the wall. 'Or on the floor. Here. Beside me. The carpet is comfortable enough.'

He placed the whiskey glass on the floor, took his jacket off and sat. The carpet was a thick pile thing, not as uncomfortable as he had imagined. He felt awkward. She was watching him. The whiskey had hit the spot already. Warmth flushing his veins. He needed to be careful. He *was* tired, he had lied. The fire and the whiskey together would knock him out.

'Tell me about you,' she said. 'Tell me what makes you tick.'

'We were talking about you.'

'Let's start with you. You're more interesting.'

'I doubt it.' Did he want to tell her anything? 'I'll tell you about a friend of mine,' he said eventually, leaning back on his hands.

'A friend?'

'Yes. Do you want to hear it?'

'Why not? What's this friend called?'

'Andrew Farrar.'

'Still alive?'

He looked closely at her. Was she being ironic, suspecting, of course, that 'the friend' was merely a cover for himself? 'No. He's dead,' he said, face impassive. 'But that's not the point.'

'I'm sorry.'

'Don't be.' He took a mouthful of the whiskey.

'Go on,' she said.

He let the liquid burn the back of his throat, savoured the sensation. 'I first met him in nineteen sixty-nine, when I was fourteen. You will have been,' he calculated quickly, 'nine. You were nine years old. Where were you then, I wonder?'

He allowed the question to hang there for a moment. She didn't reply.

'In that year,' he went on, 'my family moved down to Yorkshire.'

'From where?'

He smiled. 'From Cupar.'

'Cupar?'

'Yes. It's in Fife. The Kingdom of Fife, in Scotland.'

He broke off, eyes distant, thinking about it. Her eyes were on him, focused, concentrating. She was more interested that he was telling her this, he thought, than in the story itself. 'I had to start my life from scratch. At least, that's what it felt like. In Scotland I had friends, family, everything. In Leeds I had nothing.'

'Why Leeds?'

'My father got an engineering job there. The factory closed in Dundee, a job came up in Leeds. He moved, took his family with him. My father, my mother and me. I was an only child, you see, no brothers, no sisters. In Cupar I had been close to my cousins, but down here I had no one. At school,' he paused, trying to select what to say, 'at school I was bullied. All sorts of reasons that I won't tire you with, but mainly because my accent was different. Jock-the-cock, they called me.'

She was frowning. What had that to do with his accent? He could see her thinking it.

'Don't worry about the logic of it,' he said. 'There wasn't meant to be a reason. It was a nickname. I had it

160

through most of my late teens. To object to it meant a beating and back then I was skinny, not good with my fists. But these are trivial details, no different to most kids. And this story is not about me.'

He took another sip of the whiskey.

'At school Andrew Farrar was the only person who would speak to me. To this day I don't know why. I was tall, lanky, uncomfortable with myself. On the sports field there was nothing I could do. When they lined you up to pick teams I was always left behind. In class things weren't much better. I was average, I suppose. Average at nearly everything I touched. Andrew, by comparison, was good at everything. In fact, that's not true. He was brilliant at everything.'

He stopped, drained the glass, felt his mind relaxing. The fire was lulling him.

'At sixteen he was playing rugby for the county. He scored four straight A grades at A level. While I was struggling to scrape passes, he had a place lined up to do medicine at Cambridge. He was elected Head Boy at the school. Everyone loved him. All the girls, all the boys. He didn't have a single enemy. And yet within five months of me meeting him we were inseparable.' He looked at her. 'Why would that be? Why would he be interested in me?'

She shrugged. 'Perhaps you don't see yourself as others see you.'

'In what way?'

'You paint an ugly picture of yourself. But you can't have changed that much.'

His glass was empty. She stood and walked over to the table to retrieve the whiskey bottle. He watched the swing in her hips, the long legs. When she came back she bent down beside him and the liquid trickled from bottle to glass. Her head was six inches from his. He could reach out, touch her. Was that what she wanted? Was that what she was trying to communicate?

'Thanks,' he said.

She put the bottle down, sat down, nearer to him this time, close enough to touch him if she reached out her arm.

'Go on,' she said. 'Tell me more.'

'Are you interested?'

'Yes.'

He picked up the glass. 'Where was I?'

'Inseparable friends.'

'Inseparable friends. We shared everything. Rugby, girls, music. Everything. Of course, with most of these things I was *watching*, he was *doing*. But don't let that get in the way. For me it was more than friendship. I hero-worshipped him, looked up to him. I've done that all my life with strong characters. People say they think I'm strong, that I come across that way . . .' He faltered. Where did that thought lead?

'Tell me,' she said. 'Tell me what you were about to say.' She was leaning towards him slightly. He swallowed.

'Just that I have gone through most of my life feeling half-formed, copying. I sometimes doubt I have a personality at all.'

She moved back a little, frowning now. Was this *too* personal? Not what she had expected.

'But this isn't about me,' he said, again, too quickly. 'It's about Andrew Farrar.' He took another mouthful. 'Andrew fell in love with the girl I had adored and loved – in my own juvenile way – since the fifth year. Louise Robertson. I can remember her now, exactly as she looked then. Red hair, slightly built, graceful. She was never interested in me, not really. Not with Andrew there. Who would be? That I got anywhere with her was down to him. I didn't have a clue with women back then. He helped me.'

'Then took her off you?'

'Not quite.' He smiled, trying to make it look normal. 'For a while she was sort of,' he could feel himself colouring, '*between* us. Going out with both of us. Sometimes me, sometimes Andrew. Sometimes . . .' He couldn't find the words, couldn't make himself say it.

She said it for him. 'Both of you?'

He sighed. 'Yes. In a harmless way. By the time he was twenty they were dating. Just her and him.'

'Twenty?'

'Yes.'

'And before that it was *both* of you, this thing with *both* of you?'

'Yes.'

'I see.'

She didn't though. He went on quickly. 'Despite my interest I would admit that they were made for each other. If that makes any sense.' He paused, looked at her. 'Does it?'

'Make sense?'

'Yes. Do you think people – two people – can be made for each other? Do you think it works like that?'

'I don't know. Does it matter to the story, given you were *both* with her at some point?'

He shook his head. 'Not really.' Suddenly he felt heavy, unhappy with it all. Why had he started telling her this?

'Did he get to be a doctor?' she asked.

He stared at the fire, wanting to sleep. 'Of course.' His words sounded slurred, unclear. 'I left school and joined the police. He went to Cambridge and became a doctor. They married. Everything worked out as it should have.'

'Is that it?'

He took a breath. 'No.'

'What else then?'

He rubbed his head. 'Ten years ago, when I had just made DC, I was working out of Weetwood when we had a call to come to his house.'

'Did you know it was his house?'

'Of course.'

'You were still friends?'

'Why shouldn't we have been?' He lay back on the floor, resting his head on his arm. He felt slightly dizzy.

'Sometimes people grow apart.'

'Not us.'

'Louise as well?'

'That's right.'

'Even though you liked her?'

'Fancied her, you mean?'

'Yes.'

'That wasn't a problem.'

'So what did you find?' she asked. She wasn't going to push it.

'He had disappeared.'

She raised an eyebrow. 'Just like that?'

'Just like that. Didn't return from hospital one day. No phone call, no explanation, no trace. He just disappeared. It took her two days to report him missing.'

'Did they have children?'

'No. I learned from her – Louise Farrar, as she was then – during the course of the enquiry, that he had never wanted children, that his own father – whom I knew well – had beaten him very badly when he was little. He had told me nothing of this. Nor had she. This and other things. Maybe that had something to do with it . . .'

He didn't want to go on now. It was too revealing. He should never have started.

'Did you find out where he was?'

'Eventually.' He could feel his eyes closing.

'So tell me.'

'He was in Cornwall, picking fruit.'

'Picking fruit?'

'Yes. It took us eight months to locate him. He had walked out on her, walked out on a seventy-к-a-year job, jumped on a train with nothing but the clothes he was wearing, and got off it in Cornwall.'

He propped his head up, looked at her. In the half-light it was difficult to tell, but he thought she looked paler. He sat up, slowly.

'I'm sorry,' he said. 'It's all rubbish. I shouldn't have started telling you.'

'No,' she said quickly, interrupting him. 'Tell me.' She reached over to where his hand was lying on the carpet, placed her fingers over his. He felt a tiny thrill, like electricity passing between them. 'You're keeping bits from me,' she said.

'Maybe.'

'So why start telling me?'

He shook his head. 'I don't know. I shouldn't have.'

He saw her think it through, constructing the possibilities. 'How was he?' she asked. 'How was he when you found him?'

'He was different. I hardly knew him.'

'Did he tell you why?' Her fingers were still there, gripping his.

'Not really. It was difficult to get much sense out of him. He said when he thought back to his time in Yorkshire it was like thinking about someone else. Someone who had died.'

'He said that? He said those words?'

'Yes. I think so.'

She withdrew her hand. She looked as if she was shivering slightly.

'He said, "It's like having someone else's memories. It was never me. I never wanted to do it. I never wanted to be that person. All my life I was forced into being something I was not. One day I woke up and realised it didn't have to go on."'

He lay back again, his eyes closing.

'That's why I said he was dead,' he said. 'He might be down there now, picking fruit. But he is not Andrew Farrar. Not the person I knew.'

'And Louise? Louise Robertson?'

He sighed. 'My wife,' he said. 'My estranged wife.'

TWENTY-FOUR

Thursday, 11 April 1996, 4.40 a.m.

Already it was light.

Police Constable John Bowman stood looking into the wide, metallic sheet of grey that was the sky. He was freezing. This was spring, he thought. It didn't feel like it. He looked out along the line of probationers, cadets and soldiers, all kitted out, like himself, in identical white, sterile nylon overalls and wondered why on earth he had ever considered this for a living.

The day before he had spent ten solid hours doing what they called an 'area search'. It involved nothing more onerous than walking at an even pace across a stretch of moor, scanning the ground in front of him as far as an imaginary dividing line between himself and the two men either side of him. At first it had been so boring he had long, protracted thoughts about what it would be like to be at the end of the line, to not have the safety of someone else to one side of you. How far would you then scan to that side? As the day had progressed, however, the level of concentration required to simply move your eyes and your head, with attention, in a limited arc to either side of the body, repetitively, for hours on end, had become almost unbearable.

The soldiers had started to crack first, focused silence passing into ribald humour and guffaws. Then the cadets, freshly bussed up from the Met. His serial – WYP probationers one and all – had tried hard to maintain a level of pride, professionalism. It was their area, their patch. They wanted to succeed. But by three in the afternoon he doubted anyone was looking hard enough to spot the level of detail they required.

Predictably, they found nothing.

That was over the other side of this moor, in a place called Wainstalls. Today they had bussed them further, to a place called Cock Hill. He had never heard of it. All they had told them was that part of it was a murder scene. They didn't even say which part.

Yesterday had been gruelling. But it wasn't the worst of it. What they wanted them to do today was called a 'fingertip search'. It involved crawling, on hands and knees, head down, through sodden moor and marsh, hands submerged beneath freezing puddles of water, for, they confidently predicted, at least six hours. Looking, they said, 'for anything'. But in particular, spent cartridge cases.

They formed up in a line along the road that ran across the top of the place, next to a weather station. The weather was hard to describe. At that time of day it was constantly changing. They were so high up that most of the time there were clouds below them, in the valley. Maybe it was beautiful, maybe it wasn't. He didn't get the chance to look. They gave them coffee and then lined them up.

The search was to progress past a small fence penning in the moor about five yards from the road. The pattern was centred around a line of telegraph poles that followed a small, peaty gully down into the valley below. They walked as far as the fence, finding nothing, then climbed over it and got down on to hands and knees. He didn't know the officers to either side of him.

After about an hour they hit a patch of really wet ground. Kneeling, his legs sank into it up to his groin. He found his hands were under about six inches of brackish liquid before they were even touching 'the bottom'.. The bottom wasn't the bottom either, but a layer of mud that varied in thickness. They hadn't told him how deeply he was to push his fingers into it.

He was beginning to shiver quite badly when he felt it, a tiny sharp edge against one of his fingers. They were so numb by this point, travelling so quickly through the freezing depths, that he had to stop and go back to it to be sure. He found it again and felt it slip away. He stopped, took his hands out and tried to rub some life into them. Then he went at it again. By this point his colleagues either side were about a foot ahead of him. The mist had cleared slightly and, out of the corner of his eye, he could see the line supervisor marching towards him from about fifty feet away, no doubt to demand he get a move on. His fingers closed around it. He brought it out.

It was a spent cartridge case. He sat back on his haunches in the water. 'Object!' he yelled, remembering the word they had told him to use.

The entire line stopped. The supervisor began to run. As he reached him he held it up in the air, between his finger and thumb.

'It's a bullet, sir,' he said, feeling suddenly proud. But more importantly, feeling the whole painful experience might now be cut short.

'It's a spent cartridge case, son,' the supervisor corrected him. 'Be accurate.'

They moved into life behind the line. He was told to sit exactly where he was and the supervisor called on his radio for the SOCO team. Within ten minutes they were there. They asked him questions about the location. They moved the entire line back six feet (so that only he was left sitting there, still in the water). They began to sketch and photograph, brought out stakes with little yellow pennants, fixed them around him and began to talk amongst themselves, excitedly. All of this went on as if he wasn't even there. Finally, they took the thing off him, bagged it, told him he could get up.

He was so cold, so stiff, someone had to help him. As he walked back he saw the SOCO team replacing him, getting down on their hands and knees in the area he had been covering.

He walked back to the tea truck. That was his reward. Within ten minutes the entire line had been broken out and sent to join him. He sipped a cup of milky, sweet tea and tried to get some circulation back into his hands. The talk was that they had found another, right next to where he had been.

The supervisor came up and took some notes of his details. When he had finished he told them all to be ready in five minutes.

'It's not over yet,' he said, voice hard. 'Before six tonight we've got to cover a square mile of this shit.'

TWENTY-FIVE

He was clever, she thought, more than she had given him credit for. She stood in the front room looking at him, flat out on her floor, still asleep, fully clothed and wrapped in the heavy quilt she had thrown over him the night before. Head still on the pillow she had wedged beneath him. He was sprawled, arms flung out to either side, legs apart. He was so large he made the room look tiny, the whole house seem strange. An alien under her roof.

It was nearly seven o'clock.

It was like having someone else's memories. Had he read her unedited file? Or were the words merely a coincidence? What had been the real point to his little bedtime story?

She made them both coffee, making no attempt to be quiet. The noise didn't wake him. His mobile had been ringing, intermittently, since five-thirty. That hadn't made an impact either.

He had implied he had read only the doctored version of her file. She had to doubt that now. Which raised the question of how much else he knew.

She had thought she could control him. Feigning alarm as he made to leave, reaching out to touch his fingers. Physical contact usually did it for men. They couldn't interpret it properly. They found it hard to believe it couldn't be genuine affection, because physicality implied you would let them go 'the whole way'. There was some kind of biological factor, deeply seeded, that said sex was important for women, trivial for men.

He was attractive enough. If necessary she would have happily slept with him to keep him off her back, in a manner of speaking. *Happily* was the correct term. From the moment she saw him at his car she had, in fact, been looking forward to it. She had done it with far worse than John Munro and for far less compelling reasons. Get his clothes off, find out what he was like beneath. Maybe it would have restored a sense of life to her, fleetingly.

Then he had come out with the strange sob story. At the end, when he had told her what she had guessed from the very beginning, that Louise was his wife, she had struggled to keep her remarks kind. Even then the best she could come up with had been about it being a little better than the standard police bullshit. But he had been out of it by then, hadn't heard a thing.

When she had reached out to touch his hand, halfway through the tale, she had tried to communicate desire to him. But he had not taken it that way. She had seen that in his eyes. He was no different to any other male. If *they* wanted it, it could mean nothing, like eating a good steak. She had heard them describe it like that. But if *you* wanted it, if you were ahead of them, the aggressor, then it had to *mean* something. If it didn't, you were a *slut*.

Taking his coffee over to him, she thought briefly about whether it would work to get him out of his pants now, wake him up with it. Last night had been effective in one sense – he had not pressed her about what she had done yesterday afternoon. Anything that would make him less able to cope with her professionally would be useful right now.

Instead, she set the coffee down by his side and shook him gently. He was the kind that would be put off by her being forward. Waking up inside her would probably make him ill.

When he finally awoke he seemed genuinely confused to find himself on her floor. Then he started the apologies.

'Don't apologise,' she said. 'You did nothing.' She let this sink in. 'You did so little I was disappointed,' she added. She stood up and pulled on her jacket, not waiting for him to respond. 'I have to go.'

He sat up, eyes bleary. 'What time is it?'

'After seven-thirty. Your mobile has been ringing on and off for a couple of hours.'

'My mobile?' He searched through his clothing for it, pulled it out. 'Shit.'

'Did you miss something?'

'I don't know.'

She waited while he dialled for his messages.

'What's the rush?' he asked, one ear to the phone.

'I'm on a murder team.'

He held a hand up to her, frowning. 'Wait,' he said. 'This is important.'

She waited. No point in biting. Let him have his pretensions. He listened for nearly a minute to the messages.

'They've found two more cartridge cases,' he said eventually, placing the phone back in a pocket.

'Where?'

'Cock Hill. Roughly where Boyd said they would be.'

'So what does that mean?'

'I don't know. Probably that Mitchell didn't kill herself. Are you going now? Drink your coffee with me.'

'I told you. I'm on a murder squad. You take your time, though. The door is on a catch. Pull it shut after you.'

He smiled at her, thinking she was joking. She smiled

back at him, then turned to leave. 'Wait.' She paused. 'Don't leave like this. I need to talk to you first.'

About yesterday afternoon, she thought. 'We can talk tonight,' she said.

'Tonight? What day is it?'

'Thursday, the eleventh of April. All day.'

'What happens tonight?'

She shrugged, opening the front door. 'I don't know. If you want to talk though, I'll be here.'

TWENTY-SIX

DC Clare Isles had been waiting over half an hour before they let her into the West Yorkshire Bank in Bradford. The manager was a middle-aged man called Thompson. It had been apparent from her first conversation with him – by phone, the day before – that he wasn't going to be cooperative if he could help it. He was too busy to give her the time; contact with the police was bad publicity. Etcetera. He had tried to catch her out by suggesting an eight o'clock morning meeting, saying that was the only 'slot' he had free, probably hoping it was too early for her. But she had arrived at the main, shuttered door on time. He had not.

Not that there was anything she could do about it. All investigations depended upon public cooperation. You couldn't force them into it. Either they wanted to do something about crime or they didn't. She had expected, of course, that telling Thompson that the enquiry was about the death of a policeman would make some kind of difference. It didn't.

She had got the action because she was a woman. She was certain about that. She had been assigned to the team researching Phil Leech's background, which should have been interesting enough, though she would have preferred the Coates and Varley team. But her DS was called Nigel Davis and he was old school. She was the only woman on a six-person team and from day one every single action that had anything to do with chasing banking records had landed in her tray. The message was clear. Chasing banks was all he could trust her with. The most routine and boring work the team had to do.

Phil Leech – as far as she had been able to determine by going through the property seized from his home address, his estranged wife's address, on his person or on Mitchell's person (his wallet, in particular) – had three different bank accounts. There was a savings account with the Abbey National, a current account with the West Yorkshire and a loan account with the West Yorkshire.

Abbey National had been very helpful. Within hours she had complete transaction details going back five years faxed to her in the Incident Room. The account had fluctuated, but not in any way that she could see would be helpful to the enquiry. He had last used it, to with-draw £50, in November 1995. A grand total of £11.56 was left.

'I've been told to see you by my chiefs,' was the first thing Thompson said to her when the shutters finally rolled up after eight-thirty a.m.

'We did agree to meet at eight, didn't we?' she said.

'Yes. I'm sorry. Other commitments.'

They sat her in a room with a spare desk and left her for nearly fifteen minutes. Then a young woman appeared, dressed in their uniform.

'Can I help you, madam?'

'I think Mr Thompson is already dealing with me.'

'No. He's had to deal with something else. He's asked me to see you.'

She repeated the entire request again. The woman wrote it all down and disappeared. She didn't offer her coffee.

When, half an hour later, they finally assembled printed

records in front of her she decided she would just take them all and examine them back at the station. But that proved problematic. Thompson reappeared.

'They tell me you wish to remove these records from the bank?'

'Yes.'

'I don't think that can be done. Not without a Court Order.'

She sighed. She could try explaining that other banks regularly assisted, without Court Orders. She didn't think that would work though.

'What's the difference?' she asked. 'I've seen the stuff now. You've disclosed it.'

'Letting you take away originals is a quite different matter. I'll need to consult Head Office on that.'

'How long will it take?'

'If you come back tomorrow. I could have an answer by then.'

'Too long.'

'Well, I'm sorry, but these are our records. You cannot just—'

'They are computer print-outs. They are copies, not originals. The originals are on your system.'

'It doesn't matter. I'm thinking about my duties of confidentiality to my client.'

'You've already breached those – if you have them – by showing me this.'

'Because I was told to. Wrongly, I believe. I was not told to allow you to remove material.'

'Your client is dead.'

'He has an estate. The duty is to his estate.'

She stood up. 'I'm taking them,' she said. 'What are you going to do? Obstruct me?'

His face turned purple for a moment. She waited,

staring at him. Was he thinking about it? Was he considering getting physical with her?

'What will you do if I try to stop you?' he asked, eventually. His voice had risen a couple of semi-tones.

'I'll arrest you,' she said. A complete lie.

'I will write all this down. I will complain about you.' His voice was quivering with suppressed rage.

She nodded. 'Fine. I take it I'm not going to have to arrest you?'

He let out a long breath, between gritted teeth. 'You will have to sign for them,' he said.

'Fine.'

'Wait here. I'll have receipts prepared.'

It took another ten minutes before an older, slightly friendlier, woman appeared with several pieces of typed paper for her to sign.

'What are these?' she asked.

'Lists of the material you're removing.'

She checked through them.

'I know about these two accounts,' she said. 'The current and the loan account. But what's this?'

She pointed to a sheet of paper that read 'Records of all transactions on Account 70054384: Philip Andrew Leech.'

'That's his third account.'

'Third? I didn't know about that. I've found no cards, no documentation relating to this.'

'It's new. He opened it last month. He was having difficulty keeping within agreed limits on the main current account. His pay goes into the current account. He agreed with the manager to open another account and transfer a certain amount of living expenses into it each month. Then he would only have that amount to use.'

'But was there a card?'

'Yes. A cashpoint card. He was meant to use that instead of the other one.'

Isles opened her pocket book and found the page where she had written down the details of the cards recovered from the wallet found on Mitchell. 'We definitely don't have a card for that account,' she said, thinking about it. The woman shrugged at her.

She looked for the list of transactions on the new account. It was short. One transfer and one withdrawal.

'So he used it,' she said, thinking aloud.

'Yes,' the woman said. 'There's the first transfer from his main account at the beginning of the month. Five hundred pounds. Then one withdrawal. The day of his death, I believe.'

Isles looked at the line of numbers and figures that recorded the withdrawal. 'Explain these to me,' she said.

'That's the machine and branch code. This one is a LINK machine in Burnley—'

'Burnley?'

'Yes. Timed at six forty-eight a.m. He has withdrawn one hundred pounds—'

'You're sure about the time?'

'Yes.'

'These records are accurate? The machine couldn't give the wrong time?'

'I don't think so.'

'And it says he withdrew a hundred pounds on Tuesday, the ninth of April, at six forty-eight a.m., from a machine in Burnley?'

'Yes. Is there a problem with that?'

'He'd been dead at least two hours by then.'

The woman looked blankly at her. 'It must have been somebody else then,' she said.

'With his card and PIN.'

'Yes.'

'That's what I thought.'

TWENTY-SEVEN

Harris took her aside before the briefing.

'Has the SIO spoken to you?'

'About what?'

'About anything?'

She considered this for a moment. 'Maybe.'

'Okay. About yesterday. About getting a warrant without clearing it first. About disappearing for half the day without telling us where you were.' He seemed annoyed about it.

'No,' she said. 'He hasn't said anything about that.'

'Well, he's going to. You need to see him before you do anything else today.'

'He hasn't said that to me.'

'I'm saying it to you. Where *were* you yesterday?'

'Trying to find Oliver Williams. As I was told to do.'

'Your tray is almost buried beneath actions you haven't touched.'

'I was told – by Mr Munro – that finding Williams was the priority.'

'Do you really think you can find him *alone*?'

'Alone? What do you mean?'

'We are a team, Karen. We work as a team. I have three other detectives looking for Williams. If you don't talk to them, how can you pool what you know? For all you know you might be following up leads they've already covered.'

'I work best by myself,' she said. 'Judge me by the results.' She turned her back on him.

In the downstairs Incident Room she took a seat near the back, away from the whiteboards. Munro was already in there, talking to Marshall and Dyson. They had moved more whiteboards in, she noticed. There were two additional moveable boards flanking the two fixed ones now. On each board Munro had marked up two scenarios. She recognised his handwriting already.

Eight scenarios. Each had plus and negative points listed beneath a title. She was still reading through them when Munro turned to face them, silencing the mumbling. She calculated there were about forty detectives in the room.

He looked tired, she thought, though he had appeared to sleep very well.

'Good morning, ladies and gentlemen. Day Three of our enquiry. Briefing number two.'

She saw his eyes catch hers, register her presence, move on.

'There's been some really excellent work put in over the last forty-eight hours. I want to review where we are up to today and establish policy regarding the lines to focus on in the next forty-eight hours. There's quite a bit to get through.'

He indicated the boards behind him.

'We are presently working on the basis of eight possible scenarios. I've put them up behind me here. After this morning I want us to concentrate on two of these. I want to knock some options out, start to focus.'

He walked to the end of the line of whiteboards and placed his hand on the first. 'Scenario one. Coates somehow sets up Leech and Mitchell so that his half-brother, Luke Varley, can shoot them both. This is my preferred scenario. As you can see, however, there are only tenuous evidential connections to support it. So why do I favour it? One. Because life is like this on murder enquiries. The evidence takes time to show itself. When you have suspects in the cells the custody clock always ticks faster than the evidence comes in. Evidence in a murder enquiry grows over time.'

A slight pause, to let the lecture sink in.

'Two. Why make things complicated when they're not? Coates and Varley have a motive, possibly three motives. For none of the other scenarios is this really the case – except eight, which is really a version of this scenario. Phil Leech had been investigating Coates and Varley for nearly three years. We have photos of Leech, address details and car registration details, all recovered from Coates's premises. In other words, Coates knew who was looking at him. Leech thought it went further than that. He thought a bobby – Oliver Williams – who checked his car just over a year ago, might have been passing info to Coates. In other words, the material Coates did have on Leech's personal details might have come from the inside. Karen Sharpe turned over Williams's home yesterday.'

A quick nod towards her. Nothing personal. Just a part of his team.

'He has masses of illegally held copy records relating to police staff. Obviously, we would like to speak to him. Karen and others from Bob Harris's team are looking for him.'

She listened as he recounted the results of her search before moving on to a board entitled 'Negative Points'.

'There are weaknesses with scenario one,' he said. 'Interestingly, the gun, which can be used to link in Coates, is also a weakness. Why would anyone be stupid enough to leave a gun licensed in West Yorkshire at the scene of a murder? Complete with serial number. It has to be one of the stupidest things I have come across in four years doing this job. Admittedly the gun is licensed to a fictitious character called Peter Cryer. But the licence was processed by PC Oliver Williams.'

A ripple of interest spread through the room at this. He waited for it to subside.

'Coates could not have thought we would be dim enough not to trace this link. Especially given the fact it's his photo on the card.'

He moved to the table at the right of the whiteboard and sat on it, arms folded.

'What do I want you to concentrate on, out of all that? First and foremost – motive. Get me the material to evidence it. Remember, if we have a good provable motive, then the relative lack of physical evidence – provided there is *some* to link them both – is not so important. We need to have a story to tell to the jury. We need to be able to show that that story is possible. Get me that story.'

He stood up and stepped to the next board in line.

'Moving on. I'll skip through the remaining scenarios. Number two. This was a terrorist killing. Don't worry about that. I've spoken to SO13. No one has claimed this and it doesn't have the correct profile for an IRA job. At present then, this scenario is out.'

He picked up a marker pen and drew a line diagonally across the writing.

'Scenario three . . .'

Her attention drifted. With half a mind she watched him talking through the other scenarios, one by one, reciting what was wrong, striking through them with the pen. Her ears pricked up again when he came to something he called the 'third scene'.

'. . . For those of you who were at de-brief last night, you will have heard about our third scene. Things have moved on, however. Tell us about it, Dave.'

She saw a DS called Dave Binns leave his place at the front and step out next to Munro. His moment of glory.

'As some of you know, yesterday morning we recovered a recently abandoned and hidden motorbike from here.' He walked to the far wall and pointed to the large aerial photo. 'It's just on this picture. The area is called Widdop. Top end of a local tourist attraction called Hardcastle Craggs. By motorbike, to get from Cock Hill to here would take about fifteen to twenty minutes. It's two valleys over. The bike has had its plates removed, but the engine block number remains. Through that we've traced the original plate: F226 TCP. It comes back to a Mike Newby, from Lincoln. He's shown as the last keeper nearly two years ago. We spoke to him this morning. He says he sold it to someone called Brian nearly a year and a half ago. "Brian" paid cash, said he was from London. That's all Newby knows. The machine was advertised in *Exchange and Mart*. Newby filled in his part of the log book. "Brian" didn't. Newby is genuine. So the trail is dead. If this bike is connected, the registration isn't likely to be useful. Probably the user was running around on false plates. SOCO recovered a good quantity of blood staining from the machine. It's all off for DNA. There are two types and they would match the blood types of Leech and Mitchell.'

Another rustle of murmured interest. Munro butted in.

'Don't get ideas. Half the people in this room would match to type. Type counts for nothing.'

'SOCO are also doing fibres, soil etcetera,' Binns continued. 'There is a skid mark at the Cock Hill scene. We now know that it does *not* come from Newby's bike.

185

Wrong tyre size.' His voice was thin, hardly audible from where Karen was sitting.

'The bike has an empty tank and it ran out of petrol. That may or may not be why it was hidden behind a wall next to a road on the way over to Lancashire. It doesn't explain why the plates were removed. So far, surrounding area investigations have revealed no reports of break-ins or thefts in the immediate vicinity. No reports of anything, in fact.'

'Thanks, Dave.' Munro again. 'I think this bike will come back as unconnected. Running out of petrol doesn't fit with any scenario we have. I would guess it has been involved in petty crime. The user has stolen it, run out of petrol, abandoned it, removed the plates. For all we know it might have been abandoned a couple of days before Leech and Mitchell were killed. We can't prove anything on that score yet.'

'But there are no reports for it being stolen,' Binns said, still standing beside him. Munro looked slightly irritated that he was still there, ever so gently pushing against Munro's preferred line.

'True,' he said. 'And that also is interesting. Thanks, Dave. You can sit down now.'

A whisper of laughter. Binns returned to his seat.

'Some aspects of this enquiry are still wide open,' Munro continued. 'Because a third person looks possible – on the basis, we might think, of a hired, contract killer. Scenario eight is simply a combination of scenarios one and seven. We will keep these three scenarios going, but I reiterate we should focus on scenario one. What contract killer would get his gun from the paymaster and leave it at the scene?'

He looked at them. The argument was powerful. Certainly no one had an answer.

'I believe,' he said, 'that we will in the next few days be able to limit ourselves to scenario one. I think that Coates commissioned his brother Varley to kill them both, and that we have the right people in custody.'

He smiled. A cheeky sort of smile.

'Now you just have to prove it for me.'

TWENTY-EIGHT

He caught hold of her arm as she was passing him on the way out.

'Wait a moment please, Karen. I need to speak to you.'

At the time he was in discussion with Marshall. She waited behind them until he was finished. When he turned to her he was smiling. He had an attractive smile, she thought.

'Karen. Thanks for waiting. Did you find that useful?'

'Useful?'

'Yes. What did you think?'

'Of your performance?'

The smile vanished. 'No. Of the policy.'

'I thought you closed down too many lines too quickly.'

She saw his expression cloud. At that moment Harris passed them, stopped and said, 'You were to speak to Karen about yesterday, sir.'

Munro frowned at him. 'Yes. Thanks for reminding me, Bob.' He turned back to her. 'I do need to speak to you. But not here.' Quick glance at his watch. 'Can you come up to my room in an hour or so?'

'Of course.'

'Good. I'll see you there then.' Harris was still waiting at his elbow. 'You can come too, Bob. That would be useful.'

A mass ticking-off session, she thought.

She went up to the Coates and Varley room, sat at her desk and waited for it to empty as they scurried around chasing their actions. Within half an hour there was only herself and Harris's video man left.

Chris Greenwood, who spent his entire day looking at CCTV videos, didn't go out. Short, thin and bespectacled, the match of job to man seemed correct. There was something bookish about him. She had worked with him before, nearly three years back. He had been doing the same sort of thing then.

She walked over to him. 'Do you have the council CCTV from Keighley town centre?'

He thought about it. 'Yes.'

'I need to look at it.'

'All of it?'

'Just for a certain set of dates.'

'Why?'

'I'm trying to find a Liam Toomey. He drives a car with a Northern Ireland plate. I think he might have been in Keighley earlier in the year.' Best keep it close to the truth, she thought.

'You're not meant to be looking at Toomey. You're meant to be looking for Williams.'

She leaned over him. She wanted to be close enough for him to smell her. 'Don't be awkward, Chris. It'll save *you* having to watch it.'

He smiled at her. 'That's a persuasive line. What dates?'

She asked for everything from 3 to 27 February. A wide enough band to keep him guessing.

'That's probably a lot of stuff.'

'We have fast viewers, though. Right?'

'It's all on CD-ROM. You watch it through a computer program. And yes, you can speed it up, slow it down, whatever.'

'Can you make out registration plates on the Keighley stuff?'

'I don't know.'

'Can we enlarge the image, that sort of thing?'

'If you know how to work the program.'

'Is it easy to learn?'

'If I teach you. Still want the stuff?'

'Yes.'

'Okay. I'll set it up.'

He went off to stores, down in the basement.

She went back to her own desk, logged on to HOLMES and checked the latest information about Toomey. Harris had put another detective on to locating him. It took her ten minutes to track the actions. The detective had tried the DSS, housing, electoral roll, directory enquiries, the local health authorities and councils, and a handful of informants controlled by local proactive teams. Nothing.

She phoned the talking pages and got the numbers for ten car dealerships in Bradford. She started calling them, trying out the MIL 1122 plate on them. She had got through seven, with no luck, before Greenwood returned.

He took her to a room at the other end of the station, where they had set up viewing facilities for ordinary videos and computerised images. The room was small, a converted bedroom on the top floor. In most stations they still had bedrooms for officers in 'emergency' situations.

'I used to stay in one of these rooms,' Greenwood told her. She wasn't surprised.

He taught her how to mess around with the discs and images. It took less than fifteen minutes to get the hang of it. Then he left her to it. She waited until the door was closed, selected the disc for 21 February and started it off. There were ten cameras covering Keighley. She wanted one that covered the road into the supermarket she had used on that day.

The camera ID was superimposed on the image on the film, but there was little organisation to the disc. She had to watch a good twenty minutes of footage before she was certain she had got the positions of all ten cameras. She noted the ID of the best candidate for covering her route then started to skip through the scenes, looking out for images from that angle alone.

It took nearly an hour. In the end she found it. Her own car. The image was fuzzy, black and white; she had to expand it to be able to read the plate and be sure it was her. The time on the tape counter said 6.38 p.m. She slowed it down, watched herself turn off in the direction of the supermarket, counted two cars behind her and there it was. A motorbike, turning after her. She stopped the film, enlarged it. There was no registration plate. Not on the front. The camera angle was from the front.

She moved it on, waiting for her car to re-emerge. Twenty minutes later she was there. This time it was three cars back, turning out after her. It looked like the same machine, though it was difficult to be sure. She froze the image, enlarged it, looked at the plate.

Her heart jumped.

She took out her pocket book, checked the note she had made during briefing. There it was. F226 TCP. The same plate. The bike that had followed her nearly two months ago was the bike they had recovered yesterday.

She packed up the CDs, returned them to stores, went back to her desk. Greenwood wasn't in, though several others had by now returned. Looking at her watch she remembered the meeting with Munro. It was time.

Instead of walking along to his office, she went back down into the basement Incident Room and interrupted a meeting between Marshall and a couple of DCs to retrieve the exhibit bags for Coates. She dug around for the plastic key she had seen, the key to his locker in the gym. It was in a smaller exhibit bag. She removed it, looked carefully at it. It had a number embossed into the plastic – 633. It wouldn't do to make assumptions, she thought. She pocketed it.

Then she walked straight out to her car. Harris and Munro would be waiting for her. Just like at school. She couldn't be bothered with that.

TWENTY-NINE

Dave Scother checked the time. The ID Inspector had told him they had set the procedures up for eleven-thirty. It was eleven-fifteen.

'I'm going out for a fag,' he said. There were three DCs left in the room. Bob Harris was out, along the corridor with Munro. The detective who had worked with Leech – Karen Sharpe – had been and gone, looking, he thought, particularly attractive. But looks weren't everything. She was a hard bitch, that one. He could tell just by looking at her.

His new detective – Fisher – looked strangely at him as he stood up. 'Didn't know you smoked, sir.'

'There's a lot you don't know, son.' He watched the boy's eyes on him as he picked up the pack of surveillance photos from Anvil. 'I'll be back soon.'

Justice, he thought, wasn't always straightforward.

The Police and Criminal Evidence Act 1984 – PACE – was quite clear about ID parades. They were to be conducted by officers independent of the investigation, supervised by an independent Inspector. The investigating officers had to be kept away from the parade witnesses at all costs. In Scother's view, PACE demonstrated a typical eighties view of police integrity. A cynical lack of trust.

In Halifax they held parades in a room within the garage area, adjacent to the back yard. They told the witnesses to come in the back way, not to go to the front counter. The witnesses had to be kept away from the suspects as well. If the suspects weren't in custody they were told to turn up at the front counter. Usually there would be someone from the ID team waiting to meet the witnesses at the back door.

At the back door was also where the smokers had their fags. Smoking had been banned inside.

The ID team had called Mohammed Iqbal that morning, on the mobile number Scother had given them. They had told him to drive into the back yard and call the ID suite on his mobile once he was there. They would come and get him. Scother knew this because he had spoken to Iqbal since then. It was all part of witness care. That was how he liked to think of it. He had told Iqbal to make sure he arrived ten minutes earlier than the eleven-thirty time they had given him, just in case.

Iqbal arrived at eleven-twenty, driving into the yard in a standard drug-dealer Subaru Impreza. He didn't smile when he saw Scother standing at the back door. In fact, he made no sign of recognition at all. He was about to make the call to ID when Scother knocked on his window. He lowered it, putting the phone down.

'Mr Iqbal. I'm glad you've come.'

'You going to take me in there?'

'No. I'm not allowed to. I'm not allowed to talk to you at all. That's the rules. If the defence were to find out that I had seen you even now it might invalidate any identifications you were to make.'

Iqbal looked bored. 'Whatever.'

'They fear I would tell you which person to pick out, see. You have to do it alone.'

'You better get going then.'

'I will. There was just something else I wanted to run by you first.'

He leaned down at the car window, brought the photos into view, placing them inside the vehicle on the dashboard. 'I'll just leave those there a moment.'

The book was open at a page he had picked previously. A close-up of Varley with a sticker bearing his name directly beneath the image. Iqbal barely looked at it.

'Are you sure the bag was white?' Scother asked him.

Iqbal looked confused. 'Yeah.'

'White like the label on that photo, for example.' He pointed to the photo. Iqbal didn't look at it.

'What do you want, man?'

Scother reached in, retrieved the book. Maybe Iqbal was too thick even for this. 'Nothing. Don't worry about it.'

'I know who I'm picking out. Stop worrying.'

Scother looked sideways at him. 'You know?'

'I'm not stupid.'

'No? Does the person you are to pick out know *you*? If he does, that will fuck things up.'

'I've never met him, never spoken to him, never seen him. Apart from on that night.' He smiled. A row of blackened, broken teeth.

'So how do you know who you are picking out?'

'There's not just you has photos.'

'Ah.'

He left him to call the ID people.

An hour later he was sitting at his desk, enjoying the newspaper and a cup of coffee. Fisher appeared from the Incident Room.

'Did you hear?' Fisher asked him.

'Hear what?'

'Our witness identified Varley.'

Scother looked up at him. 'I knew he would. Good

work in finding him, son. I'll make sure the SIO knows your part in this.'

Fisher looked uncertain. 'You don't think he might have been put up to it?'

Scother frowned at him. Click, click, whirr, whirr. The kid had too many brains. 'Put up to it? Explain.'

'You don't think he works for the Khans? They could have set him up to ID Varley. Eliminate the opposition.'

Scother looked away. 'That just happens in films, son. You should recall what I told you about not giving anything to the opposition. If I were you I wouldn't go casting doubt on our own witness. The witness *you* found and brought to me.'

He looked up at him. Smiled.

'Do you fancy a pint? I think we should celebrate.'

THIRTY

Armitage actually seemed pleased to see her again. He was on his lunch when she arrived, working out in one of the weight rooms. They sat her in his office (no loose paperwork and every drawer locked, she checked) and he presently appeared wearing a loose-fitting T-shirt and shorts. The back of the T-shirt was soaked with sweat, his hair tousled where he had dried it off. As he stood at the desk beside her, she let the strong, raw odour of fresh male exertion linger in her nostrils. He had good, muscular, tanned legs, she thought. She caught herself looking at them.

'Are you married?' she asked him.

He wiped his face with a hand towel. 'Why?'

She smiled at him. Even after a workout, there was something smart about him, something neat, presentable. He looked like an American advert. Good, firm jaw-line.

'Just wondered,' she said.

She felt underdressed to impress him. He would go for the smart, painted look. Dresses and jewels. High heels. She hadn't worn a set of heels since school.

'You're not from here, are you?' he said. He sat down opposite her.

'How did you guess?'

He missed the sarcasm. 'Your accent.'

'Obviously.'

'Not obviously. Accents don't always locate people.

Mine wouldn't place me in any particular place, for example.'

'But it *would* place you in a particular class.'

'Tut-tut. This is nineteen ninety-six, Ms Sharpe. There's no such thing as class.'

'Just money.'

'Precisely. You're from London, I assume?'

'Maybe. Why do you want to know?'

He grinned at her. Perfect teeth. Like a Colgate advert. She waited for the little oral halo to appear. Their eyes were meeting all the time. Meeting, diverting. He had stopped trying to force it. Now it was all a dance. The dance of interest. Every look delivering the same biological message.

'Just curious,' he said. 'It's nice to see you again. Is it a social call this time?'

She shook her head. 'Not this time. Next time I'll bring some kit. You can show me your facilities.'

He was attractive, but it was still tedious to go through. All the flirtatious little innuendos. It was like a watered-down version of *The Benny Hill Show*. For what? He was on a string. He would do precisely what Berman's nephews told him to do.

'I came to ask a favour,' she said. She would sleep with him, she realised, colouring slightly at the recognition. If he offered and it was possible to get away with it, she would do it. Just for his body, his smile. That was enough.

'Whatever you want.' He held his hands palm upwards.

'I'm trying to find someone called Liam Toomey.' Not a flicker in his eyes. 'Have you heard the name?'

He shook his head. 'Not a member, I don't think.'

'You never heard him mentioned?'

'I don't think so.'

The name would go back to his bosses. It was a risk giving him it.

'He drives a distinctive car. A silver SLK with a Northern Ireland plate. MIL 1122.'

He shrugged his shoulders. 'In all honesty, that wouldn't be too distinctive at this gym.'

'No. But will you ask?'

'Of course.' No smile, no frown. Nothing. He was good at it.

'If you get anything, call my mobile. At any time.'

'Even if you are in bed?'

She smiled. 'Even if I'm in bed. I'll speak to you. It's important.'

'Is he connected with the murder?'

'I don't know. Maybe. Do you want to write the name and number down?'

He smiled compassionately at her. 'Do you think I could run this place without a good memory? MIL 1122. Liam Toomey. Silver SLK. Don't worry. If it's possible, I'll let you know.'

She stood.

'Was that all?' he asked.

'Yes.' She pretended to think about it. 'In fact, no. Could I look at Coates's locker again?'

'The empty one?'

'Yes.'

'Are you going to take sweat samples? What could you get from an empty locker?'

'Humour me. You'll see.'

He stood. 'As you wish, Officer. I'll clear the area.'

It was empty, of course. He stood back. She looked into it. She closed the door. Looked at the number. 542.

'This is the locker number?'

'Yes.'

199

'Where is six three three?'

'Locker six three three?' He smiled. He knew about it.

She waited. It would depend on his instructions. She guessed Coates wasn't big enough to merit outright obstruction. She guessed they would have told him not to stand in her way when it came to Coates, but not to help her either.

'Why do you ask?' he said, still smiling.

She took the key out, held it up in front of him. 'Because I have the key for it.'

He nodded. He knew what he needed to know. 'I see.' He stepped across to the other side of the room and found the locker.

'This is six three three.' She moved towards it and he stepped back. She turned the key in the lock. 'You knew about this?'

He tried to look offended. 'A slanderous suggestion. Of course not. Are you going to tell me what it is?'

'This key was in with Coates's possessions. It seems he had two lockers here.'

'A disgraceful breach of rules. I will have to speak to the sub-manager.'

She swung the door open. It was a tall locker, high enough to hang a thigh-length jacket in it. It was empty, apart from a single cardboard box, roughly the dimensions of a shoe box. She pulled a pair of sterile gloves from her pocket, rolled them on.

'Latex gloves,' he commented.

She raised an eyebrow, wearily. 'You like them?'

'Latex has a distinctive smell, don't you think?'

She nodded. 'One I associate with dead bodies. Is there anywhere I can look at this? In private.'

'You mean without me being there?'

'Hardly. You will already know exactly what's in here.'

He took her back to his office. She carried the box. Once in she took the lid off and examined the contents.

'Surprise, surprise,' she said. 'Photographs.'

'Pretty, aren't they?'

He was sitting opposite her, making no attempt to look. She ran through them, trying not to touch where Coates would have touched.

'You haven't put your prints all over these, have you?' she asked, without looking up. He didn't reply. When she looked at him he was just sitting watching her, the expression on his face asking whether she really thought he might be that stupid. 'I can't see any obvious prints at the corners,' she remarked. 'If a client rang in and asked—'

'If we could do something criminal? Like wipe fingerprints from a set of photos?'

'Yes. What's the club policy on that?'

'That depends upon the client and how much trouble he or she is in. Each case on its merits, as the lawyers say.'

'Do you have paperwork tracking ownership of this locker?'

'I'm afraid not. That is a rogue locker. Some member of staff has been granting facilities they shouldn't have.' He smiled at her. 'However, I am expecting that you will, in due course, have your friends from Scenes of Crime visit our premises and I would trust that any requests from a client of the sort you previously mentioned would not have been met in this case.'

'Not that you are saying there were any such requests.'

'No.'

She counted nearly forty images. Attached to the top one by a paperclip was the business card for a Leeds-based Private Investigation company, Nuttall's Enquiries. She had seen the name before, in Williams's paperwork.

The photographer had been clever. The first twenty or so images showed various scenes of Phil Leech, by himself, getting into his car, getting out of it. The next five showed him meeting Fiona Mitchell. Karen tried to make out where they were. The dates on the images were from mid- to late-March. They appeared to be in a pub car park somewhere, then a shopping mall. Fiona getting out of her own vehicle, walking across to Leech's car, getting in. Then a picture of them apparently hugging each other within the vehicle. Karen sighed to herself.

'Silly girl,' she said, aloud.

'It gets worse,' Armitage said.

There followed nearly fifteen photos apparently taken with a long-range lens. They were, she thought, top quality. The first five showed images taken through the windows of a dwelling house, showing Fiona and Leech moving around within. The remaining ten were nearly all of the same scene. One way or another the photographer had managed to snap them naked through what Karen recognised now was the upstairs window of Leech's house. Fiona was standing facing the window, stretching. In a series of rapid shots Leech approached her from behind and encircled his arms around her chest, cupping her breasts. She leaned back into him, they kissed. The date was 1 April 1996, April Fool's Day. Karen considered the tiny breasts, the anorexic rib cage. Poor Fiona, she thought, poor, stupid, sad Fiona.

'Very careless,' she commented, putting them back in the box.

'He's good though,' Armitage said. 'The photographer, I mean.'

'Yes. I must remember to use him sometime.' She sat down. 'What I don't understand,' she said, 'is why people *keep* these images.'

Armitage shrugged. 'In the case of Mark Coates,' he said, 'I would imagine the idea was insurance. To throw at your friend Leech if it ever came to a court case. To prove his *mala fides*. It's not just the sex that would interest him. It's her meeting him back in March. Obviously, she was *talking*, as they say. Coates would have been thinking, of course, of relatively unimportant court cases. Drugs, not murder. That's my guess. He wouldn't be interested in hanging on to that kind of image in order to confront his girlfriend with them over a little matter of infidelity.'

'No. His methods would be more drastic.'

'I agree. He wouldn't be interested in showing her proof, once he had it. He would just kick her out.'

'Is that all?'

'Perhaps a few "slaps", as they say. He wouldn't kill her.'

'Have you spoken to him?'

'I don't even know him. I know the type though. We have in this club people who are big enough or mad enough to put out a double hit, even on a policeman. Mark Coates isn't one of them.'

She nodded. 'That's what I would have thought. But they're going to love this back at base. Motive in a box.' She stood up. 'I'll call SOCO in. I need to get going. Can I leave all these with you, back in the locker, as we found them?'

'Of course.'

'What about Williams? Have you heard nothing?'

He stood up with her. 'You have my word on that,' he said. 'If he comes, I will call.'

THIRTY-ONE

'This is it,' Munro said, scanning the ten faces seated round the table in front of him. 'Decision time.'

The supervisors' meeting involved all ten Detective Sergeants or Inspectors. They were running late. He and Bob Harris had waited half an hour for Karen Sharpe. Half an hour wasted. That had knocked everything back.

He felt angry with her. It wasn't the insubordination, the disobedience. It was that she had used his presence in her house the night before. A background psychological threat. He shuddered to think about it. He had almost told her the whole thing, with all the revealing detail. Even as it was, he had told her things he had related to no one else. It was a minor betrayal and made him feel foolish.

'The custody clock will run out on our two guests over the weekend. Hence we have to get in early. We have to make charging decisions now, in this meeting.'

In front of him were a stack of bound reports. The Forensic Science Service material back from London, for both scenes. Everything was done. They had been faxed through to Wakefield, put together and biked over to him. He had half an hour before the meeting to read and consider.

'I have the forensics,' he said, tapping the top folder. 'They're mixed. Good and bad.'

All eyes were on him, waiting for it.

'There is no blood from Fiona Mitchell at the Wain-stalls scene. None at all. She was not shot or injured there. However, there *is* DNA and fibres. They could both be old – she had probably been in the car before. It is not, therefore, conclusive that she was in Leech's car that night. In her hair, on her face, in her clothing, however, we have large quantities of Phil Leech's blood. And not just blood. Brain material as well. Apart from *this* blood, the blood actually on Mitchell, there is no blood from Leech at the Cock Hill Moor scene. So Leech was not shot or injured there. Therefore – and the Blood Pattern Analysis on her clothing and the car seats supports this – she was sitting next to Leech when he was shot. The BPA places her in the passenger seat. The trajectories are from the other side. Therefore, we are one hundred per cent certain that Fiona Mitchell did not shoot Philip Leech.' He paused to make sure they had followed. 'Okay so far?'

A few nods.

'Inside her vagina, we have Phil Leech's semen. From *that* day.'

Raised eyebrows.

'That proves they were having a sexual relationship. We don't know the exact time they last slept with each other. We don't know if Coates knew about it. *Proving* Coates knew about it is more important than proving it was happening. At present we don't have that.'

He closed the top folder, opened the next one.

'We have DNA from Luke Varley on the murder weapon.'

An immediate, collective expulsion of breath from around the table. A loosening of tension. He smiled at them.

'Incredibly,' he continued, 'we also have a partial print on the gun, from Varley.'

At the far end of the table a couple of Sergeants started to whisper to each other. Excitement. The pieces falling into place. He held a hand up.

'Let me give you the full picture before you get too excited.'

He waited for silence.

'DNA from both Mitchell and Leech on the gun. But only from blood particles. No sweat, despite it being in her hand. More importantly, no DNA, fibres or anything else to link the gun to Mark Coates.'

He watched the older Sergeants beginning to frown.

'Worse still, there is nothing – and I mean nothing – no DNA, no soil, no pollen, no biologics and, as I told you this morning, no footprints or fingerprints – to place either Coates or Varley at either scene. Not a single trace of them. The forensics from the scenes say they were not there.'

They looked at him in silence.

'Is that exactly what they say?' Tony Marshall asked. 'That they were not there?'

'No. I'm exaggerating. I'm looking at what the defence will say. The actual results come back as inconclusive, obviously. No evidence that they *were* there.'

'Well, we knew that for Coates anyway, sir.' Harris speaking, from next to Marshall. 'And what we have now does in fact put Varley at the scene, because the gun is at the scene and we have his DNA on the gun.'

'But what will the scientists say? In cross-examination. The defence will ask them how it could be possible for someone to shoot, at point-blank range, two people and yet leave no trace of themselves on anything but the gun. Is it not possible he handled the gun elsewhere? That he was not at the scene? I think that will be a powerful submission.'

Harris didn't reply.

'In fact,' Munro said, 'the defence will have more than that to play with. Because there is an abundance of DNA from one other source at *both* scenes *and* on the gun.'

'Who?' Marshall again.

'We don't know.'

'Can they give us *anything* on it?' Philips, from the Background Team.

'White male. The third person – if there was a third person – was a white male.'

'A contractor?'

'Maybe. There could be innocent explanations. We shouldn't jump to conclusions. The lab tells me that DNA from someone who had been in contact with both Leech and Mitchell could have been transferred innocently to the gun, depending upon where exactly the gun came from, how it came into contact with them etcetera. It's something we will need to think about. But these are defence points, at the moment. Let's focus on what we *have* got. We have Varley on the gun, Coates linked to the gun, Varley driving from the scene at the correct time, Leech and Mitchell in a sexual relationship. We have a killer who surprises, we assume, Leech and Mitchell in the car at Wainstalls, shoots Leech and then . . . what? Mitchell has to be transported nearly two miles before she is shot three times by the killer. The same killer? How did she get from A to B? I asked this question right at the beginning. We still don't have an answer. Why did she get from A to B? What was going on? And, perhaps most crucial of all, how did the killer know they would both be there, at Wainstalls, at that time?'

He looked along the line of faces. Mostly blank.

'There will be evidence to cover all this,' he said. 'We just haven't found it yet. Either he was watching them or somebody told him. Assuming we are still running with scenario one, the only link I can think of – if we *cannot* prove some level of surveillance by Coates – is Mitchell herself. Karen Sharpe says she was hysterical when she called her. Coates was threatening to kill her. But we know Coates was sound asleep. Fiona and Coates do have an argument on the CCTV tape. But we've had that enhanced now. It's about why she isn't staying with him that night. It's not violent. There are no threats. Fiona left his house peacefully. I think it's fair to ask, was she genuinely in fear when she rang Sharpe, or was she lying?' He sat back. 'That's where we're at and it won't get any better today. Tell us about the interviews, Tony.'

Marshall opened up his policy log. 'They've both been done and both first interviews were long. Coates has also had a second. First for both was no replies nearly all the way through. A few comments from Coates. Nothing useful. We asked Coates about the link to the gun an hour ago. His solicitor replied. Said we hadn't given enough disclosure for him to be able to correctly advise his client. We told them about Williams and gave them a consultation. They came back and the solicitor read out a prepared statement. Complete denial that he has ever applied for a Section One licence. The documentation is off for DNA and prints. But that's as far as we can get it right now.'

'Varley?'

'Varley went ballistic when the parade came back positive. We thought he might. During the first interview he was very edgy. The officers took gas in with them, just in case. We didn't tell him the result until we had him back in the cells. Kicked off straight away. Yelling, kicking the door. We got the doctor in, but by then he'd calmed down. They're doing the second interview now . . .'

Munro's mobile started to ring. He took it out and looked at the number. Sharpe. She could wait. She had made him wait. He was quiet until it stopped ringing. Then he looked up at them, face serious. 'That's where we're at,' he said. 'I'll be honest with you. I don't like it.'

Looks of consternation. Even Marshall looked shocked. 'You can't be serious, boss. We have links to the gun and one of them at the scene. It's got to be a charge.'

'Loose ends,' he said. 'Too many loose ends. We don't even have a motive yet. I have so many questions about what exactly has happened here that I'm not sure I could explain it to myself. Every gap raises another possible interpretation. Someone tell it to me. Now. Tell me what happened, blow by blow, right now, exactly as we will have to give it to the Judge tomorrow when he goes for bail.' He looked around them. 'Can anyone here do that?'

The phone went off again. The same number. He looked at it, considered.

'I'll take this,' he said, standing up and moving away from the table. Immediately voices broke out behind him, discussing, arguing, complaining.

'Hello?'

'John? Karen Sharpe.'

'I'm in a supervisors' meeting—'

'I know. I have news though.'

He suppressed the urge to have a go at her there and then. 'Go on then. What is it?'

'I'm at a gym called Berman's, in Leeds. You'll know it. I've just called SOCO out. There's a locker here belonging to Coates. It's stuffed with photos of Leech and Mitchell. The last one is from the first of April. They're at Leech's home address, naked, kissing. He's had them under surveillance. He knew about them. A PI firm called Nuttall's Enquiries did the work. For all I know, they might have been watching Leech right up to the night. You need to track the PI down. Quickly. I'm still looking for Williams.'

He sighed inside himself. Was it relief?

'John? You still there?'

'Yes. That's fantastic work, Karen. Does it prove *only* that he knew about the sex, or do you think he knew about the information as well?'

'The one goes with the other. The earlier photos are from mid-March. Leech and Mitchell meeting in pub car parks, for instance.'

'I see. Good. Really good stuff, Karen.'

'No problem.'

'Are you on your way in now?'

'No. I'm sorry about this morning. I had to chase this up though.'

'Don't worry.'

'We can talk tonight.'

'Maybe. We'll see.'

He cut the line, paused for a moment, thinking about it, back still turned. The discussion was still going on behind him. He had, he thought, a team of nearly fifty detectives and yet only one of them – Karen Sharpe – had provided both of the most important leads in the entire enquiry, aside from the forensics. What did that say about her? Harris had said she had been rude to him. 'Judge me by my results,' she had said. Well, here they were.

He turned back to them. 'Well, it *did* just get better today,' he said, sitting down.

Gradually they stopped talking.

'That was Karen Sharpe.' He looked at Harris as he spoke. 'She's found surveillance photos Coates has taken of Leech and Mitchell together. It seems we can prove motive.'

They looked at him, speechless.

'She's at a gym in Leeds. Berman's. It's infamous. Coates had a locker there. The photos were taken by a Leeds PI firm called Nuttall's Enquiries. I need them chasing down and turning over. Quickly.' He looked at Harris again. 'Can you sort that, Bob?'

'No problem.'

'This changes things for me,' he said. 'I'm still not happy. But I'll put up with it.' He looked at his watch. 'Let's aim to get them both charged and over to court by four o'clock.'

THIRTY-TWO

She had barely finished talking to Munro when the mobile started to ring. She was on the M62, on her way back from Leeds. It was Armitage. She pulled over to the hard shoulder, set her hazard lights.

'Hi,' she said.

'Are you in bed?'

'If you have good news.' She stifled a yawn. She needed to be in bed, but not for what he had in mind.

'Williams was parked up outside while you were here. He saw you.'

'You're kidding me?'

'No. He rang in. I spoke to him. I told him the enquiry was about another client.'

'And?'

'He got jumpy. Wouldn't come in. Remember, I don't know the man from Adam. He was quite impatient with me. He hasn't realised the depth of his problem.'

'Fuck,' she said. She heard Armitage laugh.

'Don't worry. I have made another arrangement with him. Because we value him so much we have agreed to box the contents of his locker and deliver them to him.'

'You're going to do that?'

'That's what I've agreed. He will be parked up in a lay-by on a side road off the A64 between Tadcaster and York. His choice of venue, not mine. You take a turning north marked Catterton. He will be there at five. We will deliver it to him then.'

'You are going to meet him?'

'Hardly. I gave you my word. Perhaps you could meet him instead. He will be driving a red Citroën, F reg. It's a quiet country lane. You shouldn't have any problems.'

She checked her watch. She had two hours. 'Thanks,' she said. 'I'll be there. Have SOCO showed?'

'Yes. They're not as polite as you.'

'They're not as well trained.'

'And they're mostly male.'

'Did you enquire about Toomey?'

'Yes.'

'What was the decision?'

'That we would be delighted to assist.'

'Why?'

'I've spoken highly of you.'

'Is that all it takes?'

'I've said you understand the logistics of modern life.'

'Do I?'

'I believe so. You normally work on the Drugs Squad, right?'

'That's right.'

'My bosses have a great respect for the Drugs Squad. As I told you, Mr Rawson is an associate member. He also has spoken highly of you.'

'He doesn't even know me. When will you have something on Toomey?'

'Maybe never. I said I would ask, that's all. If I get something I'll call you. Don't wait up.'

She smiled. 'I won't. But listen, thanks for this, for Williams, I mean. This means a lot. I owe you.'

'To us it means nothing. Or at least nothing *but* that.'

'Nothing but what?'

'That you owe us.'

THIRTY-THREE

Munro could hear it as soon as they buzzed him through the first security door to the cell area. A repetitive, loud banging, echoing up the cell corridor, punctuated by four-letter words at full volume. The voice sounded hoarse, as if he had been keeping it up all morning.

He waited for Tony to push the inner gate, then walked with him to the Charge Desk, a long, wall-to-wall, chest-high counter that separated the Custody Sergeants from the prisoners. The Sergeant was Andrew Conrad whom he knew of old.

'Morning, Andy.'

'Morning, sir.'

He leaned against the front counter. There were three uniforms behind Conrad, plus a civilian detention officer, a woman. He could see their interest as he came in.

'Is that Varley?' he asked.

'That's him. He's been at it since they stopped interviewing him.'

'Is he using his head to make that racket?'

Conrad smiled. 'I wish.'

'Has he been seen by the doctor?'

'Yes. Few bruises. He'll be saying your lot did that. A cut head from the arrest. It's been stitched. The FME says he's fit to detain. He's not insane, just angry.'

Munro turned to Marshall. 'What's his grievance?' He had to raise his voice slightly, above the banging.

'He thinks we've set up the ID witness. Says Iqbal works for the Khans and he knows him.'

'Is that true?'

'Not as far as we know. Dave Scother has been looking at that side.'

Munro thought about it. This wasn't the place to question Tony about Scother. 'Remind me to talk to you about that later,' he said. Marshall nodded. 'The rest was no comment, I assume?'

'That's right.'

'Okay, then.' He turned back to Conrad. 'I want to charge them both,' he said.

Conrad sat down at the custody computer, grinning. He put on a pair of glasses.

'Do you want the facts?' Munro asked him.

'I'll take your word for it,' Conrad said, tapping at the keyboard, watching the screen. 'What's the charge?'

'Two charges. Both murder. Both between the eighth and ninth of April 1996. First victim, Philip Andrew Leech. Second, Fiona Jane Mitchell. In that order.'

'Joint charges?'

'Yes. Both charges against both defendants. Exactly the same wording.'

Munro waited while he banged the details into the machine.

'Their solicitors are up in the canteen,' Conrad said. 'Do you want them present?'

'I don't think so. What could they add?' He turned to Marshall. Tony was smiling. 'You happy, Tony?'

'Oh yes.'

'Glad *you* are. How's Coates? He seems quiet.'

'He's the bright one. Varley has some kind of history of minor mental illness. Coates is calm. He knows the system and the procedures.'

'Knows he's innocent?' Conrad paused at the screen, looking at him over his glasses.

'A joke, Andy,' he said. Conrad nodded. Munro turned back to Marshall. 'Or perhaps he only knows it's weak. He's the bright one, as you say.'

Tony scowled. 'You're meant to be happy at this stage, boss. We're getting there.'

'You all going for a drink, I suppose?' Munro asked.

'We'll be in the bar at five, sir. We expect you there.'

'Who do you want first?' Conrad asked.

'Can Varley be brought out?'

'No way.'

'Let's do him first then.'

Conrad came from behind the desk. He instructed one of the uniforms to bring the custody record and charge sheets, now rolling off the printer. Then he led them all down the cell corridor. They stood outside Varley's cell door. There was a small blackboard with his name and custody number scrawled on it, but you didn't need that to know which cell was his.

Munro reckoned he was kicking the door from the inside. He watched it moving with the blows. It was a big, heavy, solid door. Varley would injure himself like that. They had put him on constant observation as a consequence. On a chair to the right of the door sat a policeman whose task it was to check Varley every five minutes, by opening the cell door hatch, observing and questioning him. The results were then noted on a log to be attached into the custody record. The officer seemed sanguine about his task. An achievement, given the constant noise.

'Stand to either side, please,' Conrad said. 'He spits.'

They moved out of range. Conrad signalled to the officer on the chair and he reached up and unhooked the small, rectangular hatch. The metal trap slid down leaving a barred space big enough to frame a face.

'Luke Varley? This is Andrew Conrad, Custody Sergeant. Can you listen to what I have to say, please?' Conrad shouted the words.

The response was a loud blow against the door followed by a series of threats. Varley's face appeared, squeezed up against the hatch, the cut to his forehead a prominent stitched welt. Munro met his eyes, saw him register that there was a group there.

'Where's my fucking solicitor?'

'Listen to what I have to say, please.' Conrad ignored his question. 'I am now going to charge you with an offence. I am doing it here because I have determined that you are too violent to be brought out to the charge desk.'

'Fuck you!' Varley spat at him, missing. Munro watched his sputum trickling down the far wall of the corridor.

'Luke Varley. You are charged with two offences . . .' Conrad started to read out the charges.

Varley's face disappeared and the shouting started again. He was clearly distressed. Beside him Munro saw that Tony Marshall was trying to suppress a giggle.

Conrad finished the first charge. 'Do you have anything to say, Mr Varley?'

A pause, then the response. The uniform beside Conrad started to write down the string of threats, word for word.

'The first sentence will do it,' Conrad said to him. He moved on to the second charge.

A similar pantomime followed. This time the response was along the lines of 'I'd fucking shoot you all if I got the chance.' Munro thought it sounded as if he were starting to cry as he screamed the words.

'Helpful,' Marshall said, smirking.

Munro walked off.

They brought Coates out to the charge desk. His brother was still kicking off as he went through the same process in a more civilised fashion. If he knew it was his half-brother making the noise he didn't let on. Coates was so calm he wasn't even handcuffed. Munro stood beside him, curious. They had never met.

Coates wore a white, canvas custody overall. (They had taken all his clothing for analysis.) He was of average height (about five nine, for Munro), though the upper body was well built, muscular. The time spent in Berman's had paid off. He would weigh in at around 13 stone, none of it fat. The face was not unattractive, Munro thought. Clean-shaven, angular, clear complexion, thin without being bony. Certainly not a thuggish face. The hair was cut quite short. The eyes that flicked across his own were green, intelligent, alert.

They wouldn't have the chance to ask him about the photos now. But that didn't matter. When they had decided not to comment in interview it was sometimes a waste of time holding them until the clock ran out, just to throw every detail at them in advance. All it meant was that they had more time to respond to the evidence and put their defence together. The ideal was to give them enough information so that the barrister could subsequently make an application to have the jury draw an adverse inference from their silence, then keep the rest to surprise them with later.

Coates's replies were more careful. To the Leech charge he said, 'I deny it,' and to the Mitchell charge, 'She was my girlfriend. I did not kill her. I loved her.' There was no emotion in his voice as he spoke. He spoke the words slowly so that Conrad could write them out. Helpful. He had obviously planned the response.

Munro thought that was it. But as the charge sheet was handed over Coates turned to him and spoke. 'You've got the wrong person,' he said. A calm voice, stating a fact. Munro didn't reply.

He left Marshall to speak to the defence solicitors, sort out the custody decisions and get transport to take them over to the nearest Magistrates' Court. He went off to phone the Crown Prosecution Service. It was their responsibility now. His enquiry, handed over. They would want to know what was coming.

As he walked past the canteen he looked through and saw them at the bar. His detectives. The party was starting already.

Premature, he thought.

THIRTY-FOUR

Rush hour between York and Leeds wasn't quite like London, she thought. But it was still irritating. She passed Tadcaster, with its stinking brewery, at four forty-nine. Traffic was building up in both directions. She had been planning to get in early, scout the site, but the nearer she got to York the slower the pace. The road to Catterton was signposted, a tiny back lane.

She took it and drove at a steady thirty through a couple of twisting sections for a few miles. The country around her was flat, arable fields, the hedge bordering the road at head height, thin, interspaced with mature trees. Across the fields she could see a couple of farmhouses to either side. She was the only car on the road.

Plan A and Plan B, she thought. What were they? Up to the point where she saw the lay-by – on the same side of the road she was travelling in – saw the red car parked up, facing away from her, and slowed to pull in behind it, she had nothing more complex planned than to walk up to him, arrest him, have a chat. Plan A.

It was only when she was turning into the lay-by, speed right down to fifteen miles per hour, that she realised he would know what car she drove. He had taken pictures of her, stalked her, gathered details. Indeed, if Armitage wasn't lying, he had already seen her in the Volvo earlier that day.

She was close enough to see his eyes in the interior

mirror before she registered what it meant. He wasn't going to let her just walk up and arrest him. She saw his lights come on. On and off. He was starting the engine. Pull round, she thought, block him off. But it was too late for that. He was already starting to move.

She hit the accelerator.

On the speedo she had got it up to thirty-five before she hit him. Straight on, square with its rear bumper, a clean rear-end shunt. The noise was shocking. A grinding crash of metal on metal. She saw the Citroën jump, front end lifting. She felt herself flung forward against the seat belt. Bounced back against the headrest. Ahead of her the Citroën was still moving forward. The front and back windscreens were shattered. She watched the car jerk, stall, stop. She took a breath.

Then she was out. Out and running. She left her door open, dashed to his driver's door, wrenched it open. She was set to reach in and take hold of him, punch him, kick him – whatever it took. She had him now.

She looked in at him. There was no need to do anything. He hadn't been wearing a seat belt.

Oliver Williams was slumped backwards, blood pouring from his nose and mouth, eyes closed. Unconscious. His face had hit either the wheel or the glass. The glass had shattered, but hadn't come out. Just the right speed, she thought. Any faster and she would have been scraping him off the road in front.

She checked his airways, searched for a pulse. He was alive, breathing. The blood was flowing smoothly, but it wasn't going to kill him. She had seen pictures of him from the tasking. Nice clean pictures from five years before, smartly kitted out in full uniform. His nose had looked straight then. It was broken now. Somewhere in his mouth there would be pieces of the top front teeth. When it all settled down that would be painful.

Williams looked older than she had imagined, which gave her a moment's guilt. He had shortish grey hair, a 'seventies copper' face. Behind the mess he would look corrupt, she thought. He was the sort of policeman you would know was filth the minute he walked into a pub. She remembered the photos he had taken of her, the files in his home.

She walked back and checked the damage. The Volvo was virtually unscathed. Certainly driveable. The Citroën would need towing. The rear end had collapsed all too readily, crushing up against the wheels. She stood still and checked herself. Running mentally through the parts of her body. Soreness over her breastbone, where the belt had caught. Slight stiffening of the neck. Nothing else. She had been ready for it.

She closed her door and looked back along the road. In the distance, through the gaps in the hedges, she could see a car approaching. She waited for it. It passed at speed. She had a quick view of a male driver, then he was gone. No attempt to slow down. She walked to the passenger side of the Citroën, opened the door and got in.

His head was in the same position, but his eyes were open now, the breathing faster. She reached over and tilted his head forward. He groaned. She checked through his jacket pockets, extracting his wallet. The warrant card was in there. She had the right person. She sifted through the business cards, credit cards and cash. Beside her, his head was hanging forward now and she could hear the blood dripping away from his nose, falling on to his jacket. He wasn't looking at her, but she could tell he was conscious.

'It looks worse than it is,' she said. He started to breathe heavily, chest rising and falling. 'You will need medical help. There will be some pain. Your nose is broken. You have lost two teeth. But you'll be okay.' She could tell he was listening. 'Meanwhile, you're under arrest.'

Slowly, his head turned towards her.

She took a stick of pale red lip gloss from the pocket of her jacket. Flipping the sun visor down she leaned towards the mirror fixed into the back of it and started to place a light covering over her lips. It was only the second time she had used it in three years. Out of the corner of her eye she could see him watching her.

'You know me already,' she said, without looking at him, still running the gloss over her upper lip. 'I'm Karen Sharpe. I've seen your photos of me. I thought they were quite good, technically.' She looked at him, smiled. 'I admire your work.'

His eyes were glazed. He would be sick soon, she thought. It was the shock.

A car pulled up just ahead of them, began to reverse back. She got out and walked over. A single female driver. She waved her warrant card through the passenger window.

'It's an accident,' she said. 'I think he must have fallen asleep at the wheel. The ambulance is on the way. Don't worry.'

She watched her drive off.

When she got back to Williams, he was beginning to shiver. That too would be shock, which could kill, she recalled. The blood had drenched his shirt, his jacket, the tops of his trousers. He was in the same position. He looked incapable of movement. That would be the whip-lash. On the other hand, it could be his spine. She looked at her watch.

'Time we had a little chat, Ollie,' she said.

THIRTY-FIVE

'Can you talk?'

'Have you called an ambulance?'

'You *can* talk. No. I have not called an ambulance.'

'I can't feel my legs. Call one.'

'Not so fast. We need to get to know each other first.'

'Don't be fucking stupid.'

He turned his head to face her, panting for breath. The arms didn't move. They were hanging at his sides in the exact position they had been in when she found him.

'Swearing won't achieve anything,' she said. 'You are in a lady's company. Please be polite.'

'*Call a fucking ambulance. Bitch.*' Shouting at her, spittle and blood spattering her face.

She smiled at him. Took a tissue from her pocket, wiped herself. He was wincing with pain. 'Do you think you're badly injured?' she asked in a conversational tone.

'Please call an ambulance.' It was more of a whimper now.

'When you've told me a few things.'

He started to sob. 'I can't move my legs.'

'You should have been wearing a seat belt. Can you move your hands?' She reached over to his left wrist and took a fold of flesh between her thumb and forefinger, twisted it. 'Can you feel this?' He pulled his arm away. 'There you go. Not so bad. Already you can move your arm.'

'I need a doctor. Please.'

'I'll get you one. When you agree to answer my questions.'

'You fucking bitch. What questions?'

'You *do* remember me?'

'Karen Sharpe. The one from London.'

'Of course you do. You know everything about me. Where did you get my file?' He frowned. 'I can wait all day,' she said. 'I'm not in pain.'

There were tears rolling down his cheeks. 'What is this? I need a doctor. I need help. You can't question me like this.'

'This is real life, Ollie. You know me. You've read the file. What do you think? How long do you think the person you read about in that file would be prepared to sit here and watch you bleeding?'

He was shaking again. 'I'm going to be sick.'

'Until you bleed to death?'

He started to retch. She watched him. After a while a long string of bile fell into his lap.

'That will be shock,' she said. 'Shock can kill.'

'What do you want to know?'

'Where did you get my file?'

'The ACC sent for it. Four years ago. I was assistant to his staff officer.'

'So you copied it?'

'Yes.'

'You've had it that long?'

'Yes.'

'Who have you showed it to?'

'No one.'

'Tell me again.'

'No one. I didn't need to.'

'Why not?'

'I just told them.'

'Who did you tell?'

'Luke Varley.'

She nodded, thinking it through. 'Not Coates?'

'Coates as well. But he wasn't interested. He didn't know you then.'

'Varley was?'

'Yes. I think so.'

'Why?'

Williams sighed, a long shiver of a sigh that ran throughout his body. 'I'm in pain,' he said.

'Why was Varley interested?'

'He's trying to set up his own business. He hates Coates.'

She had known that from Mitchell. 'Who was he going to do business with?'

'The Irish.'

'The Irish?' She felt her scalp prickling.

'He says the Provisionals. Probably it's bullshit, someone selling him a line.'

'The Provisionals don't do drugs.'

'You would know.'

She looked out of the window, looked across the fields. It was like a nightmare. Growing, gaining pace. She turned back to him.

'Explain it to me. Why would he pay you for my details?'

'So he could use them as a sweetener. As a gesture of good faith. I'm sorry.'

'A sweetener?'

'I told him they would be interested in knowing where you were, who you were.'

'Did you know what that meant? What it might mean

for me?' She tried not to sound indignant, self-important. He was silent. 'Real life, eh?' she said.

'Real life. I'm sorry.'

'Bullshit. Did you give them a photo as well?'

'I didn't give "them" anything. I gave the information to Varley.'

'Whatever. Photo as well?'

'Yes. So they would know.'

'Know what?'

'That it was real.'

'How much did he give you for that?'

'Does it matter?'

'Humour me. I've got the phone.'

'Two hundred quid.'

'Two hundred quid? They would have given you fifty times that.'

'I was stabbing in the dark. I thought he was being rolled. I didn't think it could be genuine. Varley's a clown. I couldn't see him being up to that kind of deal. I gave him it thinking they wouldn't have a clue what it meant, because they were rolling him, because they weren't PIRA. I was fucking with him. It was small change. The guy's an idiot. I'm sorry.'

'And not Coates?'

'I offered him it. He had more sense.'

'So he knows?'

'No. Just vague hints. He wouldn't pay so he didn't get.'

'Who is Varley dealing with?'

'I have no idea. Some guy in Manchester. An intermediary. I didn't ask.'

'How did he meet him?'

'In a pub.' He started to snigger. It came out like a

mixture of tears and laughter. 'In a pub. He thinks you make deals with the IRA in a pub.'

She dug out her phone. 'You've been helpful, Ollie. Thanks.'

'You don't want to know about Coates and Leech?'

'No. Other people will ask you about that.' She dialled 999, waited for them to answer. 'You don't ride a motorbike, do you?'

'No.' He tried to shake his head. It looked painful.

'You sure?'

'Yes.'

She gave the details to the operator. 'I'm going to leave you now,' she said. 'Good luck with the legs.'

THIRTY-SIX

They clapped and cheered him as he walked into the bar. He left it until nearly seven o'clock, hoping they'd get fed up, go home to their wives and dogs. But they were still in there. About twenty-five of his detectives, plus some uniforms from Halifax itself. Mostly men. Half of them were drunk already.

He held his hands up to silence them. 'This is just beginning,' he said. 'We take applause when the Judge says life. Not before.'

Then he felt irritated with himself. Why couldn't he just enjoy it? He looked around for Sharpe. She wasn't there, of course. Harris came up to him. Even Bob Harris, normally so measured, so boring, looked the worse for wear. Letting things slip.

'Sharpe found Williams,' he told him.

Munro frowned. 'When?'

'Couple of hours ago. He's in a hospital in York.' Harris was trying not to laugh. 'He tried to get away from her so she rammed his car. He's injured.'

'What's funny about that?'

'It was her own car. Her private car.'

Munro didn't understand the joke. 'Is Sharpe okay?'

'Of course. Nothing will touch her.' A hint of bitterness in his tone.

'She got your results then?'

'And wrecked her car. It's down in the yard now.'

229

'She's been back?'

'Been and gone. Left her car in the yard, took one of the enquiry cars.'

'Why didn't you tell me she'd found Williams?'

'I didn't know. I was in here. She only phoned half an hour ago.'

Munro left him, took a pint off Marshall at the bar. 'Cheers,' he said.

Behind him he could hear his own voice, talking out of the television set. National news. They had interviewed him at the court. He had gone over with Tony to speak to the lawyer about bail. Sometimes the CPS lawyers needed their backs stiffening. The application for Coates had lasted forty-five minutes. Varley hadn't applied. Still kicking off, shouting about it. They couldn't even bring him up to the courtroom.

He went over to demonstrate to the beaks how important it was that they do as asked. High-ranking presence was enough. You didn't have to say anything. You never did these days. The CPS lawyer did it all.

The defence went on about the weakness of the evidence. The sheet Marshall had prepared for the CPS hadn't mentioned the lack of forensics linking Coates to either scene. So it couldn't have been that they had in mind. Just the usual pitch. The CPS lawyer took it in her stride. He got her name afterwards.

The main beak winked at him as he refused bail. No chance. Not for shooting a police officer. Both were remanded in custody for one week. Tomorrow, when they went up to Crown Court to appeal it, it would be different. You couldn't keep information back from a judge.

The press had been waiting outside. TV cameras,

everything. He listened to his softly inflected accent damping down their expectations. 'Early days . . . We are satisfied we were right to charge . . . This was an atrocious offence . . .' When the interview finished they cheered over in the corner. He raised his glass to them.

They felt strongly about it. A brother officer. They wanted a result. It was a disease. They bred it into you from training school onwards. To get a result. That was all that mattered. That meant a charge. Not a conviction. If the Judge kicked it out or the Jury said Not Guilty that was somebody else's fault. The poison went right up through the ranks to the Command Team. They would be calling him tomorrow trying to get half the squad back. Why do you need fifty detectives? You've got the result, they're charged. Offence cleared up. But gathering the evidence to get a conviction had barely started.

The bar at Halifax was small. With that many bodies crammed in, it quickly became noisy, smoky, hot. Filled with the stink of their sweat. He wanted to get out, see Sharpe. She wasn't like this lot. Beside him, Marshall was asking him what was the matter.

'Nothing. Nothing at all,' he said. 'This is one of the happiest days of my life.'

He saw Marshall looking strangely at him, unsure how to take the comment, suspecting the sarcasm, but not understanding why it should be there.

He didn't know himself.

He bought a round for the Sergeants and sank it quickly. They were asking him if he was out for the night now. Jokes about his single status. Ha-ha. He laughed with them, chatted to them, encouraged them. He was finishing up to go when Bernie Harris came in, the SOCO. She made straight for him. He offered her a drink. She had a sour face, but at least it was female.

'No. I came to give you some results.' She looked around her, spoke brusquely.

'Let's go out,' he suggested.

They left, heading for his office. He told Marshall he would be back soon. He had no intention of returning.

'The motorbike from scene three,' she said, once they were out of the noise, 'the one recovered by the dog.'

'Yes?'

'Even though it doesn't match for the skid mark at Cock Hill it was probably at both scenes.'

They were halfway there, in the corridor. He stopped.

'Probably? What does that mean?'

'Soil, grass, pollen. They all match. It's just that the samples aren't unique to that area. They're trying to refine it. They've gone back to all three scenes tonight to get more samples.'

'Will it get better than "probably"?'

'Maybe.'

'Maybe. Probably.'

'Yes. They tell me they can get the DNA from seeds now, match it back to exact plants.'

He looked at her, unsure whether it was a joke. 'Okay,' he said. 'Thanks, Bernie. But you needn't have come in to tell me that. It's neither here nor there – right?'

'Right. But this is different.' She handed him a folded slip of paper.

'What is this?'

'A late result from London. I keep the best till last. It's for clothing seized at Varley's house.'

He read it through.

'Gunshot residues on a grey sweatshirt,' she said. 'They match for the type of cartridge.'

He read it again, wishing he hadn't had a drink.

'On a grey sweatshirt?' he said.

'Yes. It was at the bottom of his bed.'

'He could have gone home afterwards, changed?'

'Maybe. I don't know the evidence in detail. He has fired that gun though.'

'That gun? That exact gun?'

'A 9 mm. That type of cartridge.'

'Just the type? Not definitely *that* weapon?'

'No. We can't say that. It's a positive result though. It supports your charging decision.'

'Does it? Maybe it supports nothing at all. Why is there nothing in his hair? Or up his nostrils? Or under his fingernails?'

It was the same with everything in this enquiry so far. Plus and minus. Always a downside. For everything that pointed to Coates and Varley, something pointed away.

Bernie Harris shrugged.

'Does it prove he fired it that night?' he asked her.

'Not quite.'

'Not at all.'

He saw her face harden, impatient with him. 'Whatever. That's the result. Make what you want of it.'

THIRTY-SEVEN

She felt frightened. What had been no more than a doubt, a shadow, was now a possibility, perhaps a reality.

Her car had driven badly on the way back, pulling to the nearside, strange noises from the engine. She left it in the yard at Halifax, entered the Incident Room through the rear fire doors and took a set of keys for a car slated to a DS Scother. The Incident Room was empty, the noise from the bar, which overlooked the yard, promised a long night for the diligent officers of Operation Phoenix. Scother, whoever he was, could do without publicly funded transport.

In Dyson's and Marshall's office she gathered together two of the evidence bags from Coates's and Varley's premises, and put them on to the back seat of the car. She wondered how long it would be before anyone noticed they were missing.

She drove home watching her mirrors, senselessly. It was too late for caution. The time for that was two months ago. But the fear had got to her now, was under her skin.

At an off-licence in Bingley she waited impatiently in a queue, chewing her nails. She checked her mobile, hoping Armitage would call. There were no other leads to Toomey now. She was relying on him.

The guy at the front of the queue – creating the queue – was drunk, fumbling through his pockets for enough change to pay for the three-litre bottle of cider on the counter between himself and the girl serving. The girl kept trying to move him sideways so she could serve the rest of them, but he was out of it. Karen struggled not to become involved. When the man finally shuffled past her he had an antagonistic look in his eyes. She looked away from him, frightened of what she might do.

She got up to 140 mph on the dual carriageway past Keighley. If anyone came after her at that speed she would see them straight away. There was a pounding sensation at her temples. A metallic blue Impreza pulled out behind her as she came off the roundabout at Silsden. She knew at once it was harmless. Too conspicuous. Tinted windows, headlights full on. She watched it accelerate until it was within a few feet of her rear bumper. She slowed carefully at the next roundabout, breaking gently from a distance. It remained there, almost shunting her. She wanted to jam her foot on the brakes, take it into the back of her. It took the right turn as she left the roundabout.

She pulled over and watched through the interior mirror as the Impreza roared down the road into Skipton, a quiet market town. Not for long. The drug dealers were spilling out from Keighley, moving up the valley. Leech would have followed the car, blocked it off, goaded the occupants until he had a fight out of it. She reached over for the vodka she had bought, screwed the top off, took a swig. Warm, neat vodka. She let it burn its way down to her stomach, stifling the retches.

She tried to piece together what she knew. Fiona had mentioned the Irish accent because Varley had said something to her. That was the only way to explain it. She had said it to *warn* her. Ollie Williams had told Varley something, Varley had told Fiona. But yet Fiona had called and lied to try to get *both* her and Leech out to Wainstalls. Why would she do that?

She had been too pissed to go. Leech had gone for both of them. Stood in for her. Then they had both been shot. It didn't fit. It didn't make sense. What had happened on Anvil that had triggered this?

She was missing something. Worse than that. She was missing something she had already noticed. She was sure of it.

In the house she put the vodka in the freezer and took the exhibit bags into her bedroom. Bending down beside the bed she pulled the carpet away from the skirting, revealing the boards. From under the upturned cardboard box she used as a bedside table she extracted a small key she had taped to the bottom of the box. She worked her fingers into a crack between the floorboards and levered out a stretch of planking. Reaching into the gap she groped around, then closed her fingers over the handle of a metal container. She dragged it until it was beneath the missing board.

It had a padlock. She fitted the small key, took the lock off, then opened the lid, without removing it from below the boards. Inside it, she closed her hand around the butt of an automatic pistol. She brought it out, placed it on the bed, dug around again. There were two loaded clips in the box, nine rounds in each. She placed them beside the gun, closed the box, replaced the padlock, flooring and carpet. Then she sat down on the bed and looked at it.

It seemed okay. She had worked the mechanism, cleaned it, oiled it and fired it around the middle of March. She did it every month. Every month for the last eight years. It had to work. There was no point in having it if it didn't fire. From the kitchen drawer where she kept all her paperwork she extracted the Section 1 licence that covered the weapon. Issued and renewed in London, every year. West Yorkshire didn't even know about it. She placed the licence, a credit card-sized strip of plastic with her photo, name and details, behind her warrant card in her wallet.

Back in the bedroom she buried one clip under some clothing in the single wardrobe in the room. She slotted the other into place inside the butt of the gun. She fixed the safety, then placed the weapon inside her leather jacket, top inside pocket. She hung the jacket in the wardrobe, lay back on the bed.

It was getting dark. She wasn't going to be able to sleep tonight. She could tell. She left the curtains open. They had been following her. There was a connection to Coates, Varley, Fiona, but the bike hadn't belonged to any of them. F226 TCP. She didn't know why she knew that, but she did. The person who had followed her, who had known already where she lived, was neither Coates nor Varley. And not Williams. Someone else entirely. She tried to recall the image of him, or her, in the split second where he/she had driven past her, two months ago, when her evasives had worked. But it had been too fleeting.

She realised she was listening, ears straining into the growing night, every little sound registering. The main road was nearly a mile away, yet she could hear the traffic on it, even with the windows closed. She could feel the vibrations from across the fields, coming up through the floor, entering her body.

In the past it had been like this all the time. She could remember now. Periods so stressed it had felt like her heart was twice its normal size. Every minute of every day she had been able to hear it, beating in her throat, pounding. She had thought it was an illness, but the doctor had told her it was stress.

The symptoms appeared as 'palpitations' because she wasn't used to hearing them. But this noise was always there, in the background, and this was what all human beings sounded like. Buckets of blood, powered by a sub-standard pump. Easy to stop.

She closed her eyes, letting the images come. She had tried to run from it for eight years. What she was missing was somewhere in there, locked in her own head.

She heard a vehicle turn off the road, on to the track that led to her house. She rolled off the bed. Let it come, she thought, whatever it is. She took the gun from her jacket and walked over to the window. She pulled the curtains and leaned on the ledge, the gun held below the level of the sill. She watched as Munro's car pulled into view. She felt irritated. He was a distraction.

He got out and saw her looking down at him, arms out of sight. He smiled at her. She smiled back, the gun a cold, heavy weight at the end of her arm.

THIRTY-EIGHT

As she opened the door to him she felt like a spring, wound too tight. She needed to relax.

'Can I help you?' she asked, blocking his route in.

He looked confused.

'A joke,' she said, standing aside.

She checked her watch. He checked his. Nearly ten.

'Earlier than last night,' she said.

He walked past her without saying anything, frowning.

'Where do we start?' she asked, closing the door and following him through.

He turned to face her, standing in the middle of her empty front room. 'What do you mean?'

'So long since we last met. So much catching up to do.'

She walked up to him, stood so close that she could register his discomfort. He had been drinking, not so much she could smell it, but she could see it in his eyes. Now that he was here she wanted to get hold of him, take his clothes off, distract herself.

'Would you like a drink, sir?' she asked, trying to keep her eyes serious.

'I'll have a small one of those whiskeys,' he said.

She poured him a shot that would probably equal about eight measures in a pub. Enough to guarantee his presence for most of the night, unless he wanted to call a cab.

'Sit down,' she said, pointing to one of the chairs.

He sat, jacket still on. She took a breath. What would he want to hear?

'I want to thank you for last night,' she said.

'Thank me?' He took a large gulp of the liquid.

'Yes. For being polite. For being normal. I was feeling . . .' She pretended to think about it. 'I was feeling *vulnerable*. You were nice to me. You didn't act like a dickhead.'

He nodded. 'I'm not.'

'No. I could see that the first time I met you. You have been good to me throughout this. You've been . . .' Again, the pause to weight the word. '*Careful*.'

'I've done my job, Karen.'

'Not quite. Last night was different.'

She let it hang there, stood up, extracted the vodka from the freezer. When she had poured herself one she sat down, pulled the seat closer to his. She had it so that if she relaxed her right leg it would just touch his. For the time being, she kept it away.

'Different?' he asked, finally.

'Yes. I was pissed. You could have taken advantage. You didn't.'

He took another long swig. He knew what was coming. She could see that. He just needed a little help. 'You didn't strike me as pissed,' he said.

'You were very tired. But I mean it, John. I appreciate it. Most men aren't like that.' She sat back, let her leg relax.

'Most men aren't . . .' he started, then stopped as her knee came to rest against his own. He didn't look down, didn't move his leg away. 'Most men aren't like what?'

'Happy to talk. Intelligent. With most men it's physical.' She kept her knee against his.

'I like talking to you, Karen. Sometimes you've seemed like the only sane person on this enquiry. I'm glad I met you.'

That's the spirit, she thought. Warm up. Get into it.

'I'm glad I met you,' she said.

She saw his thoughts move away from her. 'They're all back there celebrating now,' he said. 'They haven't a clue.'

He sounded bitter. She remained silent.

'It's not that simple, is it?' he asked.

'I don't know.'

'The DNA from the scenes is complicated.'

'I heard Varley was on the gun.'

'So what? He's nowhere else he should be. The more I think about it the more I'm worried that it isn't so much the evidence pointing to Coates and Varley as *me* being pointed at them. If I take my eyes off them and try to find out who is doing the pointing—'

'Bob doesn't like me,' she commented, interrupting him.

'Bob Harris?'

'Yes. He thinks I'm incompetent.'

'I don't think that's true. He just has a fixed view about the way these things should be processed. You seem like a maverick to him.'

'Do you think it's an age gap?'

He frowned, considering it. The implication was that there was no age gap between themselves. 'Maybe. He *is* older. He's a good DS though. You'd be worse off with Scother, or Davis.'

'Do you think I've been fucking it up?'

He looked alarmed. 'Me? Not at all. I've been really impressed by your initiative. If you hadn't rung in today with the information about the photos I wasn't going to charge.'

'No?'

'No. What do *you* think I should have done?'

'About what?'

'About charging or turning them out. Do you think we've got the right people?'

'Does it matter? As long as you can prove it?'

'Yes. I want the right people. You don't think that Coates and Varley are—'

'I thought it might be a sexist thing with Harris.' She interrupted him again.

'Sexist? How?'

'You know, because I'm not attractive, blonde . . .' She moved her hands in front of her breasts, coloured, looked away. 'Because I haven't got, you know, large . . .' She took a drink.

'Bob doesn't think like that,' he said, intent, serious. 'And it's certainly not true that you're not attractive.'

She smiled. An internal smile. 'You know what I mean though.'

'I don't,' he said. 'Attraction is more complicated than that.'

'Than what? Than physical appearance?'

'Yes.'

'You mean you don't find me physically attractive?'

'I do. I just said that.' He looked away from her.

'But not in *that* way?'

'What way? I do. I find you attractive. Full stop.'

'Why?'

He took another drink. The glass was almost empty already. She thought he might have missed the question. She leaned forward, pressing her leg against his.

'Why do you find me attractive?'

'I was thinking about it,' he said. He moved his leg away from hers.

'Is it that difficult?'

'No. But it's more than just physical. I want to get the words right.'

He was so serious. It could go on for ages, she thought. She would be bored before he got there.

'Do you want a top-up?'

He nodded. She stood up, poured him another dose.

'What I am drawn to,' he said, words slightly slurred already, 'is that I can't read you.'

'Meaning?'

'I can read you now, of course,' he said, looking right at her.

She frowned. 'Now?'

'You touch my leg with yours, fill me with drink, flirt . . .' He sipped at the drink, shrugged.

'I'm not flirting,' she said. 'I don't do that.'

'Not like normal people, you don't. But you do flirt. Believe me.'

'Normal people?'

'Those I can see straight through. What you are telling me now is what you are letting me have. You're controlling it. Most times I meet you, however, I haven't a clue where I am with you. Most times I feel you are laughing at me.'

'You make me sound terrible.'

'No. Just strong. You know what you want and what you don't need.'

She looked at the width of his shoulders. How were men born like that? Packed with muscle. That was what she needed.

'You don't care about lying either,' he said.

'About what?'

'About anything. Telling me you don't flirt. Whatever. Any little thing that will help.'

She finished her vodka, poured another. 'I thought you said you found me hard to read. You make me sound trivial.'

'Like I said, at the moment you're making it easy because you want something from me.'

'And what is that?'

He met her eyes. 'You tell me.'

'Company?' she suggested. 'Someone to talk to for a little while?'

She meant it ironically. He missed it, laughed. 'Good one. Because you're lonely out here, right?'

'How about because the man I worked with was shot dead three days ago and—'

'Spare me.' He interrupted her. 'You couldn't give a shit about Phil Leech.'

She sat back. She felt uneasy. It was routine stuff, but he was colder than she had given him credit for. 'That's a hard thing to say,' she said.

'Try to look hurt,' he replied, smiling at her.

'Are you trying to be cruel now?'

'Very good. You *do* look hurt. You really do.'

Control. It was amazing how far they would go to be in charge. He would rather she were crying than be led to her bed.

'What sort of freak do you take me for?' she asked. It was difficult to keep her face straight.

He laughed. 'Is that a line out of a film?'

'Don't be a bastard, John. It doesn't suit you.'

He leaned forwards, staring into her eyes. 'Have you ever felt anything for anyone?' he asked.

She looked away from him. Cue the life story. That was what he was after. He wanted more than her body. The silly bugger was interested in her as a person.

'You shouldn't laugh at me,' she said, voice cracking slightly. Still she didn't look at him.

'Answer me, Karen. I'm being serious.'

She felt his hand on her face, turning her head towards him. She looked into his eyes. He *was* being serious. She sighed.

'Answer what?' she asked. She was sick of it. It had taken too long already.

'Have you always been alone?'

'No. And I'm not a freak.'

'I didn't say that. I meant have you never been in a real relationship? A long-term one?'

'Short ones don't count?' She moved her face so that his hand fell away. 'I'm tired of this,' she said. 'You want me to tell you things. I've nothing to say.'

'You mean you don't want to talk about it? It's just too difficult for you?'

'No. I don't want to tell you.' She stood up. 'Do you want to go to bed?'

He sat back, surprised. 'To bed?' he said. 'You mean to sleep?'

'I mean to fuck.'

He stared at her, speechless.

'Someone has to say it,' she said. 'At this rate we'll be up all night just thinking about it.' She reached forward and took hold of his hand. 'I don't want you to share my life, John. I've nothing deep to give you. You can have me for one night. Will that do?'

He stood up. 'You're not even offering me that,' he said.

'What?'

'Yourself for one night. You'll share your bed with me. Your body. That's it.'

She smiled at him, ignoring the words. 'Last chance. One night?'

He moved closer. 'Yes,' he said.

She kissed him, quickly, gently, on the lips.

'Let's do it then,' she said.

THIRTY-NINE

She felt light. The first time in months she had felt so free of herself. He tried to undress her in the bedroom, in the dark. But he was fumbling, an effect of the drink. She gave up trying to let him lead it.

She switched the light on (he had switched it off), undressed herself. He was lying on the bed watching. The look in his eyes, she thought, was something like fear. She tried to soothe him, uttered platitudes about his physical beauty. But she had too much energy. She could feel it boiling in her, desperate to get out.

She bent down and started to kiss him, trying to be gentle, unbuttoning his shirt at the same time. He was a surprisingly docile kisser. She had to force his mouth wider with her tongue, get inside him. She had the feeling he would find the exchange of saliva in some way dirty. As she got his shirt off she could smell him, the warmth from his body rising around her. A raw male smell, ruined by some kind of musky deodorant or aftershave. Something his wife would have chosen, in the past.

Underneath he was rock hard with muscle. The shoulders, the chest, the abdomen – she ran her tongue around him, feeling the contours, wanting to do something more with them than all the options she had available. She tried to talk to him about working out, sport, male stuff. He was confused by her speaking in the middle of it. She started to rub herself against his thighs instead, feeling the wetness against him, waiting for him to respond.

When she got his trousers and boxers off she saw that he was huge. 'Fucking hell,' she said. 'You might have warned me.'

She was laughing and giggling, could hear herself. Her head felt so light it was as though she were on drugs. *Jock-the-cock*.

He was embarrassed by it, kept asking her, 'What? What? What do you mean? Why are you laughing?'

She tried to get it all inside her mouth, to shut him up. It was difficult, almost absurd. She started to laugh, with her mouth full of him. He started to move, to moan. Then suddenly he was sitting up, pushing her back, taking control.

She smiled at him, gave in. He switched the light off again. Why? Was it his body or hers? Which did he want to conceal? Or just his face, stripped of dignity. She waited with a total lack of expectation for his next move. He didn't surprise. Legs apart, straight in. She tried to relax. She had a fear he would hurt her if she couldn't relax herself. She held him back, arms full stretch, fingernails tweaking at his nipples. She could see a sheen of sweat building on his brow.

He started thumping at her. It was like some kind of caricature of male stupidity, the harder and faster the better. He got so carried away with it she could feel the sweat dripping off his forehead on to her breasts. She made the right noises for a while, then became bored of it. He was so big she was having to hold her legs together to stop him pushing in too far.

In the middle of it all he asked her some kind of question. She couldn't make out what it was.

'What?' she said. 'What? What are you saying?'

248

He was panting like a dog. 'Is it good?' he asked. 'Is it good for you?'

The words were garbled, distorted by excitement. She thought about lying, but only momentarily.

'It's fine. But not what I want.'

He stopped at once, in full flight. Hurt? Shocked? The bubble burst.

'It doesn't do it for me,' she said.

She pushed him sideways, rolled with him, kept him inside her. He went with it, face and breathing consumed by consternation and doubt. She tipped him on to his back and sat astride him.

'You're like a fucking whale,' she said, breath faster already.

She had to take him inside her to get contact, friction, possibilities. His pubic bone against her clitoris. She started to grind on him, feeling it mounting, looking down on him in the dark, wishing the lights were on. She reached out and held his nipples, focused on what she could see of the contorted expression on his face.

'I feel fucking great,' she said. She felt like she had just smoked a thick, fat reefer of pure sensimillia.

She could see him struggling with it. He didn't know what he was doing, what was happening. She forgot about him, concentrated, turned into her own movements. At the point she felt the orgasm starting she could see him gritting his teeth, eyes closed.

'Don't you fucking dare come before me,' she hissed. 'If you come before me this will never happen again.'

The look on his face was one of panic. He was going to bolt it, screw it up. She released a hand and slapped him, as hard as she could, flat across his cheek.

'Take your mind off it,' she shouted. 'Take your fucking mind off it!'

She felt as though she was going to pass out. She had a brief image of him, staring at her like she was a monster, startled, hand to his face where she had struck him. Then the contractions started.

FORTY

He was flat out, really like a whale – something huge lying in her bed. She stood up in the darkness and looked at him. She was still out of breath, but he was asleep already. Soon he would be snoring. She had heard him the night before, when he had been downstairs.

She moved through to the bathroom, switched the shower on, let the water run over her. She felt electric, body bright red, blood pumping through the capillaries. The sensation was so erotic, so powerful, she wanted to do it all again. He wasn't up for it. She moved her hand between her legs, sighed, tried to think about other things. Then thought, why not? Let it go, relax.

Afterwards, when she was clean, she dried herself, checked the time. Reality started to flood back to her. Nearly midnight and she was wide awake.

She walked downstairs, poured herself a glass of water, let the silence absorb her. He was no safety net. If something happened now, he would be useless. As ever in life, you could only count upon yourself. She got her jacket out of the wardrobe and brought it down, weapon back in the pocket and reassuringly heavy.

She sat down at the table and turned out one of the exhibit bags. Her mind wasn't on it, but she began to sift through the items. She came across Varley's diary, with the pieces of paper wedged between the pages, opened it, read the entries again. Then she turned to the pieces of paper.

The night silence was thick, palpable. She looked at the first bit of paper, the dealer list, and felt her heart quickening.

It had been there all along, the very first time she had looked at it. That was why she had brought these bags home. She had realised it the moment she had seen the list, had felt the hairs on her neck standing on end, as now. It just hadn't registered why. But now she knew.

She recognised the writing.

The shock hit her like a blow. The sensation was physical. Behind her eyes she could feel it rushing up at her, greying her vision. She felt like she was suffocating. She gasped for breath, tried to control it. She had held it down for so long it had grown massive. If she didn't control it, it *would* suffocate her.

She stood up, forced herself to think. All the memories were coming at her. The images were intense, burning with life. She forced herself to look at the writing again, check it, wait for her vision to clear.

She told herself there could be thousands of people with similar writing. What was it she thought she recognised?

She examined the detail, but it didn't work. She remembered none of it. But she knew nevertheless, with total certainty, that it was him, that he was here, in her life, in West Yorkshire. He had arrived without her knowing, had written out this list and given it to Varley. *This* was what it was about. It wasn't about Coates and Varley, or Leech and Mitchell. It was about *her*.

She sat down. She felt sick, as if she had been punched in the stomach. She tried again to work out what he had written, but there was nothing there. It was a dealer list, a straightforward dealer list. The amounts were large, enough to speak about supplying in bulk, but they were coded, as ever, impossible to decipher accurately. There were no clues as to places or times, no contact numbers.

She remembered her phone, found it, checked it. Two missed calls. She brought the messages up, both from Armitage. He had called while she was upstairs, otherwise occupied. In the first he said he had information for her, left a number. The second, fifteen minutes later, was longer and his voice sounded slow, luxurious:

'You promised me you would answer. I was hoping to catch you in bed. I'm going out now. You won't be able to get me. Your man Toomey is staying in Horsforth. Acre Court. I couldn't get the number. He's sold the vehicle you gave me. He's driving an old Ford now. Less conspicuous. L656 GSO. It's a white Granada. Hope this helps. I look forward to seeing you at the gym.'

She checked the time, went upstairs. Munro hadn't moved. She might have choked to death and he wouldn't have noticed. She dressed quietly in the darkness, listening to his breathing. He wouldn't wake until daylight. She wrote out a short note thanking him, explaining that she had left for work. She left it by his shoes.

Downstairs she re-packed the exhibit bags and pulled the jacket on. The gun felt cumbersome. She stood at the front door for a while looking out into the night. Total silence. The sky was thick with cloud, the moon obscured, the air still, hot, portending thunder. She could see nothing moving. She pulled the door shut behind her, got into the car. When she had it going she took the gun out and placed it in the glove compartment.

Horsforth was a suburb of Leeds. It would take her half an hour to get there.

FORTY-ONE

There had been a time when she thought she was seeing him nearly every week, when she had been convinced that every man she bumped into in the town centre or shops, or spotted in the distance at the end of a street, or passed driving in a car, or saw standing at the bar of a pub, sipping beer, provided they more or less fitted his rough appearance and dimensions, were him in the flesh: James Martin.

In the beginning, when she had been able to remember what he looked like, they had to resemble him quite closely. But that had faded. From an image of him that was saturated with every tiny detail of his manner and appearance, so sharp it was like a photograph, she quickly passed to hazy recollections and glimpses, more often triggered by smells or snatches of music than by seeing somebody that might have looked like him. In the end she was left with the mere idea of him. Then it was easier to bury him, move on from it.

She couldn't now recall how long it had been like that, 'seeing his face in every stranger'. She remembered that the detail of his appearance faded in her mind faster than the urge to embody him. At one point she had become so uncertain that even a woman, seen from the side, with long hair, the gait of a woman, a height that could never have matched his, even somebody who looked nothing like him, had in some way looked so similar that she had been forced to walk up to her and check. One tiny detail in the shape of her nose had brought it on.

When she thought of his face now she could see nothing. She wasn't even sure whether she would recognise him. She could try to direct her memory to his features, but as soon as she tried to focus in on the details – the shape of the mouth, or the nose, the colour of the eyes – the rest of the image slipped and disappeared. She could only ever retain part of him, never the whole.

As Munro had said, it was like having someone else's memories. She could be sitting listening to the radio and suddenly it would be there. Brought on by some trashy song. Whatever happened to have been number one at the time, whatever squeaky voice had been bashing out trite lines while the soldiers were delivering their headshots.

It was worse than having memories planted in your head. When she came out of the mental health unit the fight had been to build herself into someone who had nothing to do with her past. Nothing to do with Jim Martin. To suddenly recall him, cigarette in mouth, laughing at her, drinking his beer, telling a joke, to have his presence there, in her head, his smell in her nostrils, was like having a switch thrown on her personality. Snapping her back five, six years, dropping her into the body of someone who was dead. There. Immediately. With her. As if she was, then and there, in the present, *that* person all over again. As if she had never died, never been killed off.

It was like dying, over and over. Leaving someone behind, re-entering them, leaving them. Karen number one and Karen number two.

Except, back then, her name had not been Karen Sharpe.

She came down into Horsforth from Yeadon. Toomey had moved up in the world, from Manningham to Horsforth. The logic was clear. Wherever it was he was staying, Toomey wouldn't be paying. The people running him in Manchester would be footing the bill. Ultimately, the tax payer. To re-locate him into an area under the police spotlight – Harehills or Chappletown, for instance – would run the same risk.

Sutherland would have expected her to have put out requests across the force area. For all she knew, the people Munro had tasked with finding Toomey had done just that. Toomey therefore needed to be placed some-where where the local CID assumed you were straight, law-abiding, decent – until something suggested other-wise. The reverse was true in Manningham, Harehills, Chappletown . . .

She hated Leeds. There wasn't much to recommend Bradford, but Leeds had got to her from the first year she moved. Here, they had small-town pretensions. There was a Harvey Nichols and they were proud of it. You met someone from the putative gentility and it was one of the first things they told you, as if it proved they had got past picking straw from their teeth.

Outside a square mile of shopping and office space Leeds was a post-industrial sprawl like any other northern town. In recent years there had been money put into it to disguise this and to promote it as a 'second finan-cial centre'. Modern, clad structures, girder frameworks decked with concrete slabs and glass panels, 'prestige developments', were being thrown up all over the place. The slums were coming down faster than they could be roped off. In their place, mini-replicas of Bishopsgate and Docklands. Corporate HQ towers.

The centre of Leeds, on a Friday night, looked like a part of London. But not Central London. Up here they *thought* it looked like the West End, or the City. In reality the scale was more like an outlying borough – Harrow or Ealing. Small-town, commuter-belt stuff. And without the intense racial and linguistic mix. In Leeds it made them feel important to think they looked like some bit of London. They looked down on Bradford. Bradford didn't pretend to be anything but itself, slums and all. But it did have that racial mix, the cosmopolitan touch. She preferred Bradford, just.

In parts of Horsforth the lower middle incomes put names over the doors of their semis. Not quite North Leeds. But getting there. There were wealthy parts to it. But most of it was middle range. A few less choice holes as well, thrown in to remind them where they'd come from. Acre Court was middle range. Not a court, not even a cul-de-sac. Just a straightforward street with large multiple occupation houses mixed in with the semis. A good nondescript site for Toomey to lie low. That would have been their advice to him.

Right now it was dark, leafy, deserted. She drove its short length, watching for his white Granada, then parked up at one end, midway between street lights. She lowered her seat a little. He would be out, setting something up, enjoying himself, disregarding their advice. But she could wait.

There was a chance, she realised, that Toomey wasn't just one link in a chain that led back to James Martin. There was a chance that Toomey *was* Martin. She clenched her teeth and tried to think about it. She had his age from the CRO Sutherland had shown her. Twenty-five. Ten years out. But if you were hiding your ID that was a mere technicality. Two people had described him, neither description had been good or had sounded like Martin. Not as she remembered him.

But that had been eight years ago.

If Toomey *was* James Martin, there could be other, more complicated consequences. As far as she had got with it, as balanced as she could be, there were thoughts just below the surface of her control that she hadn't even been able to glance at. She knew they were there, she had always known. The background darkness was what she had learned to live within, ignore.

She felt her muscles tightening, the palpitations beginning in her chest. She pulled at the glove compartment, checked the gun was still there. Beneath it was a UK road map. She dragged it out and looked at the roads. She felt the sudden desperate fluttering of panic rising within her chest.

It was in her hands. She could reverse out of there now, get on to one of the roads she was looking at and follow it, take random diversions or drive straight to an airport. There was nothing to keep her here, nothing to hold her. She didn't even have a cat.

She took deep breaths, looked at the gun. She hadn't come searching for it. It had come to her. It would be like this throughout her life if she didn't face it. Not the threat, not the worry about what he was doing here, nor the reasons for the deaths of Leech and Mitchell.

The fear was that she would have to face up to what *she* had done.

FORTY-TWO

For Chris Greenwood the celebrations in the bar meant nothing. He didn't drink. He had been fifteen years in the job and for ten of those he had been dry. The mistakes in the first five had guaranteed he would never rise higher than DC. He had stopped caring about it long ago. He liked the job he was doing. He was grateful they let him do it. It was absorbing, sometimes intellectual, rarely satisfying (in terms of result), but always enough to keep his mind from straying. With his past he was lucky he had a job at all.

The past was the past. Something to forget. Staring at hours of poor-quality video footage watching out for details was a good way to forget.

He had taken the Burnley footage from the Wider Scene team because they wanted to have a drink in the bar. From nine o'clock through until three twenty-eight a.m. he had watched endless blurred frames at normal speed, looking for the bike, or Varley, or Varley's car, or Coates (though he had been warned that was unlikely), or anything that might have looked connected. Without success. His use of the speed-viewing facility had been limited. He wanted to get it right.

He had permitted himself one break around midnight to use the toilet and make a coffee. He didn't need much to keep him going. His home, if that was the correct word, was not particularly alluring. There was no one waiting for him.

All the same, by three o'clock his eyes were beginning to burn. When, twenty-eight minutes later, he finally spotted Varley's vehicle – at five forty-seven a.m. on 9 April according to the tape counter clock – he felt the quiet satisfaction that only this kind of painstaking work could yield. He froze it, reviewed it, noted the camera number.

After that it got quicker. He knew the cameras, where to pick up the journey. It took him an hour and a half to follow the vehicle from the point where it entered the system to the point it exited, just under half an hour later. It came in from the north of the town, roughly from the direction of Colne.

That would match the movement seen by the ID witness, who said he had seen Varley coming back down Cock Hill towards Keighley. Admittedly, nearly six hours before this footage.

He followed the car on a route through the near deserted town centre until it turned up a side street not covered. It disappeared from view for seventeen minutes, from five fifty-four until six-eleven. Then it reappeared, from the same street, same direction it had entered and took the same route back out of town. He wrote down on his log the last sighting of the tail lights, direction Colne, as being six-seventeen a.m.

He had been at briefings. He never missed. He knew what they would want to make of it. He spread out the map of Burnley he had been given by the Wider Scene team, to assist. He found the bank from which someone had withdrawn money using Phil Leech's bank card. He plotted the route, considered the camera angles. Varley could have parked up out of view, walked to the machine and back. The most natural route was all off camera, not covered by the system.

The timings would easily fit. From where he was last seen in the car (assuming it was him in the car, which it was not possible to say without enhancing the footage) to the location of the cashpoint would be no more than a four-minute walk, at most. He was in the right area. The footage was consistent in that respect. He could have used that machine.

The problem was the time. The transaction on Leech's account took place at six forty-eight a.m., nearly half an hour after Varley had left the area and the town.

He made himself another coffee and spent two solid hours checking for Varley's return at any time up to nine that morning. If he had come back, it wasn't in that car. He then began to review footage for others who might be involved. The problems mounted quickly. From the positioning of the cameras, it was possible to get from both bus and railway stations (and a variety of parking zones) to the general area in which the bank was situated, without coming under surveillance. There was a gap in the cover.

He started to make notes of the registration numbers of all cars entering and moving in a direction consistent with the possibility of meeting up with Varley, off camera. The theory that Varley had used the card wasn't going to stand. Therefore, Varley, if he had indeed taken the card (which, as he saw it, was still the SIO's favoured line), must have passed it on to someone else. That person then used it shortly after Varley was gone.

At seven he realised the time and dialled the number for Munro's mobile.

FORTY-THREE

The car turned into Acre Court just before eight o'clock. She heard it as a dull background noise, interrupting a dream she had been having for five years now, with limited variations.

She was running through a seaside town, being pursued. She didn't recognise the place, though details were familiar from her childhood. She climbed down off a short pier on to some rocks, made her way across them, panting for breath. It was a hot, still day. The sound of seagulls somewhere behind her.

The place looked northern – the buildings, the rocks, the way the people looked. But the waves at the shoreline were gentle. Hardly waves at all. More like the Mediterranean. As she ran past people, terrified, they looked up and said hello to her, as if nothing was going on.

She made it as far as some sand dunes and began to scramble through them. She became so out of breath that she fell to her hands and knees and had to pull herself up the next dune. As her hands slipped into the sand she had the thought that her pursuer wasn't behind her, but beneath her, under the sand. She began to dig frantically, stripping her nails away, leaving her fingers raw and bleeding.

The digging became more and more desperate. Suddenly her fingers touched something soft. Her heart almost froze with fear. She dug further, scooping the sand away from it. It was a face, a human face. Someone was buried in the sand. It became a rush to save a life. Every time she pulled the sand away more fell in. Finally she had the head in view, visible.

She sat back, horrified, confused. The thing she was looking at was a human head, but it had no face. No features at all. Instead the skin was smooth from the hairline to the jaw, like one half of someone's backside. No eyes. No mouth. No nose. In the background the sound of an engine. A boat? A plane?

She opened her eyes. Daylight. A murky, dark day, filled with low cloud. She looked into the wing mirror, saw the car approaching to pass her. Her mind linked the engine noise with the image. She registered the change of worlds. The passage into reality. It slowed down a few yards ahead of her. She kept still, read the plate. L656 GSO. A white Granada.

He had difficulty finding a parking spot, though there were many. In the end he had to reverse back towards her. He did it badly, almost colliding with two vehicles. She watched him stop-starting his way into a space so large she could have made it in one movement, even in a Granada. Drugs or drink, she thought. Her heart began to quicken.

She leaned over and took the gun from the glove compartment. Even if he wasn't James Martin, he was still somebody with connections. Probably not to the Provisional IRA. That didn't fit. The Provisionals smuggled petrol, cigarettes, guns. Not drugs. Until 9 February they had been on a ceasefire and the likes of Adams and McGuinness had been talking to the government. They had less politically damaging ways to collect funds than pushing filth up kiddies' noses. There had been a counter-intelligence effort that said otherwise, of course. Throughout the late

263

eighties the propaganda had painted them as criminals, drug dealers, smugglers, bandits.

If he was connected at all, Toomey would be with some failing splinter group with no other source of funding. But that would still be connected enough. Still not worth taking a chance. She placed the gun inside her jacket, kept her hand on the butt.

He had been parked up for nearly five minutes before the door opened. His car was about six down from her position, on the other side of the road. Front end jutting out into the road. He was two car lengths from the nearest street lamp, but there was a large tree in the way. As he stood on the pavement and fiddled with the car door, she couldn't make out details. Eventually he closed it and walked off in the other direction. Swaying slightly. She calculated his height as between five seven and five ten. James Martin had been five nine.

He had walked nearly fifty feet when he stopped, looked quickly behind himself, reversed direction and began to walk back towards her, still on the opposite side of the street. It could have been a checking manoeuvre, but more likely he had lost his bearings. He had only been living here two days. He passed his own car, looked across the street then began to cross. As he did so he was about forty feet distant. He came out of the shadow of the tree. Her hand tightened on the gun. She eased off the safety.

For a moment it was like being thrown back seven years. All those times she had scrutinised strangers, waiting for the features to settle, form, become him. There had been times when she had stared at someone for minutes, completely dumbfounded, not having a clue whether it was him or not. That the features didn't resemble what she recalled wasn't enough. She had to be certain. He could have aged, put on weight, lost weight, gained a limp.

Whatever. How would she know? How would she know for certain?

The man crossing in front of her, she saw now, was shorter than five nine and thin. He had short cropped hair and protuberant cheek bones. He looked young. The way he walked suggested he was worse for drink, but behind it there was also a distinctive gait, a slight rolling on to the front of his feet. It wasn't James Martin.

She let a long sigh slip from between her lips. As he crossed between the cars in front of her, she opened the door, quietly, slipped out, closed it. The morning was chill, damp. She picked out his figure crossing towards a five-storey, detached building, set back from the road. As she moved between the vehicles to follow he did not look back.

Between the door to the building and the street there was a paved-over area, the garden at one time, converted for parking space now. There were steps up to a first-floor entrance. A single full milk bottle on the top step. She came into the parking area expecting him to be inside already. He wasn't. Turned away from her, he was standing at the top of the steps fumbling with his keys, slightly bent towards the lock. She saw multiple buzzers in a fitting by the door. If he got in before her, she could buzz someone else to let her through.

She began to cross the open space towards the steps, speeding up, but still careful to be quiet. Still he didn't get the door open. The gun came out of her pocket, into her right hand. Her foot hit the first steps and she saw him pause, hearing something. She was eight feet away from him. As she took the five steps between them he began to turn. She held the gun out at arm's length, pointed directly at his head.

'Armed police,' she shouted. 'Keep still.'

She saw him jump with surprise, then turn quickly to face her. Enough of a reaction to have shot him, if this was real. She stopped with the barrel pointed directly at the middle of his face, arm straight. She was crouched, ready to move backwards.

His eyes didn't find hers. The gun was the first thing he saw. He dropped the keys, backed up against the door and raised his hands automatically, defensively. She took a step back, taking the gun out of his reach, but still keeping it at his head.

The look on his face was one of surprise, not fear. With her other hand she flipped the warrant card open and held it up for him to see. She saw his eyes flick from one to the other. The gun, then the warrant card, then back to the gun. Then, lastly, to her.

'If you do anything, I'll shoot you,' she said. 'I mean that. Keep still.'

She folded the warrant into her wallet, pocketed it. He hadn't read it properly. The expression in his eyes was hardening now, but it wasn't one of recognition. Maybe he had never seen her photo. Maybe this lead was a total dead end.

'Pick the keys up and open the door,' she said.

He found his voice. 'Am I under arrest?' Slight slurring. She saw him look behind her, registering the lack of support.

'That's right. I believe you to be armed. If you do anything that makes me fear you I will kill you. Do you understand that?'

He bent down, picked up the keys. 'Kill me? Not even try to wound me first?' A slight mocking tone. Manchester accent. A plastic Paddy.

'Don't fuck around,' she said. 'Open the door.'

He did as he was told. As he turned to the door, she

stepped closer again, lowered the gun, placed it against the middle of his back.

'I'm alone,' she said. 'I won't take any risks.'

He opened the door slowly, doing as she said. She followed him into a hallway, gun pressed against his back. Outside she had shouted at him. Inside there was no sound, no movement. If there was anyone else in the building, they hadn't heard.

'You *are* alone,' he said, arms at waist height now. 'There's nobody here but me and you.'

A kind of threat. She stepped back a pace, keeping the gun on him. With her other hand she reached backwards and took hold of the milk bottle. Then she straightened up and closed the door.

'Which one do you live in?' she asked.

'Right here.' He pointed to a door off to the left of the hall. 'What did you say your name was?'

'I didn't.' She placed the gun in his back again.

'Aren't you meant to—'

'Open the fucking door and get in there.'

He shrugged, confident now. She could smell the alcohol wafting out of his mouth. He opened the door, taking his time.

She stepped in after him, closed it behind them. 'Keep your back to me,' she said. She switched the gun into her left hand, took the milk bottle in her right.

'Have you got a warrant to be in here?'

'A warrant? You've got things wrong, Toomey. This isn't going to be like that.'

She took a breath, then stepped forward and swung the bottle at the back of his head. She put all her force into it, aiming for a spot at the crown of the skull where the hairline spiralled. A spot they had taught her to aim for. He was completely unaware, back to her, hands still slightly raised. The bottle felt like a lump of lead, cold in her hand. It struck with a dull noise. She heard him gasp slightly, his head jolted forward. She followed through, pressing downwards, exhaling. It broke. Glass and milk exploded across his hair and shoulders. She stepped back, saw his knees buckle. He took a pace forward, staggered, then he was falling.

He was unconscious before he hit the floor. She could tell by the way he landed, face first, no arms to break the fall, limp. The body bounced, then came to rest. As it stopped moving, the blood began to gush. The wound was beneath the hair. She watched the liquid pumping rhythmically down his back and face and on to the floor, mixed in with the milk.

She pocketed the gun and checked her hand. She was unharmed.

'That's what it's going to be like,' she said.

FORTY-FOUR

His mobile woke him. It took him a while to find it. It also took him a while to realise where he was. Karen Sharpe's house. In her bed. He sat up and held his head in his hands. Gradually the memories returned to him.

He looked around, realised that somewhere, buried beneath something, his phone was ringing. Apart from that noise the place was utterly silent. He was alone.

Second time she had left him in her place. He rolled out of the bed and fished around in his clothing, on the floor by the bed. The phone stopped ringing as he found it. He checked the number. Number withheld. He sat back.

Leaning against the headboard he thought about it. What had he done? His father had been as Presbyterian as they came, but had married a Catholic woman and the price she had extracted was that his education and upbringing had been as a Catholic. The children were to inherit her guilt. Consequently he had found it difficult to sleep with his wife without feeling some vague kind of guilt. And Karen Sharpe wasn't his wife.

He didn't believe in God, fate, heaven, hell. He didn't believe in anything beyond what he could see with his eyes, in this world. But the rubbish they put into you when you were little didn't go away when you ditched the theory. It just went deeper. Not only was he married, but Sharpe was on his team. He was her boss. He shouldn't have done it.

The phone rang again. Chris Greenwood. He listened to what he had to say. 'Good work, Chris,' he said. 'I'll be there within the next hour. Wait for me.'

It was only when he had washed, dressed and straightened the bed that he saw the note she had left him: 'Thanks for that. See you at the office.'

He sighed. Sex, he had been taught, was dirty, perverse and corporeal (not, therefore, spiritual and holy), something animals did to each other, an act that made humanity bestial; it was something only to be entered into in fulfilment of God's design, to create life; in that sense it was precious, sacramental, miraculous and holy – a somehow spiritual act to be preserved only for those brought together in marriage, between whom there is the gift of love.

Thanks for that.

He didn't love Karen Sharpe. But he liked her, she interested him, and there *could* be something more, given time. He wouldn't have slept with her otherwise. He wanted more from her than a blind clashing of loins in a darkened room. He wanted to *give* her more. But she had written, 'Thanks for that.' *That?* That pick-me-up? That drink? That little bit of fun? He thought back to how it had been and felt a bitter taste in the back of his mouth.

On the way in he realised that Chris Greenwood had probably been up all night getting the video evidence he had called him about. He called him, thanked him, told him to leave.

By the time he was coming up to Cock Hill it was nearly quarter to nine. The roads were open, the barriers down, no sign of the search teams, scene vans or tapings. As if it had never happened. He took the back route over to Wainstalls and then down into Halifax. As he got on to the tops the clouds closed around him like a blanket. Thick, impenetrable fog.

Marshall was waiting for him. They went up to his office and talked about Greenwood's findings. Marshall was nonplussed.

'It doesn't mean he didn't take the card. We have him at the scene. We have him driving there. He had handed it over to someone else, that's all.'

'Maybe someone has set him up.'

Marshall frowned.

'I feel uneasy about the whole thing,' Munro told him. 'Like *I* am being set up.'

'We have his DNA on the gun, sir. We have him driving from the scene at the right time. We've got him in Burnley just before the card taken from the scene is used. It hangs together. It's good.'

There was a knock at the door. He shouted for them to enter.

'Find me the owner of that bike,' he said to Marshall. 'Prioritise it.' He felt uneasy, uncomfortable. 'Someone is telling me they have done it,' he said. 'I know it.'

Marshall looked exasperated.

The door opened. A young DC he recognised but whose name he couldn't get.

'DC Fisher, sir.' He looked serious.

'What is it?'

'I need to speak to you.'

'Not now. How about after ten o'clock briefing?'

'I need to speak to you now.'

Munro frowned at him. 'Why?'

'The parade with Iqbal was corrupt.'

271

FORTY-FIVE

This was the way they used to do it. No messing around, a matter of life and death. She tore the sheeting on his bed into strips, wound them tightly, then bound his wrists behind his back. He was breathing deeply, heavily. Probably conscious and asleep. The booze kicking in. She did the same for his ankles and his knees. She wanted him immobile.

Then she took one of the pillow cases and pulled it over her head, testing it. She could see through it. She took the other one as well, pulled them both over *his* head, one on top of the other. Then she bound them in place by tying them around his neck. Tightly enough for him to be aware of it, when he came round.

When she had him like that she turned him over and pulled him back against the wall of the room, so that he was sitting up, slumped. She stood back and watched his chest heaving. He would live.

She searched his room. It took less than two minutes to find the gun. Under a holdall, under the bed. Some kind of Russian weapon, with a silencer. What had he been getting up to? She slipped the magazine out, checked it. Eight rounds, and one in the breach. She placed her own gun on the table by his bed.

The place was a bedsit, again. In the cistern of the toilet, predictably, she found a plastic-wrapped package she calculated to contain perhaps a gram of heroin. Ten to twenty deals, split and cut with a re-sale street value of £200 maximum. £50 to buy. A small enough quantity to be his own supply, if he was a user. Or a tester pack, if he was working on something. Most probably the latter, since there was no other gear in the place – no scales, wraps, syringes, burn-off. No marks on his arms.

She heard him groaning as she was examining it. She walked back through, pulled the single chair over from the window and placed it about four foot in front of him. The curtains were drawn already.

'Good morning, Liam. Did you have a nice sleep?'

The accent came easily to her. Broad Newry. Somewhere between the softer South Armagh vowels and the heavy inflection of County Down. A precise linguistic marker. Speaking it was like throwing a switch. An accent, a personality, a past.

Outside, before she had hit him, she had felt nervous, excitable. Now she felt cold. Her breath was even, her heart normal. This is what they had taught her to do. It was functional, a means to an end. You calculated the risks and acted. In this situation there were very few risks at all.

She stepped forward, bent down by him and grabbed his face through the hood. Finding his nose she pinched it until he started to shout. The sound was muffled through the hood. She found the opening where his mouth was and pushed the silencer into it, pinning his head against the wall with her free hand, ignoring his movements, waiting for him to understand the situation.

Eventually he bit down on the metal, stopped squirming. Breathing would be difficult enough when he was still. His brain would be feeding him the information now. Self-preservation. *Concentrate on breathing.* She watched the breath hissing at the material, sucking it in and out. She knew exactly what it was like, precisely how the panic mounted.

'If you stay calm,' she said, 'you will find that you can breathe. If you struggle, panic, make more than normal demands for oxygen, you'll find you are starting to suffocate.'

The words made him struggle anew, as she had expected. She held him, waited.

'I can't breathe,' he gasped at her, 'I can't fucking breathe.'

'In a minute you won't need to,' she said. 'The thing you're biting on is the silencer of your gun.'

He began to thrash so much she had to sit astride him to hold him there, to keep it in his mouth.

'I'll count to five,' she said, breathing quickly with the effort. 'If you're still fucking around at five I'll kill you.'

She got to two. He stopped. She waited until she was sure then moved back off him, taking the gun from his mouth. She watched him fighting to handle the breathing problem. It took him nearly five minutes to get to a point where he wasn't totally breathless.

'You're tied up, immobilised, hooded and helpless,' she said, sitting down again. 'By now you should be getting the hang of that. I have two guns to choose from. One of them has a silencer . . .'

'I'm bleeding,' he gasped. 'I can feel my head bleeding . . .'

'I can see that,' she said. It was gathering around his neck, where the hood was tied off, gradually seeping through the material. 'But it won't kill you like a bullet. Pay attention.'

'Why are you doing this?' Muffled words.

She sighed. 'I want specific information, Liam. I want it quickly. I haven't time to fuck around. This is like a game.

274

You probably haven't had as much practice at it as I have. The trick for you is to stay alive. The trick for me is not to have to kill you. If I kill you I get nothing from you. But killing you is the ultimate threat. In order that the threat works for everyone, sometimes you have to carry it out. Can you understand that?'

'Who are you with?'

'Did you hear my question?'

'You're not police. Who are you with?'

'Answer my question . . .'

'If you're with the Branch, they'll catch you.'

'The Branch? Been picking up the jargon. Are you Irish, Liam?'

'Yes.'

'You don't sound it.'

'My mother is Irish.'

'A plastic Paddy. Playing around with your identity. Where's your mother from?'

'O'Meath.'

'Not even a Northerner. Where do you think I'm from?'

'Belfast?'

'Belfast? Have you been to Ireland?'

'I grew up in—'

'Sometimes, being able to accurately identify someone's accent can be a matter of life and death. You don't know where I'm from because you're an amateur. I am not an amateur. This is what I do. People pay me to do it. If I step over there and shoot you through the mouth the bullet will break your spine and rupture several major blood vessels. You will be paralysed, mute and, at first, not in any pain. You won't die though. Not immediately. Depending upon just how many arteries I get and how quickly shock sets in, you will live for anything between

275

fifteen minutes and four hours. If you die after fifteen minutes you won't feel a thing. If you live longer than half an hour, you'll begin to feel it. Do you understand everything I'm saying to you?'

There was a pause before he answered. 'What do you want?'

She leaned closer to him, lowered her voice. 'I've killed people before. Everything I am describing to you I have seen. I didn't get to be Irish by reading about it in a book. Are you listening to me?'

'Take this hood off me. I've seen you already. There's no need to hood me. I can't breathe . . .'

'If you knew more about this you wouldn't be wanting to remind me that you've seen me already. The hood is there to *protect* you. You've had a glimpse of me. That's all. More than a glimpse can mean the difference between living and dying. Do you want to live?'

He was silent.

'Do you want to live, Liam?'

'What do you want to know?' A tremble in the voice. Reality sinking in now. He was almost there.

'Do you want to live?'

'Yes. I want to live.'

'Before we start, you have to believe that I will kill you, if necessary. Do you believe that?'

He didn't answer.

'I've been here before,' she said. 'There are various ways of getting you to believe it. By demonstrating it, for example. I can shoot you now, in the thigh. If I get the femoral artery, you will be dead within three hours. I can then use that time to talk to you. You will talk because you will be dependent upon me calling help. Do you want me to do that?'

His chest was heaving again. She stood up. He heard

the movement, began to shout immediately, 'No. No. I believe you. Don't fucking do it.'

She paused. 'I'm not sure . . .'

'I believe you. You're a fucking lunatic. I believe you.'

She sat down again. 'Not a lunatic, Liam. This is what sane people are like in Ireland. If you had spent more time there you'd know that.'

FORTY-SIX

'Tell me what you want to know.' His voice was rough, shaking.

'Okay. Let's start with the things I know already, to test you. What organisation are you working for?'

She heard him take a breath.

'Did you hear me?'

Silence. She began to count.

'One. Two. Three. Four . . .'

'No one. I work for no one.' Said between gritted teeth.

'You frightened they'll kill you if you say?' she asked.

'I work for me.'

'Have they trained you to say that?'

'I don't know what you mean.'

'I doubt they have. They *assume* you will talk. That's the training. You haven't been trained at all, have you?'

'I'm telling you the truth . . .'

'I believe you work for British Special Branch.' She said it flatly, waited for him to take it in. 'For a man called Sutherland. A military type. You won't know him as Sutherland. You probably haven't even met him. But I have. Have you heard of the nutting squad?'

'No.'

She could see him shaking, but that might have been the blood loss from his head.

'That's what the Republicans call their interrogation squad. They assume you'll talk if you're taken by the other side. That's no problem. But if you're *working* for the other side, well, that's when the nutting squad gets involved. Guess what nutting refers to?'

No response.

'Not crushing your balls in a nutcracker. It refers to putting one into your nut. Do you know what your nut is?'

Was he shaking his head? With the hood on it was hard to be sure of anything.

'Your nut is your head, back in the Province. I tell you what I'll do. I'll let you go and I'll pass on what I know to the Republicans. I'll give them Sutherland's details, meeting places . . .'

'You're making a mistake.'

She stopped. 'A mistake?'

'I'm with you. I'm on your side. You shouldn't be doing this to me.'

'My side? Which side is that?'

'You're with the RUC. RUC Special Branch. Or MI5. I don't know. You must be. Check with the Brits. Ask them about me. They'll tell you.'

'You *are* a Brit, Toomey. What would they tell me? That you're a snitch, an informant?'

'I'm helping them. Special Branch. British Special Branch. There's a plot to plant a bomb in Manchester. I'm trying to get them information.'

'But you're not with anyone. How would that work?'

'The Provos.' He blurted it out. She tried not to laugh. 'I'm with the Provos.'

'It's amazing how much credibility an accent can give,' she said. 'You haven't got any.'

'I'm telling the truth. I'm with the Provos.'

'The "Provos". You mean the RA?'

'The RA. Yes.'

279

'Doing what? Selling drugs?' She flipped the package of drugs on to his legs. 'That's from out of your toilet.'

Silence again.

'Last I heard, the RA wasn't into drugs.'

'The drugs are just a way in. They need drugs. I'm connected in that world.'

'The RA need drugs?'

'They all need drugs. I was in contact with a group called the Socialist Republican Army. They're big in Belfast. At the university. Or they were. I introduced them to people in Manchester. They took nearly 100 K a month off them.'

'The SRA. A bunch of students. Piss heads.'

'I know that. But they were linked to INLA once. They had credibility, theories. The IRA just had guns. The IRA decided to cut them out middle of last year. I heard about it on the news. They killed three people I knew. People I had dealt with. One of them was a friend. The press statements said they shot them because they were running drugs through Belfast council estates. Fucking hypocrites. Within weeks they were asking me to do the same.'

She sat back, thought about it. 'You're not in the IRA, are you? That was a lie.'

His shoulders were shaking. Beneath the hood he had started to cry.

'You were with the SRA, weren't you?'

Still no response.

'Did you join the SRA? Were you actually in it?'

'Yes.'

He could hardly speak. She looked at her watch, closed her eyes, counted to sixty. Give him time, she thought. When she looked at him again he was tense, but still.

'When was this?'

'Three years ago. I met someone when I was at Johns

Hopkins University. He was a friend. He got me into it, convinced me. I didn't know what I was doing.'

'You were a student?'

Suddenly he began to fit together for her.

'Yes.'

A student. Middle class. Drugs weren't the connection. It was about politics. The stupid bastard had got into it all to save the 'workers'. He had seemed cocky, sure of himself, possibly even dangerous. But all that had been going on was a reality gap. He hadn't realised which world he was moving in.

'You don't seem bright enough to be a student,' she said. 'This friend of yours. He was shot last year?'

'The fuckers shot him. I don't know what I'm doing any more.'

'And then they came to you?'

'Yes.'

'You're saying the IRA shot this friend of yours, closed down his group in Belfast, the Student Republican Army—'

'Socialist. Not Student. They were socialists.'

'Student. Socialist. Whatever. They shot him, closed it down, then moved on to you?'

'Yes.'

'Why?'

'They wanted me to take them to a fuckwit I had met in a pub in Bradford.'

'Name of?'

'Luke Varley. He had nothing to do with anything.'

She kept her features still. 'Was he your supplier for the SRA?'

'No. Varley was nothing. He wasn't the supplier of anything. My supplier ditched me when my friend was shot in Belfast. They put pressure on him—'

'The IRA?'

'Yes. He told me I had three hours to get out of Manchester.'

She pieced it together. 'The supplier was Skelly – the dealer you were working for in Manchester?' The man Sutherland had told her Toomey had fallen out with.

'Skelly. That's right. The fucker was scared shitless of them. He thought they were going to kill anybody who had a connection with the SRA.'

'And he had been shifting gear for the SRA?'

'Like I said, 100 k a month.'

'Did you expect him to laugh when they started popping his buyers? Skelly isn't a Marxist.'

'He's scum. He was in it for the money.'

'Politics breeds strange bedfellows. Who came to you?'

'From who?'

'From the IRA.'

'Someone called John Callaghan. Their man in Manchester. He told me to set up a deal between Varley and a guy in Colne. The guy in Colne would be their contact with me.'

'A drugs deal?'

'Yes.'

How had they come across Varley's name? she wondered.

'What was the name of the guy you were to see?'

'The guy in Colne?'

'Yes.'

'Bob Roberts.'

'Bob Roberts? He's not Irish then?'

'More so than Callaghan. Callaghan's from Manchester, like me. Roberts has an accent like yours.'

'Roberts probably isn't his real name, in that case. Did you meet with Callaghan?'

'Twice. He told me they were sorting out the splinter groups. The ceasefire was going to end, he said. There wasn't room for anything but the Provisional IRA. I had been part of a "banned group", the SRA. That was how he referred to it. A "banned group". He told me they would let me off if I did this deal with Roberts. I didn't have a choice.'

'When did you meet Varley?'

'The first time? Before all this?'

'Yes.'

'In a pub in Bradford. Last year. His brother was taking gear off Skelly. But Varley wanted some action for himself. He knew where it was going, asked if I could set him up with anything. I asked back in Belfast, the SRA leadership, but they weren't interested. They had enough coming through already. I met him three times. Once he had a photo with him. Some policewoman. He asked me to pass it back to them, said they'd be interested. I think he was trying to prove he was connected.'

She held her breath. Come back to it, she thought. 'You said you were working for Special Branch. When did that happen?'

'After the first meeting with Callaghan. They had the local police arrest me for some stupid theft charge and came to me in the cells. They had me in a vice, knew everything. I don't know how. They thought that Callaghan wanted to bomb Manchester. That was their interest. I took money off them, told them things. I thought it was safe.' He was starting to cry again. 'When I wanted to get out, they wouldn't let me. You fuckers are all the same. They said the same things as you have. If I backed out, they would let Callaghan know . . .'

She could see it now. Toomey wandering around Manchester, a goldfish in a pond full of pike. One step behind him Callaghan, and behind *him* Special Branch, just waiting for their chance.

'It's a tough world,' she said. 'You should have stuck to your books. Did you meet Roberts?'

'I met him in Rochdale, in a club. He didn't look right. I wasn't sure about it. I told the guy from Special Branch. He had never heard of a Bob Roberts. I got them his address—'

'How?'

'I followed him.'

'You think he didn't see that?'

'The guy's not like that. Not like Callaghan.'

'What's he like?'

'Stupid. Incompetent. I followed him to some terrace in Colne. I saw his family and shit. It was genuine.'

'What address?'

'I don't know. It's the road out to Keighley from the centre of town. From the clock tower. Number one hundred and nine.'

'The photo of the policewoman, where did Varley get that?' She tried to keep her voice even.

'He said he had a connection inside the police.'

'Did you pass it on?'

'Yes.'

'To Callaghan?'

'No. This was before. I gave it to the SRA.'

'Did you tell them who had given it to you?'

'Yes. That was the whole point.'

'Varley?'

'Yes.'

That was how they had it. Her photo and her name. The SRA would have passed it on, through the command chain, one Republican group to another, back to the people who knew her, back to the RA.

'Who gave you the gun?'

'Your lot.'

'Why?'

'I was frightened. I asked for it. I don't even know how to use it.'

She stood up. 'I'm going out to the car to get something. You stay here and keep quiet. I'll be back for you. Do you understand?'

She thought she could see him nodding. She placed his gun on the bed, picked up her own. She had everything she wanted. The complete story. All she needed now was to understand it. Only one person could do that for her and she knew now who he was and where he was.

In the car she used her mobile to call the ACR. She asked them to get a name for the road leading out of Colne in the direction of Keighley. There were two possibles. Only one had houses numbered up to 109. Bob Roberts's house, if Toomey was correct. She asked them to do a check on the electoral roll. She waited.

It was starting to rain as they came back with the answer.

'A Mr James Edward Martin.'

She checked, hearing the words like something out of a nightmare. Colne was a fifteen-minute drive from where she lived.

'James Martin? You're sure?'

'That's right.'

He hadn't even bothered to change his name. He was living in a town fifteen minutes from her and he hadn't even bothered to change his name.

FORTY-SEVEN

Munro waited three hours for Scother to show for duty. Fisher sat in his office with him for the entire time. Coates and Varley were up for Judge-in-Chambers at ten, Bradford Crown Court. He sent Marshall along to cover it. The result was irrelevant. The whole enquiry was stuffed now. Every line they had followed.

He made phone calls to try to speed up the forensics on the motorbike. He called every supervisor who wasn't in by nine and shouted at them for getting pissed in the middle of an enquiry. He felt raw, weakened, irritable. When Scother knocked on his door, he had difficulty sounding calm. He asked him in, told him to sit down.

Scother sat down on the chair in front of the desk. It was the only one left. He looked frazzled, hungover. He could tell something was up. Suspicion written across his features. Fisher was behind him, on the other chair. That disturbed him.

'Thanks for coming in, Dave,' Munro said. He looked at his watch.

'Sorry, boss.'

'You and the rest of the squad. It's sloppy, isn't it? This enquiry is at day four. There's a long way to go. I expect better of experienced detectives.'

Scother nodded. This was what it was about, he was thinking. He looked back at Fisher, thought again.

'Good detective you have there,' Munro said. 'DC Fisher.'

'Yes,' Scother agreed. Eyes wary.

'Needs to learn a few things, perhaps.'

'He's young,' Scother said, turning briefly to Fisher, smiling. Fisher was looking very uncomfortable.

'He tells me the witness Iqbal needed a little help.'

Scother frowned. 'Help?'

'Yes.' Munro picked up Fisher's notebook. 'I've got DC Fisher's notebook here.' He watched Scother lick his lips. 'I've read it. It's a little different to the statement you took.'

Scother shrugged, looked puzzled.

Munro smiled. 'But hey! So long as we get the result.'

He watched Scother relax slightly. 'It was a good result,' Scother said.

'That's right. An important result. An important plank of evidence.'

Scother nodded.

Munro put the notebook down, looked up at him, held his eyes. 'Have you *ever* heard me say anything like that?'

'Like what, sir?'

' "So long as we get a result"? Have you *ever* heard me say that?'

'No, sir.'

Munro stood up. He could feel something uncoiling within him. He stepped around the desk, moved closer to him.

'That notebook,' he said, 'contains the first description of a suspect.'

He could hear the suppressed rage in his voice, seething upwards. He was going to have to struggle not to thump him.

'Have you seen that notebook?'

287

Scother looked up at him. Paused. Considered. Shook his head. 'I don't recall.'

'You have,' Munro said. 'DC Fisher gave you it.'

'I don't remember that.'

'You threw it in the bin.'

'I don't recall that either.'

He had it now, saw which way it was going. There was a sheen of sweat on his brow. Munro walked behind his chair, stood directly behind him.

'Do you understand how difficult it will be to get a conviction against Varley for anything now? For *anything*?'

Scother twisted to look up at him. 'I'm not sure I understand.'

'Do you know what I would like to do to you?'

Scother stood up, suddenly, threatened. He turned to face him.

'I would like to smack your fucking face in.' He held his arms at his sides, rigid.

Scother stared at him. Like he was from another planet. 'If you are thinking of taking any action against me, sir, I would warn you that—'

Munro stepped towards him. 'Warn me what? Dick-head.'

Scother looked uncertain. The situation was directly and physically threatening. 'Warn you that I should have a Fed Rep present.'

'A Fed Rep? You'll need better than that. I'm arresting you.'

'Arresting me?' Shock spread across Scother's features.

'That's right. From now on you are a fucking criminal. You are under arrest on suspicion of attempting to pervert the course of justice.'

He stepped back, away from him. He had to keep his hands to himself.

'Fisher?'

'Yes, sir?'

'Go and get a uniform from the cells.'

'Yes, sir.'

He waited until Fisher was out of the door, kept his eyes fixed on Scother.

'Are you sure you wish to—' Scother started.

Munro held up his hand. 'Don't say anything. Anything you say may be used in evidence. And the rest of it. I don't remember the caution. You're the first person I've arrested in four years.'

He stood opposite him waiting. A long, awkward silence. Finally Fisher returned, a fat uniform in tow.

'What's your name, Officer?' Munro asked him, not taking his eyes off Scother.

'Robbins, sir.'

'I've arrested this man, Robbins. He's a police officer, but that makes no difference. Do you understand that?'

'Yes, sir.'

'Good. Attempt to pervert the course of justice. Take him down to the cells.'

'Yes, sir.'

He watched them leave, stepping aside to let Scother past him. Everything came down to control.

When they were gone, he sat down and caught his breath. He felt strained, stressed. Fisher was still there.

'You can go,' he told him.

'Yes, sir.'

'Next time, don't wait until after the parades.'

He looked up at him, saw the distress on his face, repented.

'Crime is crime, Fisher. Don't worry about it. You did the right thing.'

'Yes, sir.'

'Come and see me later today. When I'm calm. I'll counsel you about it then.'

'Yes, sir.'

The door had barely closed before the phone was ringing. Marshall, from the Crown Court.

'He gave them bail.'

'Who?'

'Judge Watkins. Incompetent fucker.'

'Both of them?'

'Both of them. I don't fucking believe it.'

'I do.'

Marshall barely heard him.

'We lost Varley already. Group Four let him out the back before we could get anyone on to it. I can't believe it. Some fucker had given the defence information about the DNA. We didn't stand a chance.'

'That was me.'

Silence. He listened to it.

'Sorry, sir?'

'That was me, Tony. I called them. I told the CPS and the defence.'

Again, silence.

'You can't fuck with a Judge, Tony.'

'No, sir. I'm sorry.'

'Are you on your way back now?'

'Yes.'

'Good. Do we know where Coates is?'

'Yes. I'm on to him. Varley is lost, though. Do you want me to do anything about it?'

'Get a couple of squad cars out to their houses. Keep an eye on Coates. But don't fret. They're not the problem,

Tony. They should never have been inside. It's someone else we're looking for.'

He fished out Sharpe's mobile number. She knew it already. He dialled the number. The phone was switched off. He left a message.

'DC Sharpe? John Munro. Where are you? Harris hasn't a clue where you are. Call me now. That's an order. Coates and Varley got Judge-in-Chambers. They're out. I am under the impression you think we shouldn't have had them locked up in the first place. I'd appreciate your views on who we *should* have charged.'

FORTY-EIGHT

It only began to sink in as she was nearing Skipton. It was ten-twenty a.m. Colne was fifteen minutes from her house. Coincidences like this didn't happen. He had moved there deliberately.

As the thought took hold, she felt so shocked, so ill, she had to stop the car. She opened the door in a lay-by, leaned out and emptied her stomach on to the tarmac. Afterwards she sat with her legs outside the vehicle, gasping, watching reality warp, spin, resettle. *Fifteen minutes from her house.* How long had he been there? The thought was so monstrous it made her feel drugged.

It took nearly twenty minutes before she could get control of her senses, her stomach, her breathing. Then she remembered the motorbike at Hardcastle Craggs. She started up the car and headed south before Skipton. She wanted to go the long way round, to use the route he would have used on that bike from Cock Hill, to acclimatise herself to his presence. That he was this short distance from her home was unbearable. Taking the indirect route made her feel there was more space between them.

If he had been that close for long enough, it was possible she had seen him, without knowing it. What else had she seen over the last few weeks, months, years, without realising? The possibilities were numbing.

The day was filthy. Black, fast-moving cloud, so low she couldn't see the tops of the hills. Rain sweeping across the windscreen intermittently, in vicious squalls. The sort that would lash your face red. She drove down through Hebden Bridge watching shoppers rushing from doorway to doorway, umbrellas turned inside out by the gale. Then out again following signs for Widdop, wipers on full.

The road ran along the edge of a steeply cut valley, heavily wooded. As she neared the head of the valley, it turned down towards the swollen torrent of water that normally ran through the bottom of the valley as a small stream. Over a stone bridge she saw the chapel looming out at her through the mist, the yew trees behind it. This was where he had run out of petrol, abandoned the motorbike.

Incompetent. Something had gone wrong, thrown him. It wouldn't have taken much. Unless he had changed, this wasn't what he was good at. It didn't seem like he had changed. He had given Toomey the name Bob Roberts, but he hadn't even bothered to register as that on the electoral roll. Toomey had been able to track him back to his home – an idiot like Toomey – without him having a clue.

She followed the road through hairpins until it climbed out above the valley and ran into the cloud again. The rain stopped immediately, but visibility was so restricted she had to keep her speed below twenty. The light from her headlights bounced back at her from a thick wall of mist.

Almost two miles further on she came to the pub where the witness lived, the one who had found the bike. There had been no mist that night. The moon had been almost full. He would not have risked walking so close to the pub. Assuming he had been forced to walk once the bike had stopped.

The road turned through a steep gorge she could barely make out then began to climb again. Over the last ridge of the eastern Pennines. Then down, into Lancashire. She picked up signposts for Colne. As the cloud lifted over a decaying industrial sprawl of terraces and factory chimneys, she checked the mileage. Almost nine miles from where he had abandoned the bike. Average walking pace four miles per hour. That made it three hours maximum if he hadn't deviated, got lost, hidden himself. She remembered the helicopter searching the moors the morning she had walked up to Wainstalls. It was light from almost four o'clock. Maybe that had slowed him.

Colne looked tired, dirty, wet. Sitting in a valley that ran from the eastern edge of the Pennines, it was built around the slopes of a small hill, at the summit of which, on the main street, there was a clock tower, clearly visible as she came down into the valley. Fanning out from the summit rows of identical terraced housing, like *Coronation Street*. She drove down into it.

It was easy to find the street. She followed the directions given, drove up through the town, past the clock tower and out, followed the signs for the turn-off to Keighley. It was called Cotton Tree Road. She scanned ahead of her for movement, cars or people, then slowed down and looked for the door numbers. Number 109 was right there in front of her. Too easy.

It was a normal, decent-sized terrace, slightly set back from the road, with a small garden at the front. She drove past and turned in a side road. Then she came back and parked up, facing it, from the other side of the street.

She sat behind the wheel, motionless. Rain streaking across the windscreen, her heart thumping like a drum. Everything was ordinary. She was sitting in a car in a nondescript Lancashire town, staring at a standard house on an ordinary street. All around her people were getting on with their lives, cursing the rain, running for shelter, driving carefully through the puddles and pot holes, going to work, shopping, coming home.

She opened the car door.

She could see herself doing it. As she stepped on to the road, the sound around her shrank, vanished into the background.

The silence enclosed her. Something from inside, moving up suddenly, without warning, cut her off from it all. The thing inside her head that was looking, thinking, feeling, flicking restlessly from one sensation to another – the thing that screamed at her day after day, shut up within her brain, wriggling from one object to the next so rapidly she hadn't even time to notice it – the worm that was her consciousness, suddenly became still, settled, concentrated.

All that she could hear was happening inside her and the noise was deafening; the thumping of her heart, the rasping of her breath, the blood rushing through her ears. But outside there was nothing. Just movement. It was as though she was seeing the world through a veil, a barrier that distanced her.

The images intensified. The cars passing her on the road moved soundlessly through a curtain of grey, like a slow-motion film sequence. The drops of rain striking the windscreen danced in silence, striking, exploding, bouncing, falling again.

It was as if she was inside and outside herself, all at once. She looked like a part of it, part of the normality. But inside she was panicking, the blood pumping furiously, her breath coming out in short little gasps.

She began to cross the road.

Memories. She couldn't stop them now. The first time she had met him. The last time she had seen him. All the events between, rushing at her, one after another. She began to walk towards the house, watching it unfold inside her head. *How many people have I been in my life?* She heard the thought coming to her, saw it floating past. And all the time, in the background, that one thing. Waiting for her. That one place she could not go.

Everything as it should be.

She was walking steadily, confidently, stepping over puddles, pausing to let a car pass. In silence. A fraction of an inch below the surface, something was building up. Like a scream. *Turn and run*, it said to her.

She stepped on to the far pavement and had an image of herself doing precisely that, ten years before, in Belfast. Rain thundering from the skies. A row of terraced houses in front of her. A day completely devoid of colour. The image was so powerful she had to lean against a wall to stop herself from falling. Who had she been, back then?

Then he had opened the door to her, smiled, said something about her being late.

Now she turned and pushed a small gate open, stepped on to a short path, which led to another door that he would open. For the first time in seven years she saw him in her mind as clear as day, every detail.

He was three inches smaller than her, average build, not fat, not thin. Light brown hair cut in a normal style, a face with features that fitted together, nothing too large or too small. One tooth missing from the top left side, which you could only see when he was *really* laughing. Aside from that, ordinary.

But he was comfortable with it, sure of himself. The way he walked, talked, moved, smiled, looked at her, everything he did, spoke of someone who did not want to be anyone else or anything different.

He did not need anyone else to complete the picture. What she had loved in him, above all, what had attracted her in a way that had devastated her, placed her in harm's way, almost killed her, was *just* that. That he had not needed her. James Martin had not needed anyone. When he was with her, whatever they were doing, each and every time, he was with her by *choice*, because of who *she* was.

With everybody else she had met – before and after – it had been different. They had been with her because they lacked something. That they thought she had cured that lack, filled the hole in their sad little hearts, had little to do with *her*, with what she was. Men needed to need someone. Anyone would do. They needed to feel the love gushing out of them, like sperm or faeces, some part of them they could smear across the world, a blind pathological need to *express*. When a man fell for you, it was about as discriminating as a dog pissing on a lamp post.

She reached her hand up to the door in front of her, saw her fist rapping against the wood.

It was that strength she was attracted to, that he had known who he was. She had spent her whole life feeling unformed, moving from one personality to the next, copying those around her. She felt as if she had never believed in anything. But he could tell the story of his life, cogently, engagingly, like a book, each part of his character and personality flowing from some trigger or cause, his life a series of consequences, everything making sense, no room for doubt, mapped out in advance by bitter circumstance.

Almost the first night they had spent together he had told her about the soldiers. The experience from which all others came, the seminal moment, the event that centred his life. She had felt trivial by comparison.

His family had been farmers, he said, nothing big. They didn't have huge Euro farms where he was from. Everything was little; hedgerows and ditches, tiny fields, small herds and crops. *Like the Normandy bocage.* His exact words. A hard life, supplemented, for most people, by the living to be earned smuggling goods from the 'Free State', ten miles to the south.

He had hated it, detested the life, the graft, the attitudes. The people of Forkhill had seemed like village idiots to him. He had even disliked the accent, the soft, almost southern vowels she had loved so much, recognisably different to her own way of speaking back then, though the distance between Newry and Forkhill was less than thirty miles. Between Newry and Forkhill there were greater divisions than mere geographical separation could enforce.

He came from South Armagh, a native Catholic. She came from a middle-class Protestant family who were doing nothing more than passing through. For the British army the fields and hedgerows had become the Normandy bocage reborn. South Armagh was perfect sniper country, each and every steeply hedged lane a potential ambush point.

The real problems had come later. But already, he had told her, growing up there in the sixties, before The Troubles had really kicked off, he had hated every minute of it. For as long as he could remember he had wanted nothing but to escape.

He had won a scholarship to Queen's, in Belfast. When she had started there in 1979 he had been in his final year. They had not met. He was studying English literature. His tutors, he said, were predicting good results, maybe even a First. His plans had been to get the qualification, apply to a university on the mainland for a teaching post. Get out. That year, however, the plans fell apart.

He had returned to stay with his family during the winter vacation. One night, returning from a pub in the

298

village, he had turned down the lane leading to their property to see army Land Rovers parked up outside the buildings. Walking through the dusk he had listened to the sound of their radios crackling, heard the harsh Essex accents. Immediately he feared that something had happened to his family.

That was his first thought. That the problem had been the Irish, his own countrymen. That the army were there to protect them. Starting to run, he passed the first vehicle and saw figures running at him, out of the darkness. Faces blacked out, helmets spiky with foliage, he recognised them as soldiers and tried to identify himself. They weren't listening. One of them struck him with the butt of his rifle. An almost casual action, he said.

He hit the ground, lost consciousness, woke to a scene that would never leave his memory. His face and hair wet, it took him a while to realise that they had urinated on him as he had lain there. To wake him up, they said later. They were paratroopers. Red berets. All from southern England. They had 'arrested' his father and himself under the anti-terrorist legislation.

As his eyes opened he picked out the detail and started to adjust his world view. They were standing around him, one of them had a gun angled towards his head. Others were smoking. From within the house – *his home* – not fifteen feet away, he could hear his mother sobbing and pleading. Desperate in a way he had never heard before. Behind her wailing, the sound of blows and groans.

His father was nearly sixty-five years old. But they beat him until he could no longer walk. When he was unconscious they left him, moving out to start on the son. He waited with his heart swollen, fear in his chest. Not for himself – that came later – but for his father.

The original blow had caught him across the forehead.

No permanent scarring. He lost the tooth when one of the soldiers pushed the rifle barrel inside his mouth. He could hardly hear the stream of racist insults at the time. But he remembered later. At the time he was so terrified he soiled himself.

They kicked and punched him, though the blows left no memory of pain. Worse was to come. They took him to Bessbrook Barracks and held him for three days. Illegally, as he was to discover later. But what did that matter? In Bessbrook they stood him naked against a wall and struck him until his legs gave way. Then they forced him to stand, repeated the action. He worked out much later how long this went on for. At the time he had no idea. At the time he thought they would kill him.

They seized the farm Land Rover the same night. A sniffer dog had 'selected' it. When they released him without charge, they gave him the vehicle to drive home in. 'Terribly sorry,' a Major said to him, 'but these days we cannot take chances. We have to be sure.' He had to drive slowly because his legs were so bruised he could hardly operate the clutch and brake.

All the way home all he could think of was the sound he had heard as he had been lying there. The repeated blows, the dull, thudding noise, metal and wood on flesh and bone. The first time he had heard that sound. His father's helpless groaning behind it. He had to stop the car and vomit at the roadside.

His father had not died. But three days later, when he returned from Bessbrook, he was still in hospital in Armagh. The house was still covered with blood where they had split his skull open, in front of his screaming, distraught wife.

'IRA cunt. Provo bastard,' they had shouted. Punctuating the words with blows.

His father had never had a good word to say for the IRA, old style or new. 'Them bastards should get proper jobs,' he would say. He lived six months after the incident, then died of a heart attack. In that time he said nothing of that night to anyone.

His views on the IRA did not change. A strong man, mentally. His mother was weaker. His death destroyed her. She died a year later. Depressed, ill, wasted by hopelessness. Her son – stupid James Martin – did not return to university, did not complete his degree.

But he did acquire a set of beliefs. And the beliefs made him strong.

She could remember as if it was happening now, sitting there with him, in his flat, his arm around her, him telling her this story. She could recall falling for him, there and then. How could that be? What lack in her own life had so simple a tale addressed? And addressed *despite* her being who and what she was.

If he had found out what she was doing there, if he had for a moment suspected the truth, if reality had come between them and it had come down to a choice between himself and her – a life for a life – he would not have hesitated. She knew that. *That* was what she had loved in him.

She saw the door opening, heard her heart pounding. At the exact moment his face came into view she realised her error. The thought went through her like an electric shock.

She had left the gun in the car.

FORTY-NINE

He brought in with him – from Sharpe's house – the two large exhibit bags he had found under the table in her kitchen. After he called her mobile another four times, leaving a message every time, he started to go through the bags, searching for whatever it was she had been looking for.

He emptied the contents on to the floor, crouched and started to sort the items. Almost immediately he was interrupted by the door being flung open and his office manager, Peter Dyson, rushing in, breathless.

'The DNA from the motorbike. Just off the fax machine,' he shouted. He was waving the sheets of paper.

Munro stood up slowly. 'Don't get over-excited, Pete. We know already that we've been following the wrong lines.'

Dyson frowned. Munro took the papers off him and skimmed through them. It didn't take long. He nodded to himself. All in all, he felt surprisingly calm.

'Okay,' he said, looking up at Dyson. 'Get all the supervisors in here. Now.'

'What does it say?'

'It says there is blood from Mitchell and Leech all over the bike, that the bike was at both scenes – Wainstalls and Cock Hill – and that there is absolutely no evidence on the bike to support the conclusion that either Coates or Varley have ever been anywhere near it.'

Dyson struggled with it. 'You mean no DNA from Coates or Varley? That's not conclusive.'

'It's as conclusive as it gets. But in case you wanted it spelling out, it also says that the profile matching back to the same identical unknown, from Phil Leech's car, from Fiona Mitchell's clothing *and* from the gun in her hand, is *also* present in abundance on this bike.'

He watched Dyson's jaw drop.

'Sometimes we're wrong, Pete,' he said. 'This is one of those times.'

He let him leave, sat down behind the desk, waited. He felt angry with himself, deflated, depressed. He had made classic mistakes. Classic. There was no excuse at all.

Fifteen minutes later, when they were all stuffed into his room, all eight that were available, at any rate, he wrote out the motorbike registration on a blank sheet of A4.

F226 TCP.

He held it up for them. 'I don't care if you have to personally call on all forty-three police forces in England and Wales, plus those in Scotland and the Irish republic. I want a lead on this bike and I want it fast.'

They looked at him in silence.

'The person who drove this bike is our killer. Not Coates. Not Varley.' He held up the faxed sheets of paper. 'These sheets tell you why.'

Still no response. Maybe it was Scother they were bothered about. Maybe that had got round.

'This is the DNA results from the abandoned bike. No DNA from Coates or Varley. Absolutely none. Plenty of DNA from the *same* person who left traces at *both* murder scenes *and* on the gun. That is – a third person. I want every single team suspended, as of now, and every detective working on this until we locate the owner of that bike. Do you understand?'

Nobody said anything. He stood up.

'We've been made to look fools. Someone has pointed us at Coates and Varley. Whoever it was, I know one thing for certain; he is dangerous. As yet we haven't a clue about the motive, so everything is open. *Everything.* I want you to do your jobs. Quickly. We need to track this man before he kills again.'

FIFTY

It was like standing at the end of a long tunnel, watching him. The panic flooding through her like a drug, narrowing her vision, intoxicating her with fear. She felt naked, face to face with something that could destroy her. She was paralysed, rooted to the spot. The door swung open further, revealing the entire body.

It was him. James Martin. No room for doubt. No hesitation. She recognised him at once. The breath caught in her throat. He was saying something to her, speaking. She couldn't hear a word. She felt as if she were fainting. She struggled to control it, to take in the details. His hands were empty, one on the door, the other at his side. He was standing there looking at her, three feet away, not moving, saying something. But she couldn't hear a thing past the noise of her own heart.

His face was the same face she remembered. Nothing hard in the eyes. Blue, Irish eyes. She brought her hands up and smashed them into her ears. With a noise like an explosion the sound returned, crashing into her skull. She took a step backwards, focused her eyes on him. Then had to lean forward and brace herself against the door frame. She saw him reach out and place a hand on her arm. The action was gentle, without aggression. She heard his words echoing through her ears.

'Are you all right, Karen?'

That was all he was saying. That was all. She began to breathe again, found her voice.

'You know my name?' The words sounded strangled.

'I know all your names,' she heard him say. 'You should come in. We have to talk.'

She turned slightly, thinking of running. But his hand was on her, holding her. She took a step forward. She felt hypnotised. He was leading her in. She would never get out again. She felt the internal warmth close around her, heard the door shut behind her. Now it starts, she thought. Now it starts for real.

She looked up and saw that she was already inside his home, in what must be the living room. Her eyes moved sluggishly across the details while he stood beside her and watched. She saw chairs, drawn curtains, lamp stands. Strewn across the floor, children's toys. On the walls, pictures in frames. A fireplace with ornaments. Photographs. Everything normal. Her eyes settled on one photograph after the other. There were so many. How many children? She tried to count, lost count. Were they all of the same child? Was there only one? She couldn't tell. Her brain wasn't working properly. In one photo she saw a woman with him, smiling. His arm around her. Shorter than him, blonde hair, much older.

'Who is that?'

She heard the words coming out of her mouth. As if they didn't belong to her. As if she was no longer in control of her tongue. She saw her finger pointing unbidden at the largest photo.

'The child?'

'No. The woman.'

Not the child. Not the child.

'My mother. Don't you remember?'

His accent was exactly the same as she recalled it. She turned to look at him. He was wearing a pair of loose-fitting trousers, an open-necked shirt, a grey sweater. His hair was unkempt, matted. Around his eyes there were dark lines. She gazed at his face and suddenly she could see the story there, the strain. One of his eyelids was quivering slightly, almost a twitch.

'How long have you lived here?'

She hardly dared listen to the answer.

'Six years.'

She felt as if the ground were opening up beneath her.

'F226 TCP?'

Her mouth was still going, still asking the questions. But already she knew the answers, knew she had to get out of there.

'Yes?'

'It's yours, isn't it?' A part of her brain over which she had no control was moving her tongue, forming the words.

'Yes. Have you found it?'

'*They* have found it.'

They. Distancing herself. Stepping backwards. She found the door with her hand, moved her fingers up behind her back to find the catch.

'I have to go,' she said.

'You can't. Not yet. Not now that you are here.'

Her heart was jumping like a flywheel; uneven, loping, massive. She was so frightened she couldn't even look at him.

'I have to.'

Her fingers began to twist the catch on the door.

'We are alone here,' she heard him say. 'We can talk.'

She felt the door beginning to open.

'You are not in danger, Karen.'

She pulled the handle and turned towards it. 'I'm sorry, Jim. I can't stay.'

She felt his hand on her arm again, stopping her. 'Look at me, Karen. Look at me.'

She paused. 'I want to go, Jim. This was a mistake.'

'Why? Because you are frightened of me? You know that's not it. You know what it is.'

'Let me go.'

She stood still. His hand was gripping her lightly, but still she dared not move.

'Look at me.'

She turned to look.

There was a gun in his hand. An automatic. He was holding it with ease and confidence. The ease of someone who had spent a lot of time with guns. It wasn't pointed at her, but angled lazily towards the floor. She heard herself beginning to gasp.

'Sit down, Karen. Don't panic. There are some things you have to know.'

'You are threatening me.'

'If you won't stay, I will have to—'

'Please, Jim. Please. Don't do this. Let me go.'

He brought the gun up and pointed it at her face. Her focus adjusted, centred on the barrel. Behind it, his arm, his face, the room, paled into background. She stopped breathing.

'If this is the way it has to be, then so be it.'

'I'll stay. Don't shoot.'

He nodded. Lowered the weapon. She saw that his hands and arms were shaking.

'Sit down.'

She took a breath, stepped away from the door. He moved around her and closed it again.

'Sit down.' The same instruction. This time the voice was harder.

She sat.

FIFTY-ONE

He sat across from her, the gun cradled carelessly in his lap. She kept catching sight of the children's toys. He started talking to her without any kind of introduction.

'You know most of it already. If you didn't you wouldn't have found me . . .'

He broke off, looked at the carpet at his feet. Hands still shaking.

'I have to tell you some things. I don't want to, but I have to. If you want to live you have to listen.'

He looked up at her, then reached over to a cigarette packet, lying on the carpet beside the chair. He lit one, sucked on it. She watched, on the edge of her chair, eyes moving from the gun to his face.

'Luke Varley. He passed your details back. I met him last year. November. He thought I was going to set up a drugs deal for him. Shifting "gear" to the IRA.'

He laughed, a mirthless noise, and took another drag on the cigarette.

'I've just started smoking again,' he said. 'Gave up nine years ago. But you remember that.'

She tried to control her breathing, tried to relax. He was getting more and more nervous. His eyes rarely meeting hers, shifting in his seat. If he was going to do something, she had to be ready for it.

'The IRA don't do drugs. You know that. I know that. I told him they did though. Went along with it. I even learned the vocabulary, the prices. I took two months at it. Meeting him. Finding out about him. Finding out about you, Mitchell, Leech, Coates. The whole thing. I had to be careful.'

He paused, rubbed his forehead with the hand holding the gun. He looked dirty, exhausted.

'One of the first things I found out was that you and Leech were watching Coates. It took me another two weeks to work out that Mitchell was with Leech. With Leech, with you. Informing. I planned the thing like I would have done nine years back. I watched. I waited. I gathered information. It wasn't difficult. These are different times. Different times and a different country. No one is security conscious here. I sent all the information back, like I was meant to. I tried to be normal about it. As if it meant nothing to me.'

He looked up at her, directly at her for a moment.

'Inside I was panicking. Terrified.'

He sat back, took another deep breath. It was as though the air was catching in his throat.

'I only worked out what I was going to do last week. By then there wasn't much time. Mitchell was the weak spot. I had information on her. Things I could use. If Coates found out about Leech and her, he would break her. If he found out she was a snitch, maybe worse. That was a powerful lever. I met her at the beginning of last week and put it to her. It was a risk. But I needed a way in. She knew what was going to happen.'

He stared at her, eyes suddenly challenging.

'Remember that. She knew.'

She nodded quickly, as if she understood.

'I told her the exact plan. She was meant to be in love with your partner. Phil Leech. She wasn't. She didn't care about anything but herself. I came to her with five grand in one hand and the threat of Coates finding out in the other. She didn't hesitate.'

He broke off suddenly and leaned forward, hand over his eyes. She watched his shoulders shaking, saw tears welling up, spilling out of his eyes.

'Fuck. How did I ever end up like this?'

The words were choked, barely audible. The gun was in the hand rubbing his eyes. She watched him crying, the gun pointed at the ceiling, tried to work out whether the safety was on or off.

'I was out of it,' he said, voice rasping. 'I was out. I work for the council here. I do traffic light programming for them. A stupid, boring, normal job. This isn't me.'

He was breaking down, the shaking getting worse. She tried to find her voice, but nothing would come out. Her mouth felt like cardboard, her tongue stuck against her teeth.

'I lost you. I know what it means to lose someone. I didn't want to do any of this.'

She watched as a long line of ash dropped from the cigarette on to the carpet. He was crying for minutes, shoulders shaking, little gasping noises coming from his mouth, eyes focused on the floor. She waited, a pulse beating at her temple, sweat creeping down her back. When he started to speak again it was through the tears, the words sometimes unclear.

'The arrangement was that she would set you up to go to the reservoir. He had met her there before – Leech. I had watched them. I told her to call both of you and arrange to meet up there. I told her to say that Coates had found out and she needed to get out. I gave her a time to do it. Everything. I don't know what went wrong. I couldn't get it out of her. She was meant to call me to confirm. She never did. When I got up there his car was there and I drove down to it. I didn't know why she hadn't called, but it didn't matter. It looked like she had set it up. He started to open the door as I pulled up. I had a helmet on. I couldn't see too clearly. I stepped in and shot him . . .'

He stopped. No longer crying. No longer shaking. Frozen. Shoulders slumped forward. The images shooting through his head. The gun dangling from his fingers. She held her breath and felt the silence swelling around her. He looked up, looked at her. Frowned. Wiped his eyes with the hand that had been holding the cigarette. The cigarette was on the floor, still burning slightly. She tried to keep her eyes on his.

'She started to scream when I fired. I couldn't see her from the angle I was at. The noise was very loud. I didn't have a silencer. But I could hear her screaming. I knew at once it wasn't you. I fired twice, I think. Then looked in. She was sitting there beside him, screaming. Her face looked like a mask, covered in blood, distorted. I didn't even look at him. As I pulled the trigger, my eyes were closed. I didn't see him. It was meant to have been you. That was the whole point. That you would be there, sitting there, beside him.'

She dared not move. He straightened up, took another breath, saw the cigarette on the carpet, moved one foot over to stub it out.

'Mairead would shout at me for that,' he muttered.

Her heart was pounding so loudly she thought he must be able to hear it from where he was. *Mairead. Mairead. Mairead. Who was Mairead?*

He stood up. 'Anyway. It's done. You make your choices. You follow through. You move on.' He stepped towards the fireplace, looking at the photos there. 'Right?'

He looked for an answer. She kept still, eyes wide.

313

'I have no idea what she expected. She knew what was going to happen. Worse. I had told her you were to get it as well. She *knew* I would come. Maybe she just didn't think about it like it was real. She was screaming for a long time afterwards. I was going through his pockets trying to think what to do, trying to work it out. I asked her what had gone wrong but couldn't get anything out of her. I asked her where you were. She couldn't talk. When she stopped screaming she just started to gag. I suppose she was terrified. I suppose she had never seen that sort of thing before. I have seen it. But I have never done it before. You know that. It was a first for me.'

He lit another cigarette, hands shaking so badly it took four matches before he could get it alight.

'I panicked, I suppose. I couldn't think straight. I took his wallet to try to slow things down. The investigation that would follow. Remove the ID. No free gifts. I thought things were going wrong. When I went round to the other side of the car, she wouldn't get out. I had to drag her out. I told her I was taking her away from it, walked her to the bike. She wouldn't let me touch her. She was shivering and sobbing like a little child. Christ. I don't even know how old she was.'

He turned and looked down at her, eyes filling again.

'I wasn't going to kill her. I don't know what I was going to do. Take her away. Whatever. Pay her off. I don't know. Thinking about it now it's all just one big blur. I got her on the bike, in front of me. But she was crying all the time. As we got over the top – on that crappy little dirt track – she started to shout at me. Telling me to let her go. I tried to ignore her but she was moving a lot, unbalancing the thing. She probably thought I was going to kill her too. If you look at it rationally that's what I should have done. But I wasn't thinking like that.'

He sighed, a long heavy sigh.

'At some point she was moving and struggling so much I had to stop. She jumped off and started running. She ran off the road and out on to the grass. It was a clear night. I could see her clearly. I shouted after her. We were on a road in the middle of nowhere, but I knew it was used. It would only be a matter of time before someone saw us. I started to run after her, desperate, still shouting to her to stop. She wouldn't.'

He looked up at the ceiling, biting his lip.

'She wouldn't stop. So I shot at her. Even then I don't think I knew what I wanted to do. I didn't know whether I'd hit her until I caught up with her. She kept going. She stumbled, but kept going. When I got to her she was standing still, holding her chest, gasping. I walked around her and watched her eyes follow me. She fell to her knees, then over on to her back. She was panting really heavily. I tried to look at the wound and she struggled a little. But I could see she was going. The look in her eyes was one of . . .'

He brought his hand up, bit the side of it.

'She was looking at me . . .'

The words were muffled, spat out around his hand. He was biting the hand so hard she could see blood running away from it.

'Looking at me. Into my eyes. I was standing over her. The expression was one of total incomprehension. Like a child's eyes . . .'

He took the hand out of his mouth and screwed his eyes shut. He stood like that for a while, his legs trembling. Then he took a breath, rubbed his face. The cigarette fell into the fireplace.

'I couldn't watch her dying. I didn't know how long it would take. So I shot her again. In the head. I wanted it to stop. She didn't know what I was doing. The eyes were looking at me then, but not focused. I didn't want her to suffer. I had to hold the gun with both hands to do it. Because I was crying. Shaking.'

He moved back unsteadily and sat down again. She felt as if every single muscle in her body was bunched up, contracted, straining.

'After that it's all a bit unclear. I thought I'd put the gun in her hand, make it like she had killed herself. But then I saw the wound where I'd shot her in the back. I shot her through the wound to try to conceal it. Amateur. Incompetent. Pathetic. I knew they would find out. But I couldn't think straight. I was only thinking with half a brain. Nothing had happened as I thought it would. I was shocked. I went through his wallet. There was a card in there with the slip of paper they send you with the PIN on wrapped around it. I took it. I don't know why. The wallet I left with her. I tried to get back here on the bike, but it ran out of petrol. I couldn't even plan that properly. I had to walk, in the dark. As it got light I heard the helicopter, looking for me. I had to stop twice, hide. I had arranged to meet Varley in Burnley. A back-up plan. I was going to give the gun back to him. He would get rid of it. But I'd left the gun with her. It took me nearly five hours to get back. I was late. He'd gone. I used the card from the wallet to get enough money to get a cab home again.'

He paused.

'All I can see is her eyes, looking at me. When I walked away from her, the body was still moving. Jerking. Like it was still alive . . .'

He looked up at her, eyes desperate, pleading.

'I didn't want to kill her. You have to believe that. It was fucked up. I didn't know what to do. She was innocent. It shouldn't have happened.'

'And Phil Leech? Wasn't he innocent?'

She found her voice suddenly, surprisingly. He looked at her in shock, as if he had never considered the question, never considered that she would speak to him or ask him it. She met his eyes and held the look. Finally he nodded, looking away from her.

'Yes. Once I would have said he was a fair target. A policeman. Not now. *You* are the police, too. He was innocent. But at least there was a purpose to killing him. Not so with her.'

'What purpose? Your aim was to kill me.' The words broke as she said them, the tears coming to her eyes. He looked quickly at her.

'Kill *you*? Are you mad?' He looked stunned. 'All this happened so that I *didn't* have to kill you.'

She swallowed, a tight, hard lump in her throat. He stood up and moved towards her, holding the gun out.

'This thing isn't even loaded. I couldn't kill you. If I were capable of killing you, Leech and Mitchell would still be alive.'

She shrank back from him. 'I don't know what you mean.'

'You will.' He was reaching down to her, taking hold of her wrists. 'Get up. Come with me.'

She froze, stiffened up, resisting.

'I have to show you something. Then you will understand.'

Suddenly she saw where it was going. She felt adrenalin surging at her neck. 'No. Please. No . . .'

'Yes.'

He pulled at her wrists, yanking her to her feet. She started to cry, gasping for breath, vision blurred, tears running down her cheeks.

'You can't. I can't . . .'

317

She tried to push him away, felt her head swimming. Her legs were weak, buckling. The thing was rising inside her like a flood, washing over her, pulling her under. She felt his arms on her, holding her up. He had his hand on the door, opening it.

'You have to, Karen. You know you have to. You knew it the moment you came here.'

As she sank to the floor she felt the room spinning around her, saw his face dark with concern, confusion. Her vision began to cloud and bile rose in her throat. She heard him pleading with her, saying something that she could no longer hear. Not calling her Karen. Using the name he had used eight years ago. The same words coming out of his mouth . . .

FIFTY-TWO

'He was stopped eight months ago in Warwickshire. James Martin, 109, Cotton Tree Road, Colne. A Suzuki 250cc. F226 TCP.'

Munro felt the relief like it was being injected into his blood. He looked at the detective standing in front of him, holding the slip of paper.

'What's your name, Officer?'

'DC Evans, sir.'

'That is excellent work, DC Evans. How many forces did you call?'

'Eighteen, sir. Some have still to get back to us.'

'Tell me more. Where was he stopped?'

'On the motorway. He was doing eighty-seven miles per hour. A police bike caught him, stopped him, warned him. His details checked out. He was told to register the bike within the week.'

'And they didn't follow it up?'

Evans shrugged. 'Not a priority, I guess.'

'No. Have we got someone going over there?'

'DC Philips is already in Colne, doing door to door with the local uniforms. I've told DS Harris. He's trying to raise him now.'

'Good. Get him round there. Get it checked out.' He stood up, walked to the door.

'Yes, sir. I'll let them know that—'

'Tell them to be careful. Don't approach him yet. Just

see what he looks like. Ask the neighbours. When they have some idea, get back to me. We might need to get the Firearms Support Unit out.'

'Yes, sir.'

He opened the door for him. 'In fact, let's have the FSU out now, just in case.'

FIFTY-THREE

Sinead, he called her. That had been her name. *Sinead Collins*. They were out of the house now, walking to the end of the street, his arm around her shoulder, steering her through the rain. She was trembling like a leaf, terrified.

'They gave me no option,' he told her, leaning his head towards her as if they were two lovers. 'They thought I had known. They were going to kill me. I was taken and held for seven days, interrogated. They couldn't understand how I could have lived with you for three years and not noticed something, not suspected that you were military. You were good at it, Sinead, very good. I even thought you loved me.'

She saw the gates of a cemetery ahead of them, whispered to him, 'I do love you . . .'

He didn't hear. 'That I was living here made it worse. I couldn't tell them the truth about that. I've been here for nearly six years, waiting for this, knowing it might happen. I knew some day they would find you. You don't realise how important it was to them – what you did. I wanted to be here if they came. I've watched you from a distance for years. Remembered you. Kept away. I hired a private investigator. Nearly seven years ago. I saved and I paid. It took him nearly a year to find you, through bank account details, bribing people. Then I came up here to see you. I can remember it now. I watched you drive out of a police station in Bradford. You looked different.

Taller. I don't know why. Healthier. Still beautiful. Maybe more so. You looked like a completely different person.'

She began to cry again.

'I followed you to your home address. Six years ago. Then I knew.'

She tried to focus her eyes on him, but couldn't. She felt like ice. Some kind of numbness creeping over her. In front of them the cemetery gates looked black in the rain.

'They found you when they shut down a splinter group. The SRA. Stupid students, fucking around. They shot the leaders, trashed their houses, found your photo. It had been passed back by a man called Toomey, from here. Varley had got hold of it from one of your own.'

They were inside the cemetery now, walking through it. The panic began to grip her like a vice.

'They told me to kill you. As simple as that. Kill you or face the consequences. Killing you would prove it, you see. Prove my bona fides. They didn't care that killing people wasn't my role, that I had no training for it. They didn't give a shit if I botched it or not. That was how the idea came to me. What was I to do? I couldn't kill you. I could never kill you. No one has meant more to me in my life. So I pretended to set up the deal with Varley, milked him for information, found a way in. The plan I had was to botch it. But to do it so close to success that they would have to think I had tried to see it through. So I set it up like that. You were meant to be sitting there in the car when I shot him. I was to panic and run. A simple error. I had killed the wrong target.'

He stopped and looked down at her. They had reached the end of the cemetery. Another set of gates.

'That would have done them,' he said. 'They would have believed me then. Your cover would have been blown

322

and you would move. You would be protected. That was why I killed him. That was why he died.'

He started walking again.

'I don't care about myself, Sinead. If that was all it was I would have let them drop me. For what I've done I deserve it.'

He took hold of her arm and guided her. She began to sob. 'No, Jim,' she said. 'Not a grave. If it's a grave, I don't want to see it.'

He laughed. A real burst of laughter, sudden, melodic and full. 'A grave! It's not a grave, Sinead. God, no.'

They turned out of the cemetery, crossed a street, stopped in front of a wire fence. She felt confused.

'It's a child,' he said.

Ahead of her, thirty paces away, there were children, playing under a covered area of playground. She caught her breath, felt her heart stop.

He was shouting, shouting out a name. She began to cry uncontrollably, no longer able to do anything to stop it.

'Mairead,' he was shouting, 'Mairead!'

A child separated from the group, stepped out from the shelter, hesitated, looking up at the rain.

'Come on, Mairead! Come over here.'

She began to run towards them. With every step she took, Karen felt her heart crashing in her ears, so loud that by the time the child reached the fence she was clutching her chest, face red, gasping for breath.

A child.

An eight-year-old girl. Bright, attentive eyes. Long brown hair, pulled back into two pigtails. Face wet from the rain. Shouting at Martin, calling him 'Daddy', trying to hug him through the fence. She was wearing some kind of school uniform, a red tunic, a blue skirt, tights, little black shoes.

It felt as if the universe had stopped.

'Look here now,' Martin was saying to the child. 'I want you to say hello to this lady. This is your Aunty Sinead. One day you'll get to know her properly.'

The child looked up at her, face curious. 'Why is she crying?' she asked, turning to Martin.

'She's happy,' Martin said. 'She cries when she's happy.'

The child reached out a hand to her. Karen stood looking at it, held in the air, extended towards her.

'Shake her hand, Sinead,' Martin said.

She looked away, desperate, brought her hand to her mouth, bit down on her fist. The child pushed her hand through the fencing, a funny kind of smile on her face. The fingers reached up towards her, she saw her own hand moving down, touching them, holding them. She felt the breath leaving her, her head swimming. She crouched down, bent forward, hand still gripped by the tiny fingers.

'I'm sorry,' she said.

The words barely made sense. Blurted out through saliva and tears, choked by the thing in her throat.

'I'm so sorry.'

Martin told the child to run back. She felt the fingers loosen from her own. A scream mounted in her chest.

'Oh God,' she said. Her hand felt for her throat, gripped it, held the thing in.

She waited for the waves to flood over her. She had suffered eight years of practice, controlling it. Every year, on time, on the anniversary of the day she had left them. Every year without ever being able to think it, to look at it, to see it for what it was. But never as bad as this. She waited for it to settle, remaining like that, crouched on the ground, head almost between her legs, cramped, crushed, broken.

Eventually, she felt him pulling her to her feet. 'Mairead is your child,' he was saying, 'you left us eight years ago this month. The eighth of April nineteen eighty-eight. She was only two months old. I understand why. It took me a long time watching you, thinking about it, to be able to understand. But I do now.'

She tried to see clearly, to look into his eyes, but everything was fuzzy. 'I was ill,' she said.

'I know. I know that. I was there.'

'They made me ill.'

'I know.'

'I wanted . . .' She could hardly think the thought. 'I wanted an abortion. They wouldn't let me. They said you would leave me if I had an abortion, because of the Catholic thing. So I told them I needed out. They said it would blow my cover if I left. They needed the cover intact. You were a *target*, Jim. A *target*. They left me with you, living that life, acting it out, for over three years. They should never have done it. I couldn't do it. *Nobody* could. Not for that long. When I found out I was pregnant, when I needed most to get out, they said people would die. They had set up an operation because of information that came from you. If you found out, it would blow the whole thing. You are saving lives, they said. That was what they told me. I don't even know what the information was. To this day . . .'

'The passports,' he said. 'The false names on their passports. You gave them the false names. That was how they identified them when they landed at Madrid. Without you they would still be alive today.'

It came back to her immediately. *Farrell, McCann, Savage.* Shot dead in Gibraltar. Sunday, 6 March 1988. She had found the names in his diary, the false names written beside them, the words '*Spain/Gibraltar*' in the margin, in June, nine months before. In August she had discovered she was four months pregnant. A nightmare. Trapped inside a personality she had been living for two years.

'They told me if I left and you became suspicious, it would blow the whole thing. Stay two more months, they said. You will save lives. Just two months. Always it was two months more. God help me, Jim. God help me. They thought I was *undercover*. But I was in *love* with you. I had forgotten who I was, where I was, what I was doing. I had become *her*. I had become Sinead Collins.'

The words were coming out of her in a rush, garbled, the first time she had ever said them to herself. She needed it out, in front of her. All of it.

'When I found out I was pregnant, it was as if a black pit had opened out in front of me. I had to look at it then, confront what I couldn't face, see what shouldn't have been happening. I couldn't take it. When that happened in Gibraltar, on the sixth of March, when it was finally over, I waited for a month, then left. I ended up in a mental hospital. I was so ill I tried to kill myself.'

He had turned her around, away from the school. She stopped, looked back. A teacher was calling the children in, dinner hour over. She couldn't make out the child, in amongst the others somewhere.

'I can't even remember her being born,' she said. 'I was in a mental hospital for six months. I have no recollection at all of her birth.'

'February the tenth,' he said. 'One day I'll tell you about it.'

She turned her back on the place, her face twisted with pain.

'You won't be able to see it,' he said. 'But she looks like you.'

'What have I done?' she asked. 'What have I done?'

The tears started again. She had cried so much her eyes and throat were aching.

'They should never have done it to me.'

He moved a hand up and stroked her forehead, there, standing in the middle of the street, in the rain. A gesture she remembered.

'I am picking her up early,' he said. 'In two hours' time. We can't stay here. I have a flight booked from Manchester in five hours.'

She turned to face him. Her head began to clear. 'In five hours they will be here,' she said. 'In five hours they will have every port in the country on full alert. You won't stand a chance.'

FIFTY-FOUR

Binns was telling him something about Colne and a DC Philips when the Duty Sergeant interrupted them. Two men from London, here to see him now, urgently, in the Divisional Commander's Office. He looked questioningly at Binns.

'Any idea?'

Binns shrugged.

'Good afternoon,' he said, entering without knocking. The Divisional Commander wasn't there. He moved round behind the desk.

There were two of them, both in ordinary civilian clothing. He waited for introductions.

'Francis Henry, SO13.'

'Hello. Did we speak earlier in the week?'

'Not me. One of my lot, no doubt.'

'No doubt.'

He looked over at the other one. A tall, very thin man with an erect back, a military manner. He smiled at him, a tight-lipped smile.

'Sutherland. MOD.'

He nodded. 'I see.' Best not to ask, he thought. 'What can I do for you?'

'Bad news, I'm afraid.' It was Henry who spoke. 'We're going to have to take your enquiry away.'

He sat down, irritation and anger building quickly

within him. 'I don't follow.' He tried to smile at them, keep his voice even.

'Don't get me wrong, Munro. You've done your best. Done an excellent job, in fact.'

'I don't need you to appraise my work.'

'No. Quite.'

'My enquiry is my enquiry.'

'Except it's not. It's one of ours, I'm afraid.'

He sat back, bit his lip, flexed his shoulders a little. 'What do you mean?'

'SO13 will take it. It's terrorism.'

He looked at them speechlessly.

Henry looked calm, sanguine. 'We should have identified it earlier,' he said.

'No one has claimed it,' Munro said, stuttering slightly. 'We agreed that—'

'They don't claim cock-ups. Not always. That they haven't claimed it means nothing.'

'Cock-ups? I don't get it.'

'They weren't after Leech.'

'They?'

'The IRA.'

The man was serious. He saw that now.

'Are you sure?'

'It's good intelligence.'

'From where?'

Henry smiled, inscrutable. 'It's good intelligence. They would have claimed Leech. He wasn't the target, but he is what they would consider legitimate. Crown Forces etcetera. Mitchell was a bystander though. Too much bad publicity there.'

'So who was the target?'

'Someone called Karen Sharpe.'

He felt his shoulders sagging. 'Karen Sharpe . . .'

'Yes. I believe you know her?'

'I do.'

Sutherland spoke. 'Have you heard of Operation Flavius?'

He shook his head.

'Obviously, nothing of what we are telling you today must get beyond the three of us.'

A pause. Waiting for him to confirm that he knew how to do his job. He stared at the man.

'You understand that?' His eyes were blank, unperturbed by Munro's hostility.

Munro gritted his teeth. 'I'm a Detective Chief Superintendent.'

'It doesn't matter. I've dealt with leaks eight levels higher than you—'

'Obviously,' Munro interrupted, trying to speak calmly, 'I will not repeat a thing. I know how to do my job.'

'On the sixth of March nineteen eighty-eight in Gibraltar, the SAS shot three terrorists. Farrell, McCann, Savage. They were travelling on false passports and the whole operation was triggered by information about the passports. That information came from an undercover operative, working in London.'

He looked at the man. 'So?'

'Her name was Karen Sharpe,' the man said.

Suddenly he felt stupid.

'Her real name is Helen Young. Eight years ago she was Sinead Collins, living with an IRA intelligence officer in London. Recently, we believe, the IRA discovered that and they've tracked her to here. The Gibraltar thing meant a lot in the Province. Still does. Farrell, Savage and McCann are practically martyrs over there. Leech and Mitchell were errors. Sharpe was the target.'

'Ironically,' Henry interjected, 'you would probably have detected all this if you hadn't brought her on to your enquiry. She was part of the story. You *should* have had a team on her, sifting through her background. That would have been the normal practice. None of this might have—'

'I trusted her,' Munro muttered.

'We all make mistakes,' Sutherland said, charitably. 'I met the woman myself three days ago. She fooled me. She's had a lot of practice at it. It doesn't matter though. There are wider things at stake. In London they think there's another ceasefire in the offing. We believe a group are trying to bomb a major city centre before that. Possibly Manchester. Sharpe has already interfered with things. Perhaps it's better this way.'

'Which way?' He frowned. Something about Sutherland's tone was disturbing.

'If SO13 take it,' Sutherland said. 'That way they can control things.'

'Control things?'

'Sharpe has a reputation for going off on one. We need to deal with her carefully. Make sure she doesn't muck things up. There are a lot of lives at stake.'

Henry stepped towards him. 'First things first – have you put out an all-ports alert?'

Munro looked away from them, shook his head.

'You need to do that at once. For these people.'

He handed him a piece of paper. Munro looked at it, read the top name, felt his pulse quicken.

'James Martin?' he asked, incredulous.

'Yes. He's the man she was living with in London. We believe he's now living in Yorkshire.'

FIFTY-FIVE

The world she was in had been waiting for her, inches below the surface, fifteen minutes from her house. For eight years she had carried it with her, buried it, suppressed it. At times she had even felt normal. But it had never gone away. Through all the fights it had lain there, locked in a corner of her brain, waiting. Seeing the child had unlocked it, brought it up around her like a cage. She looked at herself, at her hands, her feet, the road she was standing on. Everything the same and yet different. She would never get back out of it now.

She stood facing him in the street, her head and eyes focusing, the problems rushing at her.

The logic had changed. She was in it, everything mapped out, no choices to be made. She understood. The task now was to forget, to concentrate on what she had to do. There would be time later to remember, to deal with the torrent of images and emotions, to adjust. What should have been murky, problematic, riddled with moral options, was suddenly crystal clear. No choice at all. Or rather something beyond choice, wired into her cell structure. That she had turned her back once had almost killed her. She dried her tears. The child was her daughter. Everything else was secondary.

She couldn't trust him to deal with her. He was moving around as if nothing had happened, oblivious. No sense of urgency at all. She had to help him.

'You don't have two hours,' she said to him. 'They have fifty detectives looking for you. I will help you. But you can't wait two hours. You have to go now. You don't need baggage, you don't need anything. Just you and Mairead, right now. If you don't move now you will spend the next ten years in prison.'

He looked back towards the school, biting his lip.

'I am going to my car. I will wait outside your house. Get Mairead and bring her. Bring as much money as you have and nothing else. Do you understand?'

He nodded, eyes helpless, ceding control.

'I will drive you to Leeds/Bradford airport. You take whatever flight is available. You get out. Do you have passports?'

'Two sets. Different names.'

'Did you book the flight from Manchester in your own name?'

'Yes.'

'Bring the other set then. Fly as someone else.'

She watched him walking away from her. He could plot surveillance on targets better than the FTT. Yet he had missed the same things happening to him, forgot his security, missed the tail. He had planned to murder a police officer and set up a drugs dealer for the hit. Then forgot to fill a tank with petrol. She couldn't leave it to him. She would take him there and put him on the plane herself.

She sat in her car and picked up her messages from Munro. The last one was about the bike. They were on to it already. She bit her nails, checked the street for cars. Within half an hour it would be sealed off. Maybe less. *Move, Jim*, she thought. *Get a move on*. She switched the RT on and waited for any transmissions. If they didn't find him they would put out the all-ports alert there and then. The thing was turning. The whole lumbering machine that was Phoenix was twisting on its axis, turning to face James Martin. She didn't know whether there was time to stop it.

He was gone too long. Time was dragging, pulling at her. She bit her nails down, watched in her mirrors for movement. Finally, she saw him walking back up the street with the child, hand in hand. Steady walking pace, not running, no sense of desperation or urgency. She wanted to wind the window down and scream at them. The child was skipping through the puddles. He had his head down, shoulders hunched. She felt a lump sticking in her throat.

As they turned into the house, the radio came to life. A heavy burst of static followed by a transmission that froze her into the seat. Someone called Philips, a DC on the enquiry.

'Six one nine, Philips. I am driving into Cotton Tree Road now. Repeat; I am driving into Cotton Tree Road now.'

She waited for the acknowledgement, hunching down and staring into her wing mirror. When it came it confirmed her worst fears.

'Acknowledged, six one nine. Report that FSU unit is tasked and en route. Please hold for instructions.'

It was happening already. She was too late. She leaned towards the car door and began to open it. They were sending the FSU. She had to get them out now. Right now. As the door opened, she saw a car appear at the end of the road, slowing down. Immediately behind it another car turned in and began to accelerate towards her. At exactly the same time she saw the front door to Martin's house open and the child step out.

FIFTY-SIX

DC George Philips saw the car as he slowed to pull over. It was moving from behind his own vehicle, accelerating quickly. A blue Orion. There were parked cars on both sides of the road and the space between his own and the car opposite was tight. Even as he saw it, he knew it would hit him.

It took his wing mirror off before he had a chance to turn to look. It connected with the front end of his offside wing and drove straight through. The headlight exploded into the road, the fender came off with a grinding wrench, twisting briefly in the air before hitting the tarmac. It was still bouncing as he opened the door and stepped out.

The Orion was screeching, tyres skidding across the wet road surface not twenty feet in front of him. *Fuck*, he thought, still relatively calm, *this is all we need. A road rage incident in the middle of a firearms operation.* He reached into his pocket for his warrant card as he cleared the front of his vehicle. The driver of the Orion was already out, the car still moving slowly forwards, the driver's door open. Philips opened his mouth to warn him, then realised who it was.

Luke Varley.

Varley wasn't even looking at him. He was moving quickly to the front of the Orion, heading for the row of parked cars and houses. From a house directly opposite him Philips could see a child stepping through a doorway,

335

hand held by a man closely behind her. Varley was running straight for them.

The details came at once, everything together. He saw a woman stepping out of a car further down the street, someone he recognised, then heard Varley shouting, then noticed – properly noticed – the first thing he had in fact seen as Varley had stepped from his vehicle. It registered as a fact now, the implications stopping him in his tracks, propelling him frantically back towards his own vehicle and the radio.

Varley was armed.

The gun in his hand was a revolver, something huge, clumsy, unwieldy and powerful. He was running towards the child and the man, pointing it at them, screaming.

As Philips brought the radio to his lips and began the transmission he could see the woman sprinting from the car towards them. Even as he saw the gun in her hand he realised who it was. Sharpe, the DC from the enquiry, the one who had worked with Phil Leech. He heard the operator requesting his transmission, and muttered an obscenity.

Then it was happening.

FIFTY-SEVEN

She was running, gun in hand, safety off, ready for it. Her heart in her ears. Closing quickly on the car. Ahead of her she could see it already, see what was happening. The car was Varley's. He had stalled it across the road and was out of it, running towards the house. In his hand a gun. Beyond that, Philips – the DC they had sent to check the house – standing like an idiot, pieces of his car shattered all over the road from where Varley had driven straight through him.

She had slipped up, been careless. She should have been out there with them. She should never have let them out of her sight. She dug her heels in and put her head down, felt the energy bursting through her. She had to get clear of the cars and get a shot in before he could get to them. It was that simple.

While she was in the road her view was obscured. She could see movement past the cars, hear voices, raised, shouting. A child's high tones, screaming, crying, and men's voices, deeper, intense with anger. She ducked through a gap between parked cars and turned on to the pavement at full speed, bringing the gun up in front of her.

His shape filled the site, blocking her view of Martin and the child. She was aiming at the space between his shoulder blades, closing rapidly. His head was out of the line of fire, bent forward. She would have to stop to shoot, steady herself. But not yet. She needed to get closer.

Varley was moving, Martin somewhere behind him, all of them on the pavement leading up to Martin's house. She only had a body shot. She calculated the distance between them, watched the yards closing. She could hear Varley screaming something, torso twisted towards the front of the house, arm outstretched, pointing the gun at something. The weapon he had was a revolver. A huge silver thing, like something out of a Western. As she closed to within fifteen feet of him, she saw what he was aiming at. On the ground just outside the gateway to the house the child was kneeling on the wet paving, looking up at him. The gun was pointed directly at her face, the range less than four feet.

She stopped running, bringing herself up so abruptly her feet skidded and slipped on the wet paving.

'Move!' he was shouting at the child. 'Move, you bitch! Get into that car or I'll put your face all over that wall!'

She could see Martin, rigid, eyes terrified, arms around the child's body where he had been trying to get between them. The child's face was red and wet, her eyes screwed shut, the mouth trembling.

'Get in, Mairead,' Martin was shouting at her. 'Do as he says.'

She was less than ten feet away from him. She brought the sight up to cover his head and opened her mouth to shout at him, to tell him she was there. She had it all planned in her head, perfectly worked out. He would hear her and react. He would move to point his weapon at her, bringing it away from the child. It would be an automatic response for him. She only needed him to move the weapon inches off line and she would fire.

Martin saw her before she could shout. '*No!*' She heard him screaming at her. '*No, Karen. No!*'

His hand was reaching out towards her. She saw Varley

twist his head, the eyes finding her, widening with shock. She watched the gun waver in his hand, waited for it to move, felt her finger tightening on the trigger.

'For fuck's sake, Karen! Don't do it. He has the gun pointed at Mairead!' Martin was pleading with her, frightened, desperate.

Things began to slow down. She took a breath, felt the adrenalin surging through her, opening her pupils wide, flooding her body with strength. The option was closed off. She couldn't do it while he had the gun on the child. She needed to get the gun away from her. Varley was screaming at her now, threatening.

'*I will kill her. I will shoot her fucking face off.*'

She dropped down into a crouch, slowly, keeping the gun on his head. His features were distorted, twisted into a rictus of hatred and fear, the mouth wide, yelling at her.

'*Put the fucking gun down! Put the gun down!*'

She saw him thumb the hammer back on the pistol, felt her heart stopping, the panic tearing through her. He was mad. She couldn't be sure he wouldn't do it. She couldn't take the risk. She held her free hand up, stopping him, let the gun drop to her side. He took a step at once towards the child, caught her hair with his free hand, placed the gun against her head.

'*Get in that car now. Leave the gun on the road. I will count to five and if you are not in the driving seat, I will kill her.*'

She sucked air into her lungs, braced herself, stood up. The child was making a whimpering noise, eyes closed. She moved towards his vehicle, keeping the gun at her side, eyes on him. Inside her something was boiling, rising up through her, coiling her muscles into a white rage. She had to control it.

'*Drop the fucking gun! Drop it now!*'

She stopped. She had been trained. Martin had not. He was shouting from the pavement still, begging her to comply. She shut his shouting into the background, ignored it. This had to stop before it went any further. She saw Varley move the barrel towards the child's mouth. The metal was pressed into her skin, the child transfixed with terror. She couldn't do it. She took a breath, crouched, let the gun slip from her fingers to the ground.

She began to talk to him, trying to calm him. A hostage for a hostage. He could leave the child and take her. The rain was running off her hair, down her face. She moved towards the car and inside the open driver's door.

Martin was already at the rear door, shouting back to Varley with the same idea. 'Leave her! Leave her here. You have both of us now. Leave the child here.'

She sat behind the wheel without closing the door, her hands on the wheel, knuckles white, arms like overstrung wires. Varley was dragging the child across the paving towards them. She watched with a cold fascination, holding the desperation down, letting it bubble beneath the surface. When he got to the passenger door he opened it, pushed the child into the back with Martin then stepped inside, all in one movement. Before she could go for him he was in, twisting in the passenger seat and pointing the gun back through the seats. The child began to scream.

Something snapped in her. She started shouting at him. She couldn't help herself. The words came out without control or order, without her being able to stop them. He turned to her immediately, reacting. His arm jabbed forward, smashing the gun barrel into her face. It caught her above her left eye, a blinding pain. For a split second it was like a shutter coming down on her. She felt her legs give way, cried out, collapsed forward into the seat.

'*Drive! Now!*'

She could hear him shouting at her repeatedly. He had a handful of her hair. He was pulling her towards him, the gun hard against the back of her head. She brought her hand up and covered the eye, let her head sink forward, tried to let her senses settle, recover. He had struck her with the gun. She felt a liquid entering her veins, coursing through her body, chilling her. She began to breathe, consciously, slowly. She began to think.

'Move this car now or I'll fucking kill all of you.'

He was insane. Jabbing someone with the barrel of a gun while his finger was over the trigger. She felt her legs shaking. A fraction of a millimetre, a movement so small he wouldn't even have noticed, a slightly less stiff mech-anism, even . . . *boom* . . . She envisaged her head exploding through the driver's side window.

The child was crying uncontrollably, Varley's voice still shouting over her, mouthing obscenities. He was out of control. She needed time to recover, to deal with him carefully. She brought her hand up, closed the door. Behind her she could hear Martin talking, voice low, trying uselessly to be threatening. She turned the key, started the engine.

They moved up the street, everything blurred, travel-ling slowly. Too many things happening at once. She saw the faces of bystanders, watching, their shocked, fright-ened looks, one of them with a mobile phone held up to his mouth, reporting it.

'You little fucking slut. You thought you were so clever. Setting me up for it. The two of you together.' The gun was held inches from her temple as he ranted.

She picked up speed, tried to breathe calmly, to let the training kick in. She had lost her weapon, but his gun was on her now, not on the child. That gave her options. What was the first priority now?

Time. Give them time to react, to pick them up, to come to her. Philips had seen it all. She kept her mouth shut and drove. Her left eye was closing up, wet with blood. She could see nothing through it. She ignored the pain, shut it into the background, followed the road. He had given her no directions, he had no plan. From his point of view this was the worst possible thing he could be doing. He hadn't thought about it, just jumped into it feet first.

They came out of Colne quickly and the road began to twist. They were on the back road for Keighley. She turned through a landscape of rolling fields and dry-stone walls, dropping down into layers of hanging fog, climbing out again, the land building in folds and layers towards the heights between Lancashire and Yorkshire. Beside her, insistently, like a stuck record, he was running through the past two days, constructing the story of his betrayal, feeding the bitterness, a constant insane voice in her ear. As the cloud began to close about them, she slowed down, heart hammering. Where did he think this would end? She risked a look in his direction.

'Don't look at me! Don't fucking look at me!'

She had to engage him, speak to him, put doubt into his brain. 'This is a mistake,' she said. Her words sounded fuzzy, slurred.

'Fuck you! Shut the fuck up!'

The child began to sob.

'I can help you.'

'Not where you're going. The dead can't help.'

'Don't be stupid. Think about what you're doing. There are ways we can deal with this.'

He started to giggle uncontrollably.

'You are making a mistake, Varley.' Martin's voice, the accent strong. 'I work for people who will not forget this.'

342

Empty threats. He was past reason, past arguing. Something in his head was unhinged, unbalanced. She wondered where he had got the gun from so quickly. They had turned over every house he had a connection with and found nothing.

'Turn,' he yelled at her, suddenly. 'Turn here.'

She slowed, knocked it down a gear, turned into a wall of mist so dense she could hardly see the front of the vehicle.

'This leads up to Widdop,' she said. 'Do you want to—'

'Don't tell me where it leads. I've lived here all my life. Just drive the fucking car.'

FIFTY-EIGHT

Munro felt a shiver running down his spine. Something was happening. On the desk in front of him the phone began to ring. He looked up at Sutherland and Henry.

'Hadn't you better get that?' Henry asked.

He picked it up. It was Harris, downstairs, talking quickly, excitedly. Varley was at Colne, armed. He had taken someone hostage.

At first he was calm, catching his breath, silencing Harris, thinking. In front of him he could see Henry and Sutherland watching, irrelevant now. Harris gave him the last sighting, the last location, the probable destination. The DC they had sent over, Philips, was still with the car.

'Male or female hostage?' Munro asked him.

'Both. And maybe a child.'

He felt the blood prickling in his scalp.

Harris was in the Incident Room. He could hear him talking to someone beside him, trying to verify details. Still on the phone Munro looked over to Henry.

'An armed incident,' he said, keeping his voice steady. 'Sorry.'

Harris came back to him. 'We think it's Karen Sharpe,' he said.

Munro felt his chest tighten.

'Sharpe, a man and a child. Philips thinks the man might be James Martin.'

'Where's the FSU?'

'Already halfway to Colne.'

'X-Ray 99?'

'Holding back. Over Halifax right now.'

'Get them on to it, quickly. Track the car. Get them on top of it.'

'They are saying the weather is no good for the chopper . . .'

'Override them. Do it. I want it up there. Now.'

'The cloud base—'

'Forget it. They have infra-red imaging. Get them up. I'll see you in the garage in thirty seconds. Request code one two one. Let's go. I do not want another dead officer on my hands.'

FIFTY-NINE

Five miles out of Keighley, in the last of two unmarked FSU cars, PC Robert Fellows was staring at the mist moving past the vehicle when the radio came to life. From the front passenger seat his Sergeant, Paul Edwards, picked it up on the earpiece, answering their call sign. Suddenly the car was slowing down.

'One moment. I'll check,' he heard him say. He turned back to them. 'Anyone know this area?'

Beside him Paddy Malone had been stationed in Halifax and knew it well.

'Where's Widdop?'

Malone paused. 'Widdop? We're almost there. Five minutes from here, maximum.'

Edwards turned back to the radio. 'Acknowledging. ETA five minutes. Request channel for X-Ray 99.'

Fellows sighed, shifting uncomfortably in the Kevlar armour. They had been on since four that morning. It was his little boy's birthday that day. He was tired, he needed sleep. He was going to miss the kid's party.

'What is it?' he asked, as the car began to turn.

'A hostage job. Code one two one.'

The car accelerated quickly, pressing him back into the seat.

'That's it,' he heard Edwards say. 'Let's get there first.'

SIXTY

The gun kept sinking, moving from the level of her face to the level of her thigh. Then back up again as he realised. She could see out of the corner of her eye that it was a heavy thing, a forty-five of some sort. After a while it would become too tiring to hold it out like that, pointing at her head. A loose shot into her leg would cripple her, but it was different to a loose shot into her head. It allowed options.

'I didn't know what he was going to use the gun for.'

Was this what it was about? Did he want to justify himself to her? Was it that simple?

'I knew nothing.' He wasn't shouting any longer, but his voice was raised, tinged with hysteria. 'I was set up all the way. By him!' He jabbed the gun towards the back seat. In the interior mirror she saw the child cringe, heard Martin uttering something soothing to her. Her mind steadied, flicked across the details. They were both wearing seat belts. Varley was not.

'Shut up!' Varley yelled at him. 'Keep your mouth shut!'

He turned back to her.

'He told me he was going to use the thing to get funds, to do a robbery. The fucker even made me test the gun. Two days before. He knew he was going to leave it on her. He knew they would find forensic shit on my clothes. I will make him admit it to you.'

'I know already.'

'You know? You were with him then? You were in on it?'

His voice was incredulous. Whatever he had read in her file, he had forgotten the detail.

'I was in on nothing. I don't know what you're trying to do here, Luke. Where are you trying to take us?'

'Shut up! Shut the fuck up!'

He was going to strike her, the frustration surging up again. She slowed down, braced herself.

From the back she heard Martin speaking quickly, distracting him. 'Wherever you are we will hunt you out and kill you for this.' His voice was flaky, unsure. 'Even if you kill me, others will come for you.'

The road was climbing steadily, twisting through the moors between Colne and Cock Hill. The cloud was so thick she was pushed to keep the speed above ten miles an hour. In front of her it was so dense that she could have been anywhere.

She tried to pick her way back through her memory. She wasn't just anywhere. She was somewhere she knew. She had driven this route in the other direction not two hours before. In thirty seconds she would be at the summit of this particular stretch. From there the road levelled on to an expanse of flat heathland before falling away into a gorge. The mist in front of her began to part slightly. She slowed. His hand had dropped so much now it was resting against the seat.

She knew how this was going to be played. If they gave in to him, went along with it, it would become standard. A hostage scenario. She had seen it before, many times. They would corner him somewhere, get in a negotiator, dig in for the long haul. She knew how it worked, how long it took. She even knew the statistics. Ninety-eight per cent of hostage scenarios ended by negotiation, without injury to any hostage. But that left the two per cent who got their heads blown off. The child wasn't going to be part of that statistic. The risk couldn't be taken. She had to do something.

She saw the road levelling in front of her. She came over the top and accelerated quickly across the flat, the mist funnelling around the vehicle. Beside her she saw him look forwards, alarmed.

'Slow down.'

Now or never, she thought. She tried to catch sight of Martin's eyes in the mirror, to warn him, but he wasn't looking.

She hit the brakes, hard, jamming her feet against the clutch and brake, free hand yanking on the hand brake. The car screeched, span. She saw his arm fly upwards, then his body lurch forward. As he bounced off the windscreen she had her hand on the gun, pushing the barrel down, her free hand releasing her seat belt. She saw the door window beside him shatter as the car careered off a dry-stone wall. The door swung open as it span away, then she was across the seats and into him, arms closing round him. The damp, freezing air rushed around them and they were out, locked together, the road surface crashing up to meet them. Behind her back she heard a deafening explosion, glass breaking. He had fired the thing. For an infinitesimal moment they were held between the departing vehicle and the road, then it hit them.

Her shoulder and side struck the tarmac, driving the wind from her. She kept rolling, pulling him with her. She felt no pain. Away from her she could hear the engine revving freely, the sound receding. She was rolling downhill, down towards the gorge, gathering pace. She tried to hold on to him, twisting her hands through his clothing.

They bounced and he broke free, spinning away from her. Her hands came into contact with grass, stones. She started to brace herself.

As she got to her knees she could see nothing but the cloud, swirling around her, parting and gathering like smoke. Then she could hear him, moving from above her, headed back in the direction of the road. Going back towards the car, going for Martin and the child.

She pulled herself up and began to run, shouting at him, trying desperately to get him to turn. Her feet struck the road and for a moment the mist closed in, blinding her. She staggered forward, shouting into it. She could see the car now, no more than ten feet ahead of her. It had come to rest at the side of the road, next to a telegraph pole, all the doors open. In front of it, further along the road, she could see a figure running through the mist. A man, bulky. Carrying a child? Behind him another figure, limping.

She passed the car, sprinting, gaining on them. It was Varley who was limping. She saw him point the gun in the direction of the fleeing figure. She was still five yards behind him. She screamed at him, saw his arm recoil, heard the explosion. In front of him the figure stopped, turning at once to face him. She was close enough to see his face. It was Martin, the child held against his chest. His skin was ashen, stricken with fear, blood running across his eyes. In his arms the child was motionless, head buried in his clothing.

Varley caught them quickly, stopping no more than five feet in front of them, in the middle of the road, the gun waving madly. As she closed the last few yards, he stepped in front of Martin and pointed the gun down at the child.

'*I warned you. You chose this. I told you I would do it.*'

He was screaming at the top of his voice, his face contorted, blood across his mouth and forehead, gun shaking
in his hand. '*If that's the way you want it! If that's the way
you fucking want it!*'

She stood dead still, arms in the air, panting. Martin
was looking at her, paralysed with fear, shocked, shaking
from head to foot, doing nothing.

'*I'll blow her fucking head off!*'

Through the mist, above them, she could hear a noise.
She saw Varley thumb back the hammer on the gun. His
eyes were wide, bulging. She saw them divert, mist over,
the sound coming down to him. He paused, moved back a
step. The sound solidified, deepened, defined itself. The
thrashing of helicopter blades. Gun still placed against the
child's head he looked up into the bank of cloud.

'Fuck,' she heard him say. 'Fuck. Fuck. Fuck.'

She took a step forward, towards him.

'Stay there!' He hissed the words at her, teeth gritted,
saliva running down his chin.

'Let them go,' she said. The bundle in Martin's arms
wasn't moving. She felt her heart beginning to race and
skip, blood rushing to her head. Was the child injured?

'Let them go and we can sort this.'

'Shut up,' Varley hissed. 'Shut up.'

The helicopter was moving over them. The noise
picked up, became louder.

'They know you are armed,' she said.

'Shut up.'

'It will be the FSU.'

'What the fuck is that? FSU? What is that?'

'The Firearms Support Unit. Marksmen. They have
infra-red. Even through this shit they can see you.'

He was craning his neck back, staring up into the
cloud. '*Fuck.*'

351

The sound was coming straight towards them. High above the cloud, using the infra-red FLIR device, hunting for them. Martin looked up, the child stirring against him. She felt her heart racing to keep up with the adrenalin.

'They will have seen the car.'

She heard something like a sob in Varley's throat. The arm holding the gun was shaking, the weight of it increasing.

'Let the child go,' she said. 'Let both of them go and I will tell the truth for you.'

'*You're lying!*'

He yelled the words at her. She saw Martin step back a pace.

'You have my word,' she said. She took a step towards him. 'Take me.' She pointed to her head. 'Put the gun against my head. If you have me, they will not shoot you. I am a police officer.' Her voice was dead calm.

He looked at her, eyes only half comprehending, swamped with fear.

'Put the gun here. Right here against my head.' She had her finger there, placed against the spot.

'If you have a child as a hostage, they will kill you. They will shoot. That's the policy. That's what they are trained to do. This way you can live. We can sort it out.'

She was three feet from him, almost close enough to go for it.

'Let the child go,' she said, almost whispering, pleading with him. 'Take me instead.'

She saw him shrug, turn his back on Martin, bring the gun away. She stepped forward. 'Your choice,' he said.

Suddenly he was moving, his free hand coming out to her, catching her hair, pulling her down. He yanked her backwards, on to the grass at the side of the road. She felt a chunk of her hair separate. She struggled to turn and felt his arm closing around her, grinding into her throat, pushing her on to her knees. She let go, squirming frantically, trying to breathe. Above her, through a haze of blood and dirt, she could see him leaning towards her, pushing the gun down into her mouth.

'Keep still,' he was saying. 'Keep fucking still.'

Then he pulled her back to her feet, one hand in her hair, the other – the hand holding the gun – taking hold of the clothing at her neck. He was stronger than she thought he would be. She looked to where Martin had been and saw the mist curling and closing over the empty space.

SIXTY-ONE

'Walk,' Varley said, looking down at her. 'Walk fast.' He pushed her forwards, holding on still. The relief was coursing through her. She wanted to laugh in his face. There was no contest now. It was between her and him. The child was spared. She stumbled on the wet moor, dropped to her knees. The sound of the chopper blades grew in intensity. Above and around them the mist was moving, swirling, caught up in the vortex. Varley began to pant uncontrollably.

'Fuck. Fuck.'

'Let me go,' she said, shouting the words. 'I gave you my word. I will tell the truth.'

Behind the noise from the rotors she could hear sounds above them now, back up the hillside, on the road. Engine noises, voices, the screech of rubber on tarmac.

Varley pushed his face against hers, holding the gun at her head, still walking, struggling with the uneven ground.

'I'm not stupid,' he screamed, then broke off, released her. She fell forwards and looked back to him. He was pointing the gun in the air, trying to guess where the chopper would be. He fired two shots, one after the other. The gun recoiled so heavily he staggered backwards. The noise from the rotors continued, unaffected. She stood up, stepped forward to run, but already he was pointing the thing at her.

'Don't fucking try it! Don't even think about it.'

From somewhere out in the fog she heard the crackle of a radio.

'You dickhead,' she yelled. 'Now they definitely know where you are.'

He moved towards her, gun raised to strike her, caught hold of the clothing at her shoulder, pushing her into the wet ground. Above them the noise changed beat. He stopped.

It was rising, moving away. She listened to it, heard it veer off to the north, saw the mist close in thickly above them, looked down at her feet. She knew what had happened. She tried to concentrate, focus her ears through the barrier of cloud. He was panting so loudly it was difficult.

'It's going,' she heard him say. 'Get up. Get moving.'

'It's going because they have you,' she said. 'They are closing in around you even now.'

He looked down at her with a look of abject horror, wiping the blood away from his mouth. 'You're lying.'

'Listen.'

He shut up, caught his breath, stared helplessly into the mist.

It was moving now, sinking, gathering speed, flowing down into the valley below them. She looked across it and tried to guess distances. She could see about ten feet around them, in any direction. In places the bank was thinning, separating, in places so impenetrable it looked like a solid white sheet. Faintly, as if from a very great distance, she could hear movement through it, footsteps, breathing.

'Did you hear that?' she said. Her voice sounded loud. She felt his hand twist tighter in her hair.

A sound from below them made him turn suddenly.

'They are out there. Below us.'

355

'Shut up. Shut the fuck up,' he whispered, desperate, frightened.

From behind him a sound leapt out at them – someone running past them, panting with exertion. He pulled her round, pointed the gun towards it. The wall of mist registered the movement with a slight ripple, breath blown on a stream of smoke.

'Get up,' he said, moving the gun back to her head, not looking at her. Every little noise was making him twist now, turning his head frantically in the direction of the sound. She started to stand and at that moment a voice blasted at them out of the mist:

'*Luke Varley. Luke Varley. Remain where you are.*'

A loudhailer. She heard a scream strangled in his throat. His head moved from one direction through to the next, searching for figures, swivelling like a mad chicken.

'*You are surrounded by firearms officers. Remain where you are.*'

Above them she could hear more cars pulling up on the road.

'Move,' he said to her. His voice was breaking with fear. She stepped forward, moving downhill. He followed behind her, gun pointed at the back of her head.

'Move slowly,' he said. 'Don't try anything.'

She felt her way carefully. The ground was a mixture of stiff red grass and half-submerged sphagnum. Before each step she looked up and checked the cloud ahead of her. The further they moved downhill the thicker it became. Off to the left she heard the unmistakable sound of a weapon slide – a heavy double-click. He heard it, yanked back on her hair, stopping her dead. The sound had been very close.

'What the fuck was that?' He was almost whimpering. She looked back down the hill and saw a dark shape sliding through the mist, moving like a ghost. Even as she watched it settled down, the air closing over it. Varley pushed her forward and within two steps she could see it, not fifteen feet from them. She stopped.

'Move on,' he hissed at her.

'I can't. They are in front of us.'

He changed position, holding the gun at her head, looking to where she was pointing. 'What the fuck is that?'

The shape moved. Varley tensed, pulling back on her. The mist lifted slightly and he saw it. A marksman, flat on his belly in the marsh, a large black weapon stretching out in front of him, pointing directly at them.

Varley snatched back at her, letting go of her hair and closing his arm around her neck.

'You fucking move and I'll kill her!' he yelled. He pulled her head so that it was down on his chest, forcing her to her knees in front of him. The gun was pushing into a point in the middle of her forehead.

'Get up! Move!' He was shouting into the fog. 'Move now. Out of the way. Move or I'll kill her.'

The figure was motionless. Behind it she could see other shapes, moving forwards, creeping. Twisting her head she began to shout at them.

'Shoot him. Shoot him now!'

He jumped as she shouted, shocked, then tightened his arm around her throat. 'Shut up! You stupid fucking bitch. Shut up. Shut up or I'll do it!'

She ignored him, shouted again, 'Shoot him. He has said he will not release me. Shoot now!'

She could feel his heart leaping and thumping in her ear, the panic driving through him. She twisted herself and brought her hands up to the arm around her throat, pulling it downwards. The loudhailer boomed out again through the fog:

'Luke Varley. You are surrounded . . .'

He began to struggle with her, loosening his grip on the gun to bring his other hand over her face. She could hear him gagging and sobbing with fear, trying desperately to hang on to her. She got the arm that was around her neck up as far as her mouth. He pulled back into her and she bit into it, felt him react, cry out, then release her. She dropped to her belly and rolled. Behind and above her the world exploded.

He was shooting at her.

The sound was deafening, crashing into her ears, the light searing her eyes like fireworks. She kept rolling, came face up, saw him tracking her with the gun, walking behind her, following, face streaked with blood, sweat, tears, trying to get a good aim.

They fired three shots in quick succession. All from below her. His head snapped sideways, then erupted, arms flying wildly into the air, gun spinning off into the mist. The force of the first impact picked him up and held him momentarily in the air, suspended. The body arched, bending back upon itself – as if he were reaching out and backwards, leaping back to catch something at full stretch. Above him she could see pieces of his head spiralling upwards. A wide arc of crimson rain, hanging in the air, bright against the greyness. For a second the three things were separated, floating on the mist. The body, the blood, the pieces of him. Then they moved together, falling towards the earth, the body striking first – a sound like a bag of cement hitting concrete – the pieces falling around it like shrapnel, the blood spattering the green marsh in a fine red spray.

She stood up, breathing furiously. He had got two shots off at her. She turned her back to him, walked down the hill towards the dark shapes. They were standing up now, rising from the wet earth. Behind them noise, radios, people running. She could see the nearest one, training his gun on her, automatically. He was in a kneeling position, ready to fire again.

She walked up to him and knocked the gun away. He was kitted out in overalls with Kevlar armour and a helmet.

She pulled at his visor, shouting at him. He stumbled backwards and she kicked out at him.

'You stupid fucker! You useless stupid fucker!'

She couldn't stop. She began to punch the helmet, smashing her fists into it.

'You let him get one off. You let him get one off! He could have fucking killed me!'

Someone took hold of her from behind. The marksman moved away from her, shocked. She pulled herself free and walked back up the hill to where Varley was lying. Someone else was kneeling by him, also in overalls and helmet, trying for his vital signs. The body was twitching and quivering, a mass of tiny movements. She stood over it and looked down at the mess where his face had been. She felt bile rising in her throat, saw him standing there, gun held to the child's head, terror in the child's eyes.

'Fuck you,' she said and spat down at the broken head with all her strength.

SIXTY-TWO

Movement. Confusion. Radios echoing through the mist, armed figures appearing from nowhere, everyone shouting at once, barking instructions. They were telling her to move back, lie down, crouch. The instruction was garbled, contradictory, filled with the horror of what had happened, all the training and planning unseated, thrown into disorganisation. They weren't used to doing what they were trained to do.

She was. She stepped back, took a breath, felt the tension easing inside her. It was over.

The marksman she had struck was crouched down, helmet off, hand across his eyes. She could hear voices from above them, back in the direction of the road – tense, raised, stressed with fear. Something still happening. She knew what it would be. Down here they were trying to come to terms with thirty seconds of unleashed destruction. Up there they would be finishing off her failure, making the arrest.

Thin streams of mist stroked her cheeks, leaving her face wet, her eyes damp. She started to walk back up the slope, legs unsteady, weak at the knees. They came after her, grabbing at her, yelling warnings. The operation was still ongoing, the risk still live. She should remain where she was until they were certain it was safe.

She ignored them. She didn't care. She knew exactly what she had to do.

The whole thing was lost now. Varley had messed it up. She had tried to keep Martin and the child together because they had been together for eight years, because the child belonged with him. Because she had screwed up her life enough already. But they would be on to Martin now.

She had failed.

She made the road and turned towards the noise. The mist was flashing at her, blue and white, the two-tones of parked vehicles refracted through it. She could hear car engines, sirens, doors opening, people running. She passed a single, armed figure motionless in the middle of the road. She was walking slowly, deliberately, calmly. She knew exactly what was coming.

The mist cleared to reveal it. Martin was in the middle of them, kneeling in the road with his hands behind his head, completely surrounded. They had guns trained on his head and body and were shouting out instructions at him. One stepped forwards and pulled his arms behind his back, swiftly fixing a rigid handcuff. Another began to search him. Martin was panting, chest heaving, limbs shaking. As she stepped towards them, he looked up to her. His face was ashen, stricken with grief. Their eyes met and he began to cry.

A tall uniformed figure stepped in front of her, coming between them. His hands were raised in warning, the voice requesting identification.

'Karen Sharpe,' she said, not even looking at him, not even thinking. Her eyes looked past him, past the circle around Martin, searching for the child.

She was about fifteen feet away from them, watching. One of the FSU officers was standing beside her, holding her hand. He was speaking quietly into the radio set pinned to his collar, requesting assistance.

She stepped around the man in front of her and began

to walk over to them. From the group around Martin she could hear someone arresting him for the murder of Philip Leech. She didn't want to watch. She moved in front of the child, blocking off her view to the scene, crouching down so that her face was at her level.

The child's eyes found her and focused, then flickered in recognition.

She swallowed, took a breath and spoke, 'Your daddy is going to be all right. Don't worry.'

The eyes looking back at her were blank, uncomprehending.

'Do you remember me?'

No response. All the expression was gone from her features.

From above them the FSU officer said something about the kid being in shock. Without warning she had an image of herself when she had been that age, walking across a zebra crossing with her mother, somewhere in Newry. She had said something to annoy her mother, though she couldn't recall what. She saw her mother stoop towards her, eyes flashing in anger, the hand casually snapping out to slap her face, so hard she fell over, there and then in the middle of the road. Eight years old. She reached out a hand and closed it through the child's free hand. The fingers tightened around her own.

'I know you remember me,' she said. 'If you come with me now, we'll go away from all this. Will you do that?'

She waited. From behind her she could hear them getting Martin to his feet, requesting transport on their radios.

The child stepped forward. Karen slipped her arms around her and picked her up, turning away from the scene, holding her tightly.

'We'll see your daddy later,' she said.